"THE SAFE DEPOSIT"
and other Stories about
Grandparents, Old Lovers,
and Crazy Old Men

"The Safe Deposit"
and other Stories about
Grandparents, Old Lovers,
and Crazy Old Men

by
Isaac Bashevis Singer
Grace Paley, Anzia Yerzierska,
Edna Ferber and others

edited with an afterword by
Kerry M. Olitzky

Preface by Congressman Claude Pepper

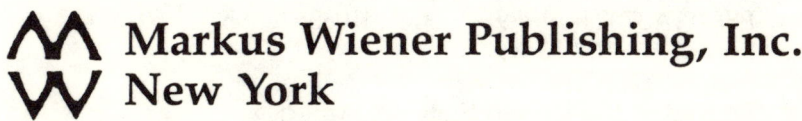 Markus Wiener Publishing, Inc.
New York

MASTERWORKS OF MODERN JEWISH WRITING SERIES
is issued in conjunction with the Center for the
Study of the American Jewish Experience, Hebrew Union
College-Jewish Institute of Religion, Cincinnati.

Copyright © 1989 by Hebrew Union College-Jewish Institute
of Religion. All rights reserved. No parts of the book may be
reproduced without prior permission of the copyright
holder. For information write to Markus Wiener Publishing,
Inc., 225 Lafayette Street, New York, N.Y. 10012

Cover Design: Cheryl Mirkin

Copy Editing: Daniel Marcus

Library of Congress Cataloging-in-Publication Data

"The Safe Deposit" and other stories about grandparents, old lovers, and crazy old men.
   (Masterworks of modern Jewish writing)
   1. Short stories, American—Jewish authors.
2. American fiction—Jewish authors.   3. American
fiction—20th century.   4. Aged—Fiction.   5. Jewish
aged—Fiction.   I. Singer, Isaac Bashevis, 1904–
II. Olitzky, Kerry M.   III. Series.
PS648.A37824   1989   813'.01083520565   59-22412
ISBN 1.55876-013-X

Printed in the United States of America

Table of Contents

Preface by Claude Pepper ix

Old Loves and New Lovers
The Safe Deposit 1
   By Isaac Bashevis Singer
The Old Man Had Four Wives 21
   By Frank Scheiner
Ben, Son of Margulies 29
   By Ruth Miller
Terrible Mistakes 45
   By Eugene Ziller
The Americanization of Shadrach Cohen 83
   By Bruno Lessing

Across the Generations
The Zulu and the Zeide 97
   By Dan Jacobson
The Crazy Old Man 117
   By Hugh Nissenson
Dreamer in a Dead Language 129
   By Grace Paley
My Father Sits in the Dark 153
   By Jerome Weidman

Living Life—Waiting for the Angel of Death
Mr. Isaacs 161
   By Seymour Epstein
Old Man Minick 175
   By Edna Ferber
The Golden Years 205
   By Sylvia Rothchild
The Open Cage 225
   By Anzia Yezierska
The Life You Gave Me 233
   By Bette Howland

Sacred Texts
Alte Bobbe 283
By Charles Angoff
The Retired Gentlemen 293
By Gertrude Berg
The Gift Horse 305
By Judith K. Liebmann
The Prayer Shawl 323
By Gloria Goldreich

Afterword by Kerry M. Olitzky 339

Acknowledgments

The following publishers have generously given permission to reprint material from copyrighted works: "The Safe Deposit," from *Old Love* © 1966, 1975, 1976, 1977, 1978, 1979 by Isaac Bashevis Singer, by permission of Farrar, Straus and Giroux, Inc., New York, NY; "The Old Man Had Four Wives" © 1950 by Frank Scheiner from *A Treasury of American Jewish Stories* by permission of Associated University Presses, Cranbury, NJ; "Ben, Son of Margulies," by Ruth Miller, from *Commentary,* 26:2 (August 1958), by permission of Ruth Miller and *Commentary* "Terrible Mistakes," by Eugene Ziller, from *Midstream* (December 1971), by permission of Eugene Ziller and *Midstream* Magazine, New York, NY; "The Americanization of Shadrach Cohen" by Bruno Lessing recently appeared in *American Jewish Archives* 37 (April 1985); "The Zulu and the Zeide," © 1956, 1984 by Dan Jacobson, from *Mademoiselle* (July 1956), by permission of Russell & Volkening as agents for the author, New York, NY; "The Crazy Old Man," from *In the Reign of Peace* © 1968, 1972 by Hugh Nissenson, by permission of William Morris Agency, Inc., New York, NY; "Dreamer in a Dead Language," from *Later the Same Day* © 1985 by Grace Paley, by permission of Farrar, Straus and Giroux, Inc., New York, NY; "My Father Sits in the Dark," from *My Father Sits in the Dark and Other Stories* © 1934, 1962 by Jerome Weidman, by permission of Brandt & Brandt Literary Agents, Inc., New York, NY; "Mr. Isaacs," from *A Penny For*

Charity © 1954, 1955, 1956, 1958, 1961, 1962, 1964, 1965 by Seymour Epstein, by permission of Little, Brown and Co., Boston, MA; "Old Man Minick," by Edna Ferber, © 1922 by the Crowell Publishing Co., 1949 by Edna Ferber, by permission of Harriet F. Pilpel as trustee & attorney for the Ferber Proprietors, New York, NY; "The Golden Years," from *A Special Legacy* © 1985 by Sylvia Rothchild, by permission of Simon & Schuster, Inc., New York, NY and *Commentary*; "The Open Cage," by Anzia Yezierska from *The Open Cage: An Anzia Yezierska Collection* © 1979 by Louise Levitas Henriksen, New York, NY, by permission of Louise Levitas Henriksen; "The Life You Gave Me" by Bette Howland from *Commentary* © 1982 by permission of *Commentary* and from *Things to Come and Go* © 1983 by Bette Howland by permission of Knopf, Inc. (all rights reserved); "Alte Bobbe," from *When I Was A Boy in Boston* © 1947 by Charles Angoff, by permission of Associated University Presses, Cranbury, NJ; "The Retired Gentlemen," from *Molly and Me* © 1961 by Gertrude Berg, by permission of Cherney Berg, Holmes, NY; "The Gift Horse," by Judith K. Liebmann, from *Orim* 1:1 (Autumn 1985), by permission of Judith K. Liebmann, Branford, CT; "The Prayer Shawl," by Gloria Goldreich, from *Moment* 10:5 (May 1985), by permission of *Moment*, Washington, DC and Gloria Goldreich.

Preface

By Claude Pepper

Elderly people are one of the great treasures of the world. They have such an abundance of wisdom and have done so many remarkable things.

At first glance, the stories appear to be just tales of ordinary people living ordinary lives. However, a closer look reveals the strength, decency and humility that are a part of these individuals and of the fiber of so many other seniors.

These characters are easy to relate to. They face the same day-to-day frustrations we all do. Yet, through hard work and perseverance, they are able to marshall their forces and triumph over obstacles.

That's what is uplifting about this collection of stories—the frank portrayal of human nature. After reading these tales, we take away a renewed belief in the positive side of human nature and the inherent goodness of people. Nothing here is sugar-coated—we see the characters for what they really are. But even so, we are inspired.

Claude Pepper
Congress of the United States of America
Washington, DC
April '89

Old Loves and New Lovers

The Safe Deposit

Isaac Bashevis Singer

Some five years back, when Professor Uri Zalkind left New York for Miami after his wife Lotte's death, he had decided never to return to this wild city. Lotte's long sickness had broken his spirit. His health, too, it seemed. Not long after he buried her, he fell sick with double pneumonia and an obstruction of the kidneys. He had been living and teaching philosophy in New York for almost thirty years, but he still felt like a stranger in America. The German Jews did not forgive him for having been raised in Poland, the son of some Galician rabbi, and speaking German with an accent. Lotte herself, who was German, called him *Ostjude* when she quarreled with him. To the Russian and Polish Jews he was a German, since, besides being married to a German, for many years he had lived in Germany. He might have made friends with American members of the faculty or with his students, but there was little interest in philosophy at the university, and in Jewish philosophy in particular. He and Lotte had no children. Through the first years they still had relatives in America, but most of the old ones had died and he never kept in touch with the younger generation. Just the same, this winter morning Dr. Uri Zalkind had taken a plane to New York—a man over eighty, small, frail, with a bent back, a little white beard, and bushy eyebrows that retained a trace of having once been red. Behind thick-lensed glasses, his eyes were gray, permanently inflamed.

It was a bad day to have come to New York. The pilot had announced that there was a blizzard in the city, with gusting winds. A dark cloud covered the area, and in the last minutes before landing at LaGuardia an ominous silence settled over the passengers. They avoided looking one another in the eye, as if ashamed beforehand of the panic that might soon break out. Whatever happens, I have rightly deserved it, Dr. Zalkind thought. His Miami Beach neighbors in the senior-citizens apartment complex had warned him that flying in such weather was suicide. And for what was he risking his life? For the manuscript of a book no one would read except possibly a few reviewers. He was glad that he carried no other luggage than his briefcase. He raised the fur collar of the long coat he had brought with him from Germany, and clutching his case in his right hand and holding on to his broad-brimmed hat with his left, he went out of the terminal to look for a taxi. From sitting three hours in one position his legs had become numb. Snow fell

The Safe Deposit

at an angle, dry as sand. The wind was icy. Although he had made a firm decision that morning to forget nothing, Professor Zalkind now realized that he had left his muffler and rubbers at home. He had planned to put on his woolen sweater in the plane and this he had forgotten, too. By the time a taxi finally stopped for him, he could not tell the driver the address of the bank to which he wanted to go. He remembered only that it was on Fifty-seventh Street between Eighth Avenue and Broadway.

Professor Zalkind had more than one reason for undertaking this journey. First, the editor of the university press that was to publish his book, *Philo Judaeus and the Cabala,* had called to tell him that he would be visiting New York in the next few days. According to the contract, Professor Zalkind was to have delivered the manuscript some two years ago. Because he had added a number of footnotes and made many alterations in the text, he decided he should meet with the editor personally rather than send the manuscript by mail. Second, he wanted to see Hilda, the only living cousin of his late wife. He hadn't seen her for five years, and her daughter had written to him that her mother was seriously ill. Third, Professor Zalkind had read in the Miami *Herald* that last Saturday thieves had broken into a bank in New York and by boring a hole in the steel door leading to the vault they had stolen everything they could. True, this theft had not occurred in the bank where Zalkind rented a safe-deposit box. Still, the news item, headlined "How Safe Is a Safe?," disturbed him to such a degree that he could not sleep the whole night after he read it. In his box were deposited Lotte's jewelry, his will, and a number of important letters, as well as a manuscript of essays on metaphysics he had written when he was young—a work he would never dare publish while he was alive but one he did not want to lose. In addition to the safe-deposit box, he had in the same bank a savings account of some seventeen thousand dollars, which he intended to withdraw and deposit in Miami. It was not that he needed money. He had a pension from his years of teaching at the university. He had been receiving a Social Security check each month since he became seventy-two; regularly, reparation money came from Germany, which he had escaped after Hitler came to power. But why keep his belongings in New York now that he was a resident of Florida?

Another motive—perhaps the most important—brought the old man to New York. For many years he had suffered from prostate trouble, and the doctors he consulted had all advised him to have an operation. Procrastination could be fatal, they told him. He had made up his mind to visit a urologist in New York—a physician from Germany, a refugee like himself.

After crawling in traffic for a long time, the taxi stopped at Eighth Avenue and Fifty-seventh Street. No matter how Professor Zalkind tried, he couldn't read the meter. Lately, the retinas of his eyes had begun to degenerate and he could read only with a large magnifying glass. Assuming that he would get change, he handed the driver a ten-dollar bill, but the driver complained that it was not enough.

The Safe Deposit

Zalkind gave him two dollars more. The blizzard was getting worse. The afternoon was as dark as dusk. The moment Zalkind opened the door of the taxi, snow hit his face like hail. He struggled against the wind until he reached Seventh Avenue. There was no sign of his bank. He continued as far east as Fifth. A new building was being constructed. Was it possible that they had torn down the bank without letting him know? In the midst of the storm, motors roared, trucks and cars honked. He wanted to ask the construction workers where the bank had moved, but in the clang and clamor no one would hear his voice. The words in the Book of Job came to his mind: "He shall return no more to his house, neither shall his place know him any more."

Now Zalkind had come to a public telephone, and somehow he got out a dime and dialed Hilda's number. He heard the voice of a stranger, and could not make out what was being said to him. Well, everything is topsy-turvy with me today, he thought. Presently it occurred to him that he had looked only on one side of the street, sure that the bank was there. Perhaps he was mistaken? He tried to cross the street, but his glasses had become opaque and he couldn't be sure of traffic-light colors. He finally made it across, and after a while he saw a bank that resembled his, though it had a different name. He entered. There was not a single customer in the place. Tellers sat idly behind the little windows. A guard in uniform approached him and Zalkind asked him if this was indeed his bank. At first the guard didn't seem to understand his accent. Then he said it was the same bank—it had merged with another one and the name had been changed.

"How did it come that you didn't let me know?"

"Notices went out to all our depositors."

"Thank you, thank you. Really, I began to think I was getting senile," Dr. Zalkind said to the guard and himself. "What about the safe-deposit boxes?"

"They are where they were."

"I have a savings account in this bank, and a lot of interest must have accumulated in the years I've been away. I want to withdraw it."

"As you wish."

Dr. Zalkind approached a counter and began to search for his bankbook. He remembered positively that he had brought it with him in one of the breast pockets of his jacket. He emptied both and found everything except his bankbook—his Social Security card, his airplane ticket, old letters, notebooks, a telephone bill, even a leaflet advertising a dancing school which had been handed to him on the street. "Am I insane?" Dr. Zalkind asked himself. "Are the demons after me? Maybe I put it into my case. But where is my case?" He glanced right and left, on the counter and under it. There was no trace of a briefcase. "I have left it in the telephone booth!" he said with a tremor in his voice. "My manuscript too!" The bank suddenly became dark, and a golden eye lit up on a black background—otherworldy, dreamily radiant, its edges jagged, a blemish in the pupil, like the eye of some cosmic embryo in the process of formation. This vision baffled him, and for some time he forgot his briefcase. He watched the mysterious eye growing both in size and in luminosity. What he saw now was not altogether new to him. As a child, he had seen similar entities—sometimes an eye, other times a fiery flower that opened its petals or a dazzling butterfly or some unearthly snake. Those apparitions always came to him at times of distress, as when he was whipped in cheder, was attacked by some vicious urchin, or was sick with fever. Perhaps those hallucinations were incompatible forms that the soul created without any pattern in the Ideas, Professor Zalkind pondered in Platonic terms. He leaned on the counter in order not to fall. I'm not going to faint, he ordered himself. His belly had become bloated and a mixture of a belch and a hiccup came from his mouth. This is my end!

Dr. Zalkind opened the outside door of the bank with difficulty, determined to find the telephone booth. He looked around, but no telephone booth was in sight. He choked from the blast of the wind. In all his anguish his brain remained playful. Is the North Pole visiting New York? Has the Ice Age returned? Is the sun being extinguished? Dr. Zalkind had often seen blind men crossing the streets of New York without a guide, waving a white stick. He could never understand where they acquired the courage for this. The wind pushed him back, blew up the skirts of his coat, tore at his hat. No, I can't go looking for the phantom of a telephone booth in this hurricane. He dragged himself back to the bank, where he searched again for his briefcase on the counters and floor. He had no copy of the manuscript, just a pile of papers written in longhand—actually, not more than notes. He saw a bench and collapsed onto it. He sat silent, ready for death, which, according to Philo, redeems the soul from the prison of the flesh, from the vagaries of the senses. Although Zalkind had read everything Philo wrote, he could never conclude from his writings whether matter was created by God or always existed—a primeval chaos, the negative principle of the Godhead. Dr. Zalkind found contradictions in Philo's philosophy and puzzles no mind could solve as long as it was chained in the errors of corporality. "Well, I may soon see the truth," he murmured. For a while he dozed and even began to dream. He woke with a start.

The guard was bending over him. "Is something wrong? Can I help?"

"Oh, I had a briefcase with me and I lost it. My bankbook was there."

"Your bankbook? You can get another one. No one can take out your money without your signature. Where did you lose it? In a taxi?"

"Perhaps."

"All you have to do is notify the bank that you lost the bankbook and after thirty days they will give you another one."

"I would like to go to the safe-deposit boxes."

"I'll take you in the elevator."

The guard helped Dr. Zalkind get up. He half led him, half pushed him to the elevator and pressed the button to the basement. There, in spite of his confusion, Professor Zalkind recognized the clerk who sat in front of the entrance to the safe-deposit boxes. His hair had turned gray, but his face remained young and ruddy. The man also recognized Zalkind. He clapped his hands and called, "Professor Zalkind, whom do I see! We already thought that . . . you were sick or something?"

"Yes, no."

"Let me get the figures on your account," the clerk said. He went into another room. Zalkind heard his name mentioned on the telephone.

"Everything is all right," the clerk said when he returned. "What you owe us is more than covered by the interest in your account." He gave Zalkind a slip to sign. It took some time. His hand shook like that of a person suffering from Parkinson's disease. The clerk stamped the slip and nodded. "You don't live in New York any more?"

"No, in Miami."

"What is your new address?"

Dr. Zalkind wanted to answer, but he had forgotten both the street and the number. The heavy door opened and he gave the slip to another clerk, who led him into the room holding the safe-deposit boxes. Zalkind's box was in the middle row. The clerk motioned with his hand. "Your key."

"My key?"

"Yes, your key, to open the box."

Only now did it occur to Dr. Zalkind that one needed a key to get into a safe-deposit box. He searched through his pockets and took out a chain of keys, but he was sure they were all from Miami. He stood there perplexed. "I'm sorry, I haven't the key to my box."

"You do have it. Give me those keys!" The man grabbed the key chain and showed Professor Zalkind one that was larger than the others. He had been carrying a key to his safe-deposit box with him all those years, not knowing what it was for. The clerk pulled out a metal box and led Zalkind into a long corridor, opened a door to a room without a window, and turned on the light. He put the box on the table and showed Zalkind a switch on the wall to use when he had finished.

After some fumbling, Zalkind managed to open the box. He sat and gaped. Time had turned him sick, defeated, but for these objects in the box it did not exist. They had lain there for years without consciousness, without any need—dead matter, unless the animists were correct in considering all substance alive. To Einstein, mass was condensed energy. Could it perhaps also be condensed spirit? Though Professor Zalkind had packed his magnifying glass in his briefcase, he recognized stacks of Lotte's love letters tied with ribbons, his diary, and his youthful manuscript with the title "Philosophical Fantasies"—a collection of essays, feuilletons, and aphorisms.

After a while he lifted out Lotte's jewelry. He never knew that she possessed so many trinkets. There were bracelets, rings, earrings, brooches, chains, a string of pearls. She had inherited all this from her mother, her grandmothers, perhaps her great-grandmothers. It was probably worth a fortune, but what would he do with money at this stage? He sat there and took stock of his life. Lotte had craved children, but he had refused to increase the misery of the human species and Jewish troubles, he had said. She wanted to travel with him. He deprived her of this, too. "What is there to see?" he would ask her. "In what way is a high mountain more significant than a low hill? How is the ocean a greater wonder than a pond?" Even though Dr. Zalkind had doubts about Philo's philosophy and was sometimes inclined toward Spinoza's pantheism or David Hume's skepticism, he had accepted Philo's disdain for the deceptions of flesh and blood. He had come to New York with the decision to take all these things back with him to Miami. Yet, how could he carry them now that he had no briefcase? And what difference did it make where they were kept?

How strange. On the way to the airport that morning, Zalkind still had some ambitions. He planned to make final corrections on his manuscripts. He toyed with the idea of looking over "Philosophical Fantasies" to see what might be done with it. He had sworn to himself to make an appointment with the urologist the very next day. Now he was overcome by fatigue and had to lean his forehead on the table. He fell asleep and found himself in a temple, with columns, vases, sculptures, marble staircases. Was this Athens? Rome? Alexandria? A tall man with a white beard, dressed in a toga and sandals, emerged. He carried a scroll. He recited a poem or a sermon. Was the language Greek? Latin? No, it was Hebrew, written by a scribe.

"Peace unto you, Philo Judaeus, my father and master," Dr. Zalkind said.

"Peace unto you, my disciple Uri, son of Yedidyah."

"Rabbi, I want to know the truth!"

"Here in the Book of Genesis is the source of all truth: 'In the beginning God created the heaven and the earth. And the earth was without form, and void; and darkness was upon the face of the deep. And the Spirit of God moved upon the face of the waters.'"

Philo intoned the words like a reader in the synagogue. Other old men entered, with white hair and white beards, wearing white robes and holding parchments. They were all there—the Stoics, the Gnostics, Plontinus. Uri had read that Philo was not well versed in the Holy Tongue. What a lie! Each word from his lips revealed secrets of the Torah. He quoted from the Talmud, the Book of Creation, the Zohar, Rabbi Moshe from Córdoba, Rabbi Isaac Luria. How could this be? Had the Messiah come? Had the Resurrection taken place? Had the earth ascended to Heaven? Had Metatron descended to the earth? The figures and statues were not of stone but living women with naked breasts and hair down to their loins. Lotte was among them. She was also Hilda. One female with two bodies? One body with two souls?

"Uri, my beloved, I have longed for you!" she cried out. "Idolators wanted to defile me, but I swore to be faithful."

In the middle of the temple there was a bed covered with rugs and pillows; a ladder was suspended alongside it. Uri was about to climb up when a stream of water burst through the gate of the temple. Had Yahweh broken his covenant and sent a flood upon the earth?

Uri Zalkind woke up with a start. He opened his eyes and saw the bank clerk shaking his shoulder. "Professor Zalkind, your briefcase has been found. A woman brought it. She opened it and on top there was your bankbook."

"I understand."

"Are you sick?" the clerk asked. He pointed to a wet spot on the floor.

It took a long while before Dr. Zalkind answered. "I'm kaput, that's all."

"It's five minutes to three. The bank will be closing."

"I will soon go."

"The woman with the briefcase is upstairs." The clerk went out, leaving the door half open.

For a minute, Dr. Zalkind sat still, numbed by his own indifference. His briefcase was found but he felt no joy. Beside the box, Lotte's jewelry shimmered, reflecting the colors of the rainbow. Suddenly Dr. Zalkind began to fill his coat pockets with the jewels. It was the spontaneous act of a cheder boy. A passage from the Pentateuch came into his mind: "Behold, I am at the point to die: and what profit shall this birthright do to me?" Zalkind even repeated Esau's words with the teacher's intonation.

The clerk came in with a woman who carried a wet mop and a pail. "Should I call an ambulance?" he asked.

"An ambulance? No."

Zalkind followed the clerk, who motioned for the key. It was underneath Lotte's jewelry, and Zalkind had to make an effort to pull it out. The clerk took him up in the elevator, and there was the woman with his briefcase—small, darkish, in a black fur hat and a mangy coat. When she saw Zalkind, her eyes lit up.

"Professor Zalkind! I went to make a telephone call and saw your briefcase. I opened it and there with your papers was your bankbook. Since you use this bank, I thought they would know your address. And here you are." The woman spoke English with a foreign accent.

"Oh, you're an honest person. I thank you with all my heart."

"Why am I so honest? There is no cash here. If I had found a million dollars, the *Yetzer Hora* might have tempted me." She pronounced the Hebrew words as they did in Poland.

"It's terrible outside. Maybe you should take him somewhere," the guard suggested to the woman.

"Where do you live? Where is your hotel?" she asked. "I heard that you just arrived from Miami. What a time to come from Florida in your condition. You may, God forbid, catch the worst kind of cold."

"I thank you. I thank you. I have no hotel. I had planned to stay over with the cousin of my late wife, but it seems her telephone is out of order."

"I will take you to my own place for the time being. I live on 106th and Amsterdam. It is quite far from here, but if we get a taxi it won't be long. My dentist moved to this neighborhood and that is why I'm here."

One of the bank employees came over and asked, "Should I try to get a taxi for you?"

Even though it wasn't clear whom he addressed, Zalkind replied, "Yes— I really don't know how to express my gratitude."

Other clerks came over with offers of help, but Zalkind noticed that they winked at one another. The outside door opened and one of them called, "Your taxi!"

The snow had stopped, but it had got colder. The woman took Zalkind's arm and helped him into the taxi. She got in after him and said, "My name is Esther Sephardi. You can call me Esther."

"Are you a Sephardi?"

"No, a Jewish daughter from Lodz. My husband's surname was Sephardi. He was also from Lodz. He died two years ago."

"Do you have children?"

"One daughter in college. Why did you come in such a weather to New York?"

The Safe Deposit

Dr. Zalkind didn't know where to begin.

"You don't need to answer," the woman said. "You live alone, huh? No wife would allow her husband to go to New York on a day like this. You won't believe me, in frost worse than this I stood in a forest in Kazakhstan and sawed logs. That's where the Russians sent us in 1941. We had to build our own barracks. Those who couldn't make it died, and those who were destined to live lived. I took your briefcase with me to the Automat to get a cup of coffee and I looked into your papers. Is this going to be a book?"

"Perhaps."

"Are you a professor?"

"I was."

"My daughter studies philosophy. Not exactly philosophy but psychology. What does one need so much psychology for? I wanted her to study for a doctor but nowadays children do what they want, not what their mother tells them. For twenty years I was a bookkeeper in a big firm. Then I got sick and had to have a hysterectomy. Dr. Zalkind, I don't like to give you advice, but what you have should not be neglected. An uncle of mine had it and he delayed until it was too late."

"It's too late for me, too."

"How do you know? Did you have tests made?"

The taxi stopped in a half-dark street, with cars buried under piles of snow. Dr. Zalkind managed to get a few bills from his purse and gave them to Esther. "I don't see so well. Be so good—pay him and give him a tip."

The woman took Zalkind's hand and led him up three flights of stairs. Until now, Professor Zalkind had believed that his heart was in order, but something must have happened—after one flight he was short of breath. Esther opened a door and led him into a narrow corridor, and from there into a shabby living room. She said, "We used to be quite wealthy, but first my husband got sick with cancer and then I got sick. I'm working as a cashier during the day in a movie theater. Wait, let me take off your coat." She weighed it in her hands, glanced at the bulging pockets, and asked, "What do you have there—stones?"

After some haggling she took off his shirt and pants as well. He tried to resist, but she said, "When you are sick, you can't be bashful. Where is the shame? We are all made from the same dough."

She filled the bathtub with hot water and brought him clean underwear and a robe that must have been her late husband's. Then she made tea in the kitchen and warmed up soup from a can. Professor Zalkind had forgotten that he had had nothing to eat or drink since breakfast. As she served him, Esther kept on talking about her years in Lodz, in Russia, in New York. Her father had been a rich man, a partner in a textile factory, but the Poles had ruined him with their high taxes. He grew so distraught that he got consumption and died. Her mother lived a few years more and she, too, passed away. In Russia Esther became sick with typhoid fever and anemia. She worked in a factory where the pay was so low that one had to steal or starve. Her husband was taken away by the NKVD, and for years she didn't know if he had been killed in a slave-labor camp. When they finally reunited, they had to wait two years in Germany in a DP camp for

The Safe Deposit

visas to America. "What we went through in all those years only God the merciful knows."

For a moment, Professor Zalkind was inclined to tell her that even though God was omniscient, the well of goodness, one could not ascribe any attribute to Him. He did not provide for mankind directly but through Wisdom, called Logos by the Greeks. But there was no use discussing metaphysics with this woman.

After he had eaten, Dr. Zalkind could no longer fight off his weariness. He yawned; his eyes became watery. His head kept dropping to his chest. Esther said, "I will make you a bed on the sofa. It's not comfortable, but when you are tired you can sleep on rocks. Ask me."

"I will never be able to repay you for your kindness."

"We are all human beings."

Dr. Zalkind saw with half-closed eyes how she spread a sheet over the sofa, brought in a pillow, a blanket, pajamas. "I hope I don't wet the bed," he prayed to the powers that have the say over the body and its needs. He went into the bathroom and saw himself in a mirror for the first time that day. In one day his face had become yellow, wrinkled. Even his white beard seemed shrunken. When he returned to the living room, he remembered Hilda and asked Esther to call her. Esther learned from an answering service that Hilda had gone into a hospital the day before. "Well, everything falls to pieces," Zalkind said to himself. He noticed a salt shaker that Esther had neglected to take from the table, and while she lingered in the bathroom he put some of the salt on his palm and swallowed it, since salt retains water in the body. She returned in a house robe and slippers. She's not so young any more, he thought appraisingly, but still an attractive female; in spite of his maladies he had not lost his manhood.

The instant he lay down on the sofa he fell into a deep sleep. This is how he used to pass out as a boy on Passover night after the four goblets of wine. He awoke in the middle of the night with an urgent need to urinate. Thank God, the sheet was dry. The room was completely dark; the window shades were down. He groped like a blind man, bumping into a chest, a chair, an open door. Did it lead to the bathroom? No, he touched a headboard of a bed and could hear someone breathing. He was overcome with fear. His hostess might suspect him of dishonorable intentions. Eventually, he found the bathroom. He wanted light but he could not find the switch. On the way back, in the corridor, he accidentally touched the switch and turned on the light. He saw his briefcase propped against the wall, his coat hanging on a clothes tree. Yes, Lotte's jewelry was still there. He had fallen into honest hands. It had become cold during the night, and he put the coat on his shoulders over his pajamas and took the briefcase with him in order to place the jewelry in it. He had to smile—he looked as if he were going on a journey. I will give it to this goodhearted woman, he resolved. At least a part of it. I have no more need for worldly possessions. If some part of Lotte's mind still exists, she will forgive me. Suddenly his head became compressed with heat and he fell. He could hear his body thud against the floor. Then everything was still.

Professor Zalkind opened his eyes. He was lying on a bed with metal bars on both sides. Above the bed a small lamp glimmered. He stared in the semi-darkness, waiting for his memory to return. An ice bag rested on his forehead. His belly was bandaged and his hand touched a catheter. "Am I still alive?" he asked himself. "Or is it already the hereafter?" He felt like laughing, but he was too sore inside. In an instant everything he had gone through on this trip came back to him. Had it been today? Yesterday? Days before? It did not matter. Although he was aching, he felt a rest he had never known before—the sublime enjoyment of fearing nothing, having no wish, no worry, no resentment. This state of mind was not of this world and he listened to it. It was both astoundingly simple and beyond anything language could convey. He was granted the revelation he yearned for—the freedom to look into the innermost secret of being, to see behind the curtain of phenomena, where all questions are answered, all riddles solved. "If I could only convey the truth to those who suffer and doubt!"

A figure slid through the half-opened door like a shadow—the woman who had found the briefcase. She bent over his bed and asked, "You have wakened, huh?"

He did not answer and she said, "Thank God, the worst is over. You will soon be a new man."

The Old Man Had Four Wives

Frank Scheiner

When I was a kid Saturday mornings were always spoiled for me. At an unearthly hour my father shook me awake, just when sleep seemed sweetest. My mother washed, dressed, and fed me while I was still in a daze. I was clothed in my best. It was the Sabbath and I had to carry my father's *talis* to the synagogue for him. A round little telescope hat was placed carefully on my head, the *talis* in its embroidered bag pressed under my arm, and I stood waiting while my father brushed his Prince Albert and shiny cylinder hat. A flick here, another flick there, and off we went, my father walking on ahead, I tagging along at his heels.

He held to a rigid construction of the Talmudical Sabbath in those days: heaven and earth could not make him bear a burden on the Lord's day of rest. Later his views were to take on a more liberal hue.

Conveniently, he came to accept the opinion of the learned *Shepser Rov*. Manhattan, he discovered, was really an island; any of the bridges across the East River, or Harlem, for that matter, could, under the circumstances, be regarded as an *eruv*. Consequently, it was no mortal sin for a pious Jew on the island of Manhattan to carry his own *talis* to the synagogue on a Saturday.

But that did not happen until I was almost full grown, until my father's generous beard after a series of evolutionary changes had finally shrunk to the proportions of a goatee and he had begun to affect a broad-brimmed Stetson that made him look strangely like a Kentucky colonel. When I was a kid, as I have said before, it was I who carried the *talis*.

Our *schul* was a simple one. No pompous ignoramus of a secular president sat enthroned in lonely splendor at the right of the Holy Ark ordering with awful eye a neatly decorous assembly. The congregation was noisy and friendly. They knew no restraint. If your heart was filled with gratefulness to overflowing, you would sing out loudly praises unto the Lord; if your bosom was heavily burdened with care, you cried out, freely, high above the others. No frowning censorious eye would turn upon you.

But, alas, if your ears were sharp they would detect a mocking, derisive echo of your broad Bessarabian *a*'s and *o*'s. Ah, that you might be sure was Silberman. Silberman the cynic, the mocker, the curly-haired Litvak. But what could one expect from his kind? In Bessarabia whence my father came, men lived well, ate well, grew stout in body and tolerant in spirit. In Lithuania, where Silberman was bred, they starved on black bread and herring. Only presumption and impudence waxed great on such a diet.

Silberman was small, dark, and quick. His nose was long and pinched, his eyes were brilliant. A stranger in our midst, prudence should have warned him, "One against many. Don't go too far!" But there was no holding Silberman back. If he was one and we were many, all the more reason then to let the vulgar barbarians know that one of the elect was among them.

Silberman was a crony of my father. And so was Melman, the old man. But the old man and Silberman never got along very well together. Not that it ever came to an open quarrel. The old man's reserve was much too great for that. He was a patriarchal old man. Not fierce or Jehovah-like. But there was a pride in him that showed itself in the deliberateness of his movements, the care with which he chose his words, and his refusal to stoop to common familiarity. His white beard, his years, and his patriarchal demeanor commanded deference. Deference from all, including even Silberman at most times. And yet it was upon the old man that Silberman made his most notorious onslaught.

I was almost eighteen at the time, quite a man in my own eyes, and went to the synagogue with my father only on the High Holidays. It happened on Yom Kippur, late in the afternoon, when the agony of the long fast grows most intense and faces are pale and drawn. All through the long day of prayer the atmosphere of reality had receded until it seemed as if a mist had risen from the ground, curling round and isolating the peaked and tented figures of old men wrapped in black-striped prayer shawls. It was hard to believe that this wailing mountain at my side was my own father, or those two there, further along the bench, Silberman and the old man.

"*Oshamnu, bogadnu, gozalnu.* We have done wrong. We were faithless. We have stolen," they wailed and beat their breasts.

How satisfying the custom of the Jews! No dark whispering in a secret closet. No groveling abnegation: "Have mercy upon us miserable sinners." No fearful shrinking from that which is and must be: "Spare us, good Lord. Good Lord deliver us."

"We are not audacious," they had begun, "and not obstinate that we said before Thee, we are just and have not sinned! We confess we have sinned! We have done wrong, we were faithless, we have stolen, used violence, borne false witness, thought evil, deceived, mocked, revolted, reviled . . ."—In a word, we are human.—"God of mercy, have mercy upon us!"

With increasing tempo, the first warm wave of contrition having passed, they continued, *"Al chait schechotonu laifonecho:* For the sins we have committed with obduracy of heart, by scorn and in error, with intention and fraud, by sinful inclination—" (The old man's woeful quaver soared high.) "For the sins we have committed by lewdness, through adultery—"

Suddenly Silberman's sharp "Ttt, ttt, ttt!" stabbed through the fervid recital. "A shame," he exclaimed. "It's a shame!"

"What's a shame?" my father asked, alarmed.

"The old man," answered Silberman with mock

concern. "To have to admit a sin he couldn't possibly commit any longer!"

Yom Kippur or no Yom Kippur, a snicker burst from all who heard.

The old man heard, too. He could not help but hear. But manfully he strove to show no sign. In a voice ever more quavery and uncertain he went on without pause. "For the sins we committed by the impurity of our lips, by dishonoring parents and teachers, by profaning the name of God, by a wicked tongue, by judging, by envy—" and so on to the bitter end, "God of mercy, pardon us, forgive us!"

At nightfall Reb David, the *shammes*, blew a long blast on the *shofar, teckeeeeeeeu-u,* and the solemn fast was ended. Hurriedly the men gathered in the little vestibule of our synagogue to await the emergence of their women-folk from the curtained segregation where they had prayed and fasted all day. The old man did not linger with the noisy group. There was no one for whom he had to wait. His wife had died the previous summer. He passed through quickly, returning the greeting of those who greeted him, distantly, coldly, his face unaccustomedly grim and unrelenting.

The following spring the war came. I joined the army, and it was more than two years before I got home again, tired and disillusioned.

I received a prodigal's welcome. My father, who had fumed and threatened when I had enlisted, was surprisingly soft and forgiving. My mother, like all Jewish mothers, wept with joy over me, fed me, and insisted on a minute account of all that had happened to me.

The story of my adventures was too meager to take long to tell, and I was grateful when the tide turned and I was permitted to inquire after this one and that one and the other I had known.

It was not long before I inquired: "How is the old man Melman?" Somehow he had been much in my mind.

"It's a shame," my mother exclaimed, suddenly indignant.

"What's a shame?"

"The old man," my mother replied.

"Why, what's happened to him?"

"For forty-two years," she began oratorically, as if she were reciting something she had committed to memory, "a man is married to one woman. They live together, suffer, thrive, raise a family, marry off children. . . . Finally she passes away, and no sooner is her body laid to rest than the old reprobate disgraces her grave—"

"You don't mean to tell me the old man has taken himself another wife?"

"One?! Three!!"

"What, all at one time?"

"No," my mother said sadly, refusing to see any humor in the situation, "one after the other. . . . They don't seem to keep with him," she added mysteriously.

"Ah," my father put in, with a wave of his hand, "that's just women's stories. He is simply unfortunate, that's all."

The next day was Saturday. My father was mildly surprised when I offered to accompany him to the synagogue. The fact was that I wanted to catch a glimpse of the old man again. My mother's words called up the image of an ancient ogre, a bluebeard brazenly flaunting his contempt in the faces of his fellows.

My mind had gone back to that afternoon when Silberman had impaled the old man on his barbaric shaft and held him up to humiliating derision. I remembered the old man's defencelessness, his horror and bewilderment. I could still see the scarlet that flooded his face in those first few moments, before he froze into an unnatural composure. But the drama, seemingly, had taken an unlooked-for turn. Silberman had picked a Tartar in the old man. Four wives!—who now would dare to accuse him of falsely confessing sinfulness and lust? Four wives! He was a hero to me, no matter what he might be to others. I marveled at his audacity. Who would have credited the old man with being capable of such a stroke of—shall I say, genius? My heart warmed to him.

Our synagogue had changed little since last I had been there. The air was warm and close and fetid, the hubbub general and unnoticed. Ostentatiously hands were stretched out to us shoulder-high, in the sabbatical manner. *"Shulem aleichem a yeed! Fin vunit kimt a yeed?"* It was good to be treated like a full-grown man.

But Silberman had to spoil it for me. He was a surprise, a shock. Somehow—because of the old man, I suppose—I had looked to find him disciplined, chastened, more subdued. Plainly, however, he was the same old Silberman. His nose perhaps a trifle more pinched, his curly black beard sprinkled with salty grey, but his tongue as sharp and biting as ever it had been. Fortunately he was no more unkind than to hail me as *"Unser groiser held!"* and laugh.

To hide my discomfort I turned away, looking about me cautiously for the old man. I could not find him and my first intimation of his presence was Silberman's acidulous half-whisper, "The old Turk's here!"

What a sad and unexpected transformation old Melman had undergone! He looked so pitifully weak and lonely. Head bowed and hanging a little to one side, he stood hesitating in the doorway for a moment, then came to us readily, apparently eager to show friendliness where he would not be repulsed. The resolute reserve that had always marked him had decayed. There was no strength or force in him at all. The hand he gave me was cold and lifeless. Valiantly he tried to form the loose folds of his mouth into a friendly smile. Weakly, feebly he smiled and never have I seen an expression of such hopeless dissolution.

How falsely we had judged him! My mother even more so than I. This was no ogre, no bluebeard. Only an old man, broken, helpless. I pitied him profoundly.

And yet when he turned to find his seat, his red-rimmed, blood-shot eyes, resting on Silberman for a moment, shone triumphantly bright. Bright, it may be, with satisfied cunning and malice. He sank into his place just as the *shammes* slapped the big wooden hand for quiet. And the *Bal Schachris* began, singing out strongly, "*Matovu ohelecho Yacov*— How beautiful are your tents, O Jacob!"

Ben, Son of Margulies

Ruth Miller

You wouldn't think that a man would come to a hospital because he had no other place to go. On the surface no one could have told that. He entered the Baker Pavilion of New York Hospital on a Sunday afternoon, the Sunday before Christmas. That should have been a clue. But you can't blame the admissions clerk. She was Sunday relief and scarcely looked at him. Anyone who is anybody is busy all week and plans his special excitements for the week end. And Christmas is for family and parties—general good cheer. Isn't that it? But he was a Jew. Christmas? No. He was a relative, in a special way, to that Samuel H. Margulies who became Chief Rabbi in Florence at the end of the last century—an influential man, a visionary, savior of the Falasha Jews. The man who had come to the hospital chose himself to be the descendant of a man who deserves a golden page in Jewish history.

And when the clerk asked his name, he said in fact, "Ben, son of Margulies." She wrote "Benson-Margulies" and introduced him to the young girl who was to accompany him upstairs. "This is Mr. Benson." He didn't hear. He had turned to say goodbye to the cab driver who dozed in the waiting room. "Goodbye, my friend. I won't see you any more."

"Goodbye, Poppa. Live and be well." The cab driver went through the revolving door, out into the world. Ben, son of Margulies the Chief Rabbi of Florence, followed the girl with his chart in her hand. Followed the girl down the long corridor, Ben—from Florence to Lvov to Stockholm to New York to Brownsville to the Manhattan Bridge to First Avenue to 68th Street to a hack stand. Into the five-million-dollar construction of white brick into an elevator. Needing finally only one small valise.

Ben was excited. As the elevator rose he felt the entire weight of himself pressing down, resisting the mechanical rise. "I live with my daughter. She couldn't take me." The girl smiled. "They do lovely things here for Christmas. They give you a turkey dinner and decorate the halls. You'll enjoy it."

"It's my gall bladder. I went to three doctors. They all said the same thing. I use Kahnweiler. A very big man." On the fifth floor the elevator stopped to take on a woman in a wheel chair with her orderly. Ben envied how they, the hospital employees, talked so easily to one another, but why not? They belonged together. Ben looked sideways at the woman and said to her, "I'm gall bladder."

She smiled sadly and shook her head. "Nowadays gall bladder is nothing."

"Nothing? I had three doctors. I have already

paid out one hundred and twenty-five dollars! Nothing." The door opened on the eleventh floor. He hung back. Soon he would be in the wheel chair and others would stand aside for him. The woman's red satin bathrobe glittered in the sunlight as she was wheeled away.

He was taken to a large clean room. A nice room. Empty of people. He was going to be the person in that room. The son of Margulies should not be in a ward.

"I'm Miss Dixon. How de do Mr. Benson."

"No—Margulies. What Benson? Do I look like a Benson?"

"Oh you're going to be a kidder. I like that. Now you just take off your hat and coat and all and I'll be back to make you comfortable."

Half an hour later he was still sitting on the chair near the door. "How do you do, sir. I'm Dr. Swope."

"Why is it always with introductions? Is it a party?"

"I thought you had this patient ready, Miss Dixon."

"Oh, Mr. Benson, sir, you're still dressed. You're supposed to be in bed, sir. Where are your pajamas?"

"What, undress, in the middle of the day? Come back at ten o'clock. At night I undress. It's then I go to bed."

"I'm so sorry, Dr. Swope. He's a comedian." Which was not a fact about Ben Margulies. He was not a comical man.

"Should I lay down finally? My pants! How do I know when I'll put on my shoes again?" The nurse giggled and he wrapped his shoes carefully in some paper towels and placed them in the valise. Five minutes later Ben was on his back between the sheets.

They examine each patient thoroughly. New York Hospital is a research hospital. If you come with an infected tooth, a broken leg, a brain tumor, it waits until after the one hundred questions. They're counting, counting. When they asked him if his mother were still alive, he wept. And were his brothers in good health; he said "The devil take them! They go to the Hot Springs every winter." "A sister?" "Dead. Dead." "What did she die of, sir?" "Gas." "What, sir?" "Gas. Her husband and all her children. Gas." "And your wife, sir?" He compressed his lips. "Are you married, sir?" "Do I ask you about your privacy? You're too young. You're wet behind the ears. Get out of here. Leave me alone."

No one could get an answer out of him after that. But they agreed with Dr. Kahnweiler. They gave him a sedative and when the night nurse flashed her light on him at four o'clock in the morning, she thought he was dead. His eyes were wide open, his jaw hung loose, and she turned swiftly to call for help. He reached out a moist hand and grabbed her. He muttered in a coarse voice: "They asked me about my wife. You tell them. Say, five years ago my wife answered me in the middle of the night, 'Ben, I hope you drop dead. I hope they carry you out in a basket!' I threw her out of the house. She wouldn't. You know what I mean? You understand a man can be sixty and still want to? She said, you filthy old—you don't need to know what she said. She went to Reno. Can you imagine such a thing with Jews? And stayed there. Ashamed to show her sour face in New York. But they take sides against me. It's my fault I'm a man? And if I tell my daughter I like my eggs soft-boiled, what do I hear? Go—go tell them." The night nurse closed the door on his shouting.

The first day it was urinalysis, blood count, blood chemistry, X-ray, temperature, pulse, tappings and thumpings. All confirming Dr. Kahnweiler who visited cheerily and in his immaculate white shirt settled the fee.

No one else came to Ben. But he did not notice this today. His condition absorbed him. Alone, he went on with the deep breathing and tried to locate his pains precisely. He pressed his fingers hard around his left wrist and went on and on counting his pulse beats. He rubbed his face a long time and stared into the mirror to watch how the red flush settled back into the yellowish pallor. He inquired about his blood pressure and tried to pay the desk clerk a dollar to show him the results of his tests. He wore proudly the huge yellow-striped terry cloth robe provided by the hospital and began to wander, peering into rooms and offices and closets, finding stainless steel, ceramic tile, inlaid linoleum. Everywhere. He clasped his hands in excitement at the thought of how much money it must have taken to build such a place. This was only one floor of who knows how many, one building of who knows how many. He tried to find out but whoever he asked kidded him from his answer. He smiled slyly because it was clear that no one really knew. His head swam with figures before he slept that night. He was counting the bills, not the amounts, that would come later, but simply the kinds of bills—electricity, laundry, water, food, paper.

In the middle of that night they found him standing in front of the massive door marked Operating Room, reading the words of the small sign: "It is forbidden to enter," reading them over and over again.

He shaved carefully for the first time in four days. Because today he was going to speak to the woman in the red satin bathrobe. He had caught glimpses of her walking slowly up and down the woman's corridor, and had approached her twice last evening but a nurse had chased him back. Now he had a plan. The public telephone booth had been installed in the men's corridor as if men had more business to keep contact with, and of course the women used it. A woman may walk and look but a man may not.

Her robe swayed past his door just after lunch and he hurried out. "I'm Ben, son of Margulies." She smiled slowly with a remembering weakness. "They said you were a Mr. Benson. But I said to myself when I saw you closer and watched you walk and heard you with the desk last night—didn't you give it to them!—I said to myself, what's in a name? I'm Dolly Freedman."

They walked together into the solarium, a large common room for use of all the patients. It was spacious with sofas and lamps and coffee tables. The wheel chairs were stored at one end. Dolly and Ben chose two and wheeled themselves over to the television set and he put in four quarters that afternoon. That night they sat in front of the windows watching the lights of the whole city of New York, looking toward the Queensborough Bridge out over Long Island City.

"See that Sunshine Biscuits? I have to pass it to where I live."

He showed Dolly he had brought eight quarters. After carefully focusing the picture he turned off the sound. Dolly enjoyed the silent comedians. He insisted the singers were best. They made the most remarkable image without sound.

"It's funny," Dolly said. "Here I sit in my nightgown and housecoat, and you are in your pajamas—it's like we're in our living room."

He leaned out of his wheel chair and patted her knee. "What satin can do for a man," he whispered. "Listen, Dolly—" he hesitated, then, "Why? you know what I mean? Why are you here? What is wrong, God forbid."

"You're gall bladder. When will they operate?"

"The day after tomorrow. They say I'm calming down. They want me to be calm. Pills and needles. To be calm. And then they cut. They are going to put a knife in me. Only they shouldn't let too much blood run out. And you? You can tell me. You can confide in me. Maybe if you're not so bad, tonight we can together disappear. I know the stairways by heart."

"Eleven floors? You're feeble-minded."

He jumped up and stood threateningly over her, shaking his fist in her face. "Shut up! You red Chinawoman!"

She wheeled her chair swiftly out of his reach. Then he dropped his hand, and his head hung down, and his shoulders sagged. Dolly got out of her chair and went to stand beside him. She said, "You're such a little guy. Look. I'm taller, you only come up to here." He raised his eyes to see—he came just to her chin. "You're thin, so thin, Ben, who takes care of you to let you go so thin the bones show?"

"No one. No one."

"Look. I'm twice your size. No one? Look."

He saw it was true. He sighed heavily. They were both weak. They sank back into their wheel chairs.

"I'm here for the treatments. It's my throat. I can't swallow. I have to eat baby food. And puddings. So every morning I go downstairs to the big machines and for fifteen minutes I take the treatment. But they don't know what it is. Look how my skin is burned from the machine." She showed him the redness and the blisters and they compared it with the whiteness of her arms.

"How could it be a woman like you never got married?"

"Listen," Dolly answered, "where do you find love? You tell me. Where do you find it?"

"My wife—she found it—if she can any woman can—a sour pickle."

"You're married?"

"Married! Divorced. Divorced. Can you imagine a Jew divorced?"

"It happens."

"But to me? Ben the son of the Chief Rabbi? A curse. This was a curse."

"Mr. Margulies, I've been fifteen years on the market. I'm a plum, an apricot, a grape—a little long out in the sun, maybe, but not spoiled. You understand me? To tell you the truth, I have my suspicions I didn't light up anyone's sky neither. So the question is, am I going to be left out of the human family? They give me treatments but for the real thing they have no medicines and no machines. They didn't ask me that. How I go for a walk with an eligible man on Queens Boulevard and try to turn the conversation to something interesting and he asks me about my pension."

Because it was Christmas Eve they were interrupted. Twelve young women from the nurses' residence walked with measured steps down the corridor carrying tall burning candles. They were singing Christmas carols for the patients. Dolly said they looked so beautiful because candlelight flatters the face. Ben said nothing. He turned up the sound of the television set. Dolly hit his wrist gently and commanded him to be polite. He liked this. He liked her to tell him to do something. The singing voices were sweet and sorrowful. As they walked slowly through the eleventh floor, wherever the patients could rise from their beds, they hurried to their doorways and leaned solemnly, wiping away tears. The muffled sobbing came from more serious beds.

Then Ben Margulies and Dolly Freedman turned to each other and tried to smile, not sentimental or nostalgic smiles because no Christmas was unlocked in their hearts; instead a bitterness, a loneliness—maybe a recognition of some impasse. Ben said, "Eh! what can they tell me?" and closed his eyes to rest.

Dolly said, "Between us nothing will happen so I can be honest with you. After all I'm not always looking. I have time for a little human friendship too. You're resting? So rest. With me you don't have to stand on ceremonies. And if I want to talk, I'll talk. Such a bargain with me a man doesn't have to be afraid to make. I've got relatives, uncles, cousins, who knows what—who needs them—they send their daughters to me—they want me to introduce them—work them into something—you know—I'm the big shot—I live in the city—she, the particular one who gets my goat, they send her in from Newark. But I'm looking for myself. I ask myself why do they send her. If it's a good thing I wouldn't introduce her; if it's a Gimbel's bargain why should I introduce her? After all it's my cousin! One Sunday she came and I took her to Riverside Drive. My feet killed me but how else do you bump into people? You never know who is looking. Well, she's married. Yes—yes, oh yes, she's married. And do you know how she did it? Florida! I have to invest four, five hundred dollars yet and get what she got. Well I don't say I wouldn't but your health comes first and as soon as I am back on my feet—maybe—we'll see. No one needs to feel sorry for me. I'll tell you the truth, I don't need sympathy. But I have a sense of humor, thank God. It's darkest before the dawn, isn't that right? I'll tell you the truth. You're sitting there quietly. Your eyes are closed. I know you don't hear me but I want to tell this to you, see, I really want to get married. You can believe me when I tell you that it's my ambition. I'm tired of working. I want someone to take care of. I could love someone in five minutes—five minutes after he says—Dolly—you know—be mine! Listen, Mr. Margulies, am I really—you know—not—desirable? I mean—it's late for this kind of thing—I don't even have much urge in that direction I think—but you see I don't believe in the after-life."

The next day, Christmas, he had to remain in bed. Intravenous. Such care they take to build me up. He began to believe in his operation too. The nurses, the doctors kept patting his shoulder and telling him it was a sad thing that he should be having this for Christmas.

But no one else came to see him and he could not go to search for her. Everyone had visitors between seven and eight. He lay weeping and lonely. Then the sounds of the families coming and going, the How-are-you's and the Good-night-darling's got to him and he began to shout at the top of his voice. "Good night darling, good night darling," over and over and everyone on the floor told everyone else to listen. The patients sat up in their beds listening, all trembling at the rasping scream of the words good night darling.

Until Dolly crept inside his room and sat beside his bed stroking his hand and telling him he would be safe. She leaned over him, smoothing his sheets, careful not to jar the iron stand nor the tube taped on his arm. She kissed his forehead and whispered, "Good night, darling." He begged, "Don't leave me. I am without anybody in this room." The room was quite empty, but a Margulies must not be in a ward.

Does it make any difference how they cut out a gall bladder? Enough that Dr. Kahnweiler knew. And the OR nurses. Yet Ben Margulies had come all this way for the one great event; all these preparations were for him—he the star! He longed to see the Operating Room where the spectacular initiation was to take place. It was like a movie, only now *he* was going to be on that very table under those very lights. The gleaming instruments had been arranged and were waiting for him.

The white-gowned, white-capped anesthetist

looked tenderly at him while adjusting the tube and he watched her face for a sign of recognition. "Feel like you're going somewhere, Mr. Benson?" she whispered.

"Wait! Wait! I have nowhere to go. No Benson!"

And then he missed it. Pentathol would not let him see any of it. His one great moment.

If you wonder what a man really feels about himself in the world, listen to him while he hovers below consciousness. The twenty doctors and nurses stand over him with their supple hands active on his body, but he, the man, has retreated to where the scalpel fails to reach. When Ben awakened from his deep anesthetic sleep he was sobbing uncontrollably, deeply satisfying sobs.

For five days the man would not emerge. The body healed marvelously, it was allowed to do its work quietly, free of all disintegrating thoughts. Two orderlies came twice each day to walk with the body, holding it up stolidly by the elbows, replacing it on the bed. The nurses laved it and fed it and gave it medicine. Dr. Kahnweiler was satisfied. But no one could get through to Mr. Margulies. Not even Dolly Freedman, who had permission from everyone to try. She combed his hair. She told him the story of her life. She told him the day the sun was shining that the sun was shining. She told him when it rained. When it was dark, she left it so, and told him how she would furnish a four-room apartment, yes, she asked him to marry her. He never spoke to anyone. Not once to Dolly Freedman, who had to leave the hospital on New Year's Day.

It was decided to stop the drugs. In the late afternoon they found him sitting in the telephone booth with a handful of coins staring at the dial.

Ben, Son of Margulies

When they coaxed him back he turned on them furiously. "When I get a telephone call I expect you to tell me. You're paid to do a job, why don't you do it? My daughter calls twice a day and you won't let her talk to me. Is it so much to let a man talk to his own daughter whose flesh and blood she is? And my brothers they came twice to see me and you wouldn't open the door. Why should you lock a man's family out?"

During the day he was quiet enough. He took his meals well. He did not interfere with the maids. He cooperated with the nurses. At night he began. They saw him pacing the floor, or standing in the middle of the room with his arms folded over his chest, as if listening to some reply. Then he would shake his fists or stamp his feet in an agony of rage. What did he say? "Dogs! Lice! Is this what a man becomes? Build big buildings. Make cars. Trucks. Airplanes. For what? Who needs it? Money. Pile it in front of the door. Will it bring five minutes a man shouldn't smell like a rotten egg?" After a week no one listened much. A new patient, scared, might ask, what is that? And hear, it's only Mr. Margulies. No one comes to see him. It gets on his nerves. But the hospital staff became used to it. His pulse was steady. No fever. Little pain. Good color. What did he say? Only he indicted the world.

Once he came out of his room huddled in that yellow bathrobe, the long belt trailing. He stationed himself outside the women's rest room, and asked, "There was a lady there by you on your side there in a red bathrobe. Is she there? There was a lady in a red bathrobe."

On Friday evening he began early. He had been

more restless that day. When the resident doctor dropped by for his regular inquiry before leaving the floor, he was puzzled by something he thought he heard Margulies say: "You can take your whole goddam America and shove it!" He prescribed a sedative. When the nurse came in with the capsule and glass of water he took it, broke it open with his finger nails, emptied it in the water and then threw the water in her face. She ran. He screamed, "Call the police! Call the fire department! Help! Help! It's poison. She gave me poison."

Two nurses closed the door on the terrifying roar. "I curse the dead! I curse the dead! And when God comes next time to ask, slam the door in his face." They were really frightened. The other nurses and the two desk clerks gathered outside the door and no one knew what to do. "I wouldn't give you two cents for the whole Coney Island!" The corridors were cleared. But from each doorway, ears, eyes—listening, watching.

The supervisor gasped: "Get emergency. For God's sake, get emergency." And they all heard the loudspeaker: "Dr. Swope, Dr. Bakely, Dr. Gumbiner, Emergency Baker 11, calling Dr. Swope, Dr. Bakely, Dr. Gumbiner, Emergency Baker 11." They came in eighty seconds from three directions. One opened the door. "No! I'm through! I quit! I wouldn't cross the street to see Theodor Herzl on a bicycle!"

"Get the guard rails up on his bed. Go on, Miss Dixon, we'll be in there with you. Gumbiner get the shot. Call 13. Tell 13 we're bringing him up." The three doctors went in together. "No shots! No shots! Nothing! Nothing! No Shots!"

The nurses crowded the door and an aide had to

tap them on the shoulder to move out of the way of the stretcher with heavy leather straps. Gumbiner came out with the hypodermic syringe empty. He signed the orderlies to wait five minutes. He stood wiping his face with a towel.

Ben Margulies was covered with blankets and it was impossible to see anything as he was wheeled out into the waiting elevator. Yet he was followed. The staff watched the indicator quiver, then swing slowly past 11, through 12, tremble, then stop at 13.

Dolly Freedman came on Sunday, wearing a pearl-gray gabardine suit and a silver feather hat. She even had a bunch of flowers. When she asked for Mr. Margulies, she was not recognized. She had to say, "I'm Dolly Freedman from the red satin bathrobe. How is our patient?" It was the maid she asked.

"Oh, Mr. Benson. I remember him in my prayers. I could tell you about Mr. Benson. He's upstairs. You know—for the—" she tapped her forehead. "When he gets out of there, it won't be back here or anywhere, I can bet you. Want to make a bet?"

So. Dolly gave the flowers for the desk. She rang for the elevator. I don't know that it was the same one that took him up. It certainly took her down. She went back the way she came. Alone, but feeling that somehow her luck was changing. "Better now than five years from now. And me maybe with a baby. And the four rooms to keep up."

Terrible Mistakes

Eugene Ziller

Meyer Kestenbaum decided to go back to work right after his wife died. He'd been retired for almost five years before that. It was autumn. The idea of spending entire days alone in that apartment, in which the presence of his wife still seemed as undiminished as if she had no more than stepped out of the house for a minute to run an errand down to the corner store—watching the year die away, seated at the livingroom window facing out on the sycamores and maples lining the curb on the street below through the still leaden winter afternoons, waiting for his own death, seemed to him to be a prospect that was more than he could bear, or would want to.

He had always been an active, gregarious man. Even in retirement he'd kept busy. He was involved in various neighborhood activities: member and officer of a social club, collector for the Heart Fund, standby volunteer to help out on special occasions at the synagogue; even canvassing for the local Democratic club during elections. So it was no surprise the whole neighborhood, practically, came to pay their respects during the week he was in mourning. They passed before him murmuring the formal trite earnest phrases of condolence, while he nodded up at them, seated on the low hard mourning bench supplied by the funeral home, his two daughters seated at his side, on mourning benches also, his son standing behind him or on his way out of the room to answer the door.

He remained in control of himself the entire week; a medium sized, spare man, sitting hunched forward a little, his slippered feet extended awkwardly before him, unshaven, in plain rumpled garments, a black yarmulke on top of his head, in the traditional, Orthodox appearance and mien of bereavement. Once or twice his voice broke when he spoke of his wife or of their life together, but that was the extent to which he showed any emotion: during that time he didn't cry *at all* in another's presence. In fact, he ended up having to console his daughters when *their* grief became unmanageable. They stayed in mourning with him the entire week. His son left after three days, explaining he was unable to stay away from his classes (he was a school teacher) any longer than that.

His son did return on the last day, when he rose from mourning. After breakfast while his children waited, he shaved for the first time that week, put on a white shirt and tie and his only suit of blue, indestructible serge, and the four of them went downstairs together, out into the bright chill October air, and walked slowly around the block, unhurrying, formal, past the mute, curious eyes of those on the street, to signify the end of mourning.

At lunch his children brought up the obligatory question immediately. They told him they knew it was too soon for him to have made up his mind, but if he decided the apartment was too much for him to handle alone, they would be more than happy to have him move in with one of them, any of them. They sounded as if they had discussed it earlier among themselves. His older daughter had made lunch. She poured coffee for him, stirring in two saccharin tablets, which was the way he liked it, without asking. The sun glared along one wall of the kitchen, on the old gas stove and porcelain sink, which had been in the apartment since they had first moved in more than eighteen years ago, at the oblique angle of midday. From several blocks away came the familiar, regular thunder of a passing elevated train, making its way across Brooklyn. At that moment, seated there among his children, in the peaceful, familiar surroundings of his neighborhood and home, he almost seemed to feel, for an instant, as though nothing had changed.

He knew better. In the evening, after everyone had left, seated alone at the kitchen table before his meager, perfunctory meal of tuna fish and a slice of toast, he looked across at the empty chair opposite him, in which his wife would sit after she had served their meals, and he broke into deep, convulsive sobbing.

He decided to stay away from the apartment as much as possible, on any pretext, for the next few months at least. He rose early now and shaved immediately, and dressed and left the apartment right after breakfast. In good weather he went to the neighborhood park about a block away and played checkers with one of the other old men who might be around and available, at one of the thick, stone, municipal tables with inlaid checkerboards, or else sat watching the young mothers strolling by with their children, or the older boys shooting basketball. Sometimes he made leather belts or comb cases from craft materials supplied by the park, when no one was around for checkers, for his grandchildren. In bad weather he played cards down at the club, the ceaseless open sound of rain or wind filling the long bare room which had served as a dry goods store earlier and now contained only, in two rows, orderly parallel clusters of bridge tables and chairs. Or he went occasionally to a movie, if it was a weekday. On week*ends* he visited his children. He had never given serious consideration to their offer: that he give up his apartment and move in with one of them. He felt they had never intended the offer seriously, but only as a gesture. His son and older daughter lived in apartments in which they barely had enough room for their own families. And while his younger daughter lived in a house which *had* enough room, he had never really felt comfortable with her husband, whom he seldom saw, even when he visited his daughter, and barely knew. Sure, he told himself. All fine and good. But where will they put me? In the case of his older daughter at least, he knew it would mean sleeping in the same room with one of his grandchildren.

But neither did he feel spending the rest of his life sitting in the park, or down at the club, at

Terrible Mistakes

unvarying, aimless games, day after day, with the other old men of the neighborhood, as he was now doing, was a prospect he liked any better; bent as he was on staying away from the apartment. It was his son who suggested the alternative of getting a job and going back to work for a while.

The first thing he said was: "At my age?"

"What do you mean, at *your* age?" his son said. "What's that got to do with it? It's how you feel that counts. You're an active man, you do things. You were never the type to just sit around. Sometimes I'd come to the house and ma'd start telling me all the things you were doing for the week—I'd get tired just *listening* to them."

"It never even entered my mind," he said, quietly.

"Why not?" his son said. "It would be a perfectly natural thing. The only difference would be, you'd be doing something you're getting paid for."

Yes. But where will I begin? he asked himself, at home that night alone, seated in the livingroom before the television set watching the eleven o'clock news. He had already decided to follow his son's advice. What he was now turning over in his mind was how to go about *finding* a job.

He started by asking around in the neighborhood. But none of the stores needed an extra clerk or someone to sweep up or to put out the stock. He tried the Democratic club next. He went directly to Harold Markowitz, the precinct captain.

"Gee, I'm sorry, Meyer," Harold said, after hearing him out, still holding on to him from their handshake. He was a genial, slack, fleshy man, with soft palms like an animal's, and clear unblinking eyes. "There's just nothing around. Maybe something'll open up after the election. God knows you got a favor coming to you, for all the work you done."

"No, I don't mean from the club, or a city job," he said, gesturing with his left, free hand. "I mean something personal. Maybe you know somebody who needs a help in their business, a clerk or a messenger, a job for a healthy, retired man."

"Gee I wish I did. You should've told me sooner," Harold said. "You used to be a painter or something, didn't you?"

"A dressmaker," he corrected the other. "I worked on better ladies garments."

"Yeah," Harold said. "Well, I didn't know you were interested in going back to work."

"I just decided last week," he said. "Since my wife died I—"

"Yeah. That was too bad," Harold said. "Be with you in a minute," he said in an aside to another, a thin redhaired man wearing a plaid flannel shirt and a tie, who had come over to them a minute before and stood waiting. "Well I'll tell you, Meyer," he went on, in the same breath practically, as if without break or digression. "I'll ask around, that's the least I can do. I'll let you know if I hear anything," and released him, finally, patting him on the shoulder with a thick hand and saying, "Excuse me," and turned to the other with that same air of complete and benign attentiveness, and moved with him among the others seated there or standing around, to another part of the room.

Meyer stood looking after them for a minute, already without any hope, illusion even, that anything tangible would result from his talk with

Markowitz. He didn't hold it against him. Listen. He is a busy man, he told himself, without resentment. He cannot have time for everyone. He was already thinking: Yes. I was a *fine* dressmaker, I almost forgot, it seems so long ago.

He had been up to his old shop only once since his retirement. Two months after he left they had asked him back to help out for a few weeks on a particularly hard garment during the busy season; but that was all. He did continue to go into the city to meet his old shopmates for lunch once or twice a month, for a while after, though. But as some changed jobs, and others retired, and the mere passage of time eroded his ties with the remainder (so that he would find himself seated opposite them in the cafeteria in the brief, glaring light of midday, before the random clutter of soiled cups and dishes containing the remnants of lunch, without anything to say to them, not a thought or observation which he hadn't made five times over in the past few months, or which was common between them and not something out of that part of his life which had begun after he'd retired and which had evolved away from them; and an abrupt, palpable, awkward silence would fall upon them, like a door closing, leaving them seated across from him like so many strangers, like people he had never seen before and had been seated among completely by accident) the meetings petered out. He had worked thirteen years for the firm; for the same owner, in the same place. He decided to take a chance and see if they had anything for him.

The same plaque bearing the company's name, *Four Star Fashions*, was still in place among the others, in the outside directory at the entrance to the building. He used the side entrance, as he had all those years he'd worked there, riding up in the freight elevator. He got out at the fifth floor. He stood in a short, dim corridor, bleak as a prison. Behind him, from inside the walls of the building, the elevator whined and creaked as it slowly made its descent. The floor was shared by his old firm and another. Their back entrances faced the elevator: broad metal sliding freight doors, to one side of which were arched, silled windows like a bank teller's. He went to the one on which *Four Star Fashions* was stenciled in mottled, flaking gilt. He stood looking in for a minute, at the small office beyond, looking for a familiar face, until the girl at the desk closest to the window asked: "Anything I can do for you?"

"Yes," he said. "Yes. I would like to see Mr. Blau, please."

"I'm sorry, but he's out in the shop right now," the girl said. "Was he expecting you?"

"I am an old acquaintance," he said. "I worked here for thirteen years. That was before your time."

"Yeah. Well," she said, looking at him without any expression, unimpressed. "He should be back in a few minutes. If you'd like to wait, just go around—"

"You don't have to tell me," he said immediately, smiling, almost with a kind of triumph, raising a hand to cut her off. "I know the way."

He stepped from the window to the freight doors, around several barrels lining the wall, filled with cloth scraps and trash. There was an opening of about six inches between the double doors. When he had worked there, they were always kept two to three feet apart, to improve the ventilation. He slid the doors apart and stepped through, into the shipping and packing section. Neither of the two men bent over the packing tables, steadily trussing long flat cardboard boxes with brown twine, so much as looked up at him. He walked through the packing section to the other end, which opened on to the main part of the shop, to stand looking out on the frantic noisy unchanged familiar vista of people seated in rows at sewing machines or bent over cutting tables, or in constant, apparently random motion up and down the aisles—which he so distinctly remembered, like an image from childhood, after almost five years. Only his boss was missing. Usually Mr. Blau was out there among them, overseeing everything, moving along the aisles and stopping to talk with this one here, making a remark to another there, inspecting a garment, fingering cloth; trailed, in the summer months, when he was home from college, by his son. This time he couldn't spot him. Before he turned away he noticed another thing, two things: there were more women among those working at the sewing machines, and more of them were black.

When he came into the office, the girl directed him to an empty chair against the wall, near her desk. While he waited, the woman at the desk across from him looked pleasantly up at him and smiled. Otherwise it was as if he wasn't even there, everyone going intently about their work. He waited patiently, barely stirring, sitting erect, his hands folded across the crown of his hat on his lap.

He had been put through this so many times in his life, he no longer felt any annoyance or exasperation.

All the while the girl continued working on the papers on her desk before her, without pause or interruption, her head downbent, preoccupied. Just her eyes occasionally flicked over to him, then immediately back down again to her papers. After about forty minutes she let her breath out noisily and put down her pencil. She rose and stepped from behind her desk. "He must be lost out there," she said in an abrupt, annoyed tone. "God knows when he could get back. I'll take you out to him."

She led him through the packing section out into the shop, up one of the aisles. He followed two steps behind, all the while looking around him for a familiar face. He saw one or two, but they were too busy working to notice him. Halfway up the aisle she said over her shoulder, "Wouldn't you know it. There he is," making a motion with one hand up ahead of her, but he couldn't see him. He saw some men in shirtsleeves and smocks moving along the aisle ahead of them; and further on, a group of others standing in a circle, blocking the aisle, some in shirtsleeves and others wearing suits or sport coats. But he didn't recognize any of them.

She led him up to those standing in a circle. They were having some kind of an argument, speaking loudly and gesturing. Even before she broke in he got a good look at the one in the middle and realized she'd made a mistake and he reached out to get her attention and tell her, but by then it was already too late. "Mr. Blau," she said in that direct, unabashed manner of hers, at the first break in the conversation. "Excuse me, but this gentleman's been waiting around for about an hour. I didn't know when you'd be getting back, so I brought him out here, if that's okay with you."

The reason he hadn't recognized Mr. Blau's *son* earlier was that he hadn't been looking for him; hadn't *expected* to see him, in this place, at this time of year, conditioned as he was during all those years when Blau's son was going to college. On top of that, his appearance had changed. He'd put on weight; around the face, along the chest and midsection, which produced a thickening effect, coarsening his features. He wore his hair longer, the way more and more men were now doing, in full waves at the temples and back of the neck, with thick sideburns. He stood there looking at the girl for a moment, more in surprise than annoyance. Then he looked at Meyer. The others stood looking at Meyer, suddenly still, remote, with an impatient, almost frustrated air, as though barely able to wait for Blau to get done with him.

"Could you make it fast?" Blau said.

"What?" he said, not immediately following the other's question.

"Could you get on with it? You took the trouble to come out here to see me. Now what'd you want to see me *about?*"

"I'm sorry. There has been a mistake," he said quietly, shaking his head. "I came up to see your father."

"Oh?" Blau said. "What'd you come up to see *him* about?"

He told him. Then he said, "You do not remember me, probably. I worked here, in this shop, for your father, for thirteen years. Over by that machine, right over there," he said, pointing up the aisle. "I remember the first time your father brought you up to the shop, when you were a little kid. You were running around—"

"Oh, stroll down mem-o-ry lane with me," one of the others sang.

"I'm sorry, but my father's not in the shop any more," Blau said.

"Maybe you can tell me when he will be back," he said.

"No. What I mean is, he's not connected with the business any more," Blau said. "He retired last year and went to Florida."

"Ahh," he said, letting his breath out slowly, as if in pain. "I did not know."

"He couldn't help you even if he was here," Blau said. "You have to go through the union."

"The *union?*" he said.

"Yep. That's the way *I* feel about it, too. But that's the way it is. These days everything goes through the union. I'm not looking for any trouble."

"What kind of trouble?" he said.

"Come on, Murray," one of the others said. "We haven't got all day."

"All right, all right. In a minute," Blau said. "Look," he said, speaking again to Meyer. "Technically you're not a union member. You're retired, you don't have a book. You know what they'd do to me if I put you on? I don't need that kind of trouble. I have enough of the regular kind."

"When I came up to help your father out four years ago, I was retired too," he said quietly.

"Well. I don't know anything about that," Blau said. "I don't know what kind of an arrangement Dad had. All I know is if I put you on, in ten seconds flat I'd have an empty shop and pickets around the building. I don't need it. Okay? So just do me a favor and go over to the union office and see *them*. Maybe *they* can help you. I can't."

Yet on his way over to the union office he felt no recrimination or bitterness. Instead, he kept thinking how much Blau's son had aged; had become harried and tough, with a trapped, unrelenting air about him, in the few years since he'd last seen him; as though he'd gone directly from his college years straight into a grinding middle age. Walking up Seventh Avenue in the leaden November air, an old man in a great worn flapping overcoat and oversized fedora, which were his formal outerwear, still grieving over the loss of his wife, jobless, at the tag end of his life practically, without help or connections, the only emotion he felt when he thought of the other was sympathy. Listen. Who can blame him? he thought. It must be a great strain, to have so much responsibility at his age. He thought: If he is not a success, it will be a great disappointment to his father.

They were no bigger help over at the union. There was no one up at the office that he knew. A secretary led him over to an official he vaguely remembered having seen at some of the general membership meetings and around union headquarters, before he retired. The other's desk was set in an open area, among others, like the desks of car salesmen or of the people in the credit and loan department in a bank. Meyer told him his reason for coming.

For a minute the other sat there looking at him without saying anything, his arms extended on the desk before him, twisting a pencil. He was a broad, muscular man, but slack, the flesh pushing up against his clothing at his waist and armpits. He let his breath out slowly, noisily.

"I'm afraid he's right," he said. "There isn't a thing he can do for you."

"All right," Meyer said. "What can *you* do for me?"

"I'm afraid I can't do very much for you, either," the other said. "The thing is you don't have your union book, and you can't work without one."

"So I will get my book *back*," he said. "I am still a member. Otherwise they would not pay me a pension."

"Well, you are and you aren't," the other began slowly. "You're a *nonworking* member. That's because you're on pension. When—"

"What are you trying to say to me?" Meyer asked in a flat, dead voice, in disbelief, staring at the other.

"What do you mean?" the other asked in turn, in a surprised, upset tone, flustered a little. "I'm trying to explain something."

"What is there to explain?" he asked.

"If you'll listen for a minute, I'll tell you," the other said. "Like I said, when you put in for your pension you give up the *working* part of your membership, so to speak. You become like a retired professor or somebody like that, you got the title but you don't do anything any more. The union appreciates all the years you put in, you know."

"I am looking for work, not appreciation," he said.

"Well, you can't have your cake and eat it too," the other said. "You can't expect us to send you a check every month if you're going to keep on working."

"Then don't send me checks," he said.

"Just like that?" the other said. "I'm sorry but it's not that simple. You can't just turn something like that off. There's a lot of hard work and organization that go into seeing that you get your check. You can't just turn it off whenever you feel like it."

"I never thought I would have trouble giving back money," he said.

"It's not that. It's that we have so many jobs for so many people, that we got to keep track of. We got to make plans for the whole industry, for years ahead of time. We'd never be able to make any plans if people could come out of retirement any time they felt like it, we wouldn't have enough jobs for the ones who really need them, the ones with kids and wives to support who don't have a check coming in on the side every month. You tell me how you would've liked it if some old guy came out of retirement and took *your* job away, when you were younger. No offense meant, I was just giving an example."

"It's all right. I understand," he said.

"Anyway, you get the point I'm trying to make? You can see it's a real problem." He sat back in his chair again, looking directly across at Meyer, pressing the eraser end of the pencil against his chin. "The thing I can't understand is, why would anyone want to come out of retirement to begin with? You wait for it your whole life practically, why would you want to throw it away? I could understand it if you were a movie star or a professional athlete or somebody like that, where you're on your own and you get a bundle just for showing up. But a working man? My God. Just think about it. No more bosses, no more getting up early weekday mornings, no more crowded cafeterias, no more subways. *No more crap!* It must be great."

"Sometimes there are reasons," Meyer said quietly.

"Well. I can't wait to find out what they are," the other said.

"You should have a long wait," he said. "You look like you should still be a young man. Forty-two? Forty-three maybe?"

"I'll tell you," the other said, bending forward, resting his forearms on the desk. "There are days around this place when I feel like a hundred and ten."

It just shows you. Everybody has his own troubles, he told himself, later on, seated at a table by the window in the cafeteria down the street. He had stopped in for a cup of coffee. He blew across the top of the cup to cool it. He remained there for a while, sitting at a table by himself, in the middle of the day, hunched forward, holding the cup before his face with both hands, watching people go by out on the street. At that moment he didn't know where to turn next.

He finished his coffee and left. On his way over to the subway he picked up an afternoon edition of the *Post*. That evening after supper he went over the want ads, for the first time in more than twenty years. The next morning he bought the *Times* and did the same thing, but with no better luck. He did that for a few weeks, almost like ritual: rose and dressed and went down to the candystore on the corner the first thing each morning, to return with a copy of the *Times* which he spread like a sheet on the kitchen table before him, and went over column after column of want ads while having his meager breakfast of instant coffee and toast.

Like ritual, each day's checking came to the same thing: there were few jobs for a man his age to begin with, and those either required some specific skill or background which he didn't have, or were too menial. By then the year had slipped into December. In the mornings, when he went down, the air had a deeper chill. He found he needed the kitchen light to read the newspapers by, when he came up. With the onset of cold weather he began to spend more time down at the club. Someone there suggested he try the New York State Employment Office or some private job agency.

It had never even occurred to him. He took the subway into Manhattan and went up to the state employment office the next day. He spent the first forty minutes filling out a long detailed application form, using a ballpoint pen chained to the table, like those in banks or in the post office, which either ran dry from time to time or released ink in sudden, dense clots. Who would even want to steal such a pen? he asked himself in exasperation, his application as full of ink smears, by the time he was through, as a child's homework paper. He spent forty minutes more seated in a hard, molded plastic chair waiting for an interview.

The interviewer was a man in his late forties, about average height so far as Meyer could tell, a little stoopshouldered, with grey hair and pale eyes. Bushy hair grew inside his ears. He wore a white shirt with a soft collar pulled into folds by his tie, and a rumpled tweed suit. A button was missing from his left cuff. Meyer was attentive to everything about the other, this being his first interview. Later on, after several weeks of making the rounds, interviewers and secretaries and receptionists alike would all blur and take on that same indistinguishable, abstract, faceless aspect of people in crowds; just as he must have—sitting there like so many before him—for the other.

The other barely looked at him during the entire interview. He studied Meyer's application for a while, asked questions from it, as if to verify the written answers, made some notes in pencil along the bottom, looked through a file. Then nothing. He didn't have anything for him at the moment, could he come back in a week or so or call in? He went slowly down the dim, narrow stairway to the street. The sun glared through the plate glass door of the entrance, into the vestibule. He stood outside, against the wall of the building, for a minute, breathing deeply. Bits of trash—candy wrappers, cigarette butts, pieces of old newspaper—blew in a circle at the base of the wall nearby. People went past him on the sidewalk in a constant stream without looking, without noticing him. Ah, he thought quietly, reasoning with himself. I should have known better. I should know by now not to start out expecting too much.

But he didn't have any better luck later in the day, making the rounds of the commercial job agencies whose ads he had circled in the *Times* that morning before he left the house. But he wasn't sorry he'd gone. He felt more active, for one thing. It filled up his day, helped pass the time. He also felt closer to the center of things, to where things were happening, when he was in Manhattan. Still it was three weeks before he went out on his first interview. After that he became less particular and went out two and three times a week. But the jobs always boiled down to one of two kinds, either messenger work or custodial, even when they seemed to be something more according to the descriptions they gave him at the agency. One time he almost gave up without having an interview because of the trouble he had finding the office. It was in downtown Brooklyn, off Fulton Street, along a cramped, shabby side street which bent in sudden angles. A cab driver finally directed him to it. He walked three blocks along parallel rows of stone, shabby office buildings of no great height, as if out of another time, with that appearance of having been converted from some other, grander purpose; that of town houses maybe.

He studied the directory in the vestibule for a minute and went up. Along the stairway the walls were cracked and bulged in places. Paint curled away from the plaster in miniature waves. Upstairs he found the office for *Metropolitan News* without any trouble. He was directed to a short, muscular man in his twenties, who rose and held and vigorously shook his hand for a full ten seconds, almost numbing it. For once the job was just what they had told him it was at the agency. The *Metropolitan News Company* operated a string of newsstands in various subway stations around the city. They needed someone for the one in the Forty-Ninth Street station.

"You don't know how lucky you are, being the first one down here," the other said. "These jobs usually get grabbed up in a second."

"I have no experience in this kind of work," he said. "I worked almost all my life as a dress operator."

"Don't worry about it," the other said, with a wave of his hand. "A kid could do it. It's like kids set up a lemonade stand on the street sometimes. All you do is sit there and keep an eye on the goods and take in the dough. You know how to make change, don't you?" This last said as a joke, the other bending forward a little; spoken with a wink and a grin.

"How many are there at a stand?" Meyer asked.

The other didn't understand the question at first, looking at Meyer for a minute with a blank expression, squinting his eyes. Then he said, "Oh! How many guys *run the stand*. Ahh, that's the beauty of it. Just *you!* It's like you're your own boss. Like it's your own business. You open it up in the morning and you close it at night, and there's no one around giving you orders or a hard time. You just keep a record of how much business you did, and give the dough and your orders for more stock to a guy who comes around every other day. I'm telling you, it's the perfect job for a conscientious, responsible, retired man like yourself."

"It sounds very good," Meyer said. "It is just the kind of a job I have been looking for."

"Okay," the other said. "Now. There's a couple of things about the job you have to know. You know, so you can do it right. For one thing we got a big problem with petty theft."

"Theft?" Meyer said.

"That's right. I don't mean *you*, the guy who runs the stand, even though we've had some of those too. I mean the ones out in front, on the platform. You got to keep your eyes open all the time, watch them like a hawk. Anyone hangs around the stand too long, tell them to move on. Let them know you got your eye on them. Even the well-dressed ones, the ones who look like solid citizens. You'd be surprised the kind of people who'll grab a lousy six bit magazine if they think no one's looking."

"I had no idea," Meyer said, in an incredulous tone.

"There's a lot of things happen people got no idea about," the other said. "This job's a regular education. Just remember, any time you get any doubts—theft losses come out of *your* pocket. That'll keep you on your toes."

"*My* pocket?" Meyer said.

"That's right. That's only fair. I told you. It's like it's your own business. You run it right or you take the loss. You can't expect the company to cover for everyone's carelessness, they wouldn't make a nickel."

"I see," Meyer said, but he didn't really believe things could be as bad as the other made them out to be. He is exaggerating, he told himself confidently, knowingly, based on what he knew personally about people. He is trying to alarm me.

"Now," the other went on. "That means you never leave the stand while it's open. You never ask anybody to watch it for you, while you take off for a minute or two, because they'll clean you out, lock, stock and barrel, you'll be lucky if you find an empty candy wrapper even, when you get back. It's happened more than once already, believe me."

"Is it such a big problem to close up the stand?" Meyer asked.

"Well, it's like this. The company has very strict rules about closing the stand," the other said. "You know, time is money. Miss one train, and there goes a couple of bucks in sales. A company can't stand too many of those, and still stay in business. The rule is, the only time you can close up is when you go out for lunch, at around eleven-thirty. That's a slow time, they found out. And just for an hour. Not longer, because they'll find out, they got a man goes around checking up, you know."

"There is a toilet in the stand?" Meyer asked.

"A *what?*" the other said. He looked at Meyer. "You're pulling my leg," he said.

"No," Meyer said. "I did not know. I was just asking."

"Hell, even if they did have one, you couldn't use it, it would mean you'd have to leave the stock unprotected."

"I cannot always arrange with my intestines to go to the toilet every day just at eleven-thirty," Meyer said.

"That's a problem," the other said. "You mean a leak, or taking a crap?"

"It makes a difference?" Meyer said.

"Well, most of the guys use bottles for taking a leak," the other said.

"Bottles?" Meyer said.

"Yeah. The widemouthed ones they sell orange juice in, so you have less of a chance of missing. They keep a bunch of them down behind the counter. If you stand over behind the magazine rack when you're doing it, no one can tell, even if they're standing right in front of the counter."

"Urinate in a bottle out in the open where people go by?" Meyer said.

"Yeah. What's wrong with that?" the other said. "You finicky or something? I'll tell you right now, this kind of work isn't for finicky people."

"It is a matter of self-respect," Meyer said.

"Because someone in your position, an old man and with not too much money, you can't afford to be too finicky. You know what I mean?" the other went on. "You know, there are one or two things *I'd* like to be finicky about, but I can't afford to be, I just learn to take them in my stride. That's the kind of a world it is."

"Well, there are some things I have managed to go through life without doing," Meyer said.

"Is one of them pissing in a bottle?" the other said with heavy sarcasm.

"I was only making a point," Meyer said.

"Yeah? Well good for you. Listen, pop," the other said abruptly, in a harsh, raised voice from which he could barely keep his sudden impatience, irritation. "You want the job or not?"

Of course he said Yes. Because what else was there? He started work the next Monday. The first day wasn't bad because another was with him, showing him the ropes: the mechanics of physically opening and closing the stand, raising and lowering the heavy wooden gate as unwieldy as a barricade; how to fill out the various inventory and sales forms; where everything was—extra forms, change sacks, coin wrappers, and, in passing, the orange juice bottles lined up underneath the counter.

But he didn't have to use them that day. Because there were two of them, they were able to alternate going to the public toilet in the subway station. The day went quickly. During slack periods he chatted with the other: alone, he could pass the time reading newspapers and magazines, the other told him. At the end of the day they checked the stock and totaled up the sales. There was a discrepancy of nine cents in their favor. The other told him he wouldn't always be that lucky.

He cut down on liquids immediately, in an attempt to avoid having to use the bottles. He did it without hope, belief in his success; merely out of that old, stubborn, reflexive assertion of his own will and independence, to his job in one sweatshop or another dressed in a suit, white shirt and tie. He drank no juice at breakfast, and went directly to the toilet on arriving at the station, before he opened the stand. At lunch he had only half a cup of coffee, no water, went to the cafeteria toilet just before returning, then managed to hold off until he closed the stand at the end of the day.

Afterward he stood at a urinal in the subway station toilet, before a wall covered with the usual obscene graffiti. Sodden cigarette butts littered the wire mesh covering the urinal drain; short, coiled hairs lay along the rim. The acrid, piercing stench of urine rose up out of it like an emanation. Usually he entered public toilets with a feeling of revulsion. He stood there now, pissing on the cigarette butts, oblivious to everything except the sensation of rapturous and untrammeled release.

When he was done he went back to the stand, to fill out the summary sheets. He sat in a cramped space no bigger than a closet, behind the lowered and padlocked gate, working in the dim light of a single unshaded bulb. From along the platform, on the other side of the gate, he heard sounds of life from time to time: passing footsteps, voices, someone coughing. In turn, he made *no* sound, so that those out on the platform were unaware of his presence there, behind the gate, inside the closed stand. He made the entries on the sheets slowly, carefully, going over everything several times, since this was the part of the job for which he had the least inclination, skill. Yet no matter how many times he went over the figures, he came up with the same thing; he was short a dollar and eighty-five cents. He sat there for a minute looking down at the sheets spread before him, letting his breath out slowly, audibly. Well, he told himself quietly, without resentment, in resignation. There is nothing else to do. He reached into his pocket and counted out a dollar eighty-five and dropped it into the cigar box with the day's take.

He didn't *have* to make up the loss from his own pocket. The other had told him they wouldn't dock him for anything under five dollars a week, provided it didn't happen too often. He made it up almost reflexively, without thinking about it. He did think for an instant about not wanting to get off to a bad start, to not give the impression he was careless, if not actually incompetent. But largely it was because he simply considered it to be his responsibility. He felt that when he accepted the job, and was placed in charge of the stand, he accepted personal responsibility for the stand in much the same way as he would for some article borrowed from a neighbor or a friend.

He began to watch those who came over to the stand more carefully. But his heart wasn't in it. He found it hard to think of everyone as a potential thief. He thought instead of those who lingered at the stand for a minute, on their way past, or after actually having bought something, as being like himself: people whose eye simply had been caught by some headline or lead story in one of the newspapers, or by the gaudy lewd myriad display of magazine covers and paperbacks, without any ulterior motive at all. If someone he was watching looked suddenly up at him, he turned immediately away, with a faintly abashed, almost guilty air, as if *he'd* been caught doing something wrong. He couldn't get up enough nerve to tell anyone to move on. Yet the feeling that some of those who came over to the stand were pitted against him, began to grow in him. He went to lunch feeling the strain of the job for the first time.

He followed his usual regimen, having no water with his meals, leaving half of his coffee, going to the cafeteria toilet just before he returned. Yet he wasn't back at the stand more than an hour, when he felt the first pangs. Usually they didn't come on until late in the afternoon, when he had only a couple of hours to go. It is only nerves, he told himself evenly, without alarm. The thing to do is try and keep calm. From that moment on he worked more methodically, moving slowly, without abrupt starts and changes of direction, like someone carrying a basin of water filled to the brim. When there was no business, he sat; careful not to bend too far forward, to avoid putting pressure on his bladder, his legs crossed in the manner of a small boy. He gave up all attempts at surveillance, halfhearted as they had been.

Even so, he noticed the boy at the outset: about fifteen, with straight blond hair which fell across his face when he leaned forward, and thin angular features, spending a little too much time over by the paperbacks. Out of the corner of his eye he could see him pick up one book, flip through it, put it down, then pick up another, with that seemingly nonchalant and random air, a little too studied, deliberate, filled with a kind of tension, to be just idle curiosity. Ah, he thought, knowingly, with a faint smile. He is looking for the dirty parts.

But he couldn't bring himself to tell him to move on. What is the harm? He will only be disappointed with what he finds, anyway, he told himself. When he looked again, a few minutes later, after a train had come into the station and he had been busy with some of the passengers, the boy was gone. But he had left the books in disarray. As soon as he was free, Meyer went over to straighten them, shaking his head in annoyance at the boy's carelessness, disregard. Straightening them, placing each title on its own stack, he saw at once that his last copy of *The Graduate* was gone. He remained there for a moment, motionless, one hand suspended in mid-air, looking down at the books with an expression as if he had just found excrement or a small dead animal among them, thinking: Who could have expected it? Only a child, and he could stand there with a straight face like that, steal it from right under my nose. How bad could he need it?

Though it was a question of the money also, what he resented just as much was being made a fool of. But there was nothing now he could do about it. All he could do was to try to see that it didn't happen again. Still it left him a little upset, shaken. On top of that the pangs in his groin had become more severe, coming now at more frequent intervals.

Like birth pains, he told himself wryly, without amusement. He realized that he would not be able to make it to the end of the day. He waited for a slack period. Yet he let several come and go by without making any attempt to relieve himself, unable to bring himself to use the bottle. Only after he bent over while reaching for a magazine for a customer, and felt a sensation as though he were dribbling in his pants, was he overcome by a sudden, ineluctable sense of urgency, of panic almost.

At the next lull, as the last customer stepped from the stand on his way out of the station, he leaned out over the counter and looked up and down the platform. It was empty except for a single figure, motionless at the far end. A man, he thought, in relief, as if it made a difference at that distance; in a fever almost, now, of desperation and abhorrence. Those on the downtown side of the station, across the tracks from him, he didn't even consider at all. He moved back inside the stand, tense, in a crouch almost, like an animal withdrawing into its burrow; listening for someone at the turnstiles or coming down the stairs. He heard no one; only the reverberations of distant trains, like summer thunder, came to him there in the tunnel. He reached down under the counter for one of the bottles in a quick, sudden motion. It was colder than he had thought, dank; giving him an unclean feeling. He held the bottle to his crotch with one hand, while he unzipped his pants with the other and began pissing into the bottle. He did everything by touch, feel, keeping his gaze straight before him, impenetrable, blank, as though urine plashing on the glass unnerved him, seeming to carry out across the platform. Actually it was barely audible. He stood so for a minute, an old man, unbending, grave, vaguely formal in the hat, dress shirt and tie, which were his working attire, his coat pushed back from his hips. He was thinking: That it should come to this. At my age. To have to stand here and relieve myself in public like this, like a child. Who needed it?

So the woman's voice took him completely by surprise. He was completely unaware of her approach. She was just suddenly there, as if she had appeared out of the air; a mild, roundfaced woman, middleaged, plump, dressed in a fur trimmed cloth coat and fur hat, speaking mildly and peacefully into him. Yet the effect was the same as if she had suddenly come up behind him and shouted in his ear. His body gave an abrupt heave and start. His hand jerked away, dislocating his aim: his urine rose in a high vagrant trajectory for an instant and played against the inside wall below the counter, pattering among the other bottles and bundles of back issue magazines stored there, wetting his hand, while he watched in a state of helpless and hopeless consternation. He stood there cringing practically, waiting for her reaction. Apparently she saw nothing, was aware of nothing out of the ordinary. Because she repeated her question in the same mild level tone without any change, flicker even, of expression. "Do you carry *The Ladies Home Journal?*" she asked. "I don't see it anywhere on the counter."

"Yes. Yes, I have it," he said immediately, reflexively, not thinking ahead; because now he'd have to get it for her. First he let his coat fall forward, across his opened pants, in a seemingly casual motion.

Then he bent and searched among the magazines and found the one she wanted and even gave her change of a dollar, in the same way: exposed beneath his coat, holding the bottle with its small accumulation of urine in his left hand, his left hand and sleeve wet where they had been sprayed; standing there among the patches and runnels of urine on the floor and on the bundles around him, with the amiable decorous patient air of any shopkeeper, as though nothing at all were out of the ordinary, he always did business this way; while the acrid piercing stench of urine, as in a public toilet, rose up about him. Actually he was terrified that at any minute she would smell something, or his coat would come open: for a minute he saw himself as one of those men he was always reading about who were arrested in the subways for indecent exposure.

But she left without any incident. He watched her go with a sense of relief. Afterward he quickly straightened things, before anyone else came over. At the end of the day, after closing the stand, the first thing he did was get rid of the soiled bundles and give the floor a good mopping. Then he sat down to make the day's entries. He discovered that, on top of everything else, he was short almost three dollars.

He made up the difference out of his own pocket, as before; but grudgingly, reluctantly, with increasing bitterness. He told himself: Another few days like this one, and I will be *losing* money for the week. He said, dour, sardonic, without amusement: They must all be passing the word around. They must be telling all their friends: the one on

Terrible Mistakes

Forty-Ninth Street is a good one. You could steal the silver from his teeth and he would never know the difference.

The next day he was tougher. He asked some of those who lingered before the stand what they wanted. Others he told to move on. And all the time he watched everyone like a hawk, with the wary and untrusting alertness of a blackjack dealer playing with strangers. Watching like that, he saw a boy in his teens come up to the stand just as a train pulled in, handle a few bars of candy one after the other, as if unable to make up his mind, then palm one of them and start to put his hand into his pocket. He immediately took a step in the boy's direction. No sooner did he begin to move, than the boy turned away. "You!" he said, but the boy was already in flight; crossed the platform in three loping strides and vanished into the nearest open door of the train, with the sureness of premeditation, to reappear a minute later in one of the windows as he made his way through the car. An instant later the doors closed, sealing him off from capture, justice, plain retribution even, then the train slid away from the platform, gathering speed.

That day he kept his losses to a dollar. It's still a dollar too much, he told himself angrily, making it up with his own money, adding up in his mind what his losses came to for the week. He thought: If this keeps up, I will have worked here for a week and have nothing to show for it. The next day he followed the same procedure, hoping for an improvement. By midday he was sure he had foiled at least four attempts, just by being openly vigilant—

by openly keeping an eye on, and harassing, those who loitered near the stand or began handling the merchandise.

So he was completely taken aback when a black child he'd been watching, a lean tense boy of about twelve, with closecropped hair and a bony nose, wearing a shabby leather jacket and frayed jeans, suddenly reached over and—in full view, without the slightest attempt at furtiveness, deception— took from their box three or four twenty-five cent candy bars and put them into his pocket, as openly as something he had paid for, and strolled almost casually from the stand, across the platform.

Meyer looked after him in amazement. Several people stood in line at the counter to be waited on. He excused himself. "Please. One minute," he said, making a gesture, as if asking for forbearance. He turned and disappeared from their view, going quickly up the narrow passageway to one side which led to the platform. He fumbled at the bolt on the door for an instant, then slid it back, shaking his head in disbelief, thinking: My God. So young to already be a thief. He stepped out on to the platform, looking around immediately for the boy. He saw him at once, up ahead, moving with that unhurrying, almost flaunting gait, toward the front of the station. A beginner, he thought. He *doesn't have* a train waiting for a getaway. The second mistake he had made was to let Meyer get between him and the exit. Nor did he once look back: either because he was confident he hadn't been seen, or in an extreme attempt to appear innocent, unconcerned as anyone else.

Meyer started down the platform after him, going past those waiting at the counter, who turned and looked after him out of blank, uncomprehending faces. He moved as fast as he could without actually running, with the abrupt, graceless, wooden motions and wasted motions of old people, his coat flared around him, trying not to attract attention. Above all he didn't want the boy to hear him, to be startled by him. He slowed down as he approached him. He covered the last twenty feet with the deliberate, tensed, stalking gait of someone approaching a bird. He didn't put a hand on him. He came up behind him, put his mouth to the other's ear, and said, composed, reasonable, as matter of fact as if making a business proposition: "Give back the candies please, and I will forget the whole thing. I will forget anything happened."

The boy whirled immediately, jerking away, half crouched, staring up at him out of wide, started eyes. "Whut?" he said in abrupt, high voice. "Whut candies? Whut you talkin about?"

"Come," Meyer said, gentle, cajoling almost. "Be a good boy. Nobody will hurt you. Give back the candies and that will be an end to it." He took a step forward, extending his hand.

No sooner did he step forward than the boy bolted. He ran in the most obvious direction, in a panic, without stratagem or cunning, back toward the end of the station. For a minute Meyer just stood there looking after him, completely taken by surprise, abashed. He had expected the whole thing to be settled calmly, rationally, since it was obviously to the boy's advantage. He glanced quickly around him, at those strung out along the station, beginning to look now in his direction out of shadowed, impassive faces. He had a sense of how ludicrous he appeared at that moment, standing there alone in the middle of the platform, in his oversized, worn hat and coat, still bent in an attitude of speaking to the boy, his right hand extended, the boy fleeing along the platform ahead of him. He knew he would look even worse chasing the boy. Nevertheless he ran after him. He ran erratically, heavily, his body jolted by each step. His footfalls made a clapping along the platform, in echo to the boy's. The boy was faster, but *he* had position. He overtook and trapped him finally at the end of the station, in the corner between the wall and the edge of the platform. When the boy turned and tried to run around him, beyond his reach, he lunged and caught and held him by one arm, surprisingly frail and sticklike inside the jacket sleeve, while the remainder of his body frantically jerked and twisted at the other end of it, like a butterfly held by one wing, in an effort to pull free.

Meyer's first thought was that the boy might injure himself, thrashing around like that. He tried to put one arm around his shoulders to restrain him, telling him all the while in a level, mollifying, insistent voice that he wasn't going to hurt him and he just wanted the candy back. The boy eluded his arm, twisting away. He dug suddenly into his jacket pocket with his free hand, then flicked it away in the direction of the tracks, the candy bars flashing for an instant in the dim light, dispersing like fireworks, to arc and disappear, as if extinguished, into the blackness of the tunnel. All the while the boy had been shouting up at him. Now Meyer heard the words. "Lemme go," the boy was saying. "I didn't do nuthin. I don't know whut you talkin about."

As if in accompaniment to the boy's voice, though lower, more controlled, he now heard another, a man's voice, to one side of him. "Say. What you want from this here boy, mister?" the other said.

Meyer turned to the other, almost in relief, grateful for an opportunity to explain. He faced a man almost his own height, but broader, square-shouldered inside a suburban coat trimmed with grey fur at the collar, wearing a narrow brimmed hat pulled forward like a visor over his eyes; black too, like the boy. "The stand," Meyer said between deep breaths, still showing the effects of his running. "I work by the newspaper stand over there. He took candies without paying."

"That's a lie! I didn't take *nuthin*," the boy said.

The other looked over at the boy, behind the lowered hat brim, lowered lids; his face completely expressionless. Then he looked back at Meyer again. "How do you know he took them candies?" he said.

"Know? How do I *know*?" Meyer asked in surprise. "I saw him."

"You could be mistaken," the other said quietly. "It could be you *thought* you saw him."

"I am not mistaken," Meyer said. "I saw him with my two eyes."

"Oh yeah? Well then, where's the evidence? You got to have evidence before you go around accusing people. Where's that candy you saying he stole?"

"Yeah. You ask him," the boy said, beginning to twist and move around again in Meyer's grasp, as if at the end of a tether. "I ain't got none of his goddam candy. Search me, you'll see. Go on and just search me."

"He threw it on the tracks," Meyer said.

"Is that so?" the other said, with a half smile, his eyes widening in mock surprise. "Now that's the kind of a answer I would never have expected to hear." He stepped to the edge of the platform and looked down. "I don't see no candies," he said, stepping back.

"Go on down on the tracks and look over by the tunnel, you'll see candies," Meyer said wearily.

"Don't you tell *me* what to do!" the other said in a fierce passionate expulsion. "This here is one nigger ain't going to take none of your white shit."

"I'm sorry. I didn't mean anything," Meyer said, completely taken aback. "I apologize."

"Think you can just go around saying anything you like to a black man," the other said. "Well them days is gone, old man. Chasing around and making accusations against this here boy like that, just because he is black."

"That is not the reason," Meyer said.

"I don't see you chasing after no goddam white boys," the other said.

"I never chased *any* boy before," Meyer said. "He is the first."

"That's right. And he is black. Like I said, you wouldn't chase no white one. Now you just take your hands off of him and let him go," the other said in a low, drawnout, constricted tone, as though speaking through clenched teeth, "or you going to get hurt."

"I cannot do that," Meyer said quietly, doggedly, looking directly back into the other's face. It wasn't that he disbelieved the other's threat. It was just that to let the boy go now would make it appear as if everything the other had said was true. "Believe me," he said as the other took a step toward him.

"The boy was stealing."

The other struck him on the chest with the flat of both hands, driving him back. He stumbled, arms flailing, the boy taking the opportunity to break from his grasp. Before he could regain his balance the other was on him again: seized him by both lapels with black iron fists on one of which a silver diamond ring winked and glittered. He drove Meyer—feet barely in contact with the ground, arms flopping, his hat tumbling finally from his head—straight back several feet into a steel pillar. He stood there before Meyer, completely carried away, devoid now of any selfcontrol; feet braced slightly apart, face contorted, shouting obscenities; driving the slack doll-like, unresisting figure in his grasp with pistonlike thrusts again and again into the pillar. Before his head finally struck the pillar and he lost consciousness, Meyer looked once across at the other with an expression of astonishment and dismay.

"Please," he said in a tone devoid of any pleading or recrimination. "You are making a terrible mistake."

The Americanization of Shadrach Cohen

Bruno Lessing

There is no set rule for the turning of the worm; most worms, however, turn unexpectedly. It was so with Shadrach Cohen.

He had two sons. One was named Abel and the other Gottlieb. They had left Russia five years before their father, had opened a store on Hester Street with the money he had given them. For reasons that only business men would understand they conducted the store in their father's name— and, when the business began to prosper and they saw an opportunity of investing further capital in it to good advantage, they wrote to their dear father to come to this country.

"We have a nice home for you here," they wrote. "We will live happily together."

Shadrach came. With him he brought Marta, the serving-woman who had nursed his wife until she died, and whom, for his wife's sake, he had taken into the household. When the ship landed he was met by two dapper-looking young men, each of whom wore a flaring necktie with a diamond in it. It took him some time to realise that these were his two sons. Abel and Gottlieb promptly threw their arms around his neck and welcomed him to the new land. Behind his head they looked at each other in dismay. In the course of five years they had forgotten that their father wore a gaberdine—the loose, baglike garment of the Russian Ghetto—and had a long, straggling grey beard and ringlets that came down over his ears—that, in short, he was a perfect type of the immigrant whose appearance they had so frequently ridiculed. Abel and Gottlieb were proud of the fact that they had become Americanised. And they frowned at Marta.

"Come, father," they said. "Let us go to a barber, who will trim your beard and make you look more like an American. Then we will take you home with us."

Shadrach looked from one to the other in surprise.

"My beard?" he said; "what is the matter with my beard?"

"In this city," they explained to him, "no one wears a beard like yours except the newly landed Russian Jews."

Shadrach's lips shut tightly for a moment. Then he said:

"Then I will keep my beard as it is. I am a newly landed Russian Jew." His sons clinched their fists behind their backs and smiled at him amiably. After all, he held the purse-strings. It was best to humour him.

"What shall we do with Marta?" they asked. "We have a servant. We will not need two."

"Marta," said the old man, "stays with us. Let the other servant go. Come, take me home. I am getting hungry."

They took him home, where they had prepared a feast for him. When he bade Marta sit beside him at the table, Abel and Gottlieb promptly turned and looked out of the window. They felt that they could not conceal their feelings. The feast was a dismal affair. Shadrach was racking his brains to find some explanation that would account for the change that had come over his sons. They had never been demonstrative in their affection for him, and he had not looked for an effusive greeting. But he realised immediately that there was a wall between him and his sons; some change had occurred; he was distressed and puzzled. When the meal was over Shadrach donned his praying cap and began to recite the grace after meals. Abel and Gottlieb looked at each other in consternation. Would they have to go through this at every meal? Better—far better—to risk their father's displeasure and acquaint him with the truth at once. When it came to the response Shadrach looked inquiringly at his sons. It was Abel who explained the matter:

"We—er—have grown out of—er—that is—er—done away with—er—sort of fallen into the habit, don't you know, of leaving out the prayer at meals. It's not quite American!"

Shadrach looked from one to the other. Then, bowing his head, he went on with his prayer.

"My sons," he said, when the table had been cleared. "It is wrong to omit the prayer after meals. It is part of your religion. I do not know anything about this America or its customs. But religion is the worship of Jehovah, who has chosen us as His children on earth, and that same Jehovah rules supreme over America even as He does over the country that you came from."

Gottlieb promptly changed the subject by explaining to him how badly they needed more money in their business. Shadrach listened patiently for a while, then said:

"I am tired after my long journey. I do not understand this business that you are talking about. But you may have whatever money you need. After all, I have no one but you two." He looked at them fondly. Then his glance fell upon the serving-woman, and he added, quickly:

"And Marta."

"Thank God," said Gottlieb, when their father had retired, "he does not intend to be stingy."

"Oh, he is all right," answered Abel. "After he gets used to things he will become Americanised like us."

To their chagrin, however, they began to realise, after a few months, that their father was clinging to the habits and customs of his old life with a tenacity that filled them with despair. The more they urged him to abandon his ways the more eager he seemed to become to cling to them. He seemed to take no interest in their business affairs, but he responded, almost cheerfully, to all their requests for money. He began to feel that this, after all, was the only bond between him and his sons. And when they had pocketed the money, they would shake their heads and sigh.

"Ah, father, if you would only not insist upon being so old-fashioned!" Abel would say.

"And let us fix you up a bit," Gottlieb would chime in.

"And become more progressive—like the other men of your age in this country."

"And wear your beard shorter and trimmed differently."

"And learn to speak English."

Shadrach never lost his temper; never upbraided them. He would look from one to the other and keep his lips tightly pressed together. And when they had gone he would look at Marta and would say:

"Tell me what you think, Marta. Tell me what you think."

"It is not proper for me to interfere between father and sons," Marta would say. And Shadrach could never induce her to tell him what she thought. But he could perceive a gleam in her eyes and observed a certain nervous vigour in the way she cleaned the pots and pans for hours after these talks, that fell soothingly upon his perturbed spirit.

As we remarked before, there is no rule for the turning of the worm. Some worms, however, turn with a crash. It was so with Shadrach Cohen.

Gottlieb informed his father that he contemplated getting married.

"She is very beautiful," he said. "The affair is all in the hands of the Shadchen."

His father's face lit up with pleasure.

"Gottlieb," he said, holding out his hand, "God bless you! It's the very best thing you could do. Marta, bring me my hat and coat. Come, Gottlieb. Take me to see her. I cannot wait a moment. I want to see my future daughter-in-law at once. How happy your mother would be if she were alive to-day!"

Gottlieb turned red and hung back.

"I think, father," he said, "you had better not go just yet. Let us wait a few days until the Shadchen has made all the arrangements. She is an American girl. She—she won't—er—understand your ways—don't you know? And it may spoil everything."

Crash! Marta had dropped an iron pot that she was cleaning. Shadrach was red in the face with suppressed rage.

"So!" he said. "It has come to this. You are ashamed of your father!" Then he turned to the old servant:

"Marta," he said, "to-morrow we become Americanised—you and I."

There was an intonation in his voice that alarmed his son.

"You are not angry—"he began, but with a fierce gesture his father cut him short.

"Not another word. To bed! Go to bed at once."

Gottlieb was dumbfounded. With open mouth he stared at his father. He had not heard that tone since he was a little boy.

"But, father—" he began.

"Not a word. Do you hear me? Not a word will I listen to. In five minutes if you are not in bed you go out of this house. Remember, this is my house."

Then he turned to Abel. Abel was calmly smoking a cigar.

"Throw that cigar away," his father commanded, sternly.

Abel gasped and looked at his father in dismay.

"Marta, take that cigar out of his mouth and throw it into the fire. If he objects he goes out of the house."

The Americanization of Shadrach Cohen

With a smile of intense delight Marta plucked the cigar from Abel's unresisting lips, and incidentally trod heavily upon his toes. Shadrach gazed long and earnestly at his sons.

"To-morrow, my sons," he said, slowly, "you will begin to lead a new life."

In the morning Abel and Gottlieb, full of dread forebodings, left the house as hastily as they could. They wanted to get to the store to talk matters over. They had hardly entered the place, however, when the figure of their father loomed up in the doorway. He had never been in the place before. He looked around him with great satisfaction at the many evidences of prosperity which the place presented. When he beheld the name "Shadrach Cohen, Proprietor" over the door he chuckled. Ere his sons had recovered from the shock of his appearance a pale-faced clerk, smoking a cigarette, approached Shadrach, and in a sharp tone asked:

"Well, sir, what do you want?" Shadrach looked at him with considerable curiosity. Was he Americanised, too? The young man frowned impatiently.

"Come, come! I can't stand here all day. Do you want anything?"

Shadrach smiled and turned to his sons.

"Send him away at once. I don't want that kind of young man in my place." Then turning to the young man, upon whom the light of revelation had quickly dawned, he said, sternly:

"Young man, whenever you address a person who is older than you, do it respectfully. Honour your father and your mother. Now go away as fast as you can. I don't like you."

"But, father," interposed Gottlieb, "we must have someone to do his work."

"Dear me," said Shadrach, "is that so? Then, for

the present, you will do it. And that young man over there—what does he do?"

"He is also a salesman."

"Let him go. Abel will take his place."

"But, father, who is to manage the store? Who will see that the work is properly done?"

"I will," said the father. "Now, let us have no more talking. Get to work."

Crestfallen, miserable, and crushed in spirit, Abel and Gottlieb began their humble work while their father entered upon the task of familiarising himself with the details of the business. And even before the day's work was done he came to his sons with a frown of intense disgust.

"Bah!" he exclaimed. "It is just as I expected. You have both been making as complete a mess of this business as you could without ruining it. What you both lack is sense. If becoming Americanised means becoming stupid, I must congratulate you upon the thoroughness of your work. To-morrow I shall hire a manager to run this store. He will arrange your hours of work. He will also pay you what you are worth. Not a cent more. How late have you been keeping this store open?"

"Until six o'clock," said Abel.

"H'm! Well, beginning to-day, you both will stay here until eight o'clock. Then one of you can go. The other will stay until ten. You can take turns. I will have Marta send you some supper.

To the amazement of Abel and Gottlieb the business of Shadrach Cohen began to grow. Slowly it dawned upon them that in the mercantile realm they were as children compared with their father. His was the true money-maker spirit; there was something wonderful in the swiftness with which he grasped the most intricate phases of trade; and where experience failed him some instinct seemed to guide him aright. And gradually, as the business of Shadrach Cohen increased, and even the sons saw vistas of prosperity beyond their wildest dreams, they began to look upon their father with increasing respect. What they had refused to the integrity of his character, to the nobility of his heart, they promptly yielded to the shrewdness of his brain. The sons of Shadrach Cohen became proud of their father. He, too, was slowly undergoing a change. A new life was unfolding itself before his eyes, he became broader-minded, more tolerant, and, above all, more flexible in his tenets. Contact with the outer world had quickly impressed him with the vast differences between his present surroundings and his old life in Russia. The charm of American life, of liberty, of democracy, appealed to him strongly. As the field of his business operations widened he came more and more in contact with American business men, from whom he learned many things—principally the faculty of adaptability. And as his sons began to perceive that all these business men whom, in former days, they had looked upon with feelings akin to reverence, seemed to show to their father an amount of deference and respect which they had never evinced toward the sons, their admiration for their father increased.

And yet it was the same Shadrach Cohen.

From that explosive moment when he had rebelled against his sons he demanded from them implicit obedience and profound respect. Upon that point he was stern and unyielding. Moreover, he insisted upon a strict observance of every tenet of their religion. This, at first, was the bitterest pill of all. But they soon became accustomed to it. When life is light and free from care, religion is quick to fly; but when the sky grows dark and life becomes earnest, and we feel its burden growing heavy upon our shoulders, then we welcome the consolation that religion brings, and we cling to it. And Shadrach Cohen had taught his sons that life was earnest. They were earning their bread by the sweat of their brow. No prisoner, with chain and ball, was subjected to closer supervision by his keeper than were Gottlieb and Abel.

"You have been living upon my charity," their father said to them: "I will teach you how to earn your own living."

And he taught them. And with the lesson they learned many things; learned the value of discipline, learned the beauty of filial reverence, learned the severe joy of the earnest life.

"One day Gottlieb said to his father:

"May I bring Miriam to supper to-night? I am anxious that you should see her."

Shadrach turned his face away so that Gottlieb might not see the joy that beamed in his eyes.

"Yes, my son," he answered. "I, too, am anxious to see if she is worthy of you."

Miriam came, and in a stiff, embarrassed manner Gottlieb presented her to his father. The girl looked in surprise at the venerable figure that stood before her—a picture of a patriarch from the Pentateuch, with a long, straggling beard, and ringlets of hair falling over the ears, and clad in the long gaberdine of the Russian Ghettos. And she saw a pair of grey eyes bent keenly upon her—eyes of shrewdness, but soft and tender as a woman's—the eyes of a strong man with a kind heart. Impulsively she ran toward him and seized his hands. And, with a smile upon her lips, she said:

"Will you not give me your blessing?"

When the evening meal had ended, Shadrach donned his praying cap, and with bowed head intoned the grace after meals:

"We will bless Him from whose wealth we have eaten!" And in fervent tones rose from Gottlieb's lips the response:

"Blessed be He!"

Across the Generations

The Zulu and The Zeide

Dan Jacobson

Old man Grossman was worse than a nuisance. He was a source of constant anxiety and irritation; he was a menace to himself and to the passing motorists into whose path he would step, to the children in the streets whose games he would break up, sending them flying, to the householders who at night would approach him with clubs in their hands, fearing him a burglar; he was a butt and a jest to the African servants who would tease him on street corners.

It was impossible to keep him in the house. He would take any opportunity to slip out—a door left open meant that he was on the streets, a window unlatched was a challenge to his agility, a walk in the park was as much a game of hide-and-seek as a walk. The old man's health was good, physically; he was quite spry, and he could walk far, and he could jump and duck if he had to. And all his physical activity was put to only one purpose: to running away. It was a passion for freedom that the old man might have been said to have, could anyone have seen what joy there could have been for him in wandering aimlessly about the streets, in sitting footsore on pavements, in entering other people's homes, in stumbling behind advertisement hoardings across undeveloped building plots, in toiling up the stairs of fifteen-storey blocks of flats in which he had no business, in being brought home by large young policemen who winked at Harry Grossman, the old man's son, as they gently hauled his father out of their flying-squad cars.

"He's always been like this," Harry would say, when people asked him about his father. And when they smiled and said: "Always?" Harry would say, "Always. I know what I'm talking about. He's my father, and I know what he's like. He gave my mother enough grey hairs before her time. All he knew was to run away."

Harry's reward would come when the visitors would say: "Well, at least you're being as dutiful to him as anyone can be."

It was a reward that Harry always refused. "Dutiful? What can you do? There's nothing else you can do." Harry Grossman knew that there was nothing else he could do. Dutifulness had been his habit of life: it had had to be, having the sort of father he had, and the strain of duty had made him abrupt and begrudging: he even carried his thick, powerful shoulders curved inwards, to keep what he had to himself. He was a thick-set, bunch-faced man, with large bones, and short, jabbing gestures; he was in the prime of life, and he would point at the father from whom he had inherited his strength, and on whom the largeness of bone showed now only as so much extra leanness that the clothing had to cover, and say: "You see him? Do you know what he once did? My poor mother saved enough money to send him from the old country to South Africa; she bought clothes for him, and a ticket, and she sent him to her brother, who was already here. He was going to make enough money to bring me out, and my mother and my brother, all of us. But on the boat from Bremen to London he met some other Jews who were going to South America, and they said to him: 'Why are you going to South Africa? It's a wild country, the savages will eat you. Come to South America and you'll make a fortune.' So in London he exchanges his ticket. And we don't hear from him for six months. Six months later he gets a friend to write to my mother asking her please to send him enough money to pay for his ticket back to the old country—he's dying in Argentina, the Spaniards are killing him, he says, and he must come home. So my mother borrows from her brother to bring him back again. Instead of a fortune he brought her a new debt, and that was all."

But Harry was dutiful, how dutiful his friends had reason to see again when they would urge him to try sending the old man to a home for the aged. "No," Harry would reply, his features moving heavily and reluctantly to a frown, a pout, as he showed how little the suggestion appealed to him. "I don't like the idea. Maybe one day when he needs medical attention all the time I'll feel differently about it, but not now, not now. He wouldn't like it, he'd be unhappy. We'll look after him as long as we can. It's a job. It's something you've got to do."

More eagerly Harry would go back to a recital of the old man's past. "He couldn't even pay for his own passage out. I had to pay the loan back. We came out together—my mother wouldn't let him go by himself again, and I had to pay off her brother who advanced the money for us. I was a boy—what was I?—sixteen, seventeen, but I paid for his passage, and my own, and my mother's and then my brother's. It took me a long time, let me tell you. And then my troubles with him weren't over." Harry even reproached his father for his myopia; he could clearly enough remember his chagrin when shortly after their arrival in South Africa, after it had become clear that Harry would be able to make his way in the world and be a support to the whole family, the old man—who at that time had not really been so old—had suddenly, almost dramatically, grown so short-sighted that he had been almost blind without the glasses that Harry had had to buy for him. And Harry could remember too how he had then made a practice of losing the glasses or breaking them with the greatest frequency, until it had been made clear to him that he was no longer expected to do any work. "He doesn't do that any more. When he wants to run away now he sees to it that he's wearing his glasses. That's how he's always been. Sometimes he recognizes me, at other times, when he doesn't want to, he just doesn't know who I am."

What Harry said about his father sometimes failing to recognize him was true. Sometimes the old man would call out to his son, when he would see him at the end of a passage, "Who are you?" Or he would come upon Harry in a room and demand of him, "What do you want in my house?"

"Your house?" Harry would say, when he felt like teasing the old man. "Your house?"

"Out of my house!" the old man would shout back.

"Your house? Do you call this your house?" Harry would reply, smiling at the old man's fury.

Harry was the only one in the house who talked to the old man, and then he didn't so much talk to him, as talk of him to others. Harry's wife was a dim and silent woman, crowded out by her husband and the large-boned sons like himself that she had borne him, and she would gladly have seen the old man in an old-age home. But her husband had said no, so she put up with the old man, though for herself she could see no possible better end for him than a period of residence in a home for aged Jews which she had once visited, and which had impressed her most favourably with its glass and yellow brick, the noiseless rubber tiles in its corridors, its secluded grassed grounds, and the uniforms worn by the attendants to the establishment. But she put up with the old man; she did not talk to him. The grandchildren had nothing to do with their grandfather—they were busy at school, playing rugby and cricket, they could hardly speak Yiddish, and they were embarrassed by him in front of their friends; and when the grandfather did take any notice of them it was only to call them Boers and *goyim* and *shkotzim* in sudden quavering rages which did not disturb them at all.

The house itself—a big single-storied place of brick, with a corrugated iron roof above and a wide stoep all round—Harry Grossman had bought years before, and in the continual rebuilding the suburb was undergoing it was beginning to look old-fashioned. But it was solid and prosperous, and withindoors curiously masculine in appearance, like the house of a widower. The furniture was of the heaviest African woods, dark, and built to last, the passages were lined with bare linoleum, and the few pictures on the walls, big brown and grey mezzotints in heavy frames, had not been looked at for years. The servants were both men, large ignored Zulus who did their work and kept up the brown gleam of the furniture.

It was from this house that old man Grossman tried to escape. He fled through the doors and the windows and out into the wide sunlit streets of the town in Africa, where the blocks of flats were encroaching upon the single-storied houses behind their gardens. And in these streets he wandered.

It was Johannes, one of the Zulu servants, who suggested a way of dealing with old man Grossman. He brought to the house one afternoon Paulus, whom he described as his 'brother.' Harry Grossman knew enough to know that 'brother' in this context could mean anything from the son of one's mother to a friend from a neighbouring *kraal*, but by the speech that Johannes made on Paulus' behalf he might indeed have been the latter's brother. Johannes had to speak for Paulus, for Paulus knew no English. Paulus was a 'raw boy,' as raw as a boy could possibly come. He was a muscular, moustached and bearded African, with pendulous ear-lobes showing the slits in which the tribal plugs had once hung; and on his feet he wore sandals the soles of which were cut from old motor-car tyres, the thongs from red inner tubing. He wore neither hat nor socks, but he did have a pair of khaki shorts which were too small for him, and a shirt without any buttons: buttons would in any case have been of no use for the shirt could never have closed over his chest. He swelled magnificently out of his clothing, and above there was a head carried well back, so that his beard, which had been trained to grow in two sharp points from his chin, bristled ferociously forward under his melancholy and almost mandarin-like moustache. When he smiled, as he did once or twice during Johannes' speech, he showed his white, even teeth, but for the most part he stood looking rather shyly to the side of Harry Grossman's head, with his hands behind his back and his bare knees bent a little forward, as if to show how little he was asserting himself, no matter what his 'brother' might have been saying about him.

His expression did not change when Harry said that it seemed hopeless, that Paulus was too raw, and Johannes explained what the baas had just said. He nodded agreement when Johannes explained to him that the baas said that it was a pity that he knew no English. But whenever Harry looked at him, he smiled, not ingratiatingly, but simply smiling above his beard, as though saying: "Try me." Then he looked grave again as Johannes expatiated on his virtues. Johannes pleaded for his 'brother.' He said that the baas knew that he, Johannes, was a good boy. Would he, then, recommend to the baas a boy who was not a good boy too? The baas could see for himself, Johannes said, that Paulus was not one of these town boys, these street loafers: he was a good boy, come straight from the *kraal*. He was not a thief or a drinker. He was strong, he was a hard worker, he was clean, and he could be as gentle as a woman. If he, Johannes, were not telling the truth about all these things, then he deserved to be chased away. If Paulus failed in any single respect, then he, Johannes, would voluntarily leave the service of the baas, because he had said untrue things to the baas. But if the baas believed him, and gave Paulus his chance, then he, Johannes, would teach Paulus all the things of the house and the garden, so that Paulus would be useful to the baas in ways other than the particular task for which he was asking the baas to hire him. And, rather daringly, Johannes said that it did not matter so much if Paulus knew no English, because the old baas, the *oubaas*, knew no English either.

It was as something in the nature of a joke—almost a joke against his father—that Harry Grossman gave Paulus his chance. For Paulus was given his chance. He was given a room in the servants' quarters in the back yard, into which he brought a tin trunk painted red and black, a roll of blankets, and a guitar with a picture of a cowboy on the back. He was given a houseboy's outfit of blue denim blouse and shorts, with red piping round the edges, into which he fitted, with his beard and physique, like a king in exile in some pantomime. He was given his food three times a day, after the white people had eaten, a bar of soap every week, cast-off clothing at odd intervals, and the sum of one pound five shillings per week, five shillings of which he took, the rest being left at his request, with the baas, as savings. He had a free afternoon once a week, and he was allowed to entertain not more than two friends at any one time in his room. And in all the particulars that Johannes had enumerated, Johannes was proved reliable. Paulus was not one of these town boys, these street loafers. He did not steal or drink, he was clean and he was honest and hardworking. And he could be gentle as a woman.

It took Paulus some time to settle down to his job; he had to conquer not only his own shyness and strangeness in the new house filled with strange people—let alone the city, which, since taking occupation of his room, he had hardly dared to enter—but also the hostility of old man Grossman, who took immediate fright at Paulus and redoubled his efforts to get away from the house upon Paulus' entry into it. As it happened, the first result of this persistence on the part of the old man was that Paulus was able to get the measure of the job, for he came to it with a willingness of spirit that the old man could not vanquish, but could only teach. Paulus had been given no instructions, he had merely been told to see that the old man did not get himself into trouble, and after a few days of bewilderment Paulus found his way. He simply went along with the old man.

At first he did so cautiously, following the old man at a distance, for he knew the other had no trust in him. But later he was able to follow the old man openly; still later he was able to walk side by side with him, and the old man did not try to escape from him. When old man Grossman went out, Paulus went too, and there was no longer any need for the doors and windows to be watched, or the police to be telephoned. The young bearded

Zulu and the old bearded Jew from Lithuania walked together in the streets of the town that was strange to them both; together they looked over the fences of the large gardens and into the shining foyers of the blocks of flats; together they stood on the pavements of the main arterial roads and watched the cars and trucks rush between the tall buildings; together they walked in the small, sandy parks, and when the old man was tired Paulus saw to it that he sat on a bench and rested. They could not sit on the bench together, for only whites were allowed to sit on the benches, but Paulus would squat on the ground at the old man's feet and wait until he judged the old man had rested long enough, before moving on again. Together they stared into the windows of the suburban shops, and though neither of them could read the signs outside the shops, the advertisements on billboards, the traffic signs at the side of the road, Paulus learned to wait for the traffic lights to change from red to green before crossing a street, and together they stared at the Coca-cola girls and the advertisements for beer and the cinema posters. On a piece of cardboard which Paulus carried in the pocket of his blouse Harry had had one of his sons print the old man's name and address, and whenever Paulus was uncertain of the way home, he would approach an African or a friendly-looking white man and show him the card, and try his best to follow the instructions, or at least the gesticulations which were all of the answers of the white men that meant anything to him. But there were enough Africans to be found, usually, who were more sophisticated than himself, and though they teased him for his 'rawness' and for holding

The Zulu and the Zeide

the sort of job he had, they helped him too. And neither Paulus nor old man Grossman were aware that when they crossed a street hand-in-hand, as they sometimes did when the traffic was particularly heavy, there were white men who averted their eyes from the sight of this degradation, which could come upon a white man when he was old and senile and dependent.

Paulus knew only Zulu, the old man knew only Yiddish, so there was no language in which they could talk to one another. But they talked all the same: they both explained, commented and complained to each other of the things they saw around them, and often they agreed with one another, smiling and nodding their heads and explaining again with their hands what each happened to be talking about. They both seemed to believe that they were talking about the same things, and often they undoubtedly were, when they lifted their heads sharply to see an aeroplane cross the blue sky between two buildings, or when they reached the top of a steep road and turned to look back the way they had come, and saw below them the clean impervious towers of the city thrust nakedly against the sky in brand-new piles of concrete and glass and face-brick. Then down they would go again, among the houses and the gardens where the beneficent climate encouraged both palms and oak trees to grow indiscriminately among each other—as they did in the garden of the house to which, in the evenings, Paulus and old man Grossman would eventually return.

In and about the house Paulus soon became as indispensable to the old man as he was on their expeditions out of it. Paulus dressed him and bathed him and trimmed his beard, and when the old man woke distressed in the middle of the night it would be for Paulus that he would call—*"Der schwarzer,"* he would shout (for he never learned Paulus' name), *"vo's der schwarzer"*—and Paulus would change his sheets and pyjamas and put him back to bed again. *"Baas Zeide,"* Paulus called the old man, picking up the Yiddish word for grandfather from the children of the house.

And that something that Harry Grossman told everyone of. For Harry persisted in regarding the arrangement as a kind of joke, and the more the arrangement succeeded the more determinedly did he try to spread the joke, so that it should be a joke not only against his father but a joke against Paulus too. It had been a joke that his father should be looked after by a raw Zulu: it was going to be a joke that the Zulu was successful at it. "Baas *Zeide!* That's what *der schwarzer* calls him—have you ever heard the like of it? And you should see the two of them, walking about in the streets hand-in-hand like two schoolgirls. Two clever ones, *der schwarzer* and my father going for a promenade, and between them I tell you you wouldn't be able to find out what day of the week or what time of day it is."

And when people said, "Still that Paulus seems a very good boy," Harry would reply:

"Why shouldn't he be? With all his knowledge, are there so many better jobs that he'd be able to find? He keeps the old man happy—very good, very nice, but don't forget that that's what he's paid to do. What does he know any better to do, a simple kaffir from the *kraal?* He knows he's got a good job, and he'd be a fool if he threw it away. Do you think," Harry would say, and this too would insistently be part of the joke, "if I had nothing else to do with my time I wouldn't be able to make the old man happy?" Harry would look about his sitting-room, where the floorboards bore the weight of his furniture, or when they sat on the stoep he would measure with his glance the spacious garden aloof from the street beyond the hedge. "I've got other things to do. And I had other things to do, plenty of them, all my life, and not only for myself." What these things were that he had had to do all his life would send him back to his joke. "No, I think the old man has just found his level in *der schwarzer*—and I don't think *der schwarzer* could cope with anything else."

Harry teased the old man to his face too, about his 'black friend,' and he would ask his father what he would do if Paulus went away; once he jokingly threatened to send the Zulu away. But the old man didn't believe the threat, for Paulus was in the house when the threat was made, and the old man simply left his son and went straight to Paulus' room, and sat there with Paulus for security. Harry did not follow him: he would never have gone into any of his servants' rooms least of all that of Paulus. For though he made a joke of him to others, to Paulus himself Harry always spoke gruffly, unjokingly, with no patience. On that day he had merely shouted after the old man, "Another time he won't be there."

Yet it was strange to see how Harry Grossman would always be drawn to the room in which he knew his father and Paulus to be. Night after night he came into the old man's bedroom when Paulus was dressing or undressing the old man; almost as often Harry stood in the steamy, untidy bathroom when the old man was being bathed. At these times he hardly spoke, he offered no explanation of his presence: he stood dourly and silently in the room, in his customary powerful and begrudging stance, with one hand clasping the wrist of the other and both supporting his waist, and he watched Paulus at work. The backs of Paulus' hands were smooth and black and hairless, they were paler on the palms and at the finger-nails, and they worked deftly about the body of the old man, who was submissive under the ministrations of the other. At first Paulus had sometimes smiled at Harry while he worked, with his straightforward, even smile in which there was no invitation to a complicity in patronage, but rather an encouragement to Harry to draw forward. But after the first few evenings of this work that Harry had watched, Paulus no longer smiled at his master. And while he worked Paulus could not restrain himself, even under Harry's stare, from talking in a soft, continuous flow of Zulu, to encourage the old man and to exhort him to be helpful and to express his pleasure in how well the work was going. When Paulus would at last wipe the gleaming soap-flakes from his dark hands he would sometimes, when the old man was tired, stoop low and with a laugh pick up the old man and carry him easily down the passage to his bedroom. Harry would follow; he would stand in the passage and watch the burdened, bare-footed Zulu until the door of his father's room closed behind them both.

Only once did Harry wait on such an evening for Paulus to reappear from his father's room. Paulus had already come out, had passed him in the narrow passage, and had already subduedly said: "Good night, baas," before Harry called suddenly:

"Hey! Wait!"

"Baas," Paulus said, turning his head. Then he came quickly to Harry. "Baas," he said again, puzzled and anxious to know why his baas, who so rarely spoke to him, should suddenly have called him like this, at the end of the day, when his work was over.

Harry waited again before speaking, waited long enough for Paulus to say: "Baas?" once more, and to move a little closer, and to lift his head for a moment before letting it drop respectfully down.

"The *oubaas* was tired tonight," Harry said. "Where did you take him? What did you do with him?"

"Baas?" Paulus said quickly. Harry's tone was so brusque that the smile Paulus gave asked for no more than a moment's remission of the other's anger.

But Harry went on loudly: "You heard what I said. What did you do with him that he looked so tired?"

"Baas—I—" Paulus was flustered, and his hands beat in the air for a moment, but with care, so that he would not touch his baas. "Please baas." He brought both hands to his mouth, closing it forcibly. He flung his hands away. "Johannes," he said with relief, and he had already taken the first step down the passage to call his interpreter.

"No!" Harry called. "You mean you don't understand what I say? I know you don't," Harry shouted, though in fact he had forgotten until Paulus had reminded him. The sight of Paulus' startled, puzzled, and guilty face before him filled him with a lust to see this man, this nurse with the face and the figure of a warrior, look more startled, puzzled, and guilty yet; and Harry knew that it could so easily be done, it could be done simply by talking to him in the language he could not understand. "You're a fool," Harry said. "You're like a child. You understand nothing, and it's just as well for you that you need nothing. You'll always be where you are, running to do what the white baas tells you to do. Look how you stand! Do you think I understood English when I came here?" Harry said, and then with contempt, using one of the few Zulu words he knew: *"Hamba!* Go! Do you think I want to see you?"

"Au baas!" Paulus exclaimed in distress. He could not remonstrate; he could only open his hands in a gesture to show that he knew neither the words Harry used, nor in what he had been remiss that Harry should have spoken in such angry tones to him. But Harry gestured him away, and had the satisfaction of seeing Paulus shuffle off like a schoolboy.

Harry was the only person who knew that he and his father had quarrelled shortly before the accident that ended the old man's life took place; this was something that Harry was to keep secret for the rest of his life.

Late in the afternoon they quarrelled, after Harry had come back from the shop out of which he made his living. Harry came back to find his father wandering about the house, shouting for *der schwarzer,* and his wife complaining that she had already told the old man at least five times that *der schwarzer* was not in the house: it was Paulus' afternoon off.

Harry went to his father, and when his father came eagerly to him, he too told the old man, "*Der schwarzer's* not here." So the old man, with Harry following, turned away and continued going from room to room, peering in through the doors. "*Der schwarzer's* not here," Harry said. "What do you want him for?"

Still the old man ignored him. He went down the passage towards the bedrooms. "What do you want him for?" Harry called after him.

The old man went into every bedroom, still shouting for *der schwarzer*. Only when he was in his own bare bedroom did he look at Harry. "Where's *der schwarzer?*" he asked.

"I've told you ten times I don't know where he is. What do you want him for?"

"I want *der schwarzer.*"

"I know you want him. But he isn't here."

"Do you think I haven't heard you? He isn't here."

"I want *der schwarzer.*" "Bring him to me," the old man said.

"I can't bring him to you. I don't know where he is." Then Harry steadied himself against his own anger. He said quietly: "Tell me what you want. I'll do it for you. I'm here, I can do what *der schwarzer* can do for you."

"Where's *der schwarzer?*"

"I've told you he isn't here," Harry shouted, the angrier for his previous moment's patience. "Why don't you tell me what you want? What's the matter with me—can't you tell me what you want?"

"I want *der schwarzer.*"

"Please," Harry said. He threw out his arms towards his father, but the gesture was abrupt, almost as though he were thrusting his father away from him. "Why can't you ask it of me? You can ask me—haven't I done enough for you already? Do you want to go for a walk?—I'll take you for a walk. What do you want? Do you want—do you want——?" Harry could not think what his father might want. "I'll do it," he said. "You don't need *der schwarzer.*"

Then Harry saw that his father was weeping. The old man was standing up and weeping, with his eyes hidden behind the thick glasses that he had to wear: his glasses and his beard made his face a mask of age, as though time had left him nothing but the frame of his body on which the clothing could hang, and this mask of his face above. But Harry knew when the old man was weeping—he had seen him crying too often before, when they had found him at the end of a street after he had wandered away, or even, years earlier, when he had lost another of the miserable jobs that seemed to be the only one he could find in a country in which his son had, later, been able to run a good business, drive a large car, own a big house.

"Father," Harry asked, "what have I done? Do you think I've sent *der schwarzer* away?" Harry saw his father turn away, between the narrow bed and the narrow wardrobe. "He's coming——" Harry said, but he could not look at his father's back, he could not look at his father's hollowed neck, on which the hairs that Paulus had clipped glistened above the pale brown discolourations of age— Harry could not look at the neck turned stiffly away from him while he had to try to promise the return of the Zulu. Harry dropped his hands and walked out of the room.

No one knew how the old man managed to get out of the house and through the front gate without having been seen. But he did manage it, and in the road he was struck down. Only a man on a bicycle struck him down, but it was enough, and he died a few days later in the hospital.

Harry's wife wept, even the grandsons wept; Paulus wept. Harry himself was stony, and his bunched, protuberant features were immovable; they seemed locked upon the bones of his face. A few days after the funeral he called Paulus and Johannes into the kitchen and said to Johannes: "Tell him he must go. His work is finished."

Johannes translated for Paulus, and then, after Paulus had spoken, he turned to Harry. "He says, yes baas." Paulus kept his eyes on the ground; he did not look up even when Harry looked directly at him, and Harry knew that this was not out of fear or shyness, but out of courtesy for his master's grief—which was what they could not but be talking of, when they talked of his work.

"Here's his pay." Harry thrust a few notes towards Paulus, who took them in his cupped hands, and retreated.

Harry waited for them to go, but Paulus stayed in the room, and consulted with Johannes in a low voice. Johannes turned to his master. "He says, baas, that the baas still has his savings."

Harry had forgotten about Paulus' savings. He told Johannes that he had forgotten, and that he did not have enough money at the moment, but would bring the money the next day. Johannes translated and Paulus nodded gratefully. Both he and Johannes were subdued by the death there had been in the house.

And Harry's dealings with Paulus were over. He took what was to have been his last look at Paulus, but this look stirred him again against the Zulu. As harshly as he told Paulus that he had to go, so now, implacably, seeing Paulus in the mockery and simplicity of his houseboy's clothing, to feed his anger to the very end Harry said: "Ask him what he's been saving for. What's he going to do with the fortune he's made?"

Johannes spoke to Paulus and came back with a reply. "He says, baas, that he is saving to bring his wife and children from Zululand to Johannesburg. He is saving, baas," Johannes said, for Harry had not seemed to understand, "to bring his family to this town also."

The two Zulus were bewildered to know why it should have been at that moment that Harry Grossman's clenched, fist-like features should suddenly seem to have fallen from one another, nor why he should have stared with such guilt and despair at Paulus, while he cried, "What else could I have done? I did my best," before the first tears came.

The Crazy Old Man

Hugh Nissenson

The old man is still alive, living in the same apartment on Jaffa Road in Jerusalem. He's very old by now, in his late eighties, blinded by a cataract in his left eye, but when I saw him last, about a week after the liberation of the Old City, he was on his way, alone, to pray at the Wall. He recognized me immediately—or so I thought—but after a few minutes' conversation on the street I realized that he confused me with Uzi because he asked if I still lived in Haifa. I let it pass, and chatted for a while. He still lived with his daughter, he said, who was married to a captain in the paratroops, and had two children. His son-in-law had fought and been wounded in the fight for the Old City, making a dash across the crest of the Temple Mount toward the Dome of the Rock.

"What's his name?" I asked.

"Seligman."

"Raphael?" I asked, and he answered in Yiddish. "Yes. You know him?"

"We've met."

He peered at me with his good eye; at my unshaven face and civilian clothes—a filthy white shirt and blue trousers I was wearing for an Intelligence job I'd just finished in the Old City.

"So you know Raphael," he said.

"He's a good soldier."

"Is he?"

"Where was he hit?" I asked.

"In the arm. Nothing. A flesh wound in the muscle up here."

Up to then I thought that I had detected pride in his voice and that he had at last recovered his sanity. But then he said, "I must go and pray for him now, and ask forgiveness."

And off he went, wearing a black felt hat with a wide brim, a long black gabardine coat, and those knee-length white stockings. In his right hand he carried a ragged, blue velvet bag embroidered with a gold Star of David, for his prayer shawl. He was the same. Nothing had changed for him in almost twenty years. I resisted an impulse to run upstairs to take a look at his apartment, imagining that that, too, had remained the same, with its wicker chairs and that hideous sideboard made from teak and inlaid with mother-of-pearl that he had bought from some Arab when he first came to the country from Russia in 1912. Instead, I strolled up King George Street and, to get out of the sun, had a cup of bitter coffee in an immaculate German café.

Later in the afternoon, driving back to G.H.Q. in Tel Aviv, I thought about the whole thing for the first time in years, watching the stream of Dan

The Crazy Old Man

buses, private cars, captured Jordanian Ford trucks with Arab license plates, and even a Russian jeep taken from the Syrians, all packed with people heading for the Wall. The rest of the Old City was still closed to civilians because of snipers and mines. I thought about Uzi, who died in 1953 in a car accident on the Tel Aviv-Haifa road, and the two Arab prisoners.

At the time, in July 1948, during the Ten Days' Fighting just before the second truce, Uzi and I were with the Haganah's Intelligence in Jerusalem, assigned to interrogate prisoners and gather information for the coordinated attack that was to be made on the Old city.

The plan was simple; a simultaneous breakthrough from the north through the New Gate by a unit of the Irgun, and from the south, by the Haganah, near the Zion Gate. The Old City wall is four yards thick here, but we had high hopes that we'd be able to breach it with a new explosive that we had never tried before. As it turned out, the stuff hardly scratched the wall's surface, and the plan failed. So, in the end, what we did was useless.

Uzi and I had been detailed to find out the exact number and disposition of the Arab forces around the Zion Gate from two Jordanian legionnaires who had been captured the day before. We had twelve hours to get the information out of them, so we took them to my apartment, which I had used as a "drop" for ammunition during the Mandate and where I now did most of my work. It was one room on the second floor, right across the hall from the old man and his daughter. They didn't bother me much. The old man was busy praying, and the girl, who was about twelve or thirteen, was very shy. Only once, in the last month of the Mandate, the old man invited me into his apartment for a glass of tea.

"I insist," he told me. "The kettle's on the stove. There, you hear? Already boiling. Sit down. I have no lemon. Sugar?"

"Thanks."

"Enough?"

"One more. Yes, that's fine, thanks."

"Keep the spoon. I have one here." He blew into his steaming glass and, with a spoonful of sugar already on his tongue, took a sip and smacked his lips. "Ah. That's a pleasure. Sugar on the tongue." He smiled. "For me, it somehow never tastes as good in the glass. A habit from the Old Country. But you, of course, were born here, weren't you?"

"Yes, in Tel Aviv."

"Tel Aviv. Is that so?" He stroked his red beard streaked with gray. "You're lucky."

"You think so?"

"I know so. You see, this is your chance. Not mine. Not an old Jew like me who came here to pray for forgiveness and die, but yours. My daughter Chanele's and yours, if you understand me."

"Thanks for the tea but I have to go out. It's almost curfew."

"No, no, wait. Just one minute. You must listen to me for just one minute and try to understand." He suddenly began to sweat. His forehead, wrinkled with concentration, glistened. "The Exile, you see, the real Exile is that we learned to endure it," he suddenly went on. "Rabbi Hanokh, may he rest in peace, once said that, and he was right. But it's all over now. I can feel it. I look at you and even

The Crazy Old Man

my little Chanele, my shy little Chanele, who dreams of becoming a courier for the Haganah. . . . Can you believe that? It's true. At twelve. That pious child. . . . All of you who were born here have had enough and will have your State. For you, the Exile is over. Not that it wasn't deserved." He wagged a forefinger. "Oh, no. Never for one moment think that. We sinned and were punished for it. It was just. But He has relented, you see, may His Name be blessed forever and ever, and, in His mercy, has given you one more chance. So you must be careful. Very, very careful.

"No, please sit down," he said, and in a lower voice went on. "When I was a boy ten years old, there was a pogrom in my town. A little town south of Kiev, and a little pogrom. Ten, twelve Jews killed, and three wounded. Nothing extraordinary, except that a Russian blacksmith raped and murdered a Jewish woman he had known for forty years. They had grown up together. Played together as children. His name was Kolya. Huge and gentle, with his eyebrows and eyelashes all burned away from the sparks that flew from his forge. After *cheder*, I would go and watch him work and sometimes he'd even share his food with me—his only meal of the day. *Talakno*, a kind of porridge made from oats and mixed with cold water. We ate from the same dish with long wooden spoons. But I saw him do it. With my own eyes, from a window in our cellar, to Sarah, who was a grandmother, the wife of Mulya the tailor. Then, while I watched, Kolya strangled her with those huge hands. I saw it all, and I learned a secret. He was human. Kolya was a human being, just like little Itzik the *shammis*, for example, or myself. There was no question of that. But he was different. And what was the difference? His violence. Violence made all the difference between us, the goyim and the Jews." He leaned toward me. His breath smelled of cloves. "And let me tell you something else," he whispered. "The Holocaust . . . Why did He relent and save a remnant from the ovens and bring them here? I'll tell you why. Because they didn't fight back."

"I've got to go," I told him. "I've got a meeting. We've just gotten a shipment of some Czech rifles."

In any case, as I said, we had twelve hours to get the information from the prisoners. It wasn't much time. We started in about nine at night, working them over according to the system that Uzi and I had found to be effective twice before. It was nothing unusual: threats, alternating with promises, and, above all, keeping them on their feet and awake. Uzi and I took turns, an hour each, while the other covered them with my old Beretta, a 1934 model I'd had for years. We kept them awake with cups of Arab coffee brewed over a kerosene stove that stank up the place, and when the coffee gave out, a couple of slaps across the face. Even so, just before dawn the older one, who was a lieutenant, fell asleep standing up.

Uzi slapped him, and all at once, without premeditation, because we weren't getting anywhere, we began beating them up. I hit the younger one in the corner of his mouth with my fist, and his eyetooth split the inside of his upper lip. We let him bleed. He was about twenty, a private, still in his khaki uniform, with the red-and-white checkered *kaffiah*, the headdress of the Legion, wrapped around his neck like a kerchief. His mouthful of

The Crazy Old Man

blood embarrassed and scared the hell out of him. You could tell by the look in his eyes. He was afraid to spit it out and mess up the floor. Finally he took off the *kaffiah* and, crumpling it up in his hand, spit into that. Then he gagged and puked in it but, still terrified, stuffed it into the breast pocket of his tunic. His lip swelled up and made it hard for him to talk.

"I don't know," he kept repeating. "I swear I don't know. I have no idea."

The lieutenant, who had a swollen right cheek, never said a word or even made a sound. He was about thirty, and good-looking, with a deep cleft in his chin and a carefully clipped little mustache. The British officers who had trained him had done a good job. He was a professional soldier and proud of it. He stood at parade rest, in the middle of the room, with his hands clasped behind his back and his feet spread about a yard apart, according to regulations. That was the way he had fallen asleep.

"The kid," Uzi whispered to me. "Our only chance is the kid."

He punched him in the stomach, and the boy doubled up and fell, knocking over a small table with his shoulder. The coffee cups and a half bottle of brandy shattered on the tile floor.

All of a sudden, there was a pounding on the door that grew louder and wouldn't stop until I opened it a crack to catch a glimpse of the old man. There were phylacteries bound to his forehead. We had interrupted his morning prayers.

"What is it? What's happening here?" he asked me in Yiddish.

"Go away," I told him. "It's none of your business."

I tried to shut the door in his face, but he had

already put one foot over the threshold, and with surprising strength threw the door wide open, looked around the room very slowly, and at me again, or rather, at the Beretta in my hand.

"Who is it?" Uzi asked. "What's he want?"

"Rosenblum," I told him. "From across the hall."

"Well, get him out of here."

The boy was still on the floor, gasping for breath, but he managed to raise himself up on his elbows to stare at the old man.

"Go on, now, beat it," Uzi told him in Hebrew.

"No," he answered in Yiddish, and he shook his head. His long earlocks waved. He understood Hebrew perfectly, of course, but as a Hassid he refused to use the holy tongue in ordinary conversation.

"Get him out of here," Uzi repeated. In the distance, maybe three or four blocks away, up Ben Yehuda Street, there was an explosion. The windows rattled. The Arabs were shelling us from the Old City. As a matter of fact, when I look back on it now, they had been shelling and mortaring us all night long, at irregular intervals. We were just impervious to it; only our bodies reacted instinctively every time there was an explosion. Everyone—even the lieutenant, I noticed with satisfaction—contracted his shoulders and ducked his head. Once, about seven in the morning, when an ambulance clanged up Jaffa Road in the direction of the King David, I went to the window to take a look. The street was strewn with rubble: broken glass, glittering in the fresh light, rolls of toilet paper, the burned-out wreck of an old Packard sedan, and fragments of the beautiful, rose-colored

The Crazy Old Man

stone, quarried from the Judean hills, from which the houses of the New City are built.

The old man had apparently completed his prayers. He unwrapped his phylacteries from his forehead—the black felt hat was pushed far back on the crown of his head—and from his thin right arm, covered with red hair.

"You were born here?" he asked Uzi.

"What of it?"

"Were you?"

"Yes, in Haifa, where I live. So what?"

"And you, if I remember, in Tel Aviv," the old man said to me.

"Yes."

He slammed the door shut behind him with his foot and stood there, with his head raised and arms folded across his chest. It was a stance that in some way resembled the lieutenant's, communicating a determination not to give in, but in his case—the old man's—to speak.

"Haifa and Tel Aviv," he repeated. "No, then you mustn't."

Uzi tapped his temple with his forefinger. The old man saw it and smiled. "You think so? 'Have I need of madmen, that ye have brought this fellow to play the madman in my presence?'" He quoted the Bible in Hebrew. I had to think a moment and then remembered. It was from Samuel, when David had feigned insanity to escape from the king of Gath. "You have need," the old man whispered in Yiddish. "You have need. Let them go."

Maybe, from the tone of his voice, the boy guessed what the old man intended; anyhow, he smiled, or tried to smile, with his swollen lip. The lieutenant yawned, delicately covering his mouth with his hand.

Then the old man was off again, spouting from Isaiah, in a hoarse, singsong voice. " 'No lion shall be there, nor any ravenous beast shall go up thereon, it will not be found there; but the redeemed shall walk there.' "

He cleared his throat. His voice was hoarse, and for the first time I noticed his bulbous nose was red. He had a summer cold.

"Let them go," he said.

Uzi dragged the boy to his feet by the collar and hit him in the stomach again. He gagged but didn't have anything else to bring up.

"Well?"

Held at arm's length, his knees sagging, the boy shook his head. Uzi hit him again and let him drop to the floor, where he rolled over on his back.

"Listen to me," the old man said. "You must listen to me."

For the next ten minutes or so, Uzi and I took turns beating the boy up while the lieutenant and the old man watched. I concentrated on his mouth, and that eyetooth finally came out.

"Don't know," he mumbled. "Don't know."

It was possible that he was telling the truth, but we had less than an hour left, and we had to make sure. Uzi hit him in the stomach once more, and then we both had the same idea at the same time. All I had done was unconsciously scratch the nape of my neck with the muzzle of the Beretta. The lieutenant, who was yawning again, lowered his hand, took a deep breath, and straightened up. He understood too.

The Crazy Old Man

"Shoot him," Uzi said in Arabic. The boy, on the floor, opened his eyes.

I made a big production out of it, unloading the magazine, counting the rounds—there were four .380 Colt cartridges—and reinserting it into the handle until it locked with a click. Then I drew back the slide, let it drive the bullet into the firing chamber, closed it, and released the safety. Except for his swollen cheek, which had turned purple, the lieutenant was as white as a sheet, but hadn't moved a muscle. I raised the gun and took aim between his eyes, but the old man grabbed it by the barrel, and I was so surprised, I let go. The lieutenant jumped to one side, to the right, toward the window, but it didn't do him any good. He was off balance, on his right knee, with his right hand on the floor, when the first round hit him in the chest, throwing him on his back. The old man walked over to him and emptied the rest of the magazine into his forehead, holding the gun a yard from his face.

"*Ai, Yah Allah,*" the boy screamed, "Oh, God," and, wringing his hands, began to talk so fast that Uzi, who was scribbling all the information down on a pad of yellow paper, made him slow down and repeat himself again and again. He told us everything we wanted to know, but I wasn't listening. I was looking at the old man, who gingerly handed me back the gun, holding it by the barrel, his little finger in the air. Then he sneezed. Before I could stop him, he walked out the door, across the hall, and into his apartment.

A week later, I was temporarily transferred to G.H.Q. in Tel Aviv to help correlate Intelligence for Operation Ten Plagues that eventually destroyed the Egyptian expeditionary force in the Negev. When I finally got back to Jerusalem, the war had been over for a month. I occasionally ran into the old man on the stairs, but we never spoke. He was usually on his way to shul, or coming back, and, still deeply absorbed in his prayers, looked right through me. His eyes were blue and slightly glazed with the madness that had made him take my crime upon himself because I had been born in the country into which his God had returned the Jews to give them their last chance.

Dreamer in a Dead Language

Grace Paley

The old are modest, said Philip. They tend not to outlive one another.

That's witty, said Faith, but the more you think about it, the less it means.

Philip went to another table where he repeated it at once. Faith thought a certain amount of intransigence was nice in almost any lover. She said, Oh well, O.K. . . .

Now, why at that lively time of life, which is so full of standing up and lying down, *why* were they thinking and speaking sentences about the old.

Because Faith's father, one of the resident poets of the Children of Judea, Home for the Golden Ages, Coney Island Branch, had written still another song. This amazed nearly everyone in the Green Coq, that self-mocking tavern full of artists, entrepreneurs, and working women. In those years, much like these, amazing poems and grizzly tales were coming from the third grade, from the first grade in fact, where the children of many of the drinkers and talkers were learning creativity. But the old! This is very interesting, said some. This is too much, said others. The entrepreneurs said, Not at all—watch it—it's a trend.

Jack, Faith's oldest friend, never far but usually distant, said, I know what Philip means. He means the old are modest. They tend not to outlive each other by too much. Right, Phil?

Well, said Philip, you're right, but the mystery's gone.

In Faith's kitchen, later that night, Philip read the poem aloud. His voice had a timbre which reminded her of evening, maybe nighttime. She had often thought of the way wide air lives and moves in a man's chest. Then it's strummed into shape by the short-stringed voice box to become a wonderful secondary sexual characteristic.

Your voice reminds me of evening too, said Philip.

This is the poem he read:

There is no rest for me since love departed
no sleep since I reached the bottom of the sea
and the end of this woman, my wife.
My lungs are full of water. I cannot breathe.
Still I long to go sailing in spring among realities.
There is a young girl who waits in a special time
  and place
to love me, to be my friend and lie beside me all
  through the night.

Who's the girl? Philip asked.

Why, my mother of course.

You're sweet, Faith.

Of course it's my mother, Phil. My mother, young.

I think it's a different girl entirely.

No, said Faith. It has to be my mother.

But Faith, it doesn't matter who it is. What an old man writes poems about doesn't really matter.

Well, goodbye, said Faith. I've known you one day too long already.

O.K. Change of subject, smile, he said. I really am *crazy* about old people. Always have been. When Anita and I broke up, it was those great Sundays playing chess with her dad that I missed most. They don't talk to me, you know. People take everything personally. I don't, he said. Listen, I'd love to meet your daddy *and* your mom. Maybe I'll go with you tomorrow.

We don't say mom, we don't say daddy. We say mama and papa, when in a hurry we say pa and ma.

I do too, said Philip. I just forgot myself. How about I go with you tomorrow. Damn it, I don't sleep, I'll be up all night. I can't stop cooking. My head. It's like a percolator. Pop! pop! Maybe it's my age, prime of life, you know. Didn't I hear that the father of your children, if you don't mind my mentioning it, is doing a middleman dance around your papa?

How about a nice cup of Sleepytime tea?

Come on Faith, I asked you something.

Yes.

Well, I could do better than he ever dreams of

doing. I know—on good terms—more people. Who's that jerk know? Four old maids in advertising, three Seventh Avenue models, two fairies in TV, one literary dyke . . .

Philip . . .

I'm telling you something. My best friend is Ezra Kalmback. He made a fortune in the great American Craft and Hobby business—he can teach a four-year-old kid how to make an ancient Greek artifact. He's got a system and the equipment. That's how he supports his other side, the ethnic, you know. They publish these poor old dreamers in one dead language—or another. Hey! How's that! A title for your papa. "Dreamer in a Dead Language." Give me a pen. I got to write it down. O.K. Faith, I give you that title free of charge, even if you decide to leave me out.

Leave you out of what? she asked. Stop walking up and down. This room is too small. You'll wake the kids up. Phil, why does your voice get so squeaky when you talk business? It goes higher and higher. Right now you're above high C.

He had been thinking printing costs and percentage. He couldn't drop his answer more than half an octave. That's because I was once a pure-thinking English major—but alas, I was forced by bad management, the thoughtless begetting of children, and the vengeance of alimony into low practicality.

Faith bowed her head. She hated the idea of giving up the longed-for night in which sleep, sex, and affection would take their happy turns. What will I do, she thought. How can you talk like that to me Philip? Vengeance . . . you really stink Phil. Me. Anita's old friend. Are you dumb? She didn't want to hit him. Instead her eyes filled with tears.

What'd I do now? he asked. Oh, I know what I did. I know exactly.

What poet did you think was so great when you were pure?

Milton, he said. He was surprised. He hadn't known till asked that he was lonesome for all that Latin moralizing. You know, Faith, Milton was of the party of the devil, he said. I don't think I am. Maybe it's because I have to make a living.

I like two poems, said Faith, and except for my father's stuff, that's all I like. This was not necessarily true, but she was still thinking with her strict offended face. I like, *Hail to thee blithe spirit bird thou never wert,* and I like, *Oh what can ail thee knight at arms alone and palely loitering.* And that's all.

Now listen Philip, if you ever see my folks, if I ever bring you out there, don't mention Anita Franklin—my parents were crazy about her, they thought she'd be a Ph.D. medical doctor. Don't let on you were the guy who dumped her. In fact, she said sadly, don't even tell me about it again.

Faith's father had been waiting at the gate for about half an hour. He wasn't bored. He had been discussing the slogan "Black Is Beautiful" with Chuck Johnson, the gatekeeper. Who thought it up, Chuck?

I couldn't tell you, Mr. Darwin. It just settled on the street one day, there it was.

It's brilliant, said Mr. Darwin. If we could've thought that one up, it would've saved a lot of noses, believe me. You know what I'm talking about?

Then he smiled. Faithy! Richard! Anthony! You said you'd come and you came. Oh oh, I'm not sarcastic—it's only a fact. I'm happy. Chuck, you remember my youngest girl? Faithy, this is Chuck in charge of coming and going. Richard! Anthony! say hello to Chuck. Faithy, look at me, he said.

What a place! said Richard.

A castle! said Tonto.

You are nice to see your grandpa, said Chuck. I bet he been nice to you in his day.

Don't mention day. By me it's morning. Right Faith? I'm first starting out.

Starting out where? asked Faith. She was sorry so much would have to happen before the true and friendly visit.

To tell you the truth, I was talking to Ricardo the other day.

That's what I thought, what kind of junk did he fill you up with?

Faith, in the first place don't talk about their father in front of the boys. Do me the favor. It's a rotten game. Second, probably you and Ricardo got the wrong chemistry.

Chemistry? The famous scientist. Is that his idea? How's his chemistry with you? Huh?

Well, he talks.

Is Daddy here? asked Richard.

Who cares? said Tonto, looking at his mother's face. We don't care much, do we Faith?

No no, said Faith. Daddy isn't here. He just spoke to Grandpa, remember I told you about Grandpa writing that poetry. Well, Daddy likes it.

That's a little better, Mr. Darwin said.

I wish you luck Pa, but you ought to talk to a few other people. I could ask someone else—Ricardo is a smart operator, I know. What's he planning for you?

Well Faithy, two possibilities. The first a little

volume, put out in beautiful vellum, maybe something like vellum, you know, *Poems from the Golden Age* . . . You like that?

Ugh! said Faith.

Is this a hospital? asked Richard.

The other thing is like this. Faithy, I got dozens of songs, you want to call them songs. You could call them songs or poems, whatever, I don't know. Well, he had a good idea, to put out a book also with some other people here—a series—if not a book. Keller for instance is no slouch when it comes to poetry, but he's more like an epic poet, you know . . . When Israel was a youth, then I loved . . . it's a first line, it goes on a hundred pages at least. Madame Nazdarova, our editor from *A Bessere Zeit*—did you meet her?—she listens like a disease. She's a natural editor. It goes in her ear one day. In a week you see it without complications, no mistakes, on paper.

You're some guy, Pa, said Faith. Worry and tenderness brought her brows together.

Don't wrinkle up so much, he said.

Oh shit! said Faith.

Is this a hospital? asked Richard.

They were walking toward a wall of wheelchairs that rested in the autumn sun. Off to the right under a great-leaf linden a gathering of furious arguers were leaning—every one of them—on aluminum walkers.

Like a design, said Mr. Darwin. A beautiful sight.

Well, *is* this a hospital? Richard asked.

It looks like a hospital, I bet, sonny. Is that it?

A little bit, Grandpa.

A lot, be honest. Honesty, my grandson, is *one* of the best policies.

Richard laughed. Only one, huh Grandpa.

See, Faithy, he gets the joke. Oh, you darling kid. What a sense of humor! Mr. Darwin whistled for the joy of a grandson with a sense of humor. Listen to him laugh, he said to a lady volunteer who had come to read very loud to the deaf.

I have a sense of humor too Grandpa, said Tonto.

Sure sonny, why not. Your mother was a constant entertainment to us. She could take jokes right out of the air for your grandma and me and your aunt and uncle. She had us in stitches, your mother.

She mostly laughs for company now, said Tonto, like if Philip comes.

Oh, he's so melodramatic, said Faith, pulling Tonto's ear. What a lie . . .

We got to fix that up, Anthony. Your mama's a beautiful girl. She should be happy. Let's think up a good joke to tell her. He thought for about twelve seconds. Well, O.K. I got it. Listen:

There's an old Jew. He's in Germany. It's maybe '39, '40. He comes around to the tourist office. He looks at the globe. They got a globe there. He says, Listen, I got to get out of here. Where you suggest, Herr Agent, I should go? The agency man also looks at the globe. The Jewish man says, Hey, how about here? He points to America. Oh, says the agency man, sorry, no, they got finished up with their quota. Ts, says the Jewish man, so how about here? He points to France. Last train left already for there, too bad, too bad. Nu, then to Russia? Sorry, absolutely nobody they let in there at the present time. A few more places . . . the answer is always, port is closed. They got already too many, we got no boats . . . So finally the poor Jew, he's thinking he can't go anywhere on the globe, also he also can't stay where he is, he says oi, he says ach! he pushes the globe away, disgusted. But he got hope. He says, So this one is used up, Herr Agent. Listen—you got another one?

Oh, said Faith, what a terrible thing. What's funny about that? I hate that joke.

I get it, I get it, said Richard. Another globe. There is no other globe. Only one globe, Mommy? He had no place to go. On account of that old Hitler. Grandpa, tell it to me again. So I can tell my class.

I don't think it's so funny either, said Tonto.

Pa, is Hegel-Shtein with Mama? I don't know if I can take her today. She's too much.

Faith, who knows? You're not the only one. Who can stand her? One person, your mama, the saint, that's who. I'll tell you what—let the boys come with me. I'll give them a quick rundown on the place. You go upstairs. I'll show them wonderful sights.

Well, O.K. . . . will you go with Grandpa, boys?

Sure, said Tonto. Where'll you be?

With Grandma.

If I need to see you about anything, said Richard, could I?

Sure, sonny boys, said Mr. Darwin. Any time you need your mama say the word, one, two, three, you got her. O.K.? Faith, the elevator is over there by that entrance.

Christ, I know where the elevator is.

Once, not paying attention, rising in the gloom of her troubles, the elevator door had opened and she'd seen it—the sixth-floor ward.

Sure—the incurables, her father had said. Then to comfort her: Would you believe it, Faithy? Just like the world, the injustice. Even here, some of us start on the top. The rest of us got to work our way up.

Ha ha, said Faith.

It's only true, he said.

He explained that incurable did not mean near death necessarily, it meant, in most cases, just too far from living. There were, in fact, thirty-year-old people in the ward, with healthy hearts and satisfactory lungs. But they lay flat or curved by pain, or they were tied with shawls into wheelchairs. Here and there an old or middle-aged parent came every day to change the sheets or sing nursery rhymes to her broken child.

The third floor, however, had some of the characteristics of a hotel—that is, there were corridors, rugs, and doors, and Faith's mother's door was, as always, wide open. Near the window, using up light and the curly shadow of hanging plants, Mrs. Hegel-Shtein was wide awake, all smiles and speedy looks, knitting needles and elbows jabbing the air. Faith kissed her cheek for the awful sake of her mother's kindness. Then she sat beside her mother to talk and be friends.

Naturally, the very first thing her mother said was: The boys? She looked as though she'd cry.

No no, Ma, I brought them, they're with Pa a little.

I was afraid for a minute . . . This gives us a chance . . . So, Faithy, tell me the truth. How is it? A little better? The job helps?

The job . . . ugh. I'm buying a new typewriter, Ma. I want to work at home. It's a big investment, you know, like going into business.

Faith! Her mother turned to her. Why should you

go into business? You could be a social worker for the city. You're very good-hearted, you always worried about the next fellow. You should be a teacher, you could be off in the summer. You could get a counselor job, the children would go to camp.

Oh, Ma . . . oh, damn it! . . . said Faith. She looked at Mrs. Hegel-Shtein, who, for a solid minute, had not been listening because she was counting stitches.

What could I do, Faithy? You said eleven o'clock. Now it's one. Am I right?

I guess so, said Faith. There was no way to talk. She bent her head down to her mother's shoulder. She was much taller and it was hard to do. Though awkward, it was necessary. Her mother took her hand—pressed it to her cheek. Then she said, Ach! what I know about this hand . . . the way it used to eat applesauce, it didn't think a spoon was necessary. A very backward hand.

Oh boy, cute, said Mrs. Hegel-Shtein.

Mrs. Darwin turned the hand over, patted it, then dropped it. My goodness! Faithy. Faithy, how come you have a boil on the wrist. Don't you wash?

Ma, of course I wash. I don't know. Maybe it's from worry, anyway it's not a boil.

Please don't tell me worry. You went to college. Keep your hands clean. You took biology. I remember. So wash.

Ma. For godsakes, I know when to wash.

Mrs. Hegel-Shtein dropped her knitting. Mrs. Darwin, I don't like to interfere, only it so happens your little kiddie is right. Boils on the wrist is the least from worry. It's a scientific fact. Worries what start long ago don't come to a end. You didn't realize. Only go in and out, in and out the heart a couple hundred times something like gas. I can see you don't believe me. Stubborn Celia Darwin. Sickness comes from trouble. Cysts, I got all over inside me since the Depression. Where the doctor could put a hand, Cyst! he hollered. Gallbladder I have since Archie married a fool. Slow blood, I got that when Mr. Shtein died. Varicose veins, with *hemorrhoids* and a crooked neck, I got when Mr. Shtein got social security and retired. For him that time nervousness from the future come to an end. For me it first began. You know what is responsibility? To keep a sick old man alive. Everything like the last supper before they put the man in the electric chair. Turkey. Pot roast. Stuffed kishkas, kugels all kinds, soups without an end. Oi, Faithy, from this I got arthritis and rheumatism from top to bottom. Boils on the wrist is only the beginning.

What you mean is, Faith said, what you mean is—life has made you sick.

If that's what I mean, that's what I mean.

Now, said Mr. Darwin, who was on his way to the roof garden with the boys. He had passed the room, stopped to listen; he had a comment to make. He repeated: Now! then continued, That's what I got against modern times. It so happens you're in the swim, Mrs. H. Psychosomatic is everything nowadays. You don't have a cold that you say, I caught it on the job from Mr. Hirsh. No siree, you got your cold nowadays from your wife, whose health is perfect, she just doesn't think you're so handsome. It might turn out that to her you were always a mutt. Usually then you get hay fever for life. Every August is the anniversary of don't remind me.

All right, said Mrs. Darwin, the whole conversation is too much. My own health doesn't take every lopsided idea you got in your head, Sid. Meanwhile, wash up a little bit extra anyway, Faith, all right? A favor.

O.K. Ma, O.K., said Faith.

What about me? said Mr. Darwin, when will I talk to my girl? Faithy, come take a little walk.

I hardly sat down with Mama yet.

Go with him, her mother said. He can't sit. Mr. Pins and Needles. Tell her, Sid, she has to be more sensible. She's a mother. She doesn't have the choice.

Please don't tell me what to tell her, Celia. Faithy, come. Boys, stay here, talk to your grandma. Talk to her friend.

Why not, boys. Mrs. Hegel-Shtein smiled and invited them. Look it in the face: old age! Here it comes, ready or not. The boys looked, then moved close together, their elbows touching.

Faith tried to turn back to the children, but her father held her hand hard. Faithy, pay no attention. Let Mama take care. She'll make it a joke. She has presents for them. Come! We'll find a nice tree next to a bench. One thing this place got is trees and benches. Also, every bench is not just a bench—it's a dedicated bench. It has a name.

From the side garden door he showed her. That bench there, my favorite, is named Jerome (Jerry) Katzoff, six years old. It's a terrible thing to die young. Still, it saves a lot of time. Get it? That wonderful circular bench there all around that elm tree (it should live to be old) is a famous bench named Sidney Hillman. So you see we got benches. What we do *not* have here, what I am suffering from daily, is not enough first-class books. Plenty of best sellers, but first-class literature? . . . I bet you're surprised. I wrote the manager a letter. "Dear Goldstein," I said. "Dear Goldstein, Are we or are we not the People of the Book? I admit by law we're a little nonsectarian, but by and large we are here living mostly People of the Book. Book means mostly to you Bible, Talmud, etc., probably. To me, and to my generation, idealists all, book means BOOKS. Get me? Goldstein, how about putting a little from Jewish Philanthropies into keeping up the reputation for another fifty years. You could do it single-handed, adding very little to the budget. Wake up, brother, while I still got my wits."

That reminds me, another thing, Faithy. I have to tell you a fact. People's brains, I notice, are disappearing all around me. Every day.

Sit down a minute. It's pressing on me. Last one to go is Eliezer Heligman. One day I'm pointing out to him how the seeds, the regular germinating seeds of Stalinist anti-Semitism, existed not only in clockwork, Russian pogrom mentality, but also in the everyday attitude even Mensheviks to Zionism. He gives me a big fight, very serious, profound, fundamental. If I weren't so sure I was right, I would have thought I was wrong. A couple of days later I pass him, under this tree resting on this exact bench. I sit down also. He's with Mrs. Grund, a lady well known to be in her second, maybe third, childhood at least.

She's crying. Crying. I don't interfere. Heligman is saying, Madame Grund, you're crying. Why?

My mother died, she says.

Ts, he says.

Died. Died. I was four years old and my mother died.

Ts, he says.
Then my father got me a stepmother.
Oi, says Heligman. It's hard to live with a stepmother. It's terrible. Four years old to lose a mother.
I can't stand it, she says. All day. No one to talk to. She don't care for me, that stepmother. She got her own girl. A girl like me needs a mother.
Oi, says Heligman, a mother, a mother. A girl surely needs a mother.
But not me, I ain't got one. A stepmother I got, no mother.
Oi, says Heligman.
Where will I get a mother from? Never.
Ach, says Heligman. Don't worry, Madame Grund darling, don't worry. Time passes. You'll be healthy, you'll grow up, you'll see. Soon you'll get married, you'll have children, you'll be happy.
Heligman, oi, Heligman, I say, what the hell are you talking about?
Oh, how do you do, he says to me, a passing total stranger. Madame Grund here, he says, is alone in the world, a girl four years old, she lost her mother. (Tears are in his disappearing face.) But I told her she wouldn't cry forever, she'll get married, she'll have children, her time will come, her time will come.
How do you do yourself, Heligman, I say. In fact, goodbye, my dear friend, my best enemy, Heligman, forever goodbye.
Oh Pa! Pa! Faith jumped up. I can't stand your being here.
Really? Who says *I* can stand it?
Then silence.
He picked up a leaf. Here you got it. Gate to Heaven. Ailanthus. They walked in a wide circle in

the little garden. They came to another bench: Dedicated to Theodor Herzl Who Saw the Light if Not the Land/In Memory of Mr. and Mrs. Johannes Mayer 1958. They sat close to one another.

Faith put her hand on her father's knee. Papa darling, she said.

Mr. Darwin felt the freedom of committed love. I have to tell the truth. Faith, it's like this. It wasn't on the phone. Ricardo came to visit us. I didn't want to talk in front of the boys. Me and your mother. She was in a state of shock from looking at him. She sent us out for coffee. I never realized he was such an interesting young man.

He's not so young, said Faith. She moved away from her father—but not more than half an inch.

To me he is, said Mr. Darwin. Young. Young is just not old. What's to argue. What you know, *you* know. What I know, *I* know.

Huh! said Faith. Listen, did you know he hasn't come to see the kids. Also, he owes me a chunk of dough.

Aha, money! Maybe he's ashamed. He doesn't have money. He's a man. He's probably ashamed.

Ach, Faith, I'm sorry I told you anything. On the subject of Ricardo, you're demented.

Demented? Boy oh boy, I'm demented. That's nice. You have a kind word from Ricardo and I'm demented.

Calm down, Faithy, please. Can't you lead a more peaceful life? Maybe you call some of this business down on yourself. That's a terrible neighborhood. I wish you'd move.

Move? Where? With what? What are you talking about?

Let's not start that again. I have more to say.

Serious things, my dear girl, compared to which Ricardo is a triviality. I have made a certain decision. Your mother isn't in agreement with me. The fact is, I don't want to be in this place anymore. I made up my mind. Your mother likes it. She thinks she's in a nice quiet kibbutz, only luckily Jordan is not on one side and Egypt is not on the other. She sits. She knits. She reads to the blind. She gives a course in what you call needlepoint. She organized the women. They have a history club, Don't Forget the Past. That's the real name, if you can believe it.

Pa, what are you leading up to?

Leading. I'm leading up to the facts of the case. What you said is right. This: I don't want to be here, I told you already. If I don't want to be here, I have to go away. If I go away, I leave Mama. If I leave Mama, well, that's terrible. But, Faith, I can't live here anymore. Impossible. It's not my life. I don't feel old. I never did. I was only sorry for your mother—we were close companions. She wasn't so well, to bother with the housework like she used to. Her operation changed her . . . well, you weren't in on that trouble. You were already leading your private life . . . well, to her it's like the Grand Hotel here, only full of *landsmen*. She doesn't see Hegel-Shtein, a bitter, sour lady. She sees a colorful matriarch, full of life. She doesn't see the Bissel twins, eighty-four years old, tragic, childish, stinking from urine. She sees wonderful! A whole lifetime together, brothers! She doesn't see, ach! Faithy, she plain doesn't see.

So?

So Ricardo himself remarked the other day, You certainly haven't the appearance of an old man, in and out, up and down the hill, full of ideas.

It's true. . . . Trotsky pointed out, the biggest surprise that comes to a man is old age. O.K. That's what I mean, I don't feel it. Surprise. Isn't that interesting that he had so much to say on every subject. Years ago I didn't have the right appreciation of him. Thrown out the front door of history, sneaks in the window to sit in the living room, excuse me, I mean I do not feel old. Do NOT. In any respect. You understand me, Faith?

Faith hoped he didn't really mean what she understood him to mean.

Oh yeah, she said. I guess. You feel active and healthy. That's what you mean?

Much more, much more. He sighed. How can I explain it to you, my dear girl. Well, this way. I have certainly got to get away from here. This is the end. This is the last station. Right?

Well, right . . .

The last. If it were possible, the way I feel suddenly toward life, I would divorce your mother.

Pa! . . . Faith said. Pa, now you're teasing me.

You, the last person to tease, a person who suffered so much from changes. No. I would divorce your mother. That would be honest.

Oh, Pa, you wouldn't really, though. I mean you wouldn't.

I wouldn't leave her in the lurch, of course, but the main reason—I won't, he said. Faith, you know why I won't. You must've forgot. Because we were never married.

Never married?

Never married. I think if you live together so many years it's almost equally legal as if the rabbi himself lassoed you together with June roses. Still, the problem is thorny like the rose itself. If you never got married, how can you get divorced?

Pa, I've got to get this straight. You are planning to leave Mama.

No, no, no. I plan to go away from here. If she comes, good, although life will be different. If she doesn't, then it must be goodbye.

Never married, Faith repeated to herself. Oh . . . well, how come?

Don't forget, Faithy, we were a different cut from you. We were idealists.

Oh, *you* were idealists . . . Faith said. She stood up, walking around the bench that honored Theodor Herzl. Mr. Darwin watched her. Then she sat down again and filled his innocent ear with the real and ordinary world.

Well, Pa, you know I have three lovers right this minute. I don't know which one I'll choose to finally marry.

What? Faith . . .

Well, Pa, I'm just like you, an idealist. The whole world is getting more idealistic all the time. It's so idealistic. People want only the best, only perfection.

You're making fun.

Fun? What fun? Why did Ricardo get out? It's clear: an idealist. For him somewhere, something perfect existed. So I say, That's right. Me too. Me too. Somewhere for me perfection is flowering. Which of my three lovers do you think I ought to settle for, a high-class idealist like me. *I* don't know.

Faith. Three men, you sleep with three men. I don't believe this.

Sure. In only one week. How about that?

Faithy. Faith. How could you do a thing like that? My God, how? Don't tell your mother. I will never tell her. Never.

Why, what's so terrible, Pa? Just what?

Tell me. He spoke quietly. What for? Why you do such things for them? You have no money, this is it. Yes, he said to himself, the girl has no money.

What are you talking about?

. . . Money.

Oh sure, they pay me all right. How'd you guess? They pay me with a couple of hours of their valuable time. They tell me their troubles and why they're divorced and separated, and they let me make dinner once in a while. They play ball with the boys in Central Park on Sundays. Oh sure, Pa, I'm paid up to here.

It's not that I have no money, he insisted. You have only to ask me. Faith, every year you are more mixed up than before. What did your mother and me do? We only tried our best.

It sure looks like your best was lousy, said Faith. I want to get the boys. I want to get out of here. I want to get away now.

Distracted, and feeling pains in her jaws, in her right side, in the small infection on her wrist, she ran through the Admitting Parlor, past the library, which was dark, and the busy arts-and-crafts studio. Without a glance, she rushed by magnificent, purple-haired, black-lace-shawled Madame Elena Nazdarova, who sat at the door of the Periodical Department editing the prize-winning institutional journal *A Bessere Zeit*. Madame Nazdarova saw Mr. Darwin, breathless, chasing Faith, and called, Ai, Darwin . . . no love poems this month? How can I go to press?

Don't joke me, don't joke me, Mr. Darwin said, hurrying to catch Faith. Faith, he cried, you go too fast.

So. Oh boy! Faith said, stopping short on the first-floor landing to face him. You're a young man, I thought. You and Ricardo ought to get a nice East Side pad with a separate entrance so you can entertain separate girls.

Don't judge the world by yourself. Ricardo had his trouble with you. I'm beginning to see the light. Once before I suggested psychiatric help. Charlie is someone with important contacts in the medical profession.

Don't mention Charlie to me. Just don't. I want to get the boys. I want to go now. I want to get out of here.

Don't tell your mother is why I run after you like a fool on the stairs. She had a sister who was also a bum. She'll look at you and she'll know. She'll know.

Don't follow me, Faith yelled.

Lower your voice, Mr. Darwin said between his teeth. Have pride, do you hear me?

Go away, Faith whispered, obedient and frantic.

Don't tell your mother.

Shut up! Faith whispered.

The boys are down playing Ping-Pong with Mrs. Reis. She kindly invited them. Faith, what is it? you look black, her mother said.

Breathless, Mr. Darwin gasped, Crazy, crazy like Sylvia, your crazy sister.

Oh her. Mrs. Darwin laughed, but took Faith's hand and pressed it to her cheek. What's the trouble, Faith? Oh yes, you are something like Sylvie. A temper. Oh, she had life to her. My poor Syl, she had zest. She died in front of the television set. She didn't miss a trick.

Oh, Ma, who cares what happened to Sylvie?

What exactly is the matter with you?

A cheerful man's face appeared high in the doorway. Is this the Darwin residence?

Oh, Phil, Faith said. What a time!

What's this? Which one is this? Mr. Darwin shouted.

Philip leaned into the small room. His face was shy and determined, which made him look as though he might leave at any moment. I'm a friend of Faith's, he said. My name is Mazzano. I really came to talk to Mr. Darwin about his work. There are lots of possibilities.

You heard something about me? Mr. Darwin asked. From who?

Faithy, get out the nice china, her mother said.

What? asked Faith.

What do you mean what? What, she repeated, the girl says what.

I'm getting out of here, Faith said. I'm going to get the boys and I'm getting out.

Let her go, Mr. Darwin said.

Philip suddenly noticed her. What shall I do? he asked What do you want me to do?

Talk to him, I don't care. That's what you want to do. Talk. Right? She thought, This is probably a comedy, this crummy afternoon. Why?

Philip said, Mr. Darwin, your songs are beautiful.

Goodbye, said Faith.

Hey, wait a minute, Faith. Please.

No, she said.

Dreamer in a Dead Language

On the beach, the old Brighton Beach of her childhood, she showed the boys the secret hideout under the boardwalk, where she had saved the scavenged soda-pop bottles. Were they three cents or a nickel? I can't remember, she said. This was my territory. I had to fight for it. But a boy named Eddie helped me.

Mommy, why do they live there? Do they have to? Can't they get a real apartment? How come?

I think it's a nice place, said Tonto.

Oh shut up, you jerk, said Richard.

Hey boys, look at the ocean. You know you had a great-grandfather who lived way up north on the Baltic Sea, and you know what, he used to skate, for miles and miles and miles along the shore, with a frozen herring in his pocket.

Tonto couldn't believe such a fact. He fell over backwards into the sand. A frozen herring! He must've been a crazy nut.

Really Ma? said Richard. Did you know him? he asked.

No, Richie, I didn't. They say he tried to come. There was no boat. It was too late. That's why I never laugh at that story Grandpa tells.

Why does Grandpa laugh?

Oh Richie, stop for godsakes.

Tonto, having hit the sand hard, couldn't bear to get up. He had begun to build a castle. Faith sat beside him on the cool sand. Richard walked down to the foamy edge of the water to look past the small harbor waves, far far out, as far as the sky. Then he came back. His little mouth was tight and his eyes worried. Mom, you have to get them out of there. It's your mother and father. It's your responsibility.

Come on, Richard, they like it. Why is everything my responsibility, every goddamn thing?

It just is, said Richard. Faith looked up and down the beach. She wanted to scream, Help!

Had she been born ten, fifteen years later, she might have done so, screamed and screamed.

Instead, tears made their usual protective lenses for the safe observation of misery.

So bury me, she said, lying flat as a corpse under the October sun.

Tonto immediately began piling sand around her ankles. Stop that! Richard screamed. Just stop that, you stupid jerk. Mom, I was only joking.

Faith sat up. Goddamn it, Richard, what's the matter with you? Everything's such a big deal. I was only joking too. I mean, bury me only up to here, like this, under my arms, you know, so I can give you a good whack every now and then when you're too fresh.

Oh, Ma . . . said Richard, his heart eased in one long sigh. He dropped to his knees beside Tonto, and giving her lots of room for wiggling and whacking, the two boys began to cover most of her with sand.

My Father Sits in the Dark

Jerome Weidman

My father has a peculiar habit. He is fond of sitting in the dark, alone. Sometimes I come home very late. The house is dark. I let myself in quietly because I do not want to disturb my mother. She is a light sleeper. I tiptoe into my room and undress in the dark. I go to the kitchen for a drink of water. My bare feet make no noise. I step into the room and almost trip over my father. He is sitting in a kitchen chair, in his pajamas, smoking his pipe.

"Hello, Pop," I say.

"Hello, son."

"Why don't you go to bed, Pa?"

"I will," he says.

But he remains there. Long after I am asleep I feel sure that he is still sitting there, smoking.

Many times I am reading in my room. I hear my mother get the house ready for the night. I hear my kid brother go to bed. I hear my sister come in. I hear her do things with jars and combs until she, too, is quiet. I know she has gone to sleep. In a little while I hear my mother say good night to my father. I continue to read. Soon I become thirsty. (I drink a lot of water.) I go to the kitchen for a drink. Again I almost stumble across my father. Many times it startles me. I forget about him. And there he is—smoking, sitting, thinking.

"Why don't you go to bed, Pop?"

"I will, son."

But he doesn't. He just sits there and smokes and thinks. It worries me. I can't understand it. What can he be thinking about? Once I asked him.

"What are you thinking about, Pa?"

"Nothing," he said.

Once I left him there and went to bed. I awoke several hours later. I was thirsty. I went to the kitchen. There he was. His pipe was out. But he sat there, staring into a corner of the kitchen. After a moment I became accustomed to the darkness. I took my drink. He still sat and stared. His eyes did not blink. I thought he was not even aware of me. I was afraid.

"Why don't you go to bed, Pop?"

"I will, son," he said. "Don't wait up for me."

"But," I said, "you've been sitting here for hours. What's wrong? What are you thinking about?"

"Nothing, son," he said. "Nothing. It's just restful. That's all."

The way he said it was convincing. He did not seem worried. His voice was even and pleasant. It always is. But I could not understand it. How could it be restful to sit alone in an uncomfortable chair far into the night, in darkness?

What can it be?

I review all the possibilities. It can't be money. I know that. We haven't much, but when he is worried about money he makes no secret of it. It can't be his health. He is not reticent about that either. It can't be the health of anyone in the family. We are a bit short on money, but we are long on health. (Knock wood, my mother would say.) What can it be? I am afraid I do not know. But that does not stop me from worrying.

Maybe he is thinking of his brothers in the old country. Or of his mother and two step-mothers. Or of his father. But they are all dead. And he would not brood about them like that. I say brood, but it is not really true. He does not brood. He does not even seem to be thinking. He looks too peaceful, too, well not contented, just too peaceful, to be brooding. Perhaps it is as he says. Perhaps it is restful. But it does not seem possible. It worries me.

If I only knew what he thinks about. If I only knew that he thinks at all. I might not be able to help him. He might not even need help. It may be as he says. It may be restful. But at least I would not worry about it.

Why does he just sit there, in the dark? Is his mind failing? No, it can't be. He is only fifty-three. And he is just as keenwitted as ever. In fact, he is the same in every respect. He still likes beet soup. He still reads the second section of the *Times* first. He still wears wing collars. He still believes that Debs could have saved the country and that T.R. was a tool of the moneyed interests. He is the same in every way. He does not even look older than he did five years ago. Everybody remarks about that. Well-preserved, they say. But he sits in the dark, alone, smoking, staring straight ahead of him, unblinking, into the small hours of the night.

If it is as he says, if it is restful, I will let it go at that. But suppose it is not. Suppose it is something I cannot fathom. Perhaps he needs help. Why doesn't he speak? Why doesn't he frown or laugh or cry? Why doesn't he do something? Why does he just sit there?

Finally I become angry. Maybe it is just my unsatisfied curiosity. Maybe I *am* a bit worried. Anyway, I become angry.

"Is something wrong, Pop?"

"Nothing, son. Nothing at all."

But this time I am determined not to be put off. I am angry.

"Then why do you sit here all alone, thinking, till late?"

"It's restful, son. I like it."

I am getting nowhere. Tomorrow he will be sitting there again. I will be puzzled. I will be worried. I will not stop now. I am angry.

"Well, what do you *think* about, Pa? Why do you just sit here? What's worrying you? What do you think about?"

"Nothing's worrying me, son. I'm all right. It's just restful. That's all. Go to bed, son."

My anger has left me. But the feeling of worry is still there. I must get an answer. It seems so silly. Why doesn't he tell me? I have a funny feeling that unless I get an answer I will go crazy. I am insistent.

"But what do you *think* about Pa? What is it?"

"Nothing, son, Just things in general. Nothing special. Just things."

I can get no answer.

My Father Sits in the Dark

It is very late. The street is quiet and the house is dark. I climb the steps softly, skipping the ones that creak. I let myself in with my key and tiptoe into my room. I remove my clothes and remember that I am thirsty. In my bare feet I walk to the kitchen. Before I reach it I know he is there.

I can see the deeper darkness of his hunched shape. He is sitting in the same chair, his elbows on his knees, his cold pipe in his teeth, his unblinking eyes staring straight ahead. He does not seem to know I am there. He did not hear me come in. I stand quietly in the doorway and watch him.

Everything is quiet, but the night is full of little sounds. As I stand there motionless I begin to notice them. The ticking of the alarm clock on the icebox. The low hum of an automobile passing many blocks away. The swish of papers moved along the street by the breeze. A whispering rise and fall of sound, like low breathing. It is strangely pleasant.

The dryness in my throat reminds me. I step briskly into the kitchen.

"Hello, Pop," I say.

"Hello, son," he says. His voice is low and dream-like. He does not change his position or shift his gaze.

I cannot find the faucet. The dim shadow of light that comes through the window from the street lamp only makes the room seem darker. I reach for the short chain in the center of the room. I snap on the light.

He straightens up with a jerk, as though he has been struck.

"What's the matter, Pop?" I ask.

"Nothing," he says. "I don't like the light."

"What's the matter with the light?" I say. "What's wrong?"

"Nothing," he says. "I don't like the light."

I snap the light off. I drink my water slowly. I must take it easy, I say to myself. I must get to the bottom of this.

"Why don't you go to bed? Why do you sit here so late in the dark?"

"It's nice," he says. "I can't get used to lights. We didn't have lights when I was a boy in Europe."

My heart skips a beat and I catch my breath happily. I begin to think I understand. I remember the stories of his boyhood in Austria. I see the wide-beamed *kretchma,* with my grandfather behind the bar. It is late, the customers are gone, and he is dozing. I see the bed of glowing coals, the last of the roaring fire. The room is already dark, and growing darker. I see a small boy, crouched on a pile of twigs at one side of the huge fireplace, his starry gaze fixed on the dull remains of the dead flames. The boy is my father.

I remember the pleasure of those few moments while I stood quietly in the doorway watching him.

"You mean there's nothing wrong? You just sit in the dark because you like it, Pop?" I find it hard to keep my voice from rising in a happy shout.

"Sure," he says. "I can't think with the light on."

I set my glass down and turn to go back to my room. "Good night, Pop," I say.

"Good night," he says.

Then I remember. I turn back. "What do you think about, Pop?" I ask.

His voice seems to come from far away. It is quiet and even again. "Nothing," he says softly. "Nothing special."

Living Life— Waiting for the Angel of Death

Mr. Isaacs

Seymour Epstein

Old Mr. Isaacs sits by the stone urn in front of the apartment house in all seasons, in almost all weather. He sits in a wooden folding chair which is placed there by his daughter, who has no time, no patience, and very little money. Like a straw doll whose stuffing has been pulled thin in spots, he bends, sags, but keeps a pair of blue, observant eyes fastened upon the world around him.

The people of the street have become accustomed to seeing him. In winter, they expect to find him there, shapeless in layers of old clothing—for he would freeze to death, sitting hours, unmoving, unless his daughter swathed him in God-knows-what: castoffs, towels, an overcoat so bleached of color that one takes it for whatever light is upon it. In frightful coldness, Mr. Isaacs can be seen gazing at the curb, as if some memory has projected itself there. A watery pendant forms at the end of his nose, freezes, and becomes an icicle. If he has a handkerchief, it is so buried in the recesses of his clothing that he has neither the strength nor the dexterity to find it. So the icicle forms, and a distant observer might think there is a diamond embedded in the face of the old man who has just turned his head toward the sun.

During the day, the life of women and children swirls around Mr. Isaacs. Children too young for school, too old for immobility, run screaming past him, having no more regard for his presence than for the huge stone urn which decorates the front of the house. Occasionally one of the children will observe a movement and, arrested in flight, will pause for a moment before the old man. At opposite poles of life, the two will stare at each other, one not having learned the dissimulation called politeness, the other having forgotten it, and for a moment there is an exchange of beautiful blankness between them.

After three o'clock, a fury seizes the street. The older ones come out of school, and a look of caution comes over the features of Mr. Isaacs. The dream passes from his eyes, and they take on the sharpness of one who has lived in danger all his life.

He must watch the skaters. The skaters take him as a natural hazard, bearing down like an avalanche, then veering sharp, as they would around a hydrant or baby carriage. Mr. Isaacs shows no sign of panic during these moments of jeopardy. He begins to nod his head, holds his cane more tightly, and when one of the skaters splays out like a crab, clutching the air, going down, ripping pants, knees, elbows, Mr. Isaacs still sits nodding his head with mechanical dispassion. The smooth, brown cane he carries is by his side—almost as if it hadn't moved.

Then there are the ball players. This madness takes the form of pounding a rubber ball against the side of the house. Here again is a presumption of accuracy on the part of the boys which sets Mr. Isaacs to nodding his head and clutching his cane. Finally the ball will thud harmlessly into his many-layered armor of rags.

"'Scuse me" is all that can be spared, for the game is fiercely competitive, and Mr. Isaacs so feebly alive that he can't be credited with much feeling.

Mr. Isaacs will then jab his cane like a sword in the direction of his tormentors.

"Hey, look, the old guy wants to talk to you."

So the young one approaches, half-curious, half-annoyed, bouncing his ball and waiting for the formulation of some half-dead complaint.

"How old are you?" Mr. Isaacs asks. His voice is surprising. It is not as one would expect it, like gravel rattling around at the bottom of a rusty barrel. It is deep and smooth, almost as if Mr. Isaacs were an orator in his day and has kept this attribute as a memento of the art.

"Eight," the boy will say, or "Ten," or "Thirteen."

Mr. Isaacs nods again. He lifts his head to the boy, revealing a face over which the flesh has grown tighter and tighter with the years. Lined, sere, but with a tautness which gives a severe aquilinity to his nose and the waxen incipience of a smile to his lips.

"Someday you will be the President of the United States," Mr. Isaacs informs the boy, with such solemn certitude that the youngster's brow furrows in

Living Life—Waiting for the Angel of Death

bewilderment. Without alteration of expression, Mr. Isaacs indicates a section of the wall well out of range. "Is there something wrong with over there?" he asks. "There's no one sitting over there you can hit with your ball, is that the trouble? Do an old man a favor. Take your friends over there to play."

All of this is intoned in the same, rich, musical voice. The boy backs away, taking fright from something behind the words spoken with senile gentleness. The lashless blue eyes follow the boy's retreat without humor, without rancor, without forgiveness.

Everybody who lives in the same apartment house with Mr. Isaacs knows a little something about him. He is the albatross hung about the neck of his ponderously overburdened daughter—and she is not the sort to take even ordinary burdens lightly.

"What can I do? Put him in a home? Even a home wants money, and for the poorhouse I'm not ready yet."

She has a natural sense of the dramatic, assuming a pose and expression the medieval painters would have given their souls to capture. Her two hands nested in her lap like a pair of obese doves, her head tilted at the angle of resignation, her eyes half-closed against the implacability of fate.

"I don't understand it," she confides to her friends and neighbors. "Here is a man who worked his whole life in the garment trade. A skilled operator. Good money I know he made. It comes time for him to retire . . . not a cent! Where did it all go? On his family he didn't spend. *This* I can tell you!"

Often Mr. Isaacs is present when his daughter

brings up these mysterious questions of the past. It is as if he does not hear her words. He does not hear most of the words his daughter utters, groans, shrieks, weeps. They are wind on the surface of a sea whose calm depths Mr. Isaacs cleaves with submarine thoughts.

"Ideas he had," accuses the daughter, turning to him with a scorn all the more complete for its blindness. "Ask him."

No one asks Mr. Isaacs. It is known that he was active in the union when it was no more than a harassed little cluster of immigrants seeking to turn stones into bread. It is known that all the early criers for justice became big men, important men, men to whom the presidents of companies offered cigars, spoke respectfully. Not Mr. Isaacs. When the great struggle was about to bear fruit, he withered on the vine, lost interest, became once again an operator on dresses whose seniority assured him almost a full year's work.

"What are you always thinking about?" yells the daughter when the repeated thrusts of her scorn blunt themselves against the blue-eyed, nodding insentience.

"Shall I go to my room?" asks Mr. Isaacs.

"Go . . . !"

But she has nowhere to consign him. He is too meek for hell, too secretive for heaven. He must stay here, in the room her two sons occupied before they rushed out like a pair of convicts in a prison break.

"Leave him alone," says the son-in-law, from behind his paper. The noise disturbs him; also, a little, his conscience. It was the old man, after all, who got him his job in the dress house.

Living Life—Waiting for the Angel of Death

So there is quiet.

What is he thinking? He does not think. There is no sequence to the pictures that slide across his mind. But the pictures are bright, although they lead to nothing, form no pattern of which Mr. Isaacs would care to say: "This is my life."

Today is an autumn day, full of clouds, presaging the season Mr. Isaacs may not survive. The shadows of clouds stimulate one set of memories; the sunlight another. Sitting in the folding chair beside the stone urn, Mr. Isaacs feels the warmth of the sun on his face and hands, and the sensation travels like an electric signal, crossing and recrossing nerves, until it comes upon the one scene it is meant to illuminate.

This is the courtyard of his father's house in Warsaw. His father is wealthy in the sense merchant Jews were allowed to become wealthy in Poland. There are a carriage and two horses in the rear of the courtyard, and the smell of the beasts and their manure mingles with the smell of cooking. On Sunday his father receives guests, and the huge wooden table in the courtyard is covered with a tablecloth like a mantle of snow. The back door of the kitchen opens upon the courtyard, and from it issue his mother and two servants carrying bowls, platters, tureens, all steaming, all redolent. They were placed on the table, their covers are removed, and a cloud of smoke like the cry "Hosannah!" rises and wafts this way and that as the breeze takes it. Just then the sun comes out, striking the glazed, bellied flanks of the bowls, and the refulgence is such as though God Himself cast down one beam of benevolence to make all present remember this day.

"Well, Mr. Isaacs . . . ?"

Mr. Isaacs looks up slowly. Vaguely he recognizes the woman before him. She is someone who lives in this house and must touch him with a word whenever she passes.

"I was sleeping," says Mr. Isaacs.

The woman looks up at the sky. "Pretty soon it'll be winter," she predicts.

Mr. Isaacs nods.

The woman shifts her bundle from one arm to the other and cautions: "Don't catch cold."

Mr. Isaacs fumbles in his mind for the pleasantness which pointless words have shoved aside. What was it? He cannot remember. A cloud covers the sun and grayness rushes into the street like a river.

Gray is the window which stands like a dirty sentinel at the end of the line of sewing machines. It offers no light, only casts a gray diffusion in its immediate vicinity. In the late afternoons of fall and winter, it becomes opaque black reflecting the yellow lights within the shop.

Here within his circle of yellow light, feeding fabric which flows in waves through his machine, he is at home. This varnished pine table, the bobbins, the spools of thread, the sewing machine with its coating of oil, the fabrics of cotton, wool, rayon, silk, jersey, faille . . . all of this combines to create a dry, friendly odor in the nostrils. His ears are attuned to the drone of two dozen machines. Occasionally the forelady comes to gather up his work.

She counts the pieces, snips a thread, and carries it off as if it were her own billowing child. At noon, he unwraps a sandwich of salami. Tonight there will be chicken soup thick with noodles and white pieces of meat. Between the familiarity of meals and the familiarity of work there is a sense of eternity.

But the calm must be shaken. He has sworn to do something, and today it must be done. He is going to speak to his employer, the dwarfish Mr. Krakow, whose strength is the strength of ten because his heart is totally impure. He is going to say: "Give me a little more money, Mr. Krakow. Two dollars. With fourteen dollars a week I can live; with twelve I cannot." He has rehearsed the scene so often that he has come to know Mr. Krakow quite well. He is a good businessman, a man with a rough sense of justice who knows the value of a good workman. Therefore he will answer: "All right, Isaacs, but let me see *work!*" Ah, he will show him work. It is settled. He gets up from his chair. Weintraub, who sits to his left and is appraised of his plans, raises his head. His mouth hangs open, and if wordless supplication had the power of human arms Isaacs would remain pinned to his chair.

He is in the office of Mr. Krakow only a short time. Nothing much is said, but inside his flesh, where it cannot show, he has been raked by the claws of arrogance. An ugly fang has pierced his heart. He sits down again at his machine. His gaze wanders to the window, and he finds there is nothing friendly in its somber filth. He turns to his machine and begins to work, but the fabric which flows through his hands is repugnant to him. He is a savage, and he is stitching the flesh of his enemy.

Mr. Isaacs

In the afternoon, the mothers come down with their infants and baby carriages. They stand in the sunlight, close to Mr. Isaacs, and talk. He hears their conversation but gives no sign of it. Their voices fly above him like birds calling to each other from different trees.

"I don't know what to buy. . . . Meat. Joe only likes meat. . . . I think she is catching cold. . . . Maybe it's adenoids. . . . She always sleeps with her mouth open. . . . Are you going shopping now? . . . Yes. . . . Come. . . . Hello, Mr. Isaacs. How are you feeling? . . . Isn't it a beautiful day? . . ."

Now he is aware that his daughter is standing next to him. She does not seem to notice him, but looks up and down the street as though it were a ship and she its commander. This way to the beauty parlor, the movies, the house of a friend; that way to the market, the shoe store, the dry cleaning store. Life is kept in balance by the choice of her direction.

"Are you all right, Pa?" she asks, her glance still ranging the street.

"Yes."

"Are you warm enough?"

He nods.

"I'm going shopping now."

She leaves his side, and for several seconds Mr. Isaacs fumbles with the skeins of past and present. His daughter's voice confuses him. It is not his wife's voice, yet beneath the sound of its own quality lie the same inflections.

Deliberately Mr. Isaacs invokes memory, and he is like a man stumbling around in the darkened rooms of his own house. Hannah is dead, this much he knows, but the transition from her life to her death is only the last in a series of gradations. He tries to think of Hannah and sees countless wax-filled glasses in which the Friday flame of holiness burns. He sees the porcelain-top kitchen table gleam dully under the ceiling light. On the center of the table is an ancient silver tray, a clean napkin, and a bread. He sees laundry dampened and rolled, waiting for the iron that heats on the stove.

They are in the kitchen. Somehow all their evenings are spent in the kitchen. The other room, the one with the leather davenport, the arm chair, the massive circular table, will last a thousand years, for its dark austerity does not invite ease-taking and the reading of a paper. So it is in the kitchen that he reads his newspaper, while Hannah unrolls a shirt and spreads it on the ironing board. She takes the iron from the stove and holds it close to her face, judging by its heat whether it is ready. She applies it to the shirt, and there is the expected and comforting hiss of steam.

When the doorbell rings he goes to the door and in the dim corridor sees a familiar face. He steps out into the corridor, closing the door quietly behind him, and there in the conspiratorial darkness, amidst the commingled smells of a dozen different suppers, the visitor addresses him in a voice that is both question and challenge.

"You heard?"

"Yes," says Mr. Isaacs.

"He fired me."

"I know. Don't worry. He will have to take you back. He will have to take you back and pay you all the money you lost when he signs with the union."

"When will that be?"

"Soon," says Mr. Isaacs.

"A week? Two? Three? The rent is paid for the month . . . but food?"

Mr. Isaacs reaches into his pocket and brings out his leather purse with the snap fastener. He gives the man five dollars.

"I will pay you back."

"I know."

"As soon as I'm working again."

"I know."

"Good night, Isaacs."

"Good night."

He returns to the kitchen, picks up his paper, and sits down again. Hannah has finished the shirt. She closes all the buttons, folds it neatly, and lays it on the mound of ironed things. Out of the corner of his eye, he watches her hand reach for the next article of clothing. It is pink, something of hers, a petticoat, and when the iron touches it there is a sibilance of steam and one spoken word—as heavy and purposeful as the iron itself.

"*Narr!*" says Hannah. . . . "Fool."

Toward six o'clock, the atmosphere of the street changes. The skaters and the ball players have departed. Here and there a window opens and a shrill voice cries: "Sidneeee! . . . *Sid*-ney!" There is a slight chill in the air. The sun has passed over the roof beneath which Mr. Isaacs sits, and a straight band of gold stretches out along the upper stories of the tenement opposite.

Pretty soon Mr. Isaacs' son-in-law will walk up the street with his evening newspaper folded under his arm, his heavy face darkened by a day's growth of beard. He will come up to Mr. Isaacs and halt there with the saturnine patience of a hospital attendant. If Mr. Isaacs is sleeping, he will tap him on the shoulder. If he is awake, he will simply nod. Then he will assist Mr. Isaacs to his feet, and with one hand under the old man's arm and the other holding the folding chair they will proceed into the courtyard littered with the day's leavings of candy wrappers, fruit cores and circulars.

They will walk up the staircase, pausing at each landing for Mr. Isaacs to catch his breath. They will come to the second floor where there is a window with a pane of stained glass. It is an oddity in the building, this pane of colored glass. No other window has it. And it is here, every evening, that Mr. Isaacs repeats the same words to himself. He cannot remember what it was that first began the ritual, but when his gaze falls upon the pane of stained glass, he asks:

"What am I waiting for?"

For it is Mr. Isaacs' notion that he is holding off death by a daily act of will. Nor does death importune, but keeps with him like a friendly dog, pausing when he pauses, and going when he goes. It crouches beside him in the living room, its muzzle resting on his shoe. It follows him into the bedroom and watches as he labors with buttons and sleeves. Then, in the isolation of his room, Mr. Isaacs feels free to address his companion in the manner lonely people adopt toward domesticated pets.

"What am I waiting for?" he repeats.

There is no time, only distance, and his own life has receded so far that all perspective is lost. Joseph in the pit, Moses striking the rock, his father's courtyard in Warsaw, Mr. Krakow's medium-priced line of garments—they are all story-pictures painted on the curving wall of memory.

Now he composes his body for sleep, or death—he knows not which. Often it is for death he decides, but in the moment of choice a figure springs up and stares at him with frightened eyes. It is a shabby figure, pathetic, neither old nor young, but one whose story is so unique, so full of failures close to Mr. Isaacs' heart, so devoid of triumphs, that Mr. Isaacs feels toward it a great compassion—and would linger one more day in a world that contains its presence.

Old Man Minick

Edna Ferber

His wife had always spoiled him outrageously. No doubt of that. Take, for example, the matter of the pillows merely. Old man Minick slept high. That is, he thought he slept high. He liked two plump pillows on his side of the great, wide, old-fashioned cherry bed. He would sink into them with a vast grunting and sighing and puffing expressive of nerves and muscles relaxed and gratified. But in the morning there was always one pillow on the floor. He had thrown it there. Always, in the morning, there it lay, its plump, white cheek turned reproachfully up at him from the side of the bed. Ma Minick knew this, naturally, after forty years of the cherry bed. But she never begrudged him that extra pillow. Each morning when she arose, she picked it up on her way to shut the window. Each morning the bed was made up with two pillows on his side of it, as usual.

Then there was the window. Ma Minick liked it open wide. Old man Minick, who rather prided himself on his modernism (he called it being up to date), was distrustful of the night air. In the folds of its sable mantle lurked a swarm of dread things—cold, clammy miasmas, fever.

"Night air's like any other air," Ma Minick would say, with some asperity. Ma Minick was no worm; and as modern as he. So when they went to bed the window would be open wide. They would lie there, the two old ones, talking comfortably about commonplace things. The kind of talk that goes on between a man and woman who have lived together in wholesome peace (spiced with occasional wholesome bickerings) for more than forty years.

"Remind me to see Gerson to-morrow about that lock on the basement door. The paper's full of burglars."

"If I think of it." She never failed to.

"George and Nettie haven't been over in a week now."

"Oh, well, young folks. . . . Did you stop in and pay that Koritz the fifty cents for pressing your suit?"

"By golly, I forgot again! First thing in the morning."

A sniff. "Just smell the yards." It was Chicago.

"Wind must be from the west."

Sleep came with reluctant feet, but they wooed her patiently. And presently she settled down between them and they slept lightly. Usually, some time during the night, he awoke, slid cautiously and with infinite stealth from beneath the covers, and closed the wide-flung window to within a bare two inches of the sill. Almost invariably she heard him; but she was a wise old woman; a philosopher of parts. She knew better than to allow a window to shatter the peace of their marital felicity. As she lay there, smiling a little grimly in the dark and giving no sign of being awake, she thought, "Oh, well, I guess a closed window won't kill me either."

Still, sometimes, just to punish him a little, and to prove that she was nobody's fool, she would wait until he had dropped off to sleep again and then she, too, would achieve a stealthy trip to the window and would raise it slowly, carefully, inch by inch.

"How did that window come to be open?" he would say in the morning, being a poor dissembler.

"Window? Why, it's just the way it was when we went to bed." And she would stoop to pick up the pillow that lay on the floor.

There was little or no talk of death between this comfortable, active, sound-appearing man of almost seventy and this plump, capable woman of sixty-six. But as always, between husband and wife, it was understood wordlessly (and without reason) that old man Minick would go first. Not that either of them had the slightest intention of going. In fact, when it happened they were planning to spend the winter in California and perhaps live there indefinitely if they liked it and didn't get too lonesome for George and Nettie and the Chicago smoke, and Chicago noise, and Chicago smells and rush and dirt. Still the solid sum paid yearly in insurance premiums showed clearly that he meant to leave her in comfort and security. Besides, the world is full of widows. Everyone sees that. But how many widowers? Few. Widows there are by the thousands; living alone; living in hotels;

living with married daughters and sons-in-law or married sons and daughters-in-law. But of widowers in a like situation there are bewilderingly few. And why this should be no one knows.

So, then. The California trip never materialised. And the year that followed never was quite clear in old man Minick's dazed mind. In the first place, it was the year in which stocks tumbled and broke their backs. Gilt-edged securities showed themselves to be tinsel. Old man Minick had retired from active business just one year before, meaning to live comfortably on the fruit of a half-century's toil. He now saw that fruit rotting all about him. There was in it hardly enough nourishment to sustain them. Then came the day when Ma Minick went downtown to see Matthews about that pain right here and came home looking shrivelled, talking shrilly about nothing, and evading Pa's eyes. Followed months that were just a jumble of agony, X-rays, hope, despair, morphia, nothingness.

After it was all over: "But I was going first," old man Minick said, dazedly.

The old house on Ellis near Thirty-ninth was sold for what it would bring. George, who knew Chicago real estate if anyone did, said they might as well get what they could. Things would only go lower, you'll see. And nobody's going to have any money for years. Besides, look at the neighbourhood!

Old man Minick said George was right. He said everybody was right. You would hardly have recognised in this shrunken and wattled figure the spruce and dressy old man whom Ma Minick used to spoil so delightfully. "You know best, George. You know best." He who used to stand up to

George until Ma Minick was moved to say, "Now, Pa, you don't know everything."

After Ma when bills, and the hospital, and the nurses and the medicines and the thousand and one things were paid there was left exactly five hundred dollars a year.

"You're going to make your home with us, Father," George and Nettie said. Alma, too, said this would be the best. Alma, the married daughter, lived in Seattle. "Though you know Fred and I would be only too glad to have you."

Seattle! The ends of the earth. Oh, no. No! he protested, every fibre of his old frame clinging to the accustomed. Seattle, at seventy! He turned piteous eyes on his son George and his daughter-in-law Nettie. "You're going to make your home with us, Father," they reassured him. He clung to them gratefully. After it was over, Alma went home to her husband and their children.

So now he lived with George and Nettie in the five-room flat on South Park Avenue, just across from Washington Park. And there was no extra pillow on the floor.

Nettie hadn't said he couldn't have the extra pillow. He had told her he used two and she had given him two the first week. But every morning she had found a pillow cast on the floor.

"I thought you used two pillows, Father."

"I do."

"But there's always one on the floor when I make the bed in the morning. You always throw one on the floor. You only sleep on one pillow, really."

"I use two pillows."

But the second week there was one pillow. He tossed and turned a good deal in his bedroom off the kitchen. But he got used to it in time. Not used to it, exactly, but—well—

The bedroom off the kitchen wasn't as menial as it sounds. It was really rather cosy. The five-room flat held living-room, front bedroom, dining-room, kitchen, and maid's room. The room off the kitchen was intended as a maid's room, but Nettie had no maid. George's business had suffered with the rest. George and Nettie had said, "I wish there was a front room for you, Father. You could have ours and we'd move back here, only this room's too small for twin beds and the dressing-table and the chiffonier." They had meant it—or meant to mean it.

"This is fine," old man Minick had said. "This is good enough for anybody." There was a narrow, white enamel bed and a tiny dresser and a table. Nettie had made gay cretonne covers and spreads and put a little reading-lamp on the table and arranged his things. Ma Minick's picture on the dresser with her mouth sort of pursed to make it look small. It wasn't a recent picture. Nettie and George had had it framed for him as a surprise. They had often urged her to have a picture taken, but she had dreaded it. He needed no photograph of Ma Minick. He had a dozen of them; a gallery of them; thousands of them. Lying on his one pillow he could take them out and look at them one by one as they passed in review, smiling, serious, chiding, praising, there in the dark. He needed no picture on his dresser.

A handsome girl, Nettie, and a good girl. He thought of her as a girl, though she was well past thirty. George and Nettie had married late. This was only the third year of their marriage. Alma, the daughter, had married young, but George had stayed on, unwed, in the old house on Ellis until he was thirty-six and all Ma Minick's friends' daughters had had a try at him in vain. The old people had urged him to marry, but it had been wonderful to have him around the house, just the same. Somebody young around the house. Not that George had stayed around very much. But when he was there you knew he was there. He whistled while dressing. He sang in the bath. He roared down the stairway, "Ma, where's my clean shirts?" The telephone rang for him. Ma Minick prepared special dishes for him. The servant girl said, "Oh, now, Mr. George, look what you've done! Gone and spilled the grease all over my clean kitchen floor!" and wiped it up adoringly while George laughed and gobbled his bit of food filched from pot or frying pan.

They had been a little surprised about Nettie. George was in the bond business and she worked for the same firm. A plump, handsome, eye-glassed woman, with fine fresh colouring, a clear skin that old man Minick called appetising, and a great coil of smooth dark hair. She wore plain tailored things and understood the bond business in a way that might have led you to think her a masculine mind if she hadn't been so feminine, too, in her manner. Old man Minick liked her better than Ma Minick had.

Nettie had called him Pop and joked with him and almost flirted with him in a daughterly sort of way. He liked to squeeze her plump arm and pinch her soft cheek between thumb and finger. She would laugh up at him and pat his shoulder and that shoulder would straighten spryly and he would waggle his head doggishly. "Look out there, George!" the others in the room would say. "Your dad'll cut you out. First thing you know you'll lose your girl, that's all."

Nettie would smile. Her teeth were white and strong and even. Old man Minick would laugh and wink, immensely pleased and flattered. "We understand each other, don't we, Pop?" Nettie would say.

During the first years of their married life Nettie stayed home. She fussed happily about her little flat, gave parties, went to parties, played bridge. She seemed to love the ease, the relaxation, the small luxuries. She and George were very much in love. Before her marriage she had lived in a boarding-house on Michigan Avenue. At the mention of it now she puckered up her face. She didn't attempt to conceal her fondness for these five rooms of hers, so neat, so quiet, so bright, so cosy. Over-stuffed velvet in the living-room, with silk lamp-shades, and small tables holding books and magazines and little boxes containing cigarettes or hard candies. Very modern. A gate-legged table in the dining-room. Caramel-coloured walnut in the bedroom, rich and dark and smooth. She loved it. An orderly woman. Everything in its place. Before eleven o'clock the little apartment was shining, spotless; cushions plumped, crumbs brushed, vegetables in cold water. The telephone. "Hello! . . . Oh, hello, Bess! Oh, hours ago. . . . Not a thing. . . . Well, if George is willing. . . . I'll call him up and ask him. We haven't seen a show in two weeks. I'll call you back within the next half-hour. . . . No, I haven't done my marketing yet.... Yes, and have dinner down town. Meet at seven."

Into this orderly, smooth-running mechanism was catapulted a bewildered old man. She no longer called him Pop. He never dreamed of squeezing the plump arm or pinching the smooth cheek. She called him Father. Sometimes George's father. Sometimes, when she was telephoning, there came to him—"George's father's living with us now, you know. I can't."

They were very kind to him, Nettie and George. "Now just you sit right down here, Father. What do you want to go poking off into your own room for?"

He remembered that in the last year Nettie had said something about going back to work. There wasn't enough to do around the house to keep her busy. She was sick of afternoon parties. Sew and eat, that's all, and gossip, or play bridge. Besides, look at the money. Business was awful. The two old people had resented this idea as much as George had—more, in fact. They were scandalised.

"Young folks nowadays!" shaking their heads. "Young folks nowadays. What are they thinking of! In my days when you got married you had babies."

George and Nettie had had no babies. At first Nettie had said, "I'm so happy I just want a chance to rest. I've been working since I was seventeen. I just want to rest first." One year. Two years. Three. And now Pa Minick.

Ma Minick, in the old house on Ellis Avenue, had kept a loose sort of larder; not lavish, but plentiful. They both ate a great deal, as old people are likely to do. Old man Minick, especially, had liked to nibble. A handful of raisins from the box on the shelf. A couple of nuts from the dish on the sideboard. A bit of candy rolled beneath the tongue. At dinner (sometimes, towards the last, even at noontime) a plate of steaming soup, hot, revivifying, stimulating. Plenty of this and plenty of that. "What's the matter, Jo! You're not eating." But he was, amply. Ma Minick had liked to see him eat too much. She was wrong, of course.

But at Nettie's things were different. Here was a sufficient but stern ménage. So many mouths to feed; just so many lamb chops. Nettie knew about calories and vitamins and mysterious things like that, and talked about them. So many calories in this. So many calories in that. He never was quite clear in his mind about these things said to be lurking in his food. He had always thought of spinach as spinach, chops as chops. But to Nettie they were calories. They lunched together, these two, George was, of course, downtown. For herself Nettie would have one of those feminine pick-up lunches; a dab of apple sauce, a cup of tea, and a slice of cold toast left from breakfast. This she would eat while old man Minick guiltily supped up his cup of warmed-over broth, or his coddled egg. She always pressed upon him any bit of cold meat that was left from the night before, or any remnants of vegetable or spaghetti. Often there was quite a little fleet of saucers and sauce plates grouped about his main plate. Into these he dipped and swooped uncomfortably, and yet with a relish. Sometimes, when he had finished he would look about, furtively.

"What'll you have, Father? Can I get you something?"

"Nothing, Nettie, nothing. I'm doing fine." She

had finished the last of her toast and was waiting for him kindly.

Still, this balanced and scientific fare seemed to agree with him. As the winter went on he seemed actually to have regained most of his former hardiness and vigour. A handsome old boy he was, ruddy, hale, with the zest of a juicy old apple, slightly withered but still sappy. It should be mentioned that he had a dimple in his cheek which flashed unexpectedly when he smiled. It gave him a roguish—almost boyish—effect most appealing to the beholder. Especially the feminine beholder. Much of his spoiling at the hands of Ma Minick had doubtless been due to this mere depression of the skin.

Spring was to bring a new and welcome source of enrichment into his life. But these first six months of his residence with George and Nettie were hard. No spoiling there. He missed being made much of. He got kindness, but he needed love. Then, too, he was rather a gabby old man. He liked to hold forth. In the old house on Ellis there had been visiting back and forth between men and women of his own age, and Ma's. At these gatherings he had waxed oratorical or argumentative, and they had heard him, some in agreement, some in disagreement, but always respectfully, whether he prated of real estate or social depravity, prohibition, or European exchange.

"Let me tell you, here and now, something's got to be done before you can get a country back on a sound financial basis. Why, take Russia alone, why . . ." Or: "Young people nowadays! They don't know what respect means. I tell you there's got to be a change and there will be, and it's the older generation that's got to bring it about. What do they know of hardship! What do they know of work—real work. Most of 'em's never done a real day's work in their life. All they think of is dancing and gambling and drinking. Look at the way they dress! Look at . . ."

Ad lib.

"That's so," the others would agree. "I was saying only yesterday . . ."

Then, too, until a year or two before, he had taken an active part in business. He had retired, only at the urging of Ma and the children. They said he ought to rest and play and enjoy himself.

Now, as his strength and good spirits gradually returned he began to go downtown, mornings. He would dress, carefully, though a little shakily. He had always shaved himself and he kept this up. All in all, during the day he occupied the bathroom literally for hours, and this annoyed Nettie to the point of frenzy, though she said nothing. He liked the white cheerfulness of the little tiled room. He puddled about in the water endlessly. Snorted and splashed and puffed and snuffled and blew. He was one of those audible washers who emerge dripping and whose ablutions are distributed impartially over ceilings, walls, and floor.

Nettie, at the closed door: "Father, are you all right?"

Splash! Prrrf! "Yes. Sure. I'm all right."

"Well, I didn't know. You've been in there so long."

He was a neat old man, but there was likely to be a spot or so on his vest or his coat lapel, or his tie. Ma used to remove these from off him, as the occasion demanded, rubbing carefully and scolding a little, making a chiding sound between tongue and tooth indicative of great impatience of his carelessness. He had rather enjoyed these sounds, and this rubbing and scratching on the cloth with the finger-nail and moistened rag. They indicated that someone cared. Cared about the way he looked. Had pride in him. Loved him. Nettie never removed spots. Though infrequently she said, "Father, just leave that suit out, will you? I'll send it to the cleaner's with George's. The man's coming to-morrow morning." He would look down at himself, hastily, and attack a spot here and there with a futile finger-nail.

His morning toilette completed, he would make for the Fifty-first Street L. Seated in the train, he would assume an air of importance and testy haste; glance out of the window; look at his watch. You got the impression of a handsome well-preserved old gentleman on his way downtown to consummate a shrewd business deal. He had been familiar with Chicago's downtown for fifty years and he could remember when State Street was a tree-shaded cottage district. The noise and rush and clangour of the Loop had long been familiar to him. But now he seemed to find the downtown trip arduous, even hazardous. The roar of the elevated trains, the hoarse hoots of the motor horns, the clang of the street cars, the bedlam that is Chicago's downtown district bewildered him, frightened him almost. He would skip across the street like a harried hare, just missing a motor-truck's nose and all unconscious of the stream of invective directed at him by its charioteer. "Heh! Whatcha! . . . Look!"— Sometimes a policeman came to his aid, or attempted to, but he resented his proffered help.

"Say, look here, my lad," he would say to the tall, tired, and not at all burly (standing on one's feet directing traffic at Wabash and Madison for eight hours a day does not make for burliness) policeman, "I've been coming downtown since long before you were born. You don't need to help me. I'm no jay from the country."

He visited the Stock Exchange. This depressed him. Stocks were lower than ever and still going down. His five hundred a year was safe, but the rest seemed doomed for his lifetime, at least. He would drop in at George's office. George's office was pleasantly filled with dapper, neat young men and (surprisingly enough) dapper, slim young women, seated at desks in the big, light-flooded room. At one corner of each desk stood a polished metal placard on a little standard, bearing the name of the desk's occupant: Mr. Owens, Mr. Satterlee, Mr. James, Miss Ranch, Mr. Minick.

"Hello, Father," Mr. Minick would say, looking annoyed. "What's bringing you down?"

"Oh, nothing. Nothing. Just had a little business to tend to over at the Exchange. Thought I'd drop in. How's business?"

"Rotten."

"I should think it was!" old man Minick would agree. "I—should—think—it—was! Hm."

George wished he wouldn't. He couldn't have it, that's all. Old man Minick would stroll over to the desk marked Satterlee, or Owens, or James. These brisk young men would toss an upward glance at him and concentrate again on the sheets and files before them. Old man Minick would stand, balancing from heel to toe and blowing out his breath a little. He looked a bit yellow and granulated and wavering there in the cruel morning light of the big plate glass windows. Or perhaps it was the contrast he presented with these slim, slick young salesmen.

"Well, h'are you to-day, Mr.—uh—Satterlee? What's the good word?"

Mr. Satterlee would not glance up this time. "I'm pretty well. Can't complain."

"Good. Good."

"Anything I can do for you?"

"No—o—o. No. Not a thing. Just dropped in to see my son a minute."

"I see." Not unkindly. Then, as old man Minick still stood there, balancing, Mr. Satterlee would glance up again, frowning a little. "Your son's desk is over there, I believe. Yes."

George and Nettie had a bedtime conference about these visits and Nettie told him gently that the bond house head objected to friends and relatives dropping in. It was against the rules. It had been so when she was employed there. Strictly business. She herself had gone there only once since her marriage.

Well, that was all right. Business was like that nowadays. Rush and grab and no time for anything.

The winter was a hard one, with a record snowfall and intense cold. He stayed indoors for days together. A woman of his own age in like position could have occupied herself usefully and happily. She could have hemmed a sash-curtain; knitted or crocheted; tidied a room; taken a hand with cooking or preparing food; ripped an old gown; made over a new one; indulged in an occasional afternoon festivity with women of her own years. But for old man Minick there were no small tasks. There was nothing he could do to make his place in the household justifiable. He wasn't even particularly good at those small jobs of hammering, or painting, or general "fixing." He could drive a nail more swiftly, more surely than Nettie. "Now, Father, don't you bother. I'll do it. Just you go and sit down. Isn't it time for your afternoon nap?"

He waxed a little surly. "Nap! I just got up. I don't want to sleep my life away."

George and Nettie frequently had guests in the evening. They played bridge, or poker, or talked.

"Come in, Father," George would say. "Come in. You all know Dad, don't you, folks?" He would sit down, uncertainly. At first he had attempted to expound, as had been his wont in the old house on Ellis. "I want to say, here and now, that this country's got to . . ." But they went on, heedless of him. They interrupted or refused, politely, to listen. So he sat in the room, yet no part of it. The young people's talk swirled and eddied all about him. He was utterly lost in it. Now and then Nettie or George would turn to him and with raised voice (he was not at all deaf and prided himself on it) would shout, "It's about this or that, Father. He was saying . . ."

When the group roared with laughter at a sally from one of them he would smile uncertainly but amiably, glancing from one to the other in complete ignorance of what had passed, but not resenting it. He took to sitting more and more in his kitchen bedroom, smoking a comfortable pipe and reading and re-reading the evening paper. During that winter he and Canary, the negro washerwoman, became quite good friends. She washed down in the basement once a week but came up to the kitchen for her massive lunch. A walrus-waisted black woman, with a rich, throaty voice, a rolling eye and a kindly heart. He actually waited for her appearance above the laundry stairs.

"Wel, how's Mist' Minick to-day! Ah nev' did see a gemun spry's you ah fo' yo' age. No, suh! Nev' did."

At this rare praise he would straighten his shoulders and waggle his head. "I'm worth any ten of these young sprats to-day." Canary would throw back her head in a loud and companionable guffaw.

Nettie would appear at the kitchen swinging door. "Canary's having her lunch, Father. Don't you want to come into the front room with me? We'll have our lunch in another half-hour."

He followed her obediently enough. Nettie thought of him as a troublesome and rather pathetic child—a child who would never grow up. If she attributed any thoughts to that fine old head they were ambling thoughts bordering, perhaps, on senility. Little did she know how expertly this old one surveyed her and how ruthlessly he passed judgment. She never suspected the thoughts that formed in the active brain.

He knew about women. He had married a woman. He had had children by her. He looked at this woman—his son's wife—moving about her little five-room flat. She had theories about children. You didn't have them except under such and such circumstances. It wasn't fair otherwise. Plenty of money for their education. Well. He and his wife had had three children. Paul, the second, had died at thirteen. A blow, that had been. They had not always planned for the coming of the three but they had always found a way, afterward. You managed somehow, once the little wrinkled red ball had fought its way into the world. You managed. You managed. Look at George. Yet when he was born, thirty-nine years ago, Pa and Ma had been hard put to it.

Sitting there, while Nettie dismissed him as negligible, he saw her clearly, grimly. He looked at her. She was plump, but not too short, with a generous width between the hips; a broad full bosom, but firm; round arms and quick slim legs; a fine sturdy throat. The curve between arm and breast made a graceful, gracious line. . . . Working in a bond office. . . . There was nothing in the Bible about working in a bond office. Here was a woman built for child-bearing.

She thought him senile, negligible.

In March, Nettie had in a sewing-woman for a week. She had her two or three times a year. A hawk-faced woman of about forty-nine, with a blue-bottle figure and a rapacious eye. She sewed in the dining-room, and there was a pleasant hum of machine and snip of scissors and murmur of conversation and rustle of silky stuff; and hot savoury dishes for lunch. She and old man Minick became great friends. She even let him take out bastings. This when Nettie had gone out from two to four, between fittings.

He chuckled and waggled his head. "I expect to be paid regular assistant's wages for this," he said.

"I guess you don't need any wages, Mr. Minick," the woman said. "I guess you're pretty well fixed."

"Oh, well, I can't complain" (five hundred a year).

"Complain! I should say no! If I was to complain

it'd be different. Work all day to keep myself; and nobody to come home to at night."

"Widow, ma'am?"

"Since I was twenty. Work, work, that's all I've had. And lonesome. I suppose you don't know what lonesome is."

"Oh, don't I?" slipped from him. He had dropped the bastings.

The sewing-woman flashed a look at him from the cold, hard eye. "Well, maybe you do. I suppose living here like this, with sons and daughters, ain't so grand, for all your money. Now me, I've always managed to keep my own little place that I could call home, to come back to. It's only two rooms, and nothing to rave about, but it's home. Evenings I just cook and fuss around. Nobody to fuss for, but I fuss, anyway. Cooking, that's what I love to do. Plenty of good food, that's what folk need to keep their strength up." Nettie's lunch that day had been rather scant.

She was there a week. In Nettie's absence she talked against her. He protested, but weakly. Did she give him egg-noggs? Milk? Hot toddy? Soup? Plenty of good rich gravy and meat and puddings? Well! That's what folks needed when they weren't so young any more. Not that he looked old. My, no! Spryer than many young boys and handsomer than his own son if she did say so.

He fed on it, hungrily. The third day she was flashing meaning glances at him across the luncheon table. The fourth she pressed his foot beneath the table. The fifth, during Nettie's absence, she got up, ostensibly to look for a bit of cloth which she needed for sewing, and, passing him, laid a caressing hand on his shoulder. Laid it there and pressed his shoulder ever so little. He looked up, startled. The glances across the luncheon table had largely passed over his head; the foot beneath the table might have been an accident. But this—this was unmistakable. He stood up, a little shakily. She caught his hand. The hawklike face was close to his.

"You need somebody to love you," she said. "Somebody to do for you, and love you." The hawk-like face came nearer. He leaned a little toward it. But between it and his face was Ma Minick's face, plump, patient, quizzical, kindly. His head came back sharply. He threw the woman's hot hand from him.

"Woman!" he cried. "Jezebel!"

The front door slammed. Nettie. The woman flew to her sewing. Old man Minick, shaking, went into his kitchen bedroom.

"Well," said Nettie, depositing her bundles on the dining-room table, "did you finish that faggoting? Why, you haven't done so very much, have you!"

"I ain't feeling so good," said the woman. "That lunch didn't agree with me."

"Why, it was a good plain lunch. I don't see—"

"Oh, it was plain enough, all right."

Next day she did not come to finish her work. Sick, she telephoned. Nettie called it an outrage. She finished the sewing herself, though she hated sewing. Pa Minick said nothing, but there was a light in his eyes. Now and then he chuckled, to Nettie's infinite annoyance, though she said nothing.

"Wanted to marry me!" he said to himself, chuckling. "Wanted to marry me! The old rip!"

At the end of April, Pa Minick discovered Washington Park, and the Club, and his whole life was from that day transformed.

He had taken advantage of the early spring sunshine to take a walk, at Nettie's suggestion.

"Why don't you go into the Park, Father? It's really warm out. And the sun's lovely. Do you good."

He had put on his heaviest shirt, and a muffler, and George's old red sweater with the great white "C" on its front, emblem of George's athletic prowess at the University of Chicago; and over all, his frock coat. He had taken warm mittens and the big cane with the greyhound's-head handle, carved. So equipped, he had ambled uninterestedly over to the Park across the way. And there he had found new life.

New life is old life. For the Park was full of old men. Old men like himself, with greyhound's-head canes, and mufflers, and somebody's sweater worn beneath their greatcoats. They wore arctics, though the weather was fine. The skin of their hands and cheek-bones was glazed and had a tight look though it lay in fine little folds. There were splotches of brown on the back of their hands, and on the temples and foreheads. Their heavy grey or brown socks made comfortable folds above their ankles. From that April morning until winter drew on the Park saw old man Minick daily. Not only daily but by the day. Except for his meals, and a brief hour for his after-luncheon nap, he spent all his time there.

For in the Park old man Minick and all the old men gathered there found a Forum—a safety-valve—a means of expression. It did not take him long to discover that the Park was divided into two distinct sets of old men. There were the old men who lived with their married sons and daughters-in-law or married daughters and sons-in-law. Then there were the old men who lived in the Grant Home for Aged Gentlemen. You saw its fine, red-brick façade through the trees at the edge of the Park.

And the slogan of these first was:

"My son and my daughter, they wouldn't want me to live in any public home. No siree! They want me right there with them. In their own home. That's the kind of son and daughter I've got!"

The slogan of the second was:

"I wouldn't live with any son or daughter. Independent. That's me. My own boss. Nobody to tell me what I can do and what I can't. Treat you like a child. I'm my own boss! Pay my own good money and get my keep for it."

The first group strangely enough was likely to be spotted of vest and a little frayed as to collar. You saw them going on errands for their daughters-in-law. A loaf of bread. A spool of White No. 100. They took their small grandchildren to the duck-pond and between the two toddlers hand-in-hand—the old and the infirm and the infantile and infirm—it was hard to tell which led which.

The second group was shiny as to shoes, spotless as to mien, dapper as to clothes. They had no small errands. Theirs was a magnificent leisure. And theirs was magnificent conversation. The questions they discussed and settled there in the Park—these old men—were not international merely. They were cosmic in scope.

The War? Peace? Disarmament? China? Free

love? Mere conversational bubbles to be tossed in the air and disposed of in a burst of foam. Strong meat for old man Minick who had so long been fed on pap. But he soon got used to it. Between four and five in the afternoon, in a spot known as Under the Willows, the meeting took the form of a club—an open forum. A certain group made up of Socialists, Free Thinkers, parlour Anarchists, Bolshevists, had for years drifted there for talk. Old man Minick learned high-sounding phrases. "The Masters . . . democracy . . . toil of the many for the few . . . the ruling class . . . free speech . . . the People . . ."

The strong-minded ones held forth. The weaker ones drifted about on the outskirts, sometimes clinging to the moist and sticky paw of a round-eyed grandchild. Earlier in the day—at eleven o'clock, say—the talk was not so general nor so inclusive. The old men were likely to drift into groups of two or three or four. They sat on sun-bathed benches and their conversation was likely to be rather smutty at times, for all they looked so mild and patriarchal. They paid scant heed to the white-haired old women who like themselves were sunning in the Park. They watched the young women switch by, with appreciative glances at their trim figures and slim ankles. The day of the short skirt was a grand time for them. They chuckled among themselves and made wicked comment. One saw only white-haired, placid, tremulous old men, but their minds still worked with belated masculinity like naughty small boys talking behind the barn.

Old man Minick early achieved a certain leadership in the common talk. He had always liked to hold forth. This last year had been of almost unendurable bottling up. At first he had timidly sought the less assertive ones of his kind. Mild old men who sat in rockers in the pavilion waiting for lunch time. Their conversation irritated him. They remarked everything that passed before their eyes.

"There's a boat. Fella with a boat."

A silence. Then heavily: "Yeh."

Five minutes.

"Look at those people laying on the grass. Shouldn't think it was warm enough for that. . . . Now they're getting up."

A group of equestrians passed along the bridle path on the opposite side of the lagoon. They made a frieze against the delicate spring greenery. The coats of the women were scarlet, vivid green, arresting, stimulating.

"Riders!"

"Yes."

"Good weather for riding."

A man was fishing nearby. "Good weather for fishing."

"Yes."

"Wonder what time it is, anyway." From a pocket, deep-buried, came forth a great gold blob of a watch. "I've got one minute to eleven."

Old man Minick dragged forth a heavy globe. "Mm. I've got eleven."

"Little fast, I guess."

Old man Minick shook off this conversation impatiently. This wasn't conversation. This was oral death, though he did not put it thus. He joined the other men. They were discussing Spiritualism. He listened, ventured an opinion, was heard respectfully and then combated mercilessly.

He rose to the verbal fight, and won it.

"Let's see," said one of the old men. "You're not living at the Grant Home, are you?"

"No," old man Minick made reply, proudly. "I live with my son and his wife. They wouldn't have it any other way."

"Hm. Like to be independent myself."

"Lonesome, ain't it? Over there?"

"Lonesome! Say, Mr.—what'd you say your name was? Minick? Mine's Hughes—I never was lonesome in my life 'cept for six months when I lived with my daughter and her husband and their five children. Yes, sir. That's what I call lonesome, in an eight-room flat."

George and Nettie said, "It's doing you good, Father, being out in the air so much." His eyes were brighter, his figure straighter, his colour better. It was that day he had held forth so eloquently on the emigration question. He had to read a lot—papers and magazines and one thing and another—to keep up. He devoured all the books and pamphlets about bond issues and national finances brought home by George. In the Park he was considered an authority on bonds and baking. He and a retired real estate man Mowry sometimes debated a single question for weeks. George and Nettie, relieved, thought he ambled to the Park and spent senile hours with his drooling old friends discussing nothing amiably and witlessly. This while he was eating strong meat and drinking strong drink.

Summer sped. Was past. Autumn held a new dread for old man Minick. When winter came where should he go? Where should he go? Not back to the five-room flat all day, and the little back bedroom and nothingness. In his mind there rang a childish old song they used to sing at school. A silly song:

> "Where do all the birdies go?
> *I* know. *I* know."

But he didn't know. He was terror-stricken. October came and went. With the first of November the Park became impossible, even at noon, and with two overcoats and the sweater. The first frost was a black frost for him. He scanned the heavens daily for rain or snow. There was a cigar store and billiard room on the corner across the boulevard and there he sometimes went, with a few of his Park cronies, to stand behind the players' chairs and watch them at pinochle or rum. But this was a dull business. Besides, the Grant men never came there. They had card rooms of their own.

He turned away from his smokey little den on a drab November day, sick at heart. The winter. He tried to face it, and at what he saw he shrank and was afraid.

He reached the apartment and went around to the rear dutifully. His rubbers were wet and muddy, and Nettie's living-room carpet was a fashionable grey. The back door was unlocked. It was Canary's day downstairs, he remembered. He took off his rubbers in the kitchen and passed into the dining-room. Voices. Nettie had company. Some friends, probably, for tea. He turned to go to his room, but stopped at hearing his own name. Father Minick. Father Minick. Nettie's voice.

"Of course, if it weren't for Father Minick I would have. But how can we as long as he lives with us.

There isn't room. And we can't afford a bigger place now, with rents what they are. This way it wouldn't be fair to the child. We've talked it over, George and I. Don't you suppose? But not as long as Father Minick is with us. I don't mean we'd use the maid's room for a—for the—if we had a baby. But I'd have to have someone in to help, then, and we'd have to have that extra room."

He stood there in the dining-room, quiet. Quiet. His body felt queerly remote and numb, but his mind was working frenziedly. Clearly, too, in spite of the frenzy. Death. That was the first thought. Death. It would be easy to die. But he didn't want to die. Strange, but he didn't want to die. He liked life. The Park, the trees, the Club, the talk, the whole show. . . . Nettie was a good girl . . . the old must make way for the young. They had the right to be born. . . . Maybe it was just another excuse.

Almost four years married. Why not three years ago? . . . The right to live. The right to live. . . .

He turned stealthily, stealthily, and went back into the kitchen, put on his rubbers, stole out into the darkening November afternoon.

In an hour he was back. He entered at the front door this time, ringing the bell. He had never had a key. As if he were a child they would not trust him with one. Nettie's women friends were just leaving. In the air you smelled a mingling of perfume and tea, and cakes, and powder. He sniffed it, sensitively.

"How do you do, Mr. Minick," they said. "How are you! Well, you certainly look it. And how do you manage these gloomy days?"

He smiled genially, taking off his greatcoat and

revealing the red sweater with the big white "C" on it. "I manage. I manage." He puffed out his chest. "I'm busy moving."

"Moving!" Nettie's startled eyes flew to his, held them. "Moving, Father?"

"Old folks must make way for the young," he said, gaily. "That's the law of life. Yes, sir! New ones. New ones."

Nettie's face was scarlet. "Father, what in the world—"

"I signed over at the Grant Home to-day. Move in next week." The women looked at her, smiling. Old man Minick came over to her and patted her plump arm. Then he pinched her smooth cheek with a quizzical thumb and forefinger. Pinched it and shook it ever so little.

"I don't know what you mean," said Nettie, out of breath.

"Yes, you do," said old man Minick, and while his tone was light and jesting there was in his old face something stern, something menacing. "Yes, you do."

When he entered the Grant Home a group of them were seated about the fireplace in the main hall. A neat, ruddy, septuagenarian circle. They greeted him casually, with delicacy of feeling, as if he were merely approaching them at their bench in the Park.

"Say, Minick, look here. Mowry here says China ought to have been included in the Four-power Treaty He says—"

Old man Minick cleared his throat. "You take China, now," he said, "with her vast and practically, you might say, virgin country, why—"

An apple-cheeked maid in a black dress and a white apron stopped before him. He paused.

"Housekeeper says for me to tell you your room's all ready if you'd like to look at it now."

"Minute. Minute, my child." He waved her aside with the air of one who pays five hundred a year for independence and freedom. The girl turned to go. "Uh—young lady! Young lady!" She looked at him. "Tell the housekeeper two pillows, please. Two pillows on my bed. Be sure."

"Yes, sir. Two pillows. Yes, sir. I'll be sure."

The Golden Years

Sylvia Rothchild

If anyone had told Simon Halpern a year ago that he would soon spend every day sitting on a park bench instead of in front of a sewing machine, he would surely have laughed. "What will I do all day?" he asked when his wife suggested that he retire. "Do you want to make a rag out of me? What kind of person can sit with empty hands all day?"

"You don't earn any more than you would get if you stayed at home," she reminded him.

"So I don't earn as much as I used to; would you like me to go out and steal a little more?"

"We won't talk about it any more," his wife answered; "be well, and work as hard as you like."

Three days before his seventieth birthday, however, he came home from work early with the fingers of his right hand stiff and immovable. He insisted that it would be all right in a few days. But his hand did not improve. No one believed it would and after a few weeks, though he still assured everyone that he would be back at work soon, he too doubted that it would be possible.

Simon did not change his routine any more than was necessary. His wife knew that he could not. He awoke at five-thirty just as he had done for fifty years. Each morning he was surprised anew to remember that he had no place to go, that the keys to the shop were returned to the boss, that the subway would grind out of the station without him. It was Sunday every day of the week but he refused to think about it. He washed and shaved carefully, brushed his thin iron-gray hair with the wispy, ivory-backed brush his wife had given him before his marriage. Then he took his false teeth from the glass where they were soaking all night, and put them in his mouth deliberately. They had never fitted properly and his gums were always sore where they rubbed against them but he wore them stubbornly even though no one but his family would see him.

He took his prayer shawl and phylacteries from their velvet cases, wrapped his prayer shawl around his shoulders, and wound his phylacteries carefully around his left arm and again on his brow. Then he said the morning prayer. He loved the morning meeting with his God better than any other. Praying while the streets were empty and the houses still with sleep made him feel as though he alone in the world had the Lord's attention.

Though he relished the privacy of the morning, he didn't mind sharing it with his two-year-old grandson. Many mornings the little boy would climb out of his crib without waking his mother and run into the kitchen to see his grandfather. Simon would take a fresh diaper off the line that was strung across the bathroom and struggle with his stiff fingers until he changed the boy's pajamas. Then he would reach into the oven where his wife stored the cookies she baked each Friday and give the child one for each hand. He would help him up into a kitchen chair before he began his prayer, turning frequently to look at the soft round face still puffed with sleep. The boy couldn't sit still for long. He would jump down and pull his grandfather's trousers and the fringes of his shawl. Sometimes Simon prayed with the boy perched on his shoulder like a monkey. If the child moved or tried to turn the pages of the prayer book, Simon made a humming noise with his lips closed and didn't interrupt the prayer.

As soon as the boy had been dressed and given his breakfast, Simon would wheel him down to the park in his stroller. They didn't stop at the shelter where all the men gathered, but stayed in the sun where there were mothers and other little children. When the weather was warm, he would lie down on the grass and let the boy jump all over him. He would snatch him up in the middle of their play and kiss the nape of his neck, bite into his buttocks and pretend to devour him.

On rainy days they sat together at the bedroom window, watching the cars, or they squatted on the linoleum in the living-room to build houses of blocks and dominoes. His daughter Evelyn came into the room every few minutes to say, "Watch yourself, Pa. You'll hurt your hand, Pa." Or she would call from the kitchen, "Why don't you leave him alone for a minute, Pa. Don't kiss him so much!" Simon often thought that if not for the baby the first months at home would have been unbearable. He kept hoping that he could make the little boy his; that with sheer love alone he could woo him to his way of life.

But they didn't let him have the boy long enough. Once he overheard his daughter telling a friend on the phone: "If we can only get Allan away from Pa. It drives me crazy. He gave the baby a glass of coffee this morning. Imagine! If he turns over in his crib, Pa is there to see what's the matter. It makes me so nervous." Three months later his son-in-law came home from Japan and resumed his civilian life and they went to California to live.

Simon was miserable, though people kept congratulating him on having his apartment to himself, on no longer having his sleep and meals disturbed. He and his wife found themselves in an endless, frightening silence. She suffered from arthritis and was in bed a good part of the day. She would lie down as soon as her work was done. He sat in the chair beside her bed reading the Yiddish newspapers he bought every day. Sometimes the whole afternoon would pass while she lay dozing in the bed and he sat at the window, listening to the bathroom faucet drip, the radiators knocking, and the footsteps of the people who lived above them.

One afternoon he offered to cook the supper, just to relieve the monotony of the day. He bought what was necessary at the corner grocery store and made a *mamelige,* a pudding of yellow corn meal, which they had not eaten since Evelyn came to stay with them. "How can you eat that? It's as heavy as lead," she would complain. He thought of her as he poured the melted butter over it and heaped little mounds of farmer's cheese and sour cream next to it. Then he broiled a herring on top of the stove, ignoring, as his wife could not do, the grease that splattered all over the stove and wall. "Gussie," he called, "it's ready." He blessed the bread and the two began to eat. They struggled with the portions he set for them. The *mamelige* was lumpy and the herring burned the blisters in his mouth. After four or five bites, he pushed the dish aside and his wife watching him did the same.

"It's good, Simon, it's very good, but I'm just not hungry. One doesn't get an appetite lying in bed."

"No," he said, "It's not your fault. It isn't good; it isn't good at all. Tell me why is it that in America nothing has any taste?"

"Why pick on America?" she asked. "Things have a taste here. It's we who have no taste. Who says food has to taste good to people who have no teeth, no hands, no feet? Don't pick on America. America has nothing to do with it."

Simon went back to the park the next day. He felt foolish going by himself just to sit, but he found forty or fifty men there already. They sat on the benches under the shelter near the mall where the band played in the summertime. Some read newspapers; some played checkers or cards; some talked excitedly in little groups and others sat with blank pallid faces neither looking nor seeing. He found an empty bench and sat down to read his paper. When he was finished he got up and walked slowly around the walks with his hands locked behind his back, stooping forward as though he were looking for something on the ground. It was hard to make the morning pass just walking, and he finally returned to the shelter to find someone to talk to.

A plump, bearded man sat beside him and smiled. "You're a newcomer here, aren't you?" he asked Simon. "What are you on?"

"What do you mean—'on'?" Simon asked.

"On," said the man. "On old age, on pension. I mean where do you get money so you can sit in the park?"

Simon was embarrassed. It was not proper to ask a workingman what he earned; that was his own business. Why should a total stranger ask him such a question?

"Don't be ashamed," his bearded friend went on. "We're all the same here. Take me, for instance. I used to have a little grocery store, but now I'm on assistance for the blind. I can't complain; they're very nice to me."

But Simon couldn't bring himself to answer him. Instead he asked where the nearest telephone was and went home.

He was about to cross the wide avenue that ran along the park when a car pulled up in front of him. "Simon," his brother called, "what are you doing here in the middle of the day? Jump in. How are you feeling?"

Unwillingly, Simon settled himself in the car beside his brother. "I heard that you finally got smart and joined the loafers," he said with the cigar still in his mouth. "Shall I take you home?"

"Yes," said Simon, "I'm going home." They were in front of the house in two minutes.

"I can't stop now, but tell me, Simon, how are you doing? Do you need some money?"

"I'm doing fine. Everything I have is God's and mine. I don't owe anything and I don't want to owe. I'm satisfied."

"That's also doing? I probably give more away a week than you earn."

Simon fumbled with the door handle but could not open it. "If you had listened to me you wouldn't be a failure."

"You think every workingman is a failure. But there are lots of them in America and I'm there with the others. If I'm satisfied with my life, what do you want from me?"

His brother helped him open the door. "Give my regards to Gussie," he said.

"Who took you home?" his wife asked when he came in.

"Hymie," he said.

"In a new car?" she asked.

"I don't know. All cars look the same."

"It's a new car, Sarah told me. He bought her a new squirrel coat too."

"With all the fat on her she needs a fur coat to keep her warm?"

"It's not what you need but what you want," his wife said quietly.

"I'll tell you what Hymie wants. A little sense and understanding; a little appreciation of what is right and wrong; a few feelings that can't be bought with money. I wouldn't trade one week of my life for all of his, with his comforts."

"No one is asking you to," his wife said with a finality he could not break.

Simon avoided the bearded man the next day and sat down next to a drawn, sick-looking man wearing an old torn overcoat that was tied together with a safety pin. He greeted him with a nod but when Simon offered him part of his paper he did not answer. Simon decided that he must be deaf and sat down on a bench opposite him to read. He was almost finished when the bearded man came over and greeted him like an old friend. "Come with me," he said, "I want you to hear something. It's better than the theater when this bunch gets together. It's something to hear." Simon folded his paper and stuffed it into his pocket and followed him along the walk until they stopped in front of two men who were shouting at each other. One was short and heavy with a thick shock of white hair. He waved his hands wildly as he spoke to a tall, thin man wearing a new hat and coat, well-creased trousers, and polished shoes.

"Tell me one thing," the short man shouted. "Tell me, do you believe Adam was the father of his people, tell me do you believe it?"

"All right, so I believe it," the man answered.

"Then agree that today Abraham would be thrown in jail in no time. For what was he? He was the first troublemaker; he was the first revolutionary. He didn't listen to his father; he smashed the idols; he couldn't be satisfied with what he had. Today, you'd holler Communist. What I'm saying is that Jews aren't supposed to be satisfied. They're supposed to complain. They're supposed to make the world better."

"With your ideas you'll make the world better? I could live without it being so much better," he said, putting his hands into his coat pockets.

A short bald man who was on the outside of the circle, listening, pushed himself forward and in a hoarse, raucous voice called out, "The world will never change and you Communists won't make it any better. Cain killed Abel and since then there's always been fighting and struggling and there always will be fighting and struggling. I'm eighty years old and I've seen something in my time."

The tall man answered first, "You're calling me a Communist? Why don't you listen to what goes on and see who the Communist is here?"

The short man spat on the grass. "What a repulsive bunch you are. You're dead already and you don't know it. Everyone's dead in America. Even my own sons. In my house the father is the revolutionary and the sons are the reactionaries. Is that normal? In my house the television is the Bible and the ballplayers are the prophets. For that I say, 'Thank you, America.'"

The circle broke up and someone murmured, "It's a pity he can't afford a ticket right back to his home town. There he would really lick off a good bone; America isn't good enough for him, the big shot."

"*Nu*," said the bearded man to Simon, "didn't I tell you? What do you think?"

"I don't like Communists," said Simon, "but I like to listen. It's like being back in the market."

"You haven't heard anything till you hear Grossman."

"Who is Grossman?"

"Grossman, you don't know Grossman, he used to be a millionaire. He owned all the Osman furniture stores; even now he's still worth ten thousand. But such a *nudnik* you have to go far to find."

"So what is there to hear if he's such a *nudnik*?"

"Nobody lets him alone, that's the thing. For instance, yesterday after you went away, we were holding our sides laughing. Grossman came along and starts with his story. Grossman has only one story, about his store from the rag business, the apartment on Riverside Drive, summers in Atlantic City and winters in Florida; anything to make us drool. Sometimes he even tells it in English. That's how it was yesterday. He went on and on about the same old thing when Klonsky, he's the one with the white hair you just heard talking, Klonsky asks him, 'Mister,' he says, as if he doesn't know his name. 'What's the matter you can't speak Yiddish so everyone can understand you?' Grossman doesn't flicker an eyelash. He just starts the whole thing over in Yiddish, right from the beginning. I thought Klonsky was going to pull all the hair out of his head. 'Enough!' he shouts at him. 'We just heard the whole thing; once, twice, ten times, fifty times is surely enough.' Then he rubs a little salt on, 'Don't forget,' he tells Grossman, 'millionaires are a dime a dozen in America. All you need is a newspaper stand, a dry-goods store, even a wagon that sells knishes or sweet potatoes and you're all set.' I'm telling you this is the life."

The man in the torn overcoat sat on the bench opposite Simon every day but they never spoke to each other. One morning Simon was surprised to find him with his face red and swollen as though he had been crying. He couldn't help but glance up from his paper every few minutes to look wonderingly at the unhappy face opposite him. Then he saw that there were tears streaming down the man's face though he made no sound and the expression on his face was unchanged. Simon got up and sat down beside him. "What is the matter?" he asked quietly, not expecting an answer.

"They're sending me away," he said in a whisper. "This is my last day here. Tomorrow they pack me up, and away." The tears then came too quickly and he stopped talking.

"Where?" asked Simon. "Who is doing this?"

He tried to swallow his sobs that emerged like belches. "My own children want to bury me alive. They're sending me to a home." And the tears streamed again.

Simon put his hand on his shoulder. "Don't be foolish," he said. "That's not burying alive. Hundreds and thousands of people are in homes and they live until they die. What's so terrible? Stop crying. It's not such a terrible thing. You may even like it there."

"No," said the man. "No one will come to see me. I'll be as lonely as a stone, all the days and nights. My children won't come and who else do I have? I was the youngest in my family, all, all gone." He almost choked as he pressed the sobs down.

"I'll come," said Simon. "I'll find a few other men here and we'll come to see you. Stop crying." The man moved to the end of the bench to make room for a few other people who had stopped to talk and he huddled there, taking deep breaths to control his tears.

Before Simon left the park, he took out his address book. "What's your name?" he asked the stranger.

"Ziskind," he answered, "Abraham Ziskind."

"And to what home are you going?"

Living Life—Waiting for the Angel of Death

"To Carole Street, near the market," he answered.

"Oh, I know," said Simon. "I've never been there, but I know."

Two weeks later Simon persuaded his friend to go to the home with him. He didn't know the man's name, but when talking to his wife he called him "the Beard." They walked together through the most crowded streets in the neighborhood, past pushcarts, and trucks, down a street where there were not even alleyways between the apartment houses and the street was a gully flanked by two walls. The home was an apartment house like all the others. There were the two marble steps, the same grillwork on the doors and only a small sign saying *Moshav Zekanim* to distinguish it from the houses next to it and opposite it.

"So this is the place," Simon said. "Every year a collector comes and I give him two dollars and I never knew where it went."

They pushed the heavy door open and in the small lobby where the other houses had doorbells and letter-boxes there was a hole in the wall, about a foot square. A woman stuck her head out and asked, "What do you want?"

"We came to see Mr. Ziskind," Simon said.

"In Room Fourteen," she answered, and her head disappeared from view.

They stood on the threshold looking for someone who would know where Fourteen was. It was quiet except for the noise of pans rattling and water running somewhere in a kitchen and for a moment neither Simon nor the Beard realized that there were several people in the hallway. Under the steps at the back, where there was a door leading to the basement, a shriveled, toothless old lady with a kerchief on her head sat on an apple box. In folding chairs on both sides men and women sat staring into space like wax figures. A voice at Simon's right called out, *"Vehmen zicht ihr?"* and the Beard answered.

"Ziskind, Room Fourteen."

"Upstairs, the second floor," was the answer.

When they turned to see where the voice was coming from they saw the entrance to a small synagogue, where several men were sitting.

They took the steps slowly. The Beard held the banister on the right and Simon held on to the wall. The wall was rough where the paper was torn off in large strips and the steps were worn into shallow bowls. At the turning point on the staircase they left the smells of the first floor—strong odors of disinfectant, food, garbage, and the musty smell of old books from the synagogue—for the dusty smells of carpeting, old sweaty clothes, and improperly washed bathrooms. The Beard held his nose and said, *"Pfui."*

"Never mind," said Simon. "Smell your share and go along."

There was no one in the first room they passed. The next was so crowded with furniture that they had to look carefully before they saw Ziskind sitting with his hands folded and his head down. He wore a skull-cap on his head and dirty tweed jacket over uncreased rayon trousers. He looked as if he had not shaved since he had come to the home. Only a little gray light came down the shaft from the skylight into his room. There was a wall only two feet from his window so that there was nothing to look out upon.

"Hello, how are you?" Simon asked with forced cheerfulness.

Ziskind looked at them for a minute as if wondering whether to answer. "I am just as you see me, just as I look, that's how I am."

Simon and the Beard looked at each other significantly. He looked dreadful, as if he were not much longer for this world. They stayed with him for half an hour. Simon talked all the time and Ziskind seemed apathetic. When they stood to leave, however, he jumped and seized Simon's right hand in both his own and said, "I thank you for coming. I didn't think anyone would ever come. God will repay you. Please come again, I beg you."

Simon and his friend didn't talk about the home to the other men but it was on their minds for many days. The Beard, seemingly out of the blue, would ask him, "What kind of slop do you suppose they give them to eat there?"

"How should I know?" Simon would ask irritably, annoyed that he was forced to think about it.

When his wife asked how it was, he said, "How should it be, a lot of old people, that's all."

It rained for a week after they had gone and then Simon's hand became very painful. A month passed before he and the Beard went to see Ziskind again. They found the entrance hall crowded with women and for a moment they thought they had come to the wrong building. Then they noticed the old folks, dressed in good clothes. "*Oi*, it must be a funeral," was the Beard's decision. They went upstairs and found Ziskind just where they had left him.

"What going on? Somebody went away? Who are all the women?"

"It's nothing; some kind of party. They're charity ladies," said Ziskind.

"So what are you doing here alone when there's a party?" the Beard asked.

"If they want me, they can come and call me," Ziskind answered petulantly.

"Don't be foolish," said the Beard. "If it's a party, maybe there's some schnapps or wine, and lots of pretty young women are there already. Don't be an old fool. Let's go down."

They pulled Ziskind, still unshaven, in dirty, crumpled clothes, down the stairs. The old people were already in the dining-room and the women were carrying teacups, glasses, and plates.

"Here are some more," one of the women called as she ran to greet them. "Come, come, come," she said, holding Simon by the arm. "Now don't worry, we saved some cake for you, you're not too late. Simon tried to shake her hand off, but she held him tightly as if he were a little child that might run away. She led them to one of the long tables that were used for meals and pulled the chairs out for them. Another woman in a large feathered hat stood at the head of the room. "My dear friends," she said slowly as though she didn't expect to be understood. "We have come to celebrate some birthdays with you. We want you to know that even in your golden older years you can still have happy birthdays. Let us all rise and sing happy birthday to Mrs. Bella Gold, Mr. Abraham Selkin, Mrs. Celia Kroll, and Mrs. Molly Greenstein." Some of the people stood up, but only the guests sang. Then a large cake was brought in and pieces were carried to everyone, with glasses of tea. One of the guests played the piano while the tea and cake were devoured.

"Aren't you eating your cake?" the Beard asked Simon.

"It'll stick in my throat. What kind of foolishness is this? Let's go."

"Wait another minute," said the Beard and proceeded to drink Simon's tea and eat his cake.

"Mr. Goldman," announced the woman at the piano, "will now play for you on his violin."

Mr. Goldman, one of the members of the home, shuffled forward with his violin. He scratched at it for a few minutes and then sat down. Then a tiny woman sang a long song in a thin wavering voice. She had scarcely finished when a man stood up and told an obscene story. Simon got up to leave but the Beard kept motioning for him to sit down.

"What's your hurry, we can stay another minute," he begged.

Ziskind still sipped his tea, looking around at the guests as if they had descended from Mars. Behind him, four women were filling little brown paper bags with candy, nuts, and tangerines. Simon remembered filling such bags himself for his grandson's birthday party a few months before.

The people laughed at the story-teller and he was so encouraged that he did a *kazatska* and then sang a *double-entendre* song called "But I Don't Know How" in a flat, tuneless voice. Simon felt himself quivering with exasperation and shame. He squirmed out of the narrow place behind the chairs and went toward the door. He had almost reached

The Golden Years

it when he heard a woman's voice call him, "Mister, wait!" He didn't turn and she ran all the way out to the lobby with a little paper bag in her hand. She caught his sleeve breathlessly, and said, "You didn't get your candy, here it is."

"Let me alone," he waved his hand at her; "I don't need any candy." Then he let the door slam behind him.

When he stopped for a traffic light he looked back and saw the Beard hurrying after him as fast as his fat legs would take him.

"What was your hurry?" he asked breathlessly. "You could have waited another minute. We came together, let's go home together."

"I can't stand to see old people get up and make fools of themselves like children. It makes me want to sink into the ground."

"Don't take it to heart, it was just a party. Nothing would be better? At least it shows the women have some respect."

"That's also respect, to make fools of people?"

"Is it their fault if the people are fools? Beggars can't afford to be so proud."

"But when a beggar loses his pride, what is he? A common beggar; it's the beggar that can't afford to lose his pride. And without pride, there's no respect."

"Take that up with Klonsky, I'm not a debater," said the Beard.

When Simon stopped at the bakery on the corner of his street, the Beard continued on to his house. Simon bought a pumpernickel and some rolls and hurried down the block and into the hallway, feeling a little guilty because he had been away longer than usual. He didn't notice the ambulance in front of the house. He climbed the steps to the first floor, pulled his key out of his pocket and pushed it into the lock. It didn't turn properly and he put the bag under his arm and tried to use both hands. Then he realized that he had been closing it instead of opening it. He wondered why his wife had left the door open. He had only opened it a crack when he knew that something was wrong. He heard no voices but he sensed at once that there were people in the house.

He walked through the long foyer quickly but not until he reached the entrance to the kitchen did he see the woman from the apartment next to his standing with her hand on the sink. Opposite her a blond young man in a white coat sat in Simon's chair at the kitchen table.

"What are you doing here? What's the matter? Where's my wife?" Simon felt his voice as one does in a nightmare.

"I'm sorry, Mister, but your wife had a heart attack an hour and a half ago. There was nothing we could do when we came. I'm sorry."

"Nothing is the matter with my wife's heart. She has arthritis."

"Sorry, Mister."

"But I was only gone a little while. See, I have the rolls. I was only gone a little while."

Simon stood at the door of their bedroom, his face twisting as if he were struggling to catch his breath.

"Look, Mister, I'm sorry to bother you but would you please sign this form. I've been here an hour already. It'll just take a minute."

Simon sat down to sign. When he finished, the

doctor folded the paper and put it into his breast pocket. He put his hand on Simon's shoulder and went out quietly on rubber-soled shoes.

The neighbor still stood near the sink. "She got scared and knocked on my door. I called the emergency. Is there anything I can do?"

"No," said Simon; but then added, "Please send telegrams to my daughters." He hunted in his little book for an address in Washington and another in California. "Please call the synagogue for me, too." The woman took the slips of paper and hurried out. She seemed relieved to have reason to go.

When she left, Simon sat down on the edge of his bed. He reached over across the narrow aisle between the beds and uncovered his wife's pale peaceful face.

"So you are the lucky one," he said. "You found favor in His eyes. Oh, that I too could be there safely beside you."

Then he covered his face with his hands to hide the tears, "*Mamele, Mamele,* what will I do now?"

The Open Cage

Anzia Yezierska

I live in a massive, outmoded apartment house, converted for roomers—a once fashionable residence now swarming with six times as many people as it was built for. Three hundred of us cook our solitary meals on two-burner gas stoves in our dingy furnished rooms. We slide past each other in the narrow hallways on our way to the community bathrooms, or up and down the stairs, without speaking.

But in our rooms, with doors closed, we are never really alone. We are invaded by the sounds of living around us; water gurgling in the sinks of neighboring rooms; the harsh slamming of a door, a shrill voice on the hall telephone, the radio from upstairs colliding with the television set next door. Worse than the racket of the radios are the smells— the smells of cooking mixing with the odors of dusty carpets and the unventilated accumulation left by the roomers who preceded us—these stale layers of smells seep under the closed door. I keep the window open in the coldest weather, to escape the smells.

Sometimes, after a long wait for the bathroom you get inside only to find that the last person left the bathtub dirty. And sometimes the man whose room is right next to the bath and who works nights, gets so angry with the people who wake him up taking their morning baths that he hides the bathtub stopper.

One morning I hurried to take my bath while the tub was still clean—only to find that the stopper was missing. I rushed angrily back to my room and discovered I had locked myself out. The duplicate key was downstairs in the office, and I was still in my bathrobe with a towel around my neck. I closed my eyes like an ostrich, not to be seen by anyone, and started down the stairway.

While getting the key, I found a letter in my mailbox. As soon as I was inside my room, I reached for my glasses on the desk. They weren't there. I searched the desk drawers, the bureau drawers, the shelf by the sink. Finally, in despair, I searched the pockets of my clothes. All at once I realized that I had lost my letter, too.

In that moment of fury I felt like kicking and screaming at my failing memory—the outrage of being old! Old and feeble-minded in a house where the man down the hall revenges himself on his neighbors, where roomer hates roomer because each one hates himself for being trapped in this house that's not a home, but a prison where the soul dies long before the body is dead.

My glance, striking the mirror, fixed in a frightened stare at the absurd old face looking at me. I tore off the eyeshade and saw the narrowing slits where eyes had been. Damn the man who hid the bathtub stopper. Damn them all!

There was a tap at the door and I ignored it. The tapping went on. I kicked open the door at the intruder, but no one was there. I took my ready-made printed sign—Busy, Please do not disturb!—and hung it on the door.

The tapping began again—no, no, no one at the door. It was something stirring in the farthest corner of the molding. I moved toward it. A tiny bird, wings hunched together, fluttered helplessly.

I jumped back at the terrible fear of something alive and wild in my room. My God, I told myself, it's only a little bird! Why am I so scared? With a whirring of wings, the bird landed on the window frame. I wanted to push it out to freedom, but I was too afraid to touch it.

For a moment I couldn't move, but I couldn't bear to be in the same room with that frightened little bird. I rushed out to Sadie Williams.

A few times, when her door was open, I had seen parakeets flying freely about the room. I had often overheard her love-talk to her birds who responded to her like happy children to their mother.

"Mamma loves baby; baby loves mamma; come honey-bunch, come darling tweedle-dee-tweedle-dum! Bonny-boy dearest, come for your bath."

Her room was only a few doors away, and yet she had never invited me in. But now I banged on her door, begging for help.

"Who is it?" she shouted.

"For God's sake!" I cried, "A bird flew into my room, it's stuck by the window, it can't fly out!"

In an instant she had brushed past me into my room.

"Where's the bird?" she demanded.

"My God," I cried, "Where is it? Where is it? It must have flown out."

Sadie moved to the open window. "Poor darling," she said. "It must have fallen out. Why didn't you call me sooner?"

Before I could tell her anything, she was gone. I sat down, hurt by her unfriendliness. The vanished bird left a strange silence in my room. Why was I so terrified of the helpless little thing? I might have given it a drink of water, a few crumbs of bread. I might have known what to do if only I had not lost my glasses, if that brute of a man hadn't hid the bathtub stopper.

A sudden whirring of wings crashed into my thoughts. The bird peered at me from the molding. I fled to Sadie Williams, "Come quick," I begged, "the bird—the bird!"

Sadie burst into my room ahead of me. There it was peering at us from the farthest corner of the molding. "Chickadee, chickadee, dee, dee, dee!" Sadie crooned, cupping her hands toward the bird. "Come, fee, fee, darling! Come, honey." On tiptoes she inched closer, closer, closer, cooing in that same bird-voice—until at last, in one quick, deft movement, she cupped the frightened bird in her hands. "Fee, fee, darling!" Sadie caressed it with a finger, holding it to her large breast. "I'll put you into the guest cage. It's just been cleaned for you."

Without consulting me, she carried the bird to her room. A little cage with fresh water was ready. Shooing away her parakeets, she gently placed the bird on the swing and closed the cage. "Take a little water, fee, fee dear," she coaxed. "I'll get some seed you'll like."

With a nimble leap the bird alighted on the floor of the cage and dipped its tiny beak into the water.

"It drinks! It drinks!" I cried joyfully. "Oh, Sadie, you've saved my baby bird!"

"Shhh!" she admonished, but I went on gratefully. "You're wonderful! Wonderful!"

"Shut up! You're scaring the bird!"

"Forgive me," I implored in a lower voice. "So much has happened to me this morning. And the bird scared me—poor thing! I'll—But I'm not dressed. May I leave my baby with you for a while longer? You know so well how to handle it."

Back in my room, I dressed hurriedly. Why did I never dream that anything so wonderful as this bird would come to me? Is it because I never had a pet as a child that this bird meant so much to me in the loneliness of old age! This morning I did not know of its existence. And now it had become my only kin on earth. I shared its frightened helplessness away from its kind.

Suddenly I felt jealous of Sadie caring for my bird, lest it get fonder of her than of me. But I was afraid to annoy her by coming back too soon. So I set to work to give my room a thorough cleaning to insure a happy home for my bird. I swept the floor, and before I could gather up the sweepings in the dustpan, another shower of loose plaster came raining down. How could I clean up the dinginess, the dirt in the stained walls?

An overwhelming need to be near my bird made me drop my cleaning and go to Sadie. I knocked at the door. There was no answer, so I barged in. Sadie was holding the tiny thing in her cupped hands, breathing into it, moaning anxiously. "Fee, fee, darling!"

Stunned with apprehension I watched her slowly surrendering the bird into the cage.

"What's the matter?" I clutched her arm.

"It won't eat. It only took a sip of water. It's starving, but it's too frightened to eat. We'll have to let it go—"

"It's my bird!" I pleaded "It came to *me*. I won't let it go—"

"It's dying. Do you want it to die?"

"Why is it dying?" I cried, bewildered.

"It's a wild bird. It has to be free."

I was too stunned to argue.

"Go get your hat and coat, we're going to Riverside Drive."

My bird in her cage, I had no choice but to follow her out into the park. In a grove full of trees, Sadie stopped and rested the cage on a thick bush. As she moved her hand, I grabbed the cage and had it in my arms before either of us knew what I had done.

"It's so small," I pleaded, tightening my arms around the cage. "It'll only get lost again. Who'll take care of it?"

"Don't be a child," she said, coldly. "Birds are smarter than you." Then in afterthought she added, "You know what you need? You need to buy yourself a parakeet. Afterwards I'll go with you to the pet store and help you pick a bird that'll talk to you and love you."

"A bought bird?" I was shocked. A bird bought to love me? She knew so much about birds and so little about my feelings. "My bird came to me from the sky," I told her. "It came to my window of all the windows of the neighborhood."

Sadie lifted the cage out of my arms and put it

The Open Cage

back on the bush. "Now, watch and see," she said. She opened the cage door and very gently took the bird out, holding it in her hand and looking down at it.

"You mustn't let it go!" I said, "You mustn't . . ."

She didn't pay any attention to me, just opened her finger slowly. I wanted to stop her, but instead I watched. For a moment, the little bird stayed where it was, then Sadie said something softly, lovingly, and lifted her hand with the bird on it.

There was a flutter, a spread of wings, and then the sudden strong freedom of a bird returning to its sky.

I cried out, "Look, it's flying!" My frightened baby bird soaring so sure of itself lifted me out of my body. I felt myself flying with it, and I stood there staring, watching it go higher and higher. I lifted my arms, flying with it. I saw it now, not only with sharpened eyesight, but with sharpened senses of love. Even as it vanished into the sky, I rejoiced in its power to go beyond me.

I said aloud, exulting, "It's free."

I looked at Sadie. Whatever I had thought of her, she was the one who had known what the little bird needed. All the other times I had seen her, she had remembered only herself, but with the bird she forgot.

Now, with the empty cage in her hand, she turned to go back to the apartment house we had left. I followed her. We were leaving the bird behind us, and we were going back into our own cage.

The Life You Gave Me

Bette Howland

So my father is going to be all right.

That's what my mother said as soon as we met at the airport. That's what the doctor said when he came out of surgery. That's what my father said himself, just before he went in, making it snappy over long distance. "This is costing you money."

That's what I thought all along.

He's always been all right before.

1.

Before. That would be ten years by now. The voice over the telephone sounded encouraging.

"Missus Howland? Bette Howland?"

Uh huh, he's selling something, was my first thought. What'll it be? Magazine subscriptions? Rug shampooing? I can never make up my mind what to do about telephone solicitors. Is it better to say no thanks and hang up on the spot, so they don't waste any breath? Or to stand there, frowning, with the phone to your ear, and let them finish?

I stood there.

"This is Reverend Nightsong? Chaplain at Covenant Community Hospital?"

Still inquiring.

Didn't I tell you? Collecting for charity. But what's he calling me for? What does he want from me? How did he ever get hold of my name?

"I'm calling about your father? He had an accident?"

"How?"

Owww.

A grappling hook got tangled in seaweed.

"Now take it easy now. Don't go getting all excited. There's nothing to upset yourself about. He fell? Off a ladder? Fixing the roof? It looks like he maybe cracked a couple of ribs, he broke his nose. Things like that. We should know pretty soon. They're still checking him over."

Oh yes. Wasn't that just like him? Easy to picture my father up on a ladder. The wide back and heavy shoulders. The polar bear neck. The legs powerful, foreshortened, condensed by their own strength and weight. That's nothing new.

But wait a minute. What's going on here? I don't get it. My parents sold their house ages ago, before my father retired. What roof? What house? What business does the old man have—climbing ladders?

Reverend Nightsong spoke.

"We thought you might want to come down?"

"Now?"

I was still frowning. My father does that. Talks

into the telephone as if he's getting a bad connection or bad news. His thick forehead bunched; the phone squeezed to his raspy cheek; raising his voice to make himself heard in the next room, the next world. He says he can't help it, he's used to working in the plant, shouting over the machines. I believe him. I got sent every now and then to collect his paycheck. Through all the open transom windows the noise made a tunnel: clubbed, bludgeoned, plundered air.

He doesn't know his own strength, says my mother.

We have the same deep vertical groove over one eyebrow: more than a frown—almost a scar.

"You mean right now?"

"Well, yes. Now. Now would be good. Now, that is, if it's all right with you."

"Yeah, sure," I said. "Okay. Now."

2.

It was a warm bright day. Earlier a pair of window washers had been at work, ropes and planks butting the cemented slabs of the building. I heard voices, looked out, down they came. Thick boots, army pants, cigarette butts in curly beards. The sponges slopped and blurted. Water slurred. It ran on the glass as over stones glazed in a stream.

The sky looked like that. Transparent. Luminous.

Out of the clear blue sky it came to me: what if my father was dead?

Why didn't I think of it? That's what they had called me for. That's what it was all about. The Chaplain. No wonder. You know yourself how they are; they never tell you the truth. They don't like to break the news over the phone.

I pictured a form under a white sheet; my father laid out like a large piece of furniture. The hulk of the chest, the humps and ridges of aprons pushing carts, passing out drinks, paper napkins, sliding stacked snack trays over our seats. Their faces leaned and smiled, sunny with makeup. Ice cubes faintly tinkled in plastic glasses. Smokers in the rear section had lighted up, cigarette fumes seeping through the compartment; stale traces, a bluish tinge, leaking like the trail of a dye-marker.

The aisle was lit with a wintry brightness.

"It's awfully bad luck," she kept saying. "It's really a very bad break."

Somehow she had been expecting to deal with these matters one at a time.

She was in her fifties (I'd say); round face, pouchy chin, small neat-tipped mobile nose. Bifocals. Frizzy gray hairs straggling from a smooth dark bun. (By no means as much tinsel as I have. Premature gray runs in my mother's family. We like to call it premature.)

She picked up her sandwich in plump ringed fingers and eyed it suspiciously. "Wonder what's in this? Ugh. Don't you hate airplane food?"

She put it back on her plate and began to dissect it with her fork.

I told her that my parents had only recently moved to Florida, after talking about it for years.

"Mine were that way, too," she said. "Kept putting it off."

Now they loved it; they were only sorry they hadn't made the move much sooner.

"Just like mine," she said. "Same with mine. Don't I know."

Luckily they were barely seventy; still in good health; still plenty able to enjoy themselves.

"Oh, mine were, too," she said. "Mine were, too."

She was glancing at the window, not really looking out, the light settled—a kind of sediment—in the thick bottoms of her lenses. She didn't need to look; she knew the terrain. She had been here before, she had covered this ground. She was drawing me a map.

Each time she spoke, she nodded and swallowed—as if given permission—and poked at her lips with the paper napkin:

"Mine too. Mine too."

I didn't say that my father had undergone surgery that morning.

It was an emergency. A couple of nights before he had started to hemorrhage. He was in bed; he got up and put his pants on and drove himself and my mother to the hospital. She drives now; but not with him in the car. By the time they got there, some twenty minutes later, the pants, the front seat, and the assortment of rags he keeps in the car for old times' sake (torn blankets, discarded beach towels; there's not much place for his junk in their new apartment, their new lives) were soaked through; sticky-bright; red with burst blood. He had almost no pulse. He had been on intravenous feedings and transfusions. The doctors were expecting to remove a section of the colon. They were pretty sure it would be malignant. But if all went well and there no complications; they were pretty sure he would be cured completely.

Who knows why they kept putting it off?

My father had been retired for years, had elected

to take an early retirement first chance he got. It was something new. Now there are bonuses; then there were penalties. It meant a considerable sacrifice of pensions and benefits. But he didn't want to be one of those, as he put it—as he was bound to—Living On Borrowed Time. Besides, he had always hated his job. Not that he ever said so. Not that he had to.

I used to wake to the trudge of a shovel: my father scraping the coal pile, getting the fire going in the furnace, in the basement. Hollow pipes carried it all through the house. The hoarse flinty rumbles had something of the ring and register—the grumbling resonance—of his voice, and I would think of him as down there talking to himself.

Down in the dumps.

That was not just a figure of speech, with my father.

Outside it would still be dark. The snow on roofs, gutters, fences, clotheslines, nothing but gloom. The air was black-and-blue with cold.

That was when we lived on the West Side of Chicago, a neighborhood of two story houses, mostly frame. In winter the sidewalks were blasted black from the dust of coal delivery trucks, clinkers and ashes sprinkled on snow and ice; in summer, from the squashed juices of the mulberry trees. Our house faced west, windows smeared with angry red sunsets. I remember the day we moved in. I mean the day my father moved us in; everybody else watched, neighbors old and new. Hauling it all down three flights from our old flat, tying it up on top of his car, hauling it back up those skinny steps, the porch on stilts. Crushing his burdens to himself, hugged and squeezed in his hairy arms, with his crouching legs and a familiar grim gripping look on his face, he might have been in a wrestling match. A contest of wills.

I wouldn't want anyone to get the idea that my father was ever a showoff, a musclebound type, like those body-builders and pumpers of iron in the slick magazines; arms and chests molded in epoxy. You didn't notice his muscles. Width. Heft. Pelted neck. Hairy withers. Ruddy flesh—almost raw. Smell of head sweat. (It was running from the roots of his curly hair in shining creeks.) And always, always that impression he gave, and still gives, of being laden with strength. Loaded down with it.

When everything was piled up in what was going to be our new front room—all our misplaced, mismated store: boxes, bedsprings, bureau drawers, chairs upside down on the table, all looking pretty dismal and discouraging, dashed with light from bare dirty windows—my father took my sister on one knee and me on the other. He made a speech:

From Now On. Got to Get Organized. Turn Over a New Leaf. All Pitch In. Do Our Part. Listen to Your Mother. Treat Each Other Right. Make a Fresh Start.

The dresser with the tilted mirror found its way upstairs to the bedroom; the wooden ice-chest wound up in the kitchen; everything else stayed where it was. If not those self-same boxes and drawers, headless lamps, black-bagged vacuum cleaners (why three Hoover uprights and no rugs? not that any of them worked), then others. There was always more where that came from. Still, my mother talked about "redoing"—as if anything had ever been done. That was what everybody else said, and she wanted to be like everybody else. From my friends' houses I knew the sort of thing she had in mind. Carpets you couldn't walk on, sofas you couldn't sit on, drapes you couldn't draw (the sun might fade the carpets and upholstery). Something too good for us to use. When she got her carpets, she said, "The Traffic" would take their shoes off at the door. When she got her towels, "The Traffic" would dry their hands on paper. When she got her bedspreads, "The Traffic" would hang up their clothes.

"The Traffic": that was us.

She was giving aid and comfort to the enemy.

We must have lived in that house a dozen years (which surprises me; I thought it was a hundred), and all that time it looked as if we had just moved—or were just about to. How could she ever "have anything"?

After they sold the house and my father retired, they moved a lot: Lock Stock & Barrel; which was about all they had to their name. They were like fugitives keeping just one jump ahead of the law. So when they decided, after years of this, to move to Florida, everyone pooh-poohed:

A Retirement Village? Were they out of their minds? All those *old people?* Phooey. And what would they do with themselves? Sit around and play cards? And the houses—all alike. How can you tell them apart? (A good thing they don't drink; they'd never find their way home.) Like living in a fishbowl. No privacy. Everybody knows everybody's business. They'll get tired of it. Don't worry. Just like all the other times. They'll be back.

When it comes to decisions, my parents like to change their minds a few times; otherwise they

The Life You Gave Me

don't feel right about it; same way a dog likes to turn around and around before it lies down.

But they put a couple of boxes in somebody's basement, and a couple more in somebody's attic, and piled the pots and pans and the portable TV into the back of the car and drove down. To Live Happily Ever After. From Now On.

All at once the clouds ended. Came skidding to a halt, at an edge of blue sky, as banks of snow and ice stop at the blue edge of the sea. I saw a curved shore, a stiff-frozen surf. I knew it was an illusion, but the illusion was complete. The plane was moving through light as a boat through water. The air was vibrating with clarity and brightness; the nose cones of the jets were tingling with it—ringing out—as if they had been struck with tuning forks.

The engines roar.

The light is loud and clear.

"Bad luck," she said. "A very bad break."

Sometimes I wonder what we look like, to stewardesses? Passengers, strapped into our seats, our trays down in front of us? Infants in high chairs, maybe? Clamoring to be fed? Here we were, side by side, the two dutiful daughters—she with her prompt, obedient manners, close-mouthed possessive nibbles that made me think of a squirrel in the grass; me with my napkin tucked under my chin (where it belongs).

So here I am at last. This is it; this is what it's like; I finally made it. Not just what I expected though. Hard to say just what that was. Maybe I thought the scenery would be better? Panoramic? Valleys, vistas, mountain peaks? Pearly clouds, purple distances? The sun sending down planks of light? Yes. That's right. A *view*. This is pretty flat, you know,

Will this be me in ten years' time? Then what? What if I am in her shoes? And is there any reason to think that I won't be? She doesn't know what to do because she doesn't want to do it. Easy for me to say. But what will I do?

"I know it sounds awful," she said. "It's a terrible thing to say. And yet. Right now. If one of them, at least. Isn't it crazy? You always think it's the worst thing that can possibly happen. And then all of a sudden it seems like the best thing."

It's just the only thing.

"But my parents are very happy," I said.

She nodded and swallowed and patted her lips: "Give 'em ten years."

3.

And now for the hard part. My father and I were not on the best of terms, not on the worst. No finalities, no formal estrangements. Words had been spoken—plenty of words; but not the most bitter. Not the Last. Nothing that couldn't be taken back.

We hadn't shot all the arrows in our quivers.

In his heart of hearts (I truly believe) my father held this against himself. Does a man have to live in this way? Should a man put up with such things? Disappointment, disaffection, disobedience? Unnaturalness between parents and children? Strictly observant Orthodox Jews have ways of dealing with offenders, settling matters once and for all. They know how to cut their losses. An offspring who has transgressed, sinned against the tribe and tradition, can be read off—cast out—given up for dead.

The prayers are recited; the period of mourning is observed; the tears are shed.

Goodbye and good riddance.

My father admired these methods, and had long been threatening to use them. He had been threatening as long as I could remember. *How Sharper Than a Serpent's Tooth It Is to Have a Thankless Child.* That was one of his favorite expressions. (I could tell from his lofty look he wasn't making it up, either.) If I heard it once, I heard it a thousand times, and never without a thrill—a shiver—of guilt and shame; a sense of my destiny. This was prophecy.

Wasn't it his right? Wasn't it his duty? Give him one good reason why he shouldn't.

Was he a Jew for nothing?

There was only one hitch. My father is not a strictly observant Orthodox Jew. He does as others do. Sometimes he Observes. Sometimes he Looks the Other Way.

He observes—when he observes—in the Orthodox fashion. He walks to the synagogue in skullcap and prayer shawl and stands up and prays with the book in his hands. The small smooth circle on his head and the sprinkled drops of his brilliantine make him look stiff and anointed. His hoarse gristly throat locked in necktie and collar, his eyes blue and blinking above grouty cheeks. The room sways; fringes quiver; my father's rough raspy voice gets rougher and louder. When he turns the page, or loses his place, it drops to a mutter; his chin drops to his chest.

His lip is full, solemn—exposed.

Even these days, down in Florida, he insists on walking to the synagogue; two or three miles of heat, open highway, diesel trucks, pot holes, exploding tires; mag-wheeled pick-ups sporting the spokes of the Confederate flag on their bumpers, and horns that hoot 'n toot and whistle "Dixie." He persists: there is no Orthodox synagogue to walk to. And my mother comes stumbling after, in billowy skirts and high heels, scared to death he will get knocked down and run over if she's not there to keep an eye on him. What a target. His broad, brunt-bearing shoulders draped in stripes and white silk, his curly hair whitened, thickened; the glasses pressing his cheeks. Every few minutes she stops to lean on him for support, to rattle the stones out of her shoes, to ask an old question:

Why can't he take the car and drive?

Why can't he be like everybody else?

But this went on only a few days out of the year: on Rosh Hashanah, Yom Kippur, and those occasions (ever increasing) when my father recited prayers for the dead. Of other holidays, my sister and I scarcely heard the names. We fasted on Yom Kippur, kept Passover faithfully, didn't mix meat and milk at the table or eat of "any abominable thing." But we didn't keep kosher. No separate sets of dishes, no meat ritually slaughtered, no chickens hanging by their feet in the kosher butcher's windows—in dishonor—with twisted necks and pincered wings. My parents lighted candles in memory of the dead; pink-labeled glasses filled with a white wax that sizzled. Afterward we used them for drinking glasses; they matched and made a set. (Just about the only thing that did.) But in our house prayers and blessings were not said. I never saw my mother light candles on Friday night. Her own mother did. The old lady would mutter the prayer hastily to herself, under her breath, holding both hands up to her face; as if, I thought, the flames might be too bright for her. They never seemed that bright to me. Still I saw their reflection—refraction—in her eyes.

Once, on a trip, we visited the family of my uncle's bride; Pennsylvania Dutch Quakers living in the Lebanon Valley. They were plain, but not like the Amish farmers we had seen along the way, with their clip-clopping horses and tipping buggy whips. Mr. K. wore buttons on his pants, drove a car, used farm machinery. He was a tall wide old man and his hair had the solid whiteness of a salt lick. And his wife, for all her starched cap and long apron, did not look as reticent as the Amish wives—sheltered under their bonnets and wagon canopies, the horses waiting, horse-patient, with black flies on their eyelids and black blinders. She was robust and smiling and her cheeks were broad and bright as crockery. (They really did remind me of all those cups and bowls, glazed and blazoned with slogans, selling at every roadside stand: "Too Soon Old and Too Late Smart," "The Butter Is All.")

It was August, and it was hot. The cows were mud puddles under a tree. The grass was so blurred with heat it didn't look cool; gassy, rather, effervescent, something like the green light burping up the sides of juke boxes, or that sweet soda pop, in vogue at the time, called *Green River*.

The house seemed lighter inside than out. Crisscrossed windows, white cloth, china cabinets gleaming with glass, silver, pewter that had been in the family two hundred years. Platters heaped with fresh tomatoes, fresh peaches—sliced, juicy running with their own ripeness—and dark sizzling meat.

We sat down to eat.

The meat had a strange flavor I had not tasted before. As soon as I bit in I knew something was wrong. I stopped and looked up, mouth full, head over my plate. I wasn't the only one; my mother and my little sister were looking up too. We glanced at each other and we glanced at my father. He wasn't looking at anyone. His fork was lifted and his eyes were lowered. He seemed to crouch over the table, his head so low between his big shoulders I could see the back of his neck—which was as wide as a brick; and his ears—which were as red.

Curtains fidgeted at the windows. An electric fan blew on us as on hot soup. Our host and hostess were fanning us too, flapping at our faces with fly swatters, dish towels, anything that came to hand. Their glasses beamed—almost urgently solicitous. Beads of sweat prospered on their brows.

Through the screen I could see fields wavering vaguely in the heat, and the raised hackles of the hills.

My father laid down his fork and raised up his eyes.

"Very good," he said, reaching for the water glass.

He nodded. He gulped.

"Very good."

His jaws moved on their haunches; his molars collided. At once, as at a signal, we all began to chew. Life was going to continue.

Naturally, we knew better than to bring up this subject when we got back to the car. (Just as we knew not to talk when my father was shifting gears: there was something wrong with the transmission.) And what was there to say? That he had eaten ham—pig—for that is what it was; had permitted his wife and daughters to eat, rather than to give offense? No, there was more to it. For himself, my father would not have been so touchy. What he couldn't bring himself to do was to let on—let these good kind people know that they were the ones who had given offense.

God knows they never intended. Their daughter had up and married a Jew; she had gone off to live in the big city; of that much they were aware, but they had a pretty hazy notion of what it might mean. They were different, too. The world was divided into town folk and country folk, and those who were plain and those who were not; and they had trouble keeping track of what set them apart from everybody else—without worrying about every quibbling little distinction, what the fuss was about, among all the rest.

So far so good. That much a Jew could understand. But there was something else. I felt it then, and I can try to say it now. The china cabinets, the criss-crossed windows; the white farmhouses, bricked chimneys; the fenced fields; the animals harbored under the trees. (Through the screen there was the stillness of a canvas someone had painted on in numbers.) They had all that to uphold them in their ways, sustain them in their differences. Our connection seemed more puzzling. We had nothing but this: the grip of our rituals.

Sometimes it's hard to know the right thing to do.

I'm sure my father held this against himself also.

And yet he had no use for Conservative, much less Reform, practices which would at least have let him off the hook. There are some rules that are no good if you make them up as you go along.

And still, you see what comes of it, living with compromise. (As if it is his fault that there are things we have to live with—and things we have to live without.) Let that be a lesson. If only he had been religious enough—righteous enough—man enough—*mad* enough. But who was he to perform such sonorous rites over me? Chanting Prayers for the Dead? Weeping and rocking and tearing his beard?

How would it look?

What would he tear?

He doesn't even have a beard.

So my father remains at a loss to express his dissatisfaction. He tries. When he wrote his will, he cut me out of it. (I know; he showed me; he couldn't wait.) Not What a Daughter Should Be, read the clause, in a style I think I recognize by now. That was when at long last it dawned on me.—Dummy! I am, and always have been, just the sort of daughter he wanted.

What with one thing and another, all things considered—the times we live, the Spirit of the Age—I am What a Daughter Should Be. Just What a Daughter Should Be. Just that and no more.

It's nothing to brag about.

4.

It was raining a little, a fresh scented drizzle; it might have been salt spray blowing from the ocean. The breeze felt soft as a scarf. I saw it drifting round my mother as she stood in front of the spotlighted palms, floating through the folds of her skirt, the white filaments of her hair. The trees leaned, inside out like beach umbrellas. People were rushing to make their planes, lugging armloads of grapefruit. Grapefruit grapefruit everywhere. In string bags, in plastic, packed in crates on crinkly green cellophane. Bald, thick-skinned grapefruit; yellow, uniform; perfect spheres. That was how to tell who was coming from who was going. The ones trying to take home replicas of the sun.

My mother looks like someone in disguise.
    She is stained teak-color from the Florida sun, so tan her lipstick seems to be glowing in the dark. (Purple-pink; bougainvillaea). Her hair is cut short, shingled, clinging to her cheeks—her face enclosed in its white petals—like the fancy rubber bathing caps ladies wear down here. Her shoulders stoop. (Since when?) Her elbows stick out. (How long has this been going on?) Her legs, big knee-knobs, are two thick black bones.
    I recognized her anyhow. I always have, so far.
    It was late—too late to go to the hospital tonight—the air so thick, spongy, saturated, I felt I could stop right then and there and peel it off me in layers, like the Northern sweaters I was wearing. But my mother was hurrying to the car. She walks fast—especially now; luggage or no luggage it would be hard to keep up with her. Her high heels were striking the sidewalk. She wears steel taps on her heels; it emphasizes her pace. Each step rings out—announcing her. I've been hearing this for years without reckoning why you can hear her coming. It's a practical matter, though; it saves shoe

leather. All foresight, that's my mother. Alas, no hindsight.

She stopped. "I don't want you to say anything about that."

"About what?" I said.

"About that. You know what. What you just said. I don't want you saying anything about it to him."

The biopsy report wasn't back yet.

"But what do you mean? Is there something else? Is there something wrong? There's nothing to hide?"

"Never mind. I just don't want him worrying, that's all. He doesn't need to know anything about it."

"But Mother," I said.

"No buts about it," she said. "You're not to say anything, and that's that. That's all there is to it."

My mother may be short, but she has the manner, the bearing, the imperious white head and noble features (Roman coin? Indianhead nickel?) of a woman who is used to getting what she wants. Having her own way. And she has the reputation, besides. "Won't take NO for an answer." And yet—as far as I know—and except in the most trivial circumstances—she never gets what she wants; she never has her own way (whatever that is). Nobody ever listens to her.

She doesn't let that stop her. There's no harm in trying. And maybe, if she can just keep it up long enough—. Meanwhile, it's true, she doesn't take NO for an answer. She doesn't take answers.

She went tap-tapping on, elbows sharp and crooked and ready at her sides, head thrust forward—sleuth-like, I thought—its whiteness all but phosphorescent under the eerie purple of the arc lamps. In the spotlights, the palms dipped their green pennants. Her heels clipped the cement. Her pleated skirts whipped where her hips used to be. The drummer no one is marching to.

She glanced at me over the hill of her back: "You'll do as I say," she told me.

Once, when my sister and I came downstairs to go to school, my father was still sitting at the table, stirring the spoon in his coffee, one arm white with bandages, in a sling. He had cut his wrist on the power saw; the blood came up in black bullets, sputtered the ceiling; he knew he had hit an artery.

He tied the arm in a tourniquet—tightened it in his teeth—and drove to the Emergency Room.

"That was a Close Call," he said, shaking his head. "Thought I was a Goner."

(He did not smoke or drink or use what he called "terminology." "There'll be no terminology in this house!" But he had plenty of terms of his own. Customers, Characters, Fakers, Jokers, Bellyachers, Stinkers, Schemers, Dreamers, Screwballs, So-and-Sos, and Yo-Yos. Just to give an idea; a partial listing. But the greatest of these was Goner. *Goner! Goner!* The very word was like a bell.)

And he widened his blue eyes and whistled appreciatively and went on stirring. (He was awfully fond of sugar; kept heaping it in until there was nothing left in his cup but silt—sand—glittering sludge.)

Later my mother took me aside.

"You didn't even say you're sorry," she said. "Daddy was very hurt. What's the matter with you? Haven't you got a mouth on you? Can't you talk? *I'm sorry you hurt yourself, Daddy.* Is that too much to say? I want you to go to him. Right this minute. I want you to tell him. Say you're sorry you didn't say you're sorry."

My mother of course was the family interpreter. She translated—explained—excused us to each other. That was her job, and she had her work cut out for her; but I used to think she made most of it up:

   He doesn't mean it.
   This hurts him more than it hurts you.
   You know he really loves you.
   He's *still* your father!
   You see what I mean. Who'd fall for that?

And just because she said something was so didn't mean it was so. Maybe my father had said something, and maybe he hadn't. Maybe she *thought* he was hurt. Maybe—she thought he *ought* to be hurt. Because it—and this most likely wasn't just that my mother put words in our mouths; she wanted to "redo" us.

   She's so sensitive.

That was her excuse for me. That was how she sought to put an end to their quarrels. "Can't you see she's sensitive?" But I knew I wasn't sensitive; unless it meant throwing up. And I didn't want their quarrels to end, not in that way. I wanted an end that would be an end, for a change; something dramatic, drastic. I didn't care what or how.

   "Don't provoke him." That was another one. I guess she liked to think that he could be provoked, because that implied an opposite. But my sister and I knew better; we knew there was no opposite. Our father's wrath was made of sterner stuff. We had simply got in the way of it; we were too small for it, it preceded us. Not that that didn't make us feel smaller.

"You're asking for it. You've got one coming. You're going to get a going over."

He leaned on his elbows over his newspaper, not bothering to lift his eyes from the page. We could see the blue roving from the bottom of one column to the top of the next. When he wasn't shouting at the top of his voice, stretching his throat and straining his vocal cords, his tone was something more felt than heard: a vibration in the floor, through the soles of your feet, like the grunts coming up from the basement.

Sure, don't provoke him. Go tell the trees not to provoke the wind. All that quaking makes it nervous.

These scenes are lapped by lurid flames of memory.

I seem to recall them taking place down in the basement, next to the coal pile. Spiders spilling down the walls, the pipes furred with dust, his head banging into the dangling light bulb so it swayed violently on its wire. The furnace swelling and glowing with cast-iron heat, orange as the fire inside it. But I know darn well that can't be; it was never that way. It all took place in the kitchen, only the kitchen; the smell of wiped oilcloth, still wet; dishes slanting in the drainboard; the pink-labeled glasses rinsed out and turned down. The light as dull as waxed linoleum.

I was the older one, so I went first. My little sister would cling to my mother's legs, hiding her face in my mother's apron and pleading:

Don't hit her! Don't hit her!

She kept peeping out to look and hiding again.

But what earnestness. What passion. What big beautiful tears slipped and spilled down her big beautiful cheeks. Oh, how she sparkled. She was weeping zircons.

Meanwhile, my father would be counting the strokes of the strap with words: lip gripping, eye squinting, forehead bunched in a frown. A man taking aim, taking measure, playing a hunch:

Let . . . That . . . Be . . . Lesson . . . Next Time . . . Know Better. . . .

At least I hoped he was counting.

The strap cracked and snapped against the leg of the table, the chair. That scared me. I could hear how hard he was hitting. And that just went to show how he was *restraining himself*. It was understood he was forever *restraining himself,* his a power that must be held in check.

This hurts him more than it hurts you!

He was a man who didn't know his own strength.

Then we changed places. Now it was my little sister's turn to bend over; mine to cling to my mother's legs and plead.

Don't hit her. Don't hit her.

How half-hearted it sounded, even to my ears. I never put up the defense for her that she put up for me. The most I could manage was a few snotty sniffles and a couple of sticky hiccupy secondhand tears.

Sensitive.

Why do I keep saying *little?* My sister was younger, yes; and she must have been little when she was born; but all I know is, when I had the mumps, my parents thought I was her—because my face got so fat—and switched us in our cribs. She was bigger and stronger and at five or six more precocious; not only did she paint her nails magenta (my mother hoped it would keep her from biting them, which it didn't), she shaved her legs. That was her own idea; by that time we shared a bed, and crude stubble scratched me to pieces. She was a great climber of trees and swinger from branches, and naturally, as the tomboy, our father's favorite. He had been disappointed when his first-born did not turn out to be a boy. That was an open secret. On the other hand, I had a secret of my own. I knew I had spared him a much greater disappointment. Such a boy as I would have been.

Toward books his attitude was lofty; as of something he had sworn off, a reformed zealot. He had read a book or two himself, namely *Oliver Twist* and *The Merchant of Venice*—high-school requirements—and he had a theory about the great and famous writers. Therefore, whenever he spotted me, sitting over the hot-air register (the only warm place in the house; the grill left red welts on my legs, checks and boxes just like the ones we used to draw for the game of X-and-O, and I figured people would be able to play on them for the rest of my life)—whenever he spotted me, with yet another pile of pages open on my lap—he would hitch up a mighty eyebrow and bunch up his forehead:

"What now? Not another anti-Semite?"

And yet he liked to quote poetry: Shakespeare, Longfellow, John Greenleaf Whittier and James Whitcomb Riley; slogans, famous last words, scraps of wisdom from Abe Lincoln and Ben Franklin's *Almanac*. We liked especially one lively version. You know how it goes:

> For want of a nail the shoe was lost.
> For want of a shoe the horse was lost.
> For want of a horse the rider was lost.

But he never stopped there. He went on. And on. A roaring voice, a rising pitch, a rousing rhythm; brows rollicking, carousing, even his eyes razzle-dazzle, as when he teased us:

> The battle was lost.
> The war was lost.
> The country was lost.
> The Cause was lost.

My sister and I listened with thralled faces. (One of the reasons we were so crazy about him—for of course we were crazy about him—one of the reasons, strange to say, was he was no disciplinarian. He gave us our lickings once a week almost without fail, but he never told us to go to bed.) After all the hoarseness, the shouting, the excitement of battle, his voice would drop to a rumble—all the way to the basement. Rumbling, shuddering. Everything came tumbling down:

The Cause! The Cause!
   (We had no idea what a *Cause* was.)

And all . . .
        For want . . .
                Of a nail.

It would be nice to be able to report that my mother's accusations were unfair; that I had been struck dumb from depth of emotion, sympathy for my father, fear for his injuries. But no one would fall for that either. The fact is, it had never even crossed my mind that my father could hurt himself. Let alone that anyone else could. Let alone that I could. It never even crossed my mind that he could ask—want—need my sympathy.

There was a diagonal wriggling thing on the inside of his forearm—a fat shiny pink scar-worm—from his wrist halfway to his elbow, for years and years. For all I know it's there still.

5.

All night it rained.

A newsreel rain; so I saw it in my sleep. Rain slashing through the dark, slanting against the windows, lashing the glass like the shackled leaves of the palm trees. Rain hosing down red tile and pink stucco and wrought-iron balconies; capsizing boats; swatting shutters; stropping trailer camps and truck farms and sousing ten thousand lonely gas pumps. The palms and palmettos were kneeling in the rain. Everything turned inside out—even the waves.

The morning was dark; the sky low and gray, the streets sleek and streaked with light. It took me a minute or two to realize they were flooded. The parked cars covered up to hubcaps, even bumpers. The neighbors were standing out on stairs and porches, squinting up at the sky. Helicopters were flying low, blades beating; the air was thick with sound. They were like boats out fishing.

The first floor neighbors were busy—dragging out soggy, swollen, rolled-up carpets, putting out kitchen chairs to dry.

A car was coming through slowly, nudging the

sluggish water. Everyone clapped. It got slower and slower and chugged to a stop in the middle of the street. The driver got out—naked legs, eddies of wet hair, pants to his knees—and ran off, plinking and plunking in and out of puddles, hiding, holding the shoulders of his jacket up over his head, like a mobster or a convicted public official, trying to duck the newsreel cameras.

The palm trees swayed, waving sliced streamers, tattered banners. Each and every leaf—notch—blade—was dripping light-sap. Tipped with pods of light.

There was some discussion of the relative advantages of first floors and second floors.

On the first floor you get more dampness, more bugs, more noise, and—as you see—you can expect now and then a little excitement. On the second floor, you can't use the screen porch as an outside entrance, and it might be a little hotter: it is believed that the builders skimped on the roofing insulation. (It is believed that builders skimp where they can, wherever you can't see, wherever they can get away with it. That is the nature of builders, especially in South Florida.)

In spite of that, it is clear that the second floor would have the advantage over the first, but for one thing. It's the second floor. You have to walk up. That's fine for now. But for *how long?*

Builders in South Florida are like God in the universe. Their handiwork is everywhere, but they are nowhere to be seen. They move on, leaving their paradise never quite finished.

The helicopters kept passing through misty swamp. The sun had disappeared; favors with-

The Life You Gave Me

drawn. They had discovered a leak in the roof; another defect in the plans.

This particular development is now five years old; the ones who have been here that long are the old-timers. It started out as a row of single-story, white-stuccoed duplexes. They were prefabs, and must have looked pretty bare to begin with. I wouldn't be surprised if—in spite of wear and tear, water stains, dry rot, mildew—they look better now. Because now they are drenched in green; bunches and clusters of thick subtropical vegetation; names like seagrape, nickerbean, cocoplum, cabbage palm. (I've been reading the botanical labels on the nature trails again. Strange bedfellows.)

And there is plenty of space. They are on the canals, which are everywhere in South Florida; from muddy ditches, humble fishing holes—hardly enough for an alligator to wallow in (if that's what alligators do)—to the Intracoastals, wide enough for drawbridges and seagoing vessels. People drive their golf balls into them and sometimes their cars.

But that was before The Boom. The new developers (the first had gone broke and everyone seems to think it served them right) put up two-story structures; now there were four to each unit. And they built them closer. Pretty soon they weren't prefabs any more; but they kept getting closer. They didn't face any canals, either; they faced each other: over archways, walkways, stairways; and there was less and less space in between for anything green. Crimson hibiscus; spikey Spanish bayonet; the feathery shaft of the coconut palm.

Now you pay extra for a view. The golf course,

with its mounds and flags and thistled grass; or the distant stands of gray-green scrub oak and pine. The scrawny scruffy forest primeval of Florida. They look as if they might have been trees once, but drowned and died and these are their ghosts.

Still, the crows seem to think they are trees.

Someone will buy them and chop them down too.

The sections have names like Seville, Tuscany, Isle of Capri. Each condo has a letter, each apartment a number. So it is no wonder; what with fourteen thousand people living here, if some visitors have a hard time finding their way. Everyone has stories of would-be guests who drive through the gates, past the guards in their kiosks, into the midst of all the look-alike buildings, parked cars, gridded streets, white lines, yellow stanchions; shiny brown Dempster Dumpster on each and every corner. And pretty soon they get lost; they give up; they go home. Maybe they call next day to apologize.

Everybody laughs at such tales. They know what it looks like: like every other development. Construction is everywhere, spreading westward, from the ocean, the Intracoastals, the Interstate; the setting sun winks and shimmers in the empty eyeholes of new buildings. White. That is the color of Florida. In spite of the blue of ocean and sky, and the green of practically everything else. The white of limestone and fossilized seashell, that's what the whole state is made of. It gets dug up, crushed for lime and cement, for roads and bridges, for sparkling white high-rises from the strip of Miami Beach to the rim of Lake Worth. It is the color of clouds and golf balls and gulls' gliding wings; of concave sails and pretty white yachts leaving pretty white wakes. And Florida is so flat; it seems intentional. God must have meant it for condominiums. All those raw roofs rising where the spooky trees used to grow; almost, like them, a mirage—the white dust scarcely settled. And all those billboards, promising that the Best Is Yet To Be.

And so?

So what! This is Florida.

What could be easier than to heal this landscape; repair the breach, the damage and disruption, cranes, bulldozers, quick construction, transplanted population? The flora down here are nothing like what you expect up North: shy crocuses, shrinking violets, all those tendrils so bashfully wrapped up in themselves, peeping from leaves. These are tropical plants; they know how to compete. They shriek green; they screech it. You can see they belong to a more primitive age—when reptiles flew; pterodactyl plants, ridged and spiny, still can't make up their minds whether to wear feathers or fins. And none of your pale bulbs, either, that never see the light of day, and roots reaching deeply, secretively underground. In Florida, plants carry their roots with them, a whole forest crawling on its belly, recumbent trunks with roots that noose and lasso. They have claws, tusks, fangs, beaks. They can take anchor anywhere—the shallowest places; an inch or two of soil; on water; on other plants; on nothing at all—on air. The Spanish moss that beards the scenery—all those hanks of gray hair hanging like scalps from arthritic trees—that's an air plant. And so is that thing that might be the greasy-green cluster on top of a pineapple; it favors and festoons the gawky cypress. And what about the mangrove? Its roots grow up, not down; creep, crawl, grope, feel, latching onto whatever happens to come along—treasure troves of drift and debris. The Strangler Fig does what you might expect. And the banyan—the beautiful, beautiful banyan (said to be the tree under which the Buddha found enlightenment, and why not?)—the banyan, with its tiers of leaves, puts down roots like trunks, porticoes; a verandah-tree, spreading green dominions. Looped, coiled, draped, doubled; enough rope to hang itself, or to let down a ladder from heaven.

But the palm, the palm, is the original prefab plant. Height means nothing; the roots are only a handful, bunches of grass yanked up by the hair. All you have to do is dig a hole and aim a spotlight at it.

It's not true, what people say, about the toilets and the telephones. You can hear the phones ringing, sure, if the windows are open; and if the speaker happens to be a woman—the gravelly, abrasive, mannish voice some women get as they grow older (seagulls on social security?)—yeah, sure, you can hear that too. But you don't hear the plumbing. Absolutely no. That's a lie.

I'll tell you what you do hear. You hear everyone getting up in the middle of the night. Everyone has to, at least once.

Maybe you hear creaking: footsteps. A thud: the seat going up. Silence. Then you wait. A drip. . . . A drop. . . . An experimental dribble. . . . More silence. Hey you. You up there. What happened? What are you waiting for? Did you fall back to sleep Do you have to, or don't you? Are you going to do something and get it over with, or are you just going to stand there and think about it? Ah. That's right. That's better. That's more like it.—Did you get out of bed for nothing?

What's public about that? What could be more private? Just people minding their own business. We have heard the chimes at midnight.

The guards in their kiosks with their caps and badges, waving you on with their clipboards, are a necessity, yes. People here are from the urban North; lower-middle, middle-middle class Jews, Italians, Poles, other so-called ethnics—and they know all about it. That's the way we live now. In the older retirement areas, down in Miami, built before the days of guards, and gates, the residents are sitting ducks. They may as well be on a Game Preserve. They are attacked—as the old are everywhere—with a ferocity that suggests other intentions: a kind of desecration, a destruction, of our symbols (no matter how decrepit).

Nowhere are there more old people than in South Florida. And nowhere is the contrast greater between youth and age; I don't know why. It's instructive to watch the aged, sitting on benches at the beach, watching the youth go by. They come down for spring vacation with their surfboards under their arms—chained, fettered to them. So tall, so tan, so firm of flesh, so sound of limb, so white and solid of tooth and bone. Their sun-bleached, moon-blanched, wheaty-blond hair; their eyes as blue as their cut-off jeans. Meanwhile, here sit all the old ladies with freckled arms and wattled elbows and crimpled blue hair that looks, I swear, as if they get it done in funeral parlors. And all the old gents lined up, with their hooked backs, their shoulders squatting at their ears. All the plastic teeth, the pink rinds for gums, the glasses so thick they give off a black vindictive sparkle. Pelicans perched on the shore—scythey necks sunk into their feathers, beaks buried in their breasts.

The waves roll in in generations, heaping up entangled sealife. Oozy weeds, unmolded jellyfish, driftwood and pickle jars toothed with barnacles, the deflated balloons—blue plastic bubbles, on strings—of the man-of-war. Also: styrofoam buoys, hair coconut noggins, frisbees, light bulbs, bottles, gym shoes. Bottles I can understand (but how come no notes in them?), and maybe gym shoes; but light bulbs? Why light bulbs?

The air is bright, particulate; the glint and grit of white sand. The gulls flap up, spilling wings—scraps of light—glittering currents. The sky scatters blessings.

You have to understand. It's not just that the climate is nice, the weather sunny and warm—blue-skied, cloud-scudded. It's the air: it floats. One sniff and you're grateful. It smells of orange groves and salt water and best of all, earth, pungent and potent as under the glass roofs of greenhouses. It's not just balmy: it is balm. Healing. A restorative. Heart's ease. Help for pain.

Who can blame them? Who would want to leave this?

We get it all wrong. Beauty is here to stay. Beauty doesn't vanish. We do.

The guards at this development tend to be older than the residents. That is a fact. My father gave a lift to one who—taking off his cap and rubbing his white hair first this way and then that—owned up

The Life You Gave Me

to eighty-six. He said he was getting "mighty sick and tired of retirement." Since then my father has been considering: what to do in case of emergency? What if violence should threaten? What if there should be an attack? How will he, my father, protect these poor old souls—the guards—and come to their rescue?

The guards in their kiosks are a necessity, maybe; but first and foremost, they are symbolic. Everybody knows it. The residents themselves call all this "The Reservation." This is the line of demarcation, the border. "How long are you here for?" "What's the weather doing back there?" That's what they all want to know. Because it's nothing down here; that's not what they're keeping out. It's what's back there; something they have left behind them.

More than dirt, crime, crowding, corruption; more than hard winters, blithering snows, icy streets, cars that won't start, sidewalks that need shovelling. It's a notion of life. Something they want to forget. Something bleak and somber they have traded in for things undreamt of in their philosophy.

It's The Future.

All their lives they believed in The Future; they struggled and slaved and sacrificed for The Future. Not that they had much choice; it was understood they had been born too soon. Things were going to get better.—In The Future. The Everlasting Future. And now all of a sudden they see the truth. The Future? What Future? Is there even going to be such a thing? For the first time in their lives—for once and once only—it's an advantage to have been born too soon. They won't have to stick around for The Future. They leave it to us. See how we like it.

Right here, right now, right inside these gates—this thin line of trees—they have just as much of The Future as they want. They have caught up at last with American life, and they are going no farther.

The Future stops here.

Enough is enough.

6.

My mother was on the telephone saying something about a flood. In her shortie nightgown, shoulders lifted, shrugging—the better to keep the thin straps up—her back a pair of brown water wings. The white curls were clipped to her cheeks. When she saw me coming she put her hand up in front of her mouth. She can't help it; it's a reflex, an instinct; she hides her mouth when her teeth are out.

It makes her look timid, flinching, someone stifling a scream, warding off a blow.

"It's true. I really mean it," she said. "It's not just here. It's not just us. It's everyone. Everywhere. No one can get anywhere today.—I don't think he believes me," she said to me, talking behind her hand. "Right away he blames me. He thinks there's something the matter with the car."

This is something new, so I guess the teeth must be too. A complete upper plate? When did this happen? Her lip is pinched, puckered; she is trying to hold a bunch of pins in her mouth.

That's the way she talks: lips mincing, afraid to move; afraid she'll lose all her pins.

"What? The doctor was there? Well good for him. Can I help it if the doctor was there? Maybe there's no flood where he is. Maybe he came in a boat. He can afford it, I'm sure. He said what? Back already? So soon? Oh, it was? Oh, it was. Oh. It was."

She held out the phone, her hand to her mouth, pumping up her little scarified eyebrows, biting down on her pins. Her hand is large and bumpy; she wears knuckles as other women wear rings.

" 'S all right. 'S all right."

A deep basement grunt.—The old repercussions.

Don't keep saying it's all right. It's not all right. We want to be with you.

"Take your time," he told me.

My mother hides her mouth; I don't know where she hides her teeth. I haven't seen anything pink-and-white blooming in water glasses. Maybe she keeps them under her pillow? Even while she sleeps, she hides her mouth; she pulls the covers to her nose, lying on her back, her hands—pawlike—gripping the sheets. I don't call this vanity. It's not the ugliness of old age she wants to keep to herself, it's the affliction.

There is such a thing as self-defense.

I didn't mean to pry, but I saw. I saw anyway. I looked in while she was sleeping. The covers had slipped down, her mouth had slipped open; sagged to one side—ajar—the way it does when she sleeps. It's funny, you don't realize how much of a face is mouth: the armature, the support. It was the rest of her face that had collapsed; almost her whole face was the mouth—the dreadful minced lips. It looked big, bigger than ever.

It looked like an exit.

"I told you not to say anything," she said. "I told you not to. Who asked you to?"

Her eyes are light brown, a yellowish tinge. Now that her skin is so tan, they are the same color as her face. The part—behind her hand—that is illuminated, moving.

I get a funny feeling in my parents' new home. Everything is new. Carpets, drapes, end-tables with lamps on them; sofas with arms for cozying up to, cushions to get chummy with. There is even a china cabinet—glass doors, shelves for displaying, knick-knacks (what people down here call "momentoes"). Things that rattle and chink and catch the light. Candlesticks, candy dishes, figurines, a wine decanter. But where did it all come from? That is the question. Your guess is as good as mine.

People "redo" when they move to Florida; it's part of the ritual. I thought at first there were no cemeteries in the state; there are, you don't see them. They look like the farm fields they were just the other day; still standing, right next to them, surrounding them, without fences, the crops planted in parallel rows. (The cemetery gates, with their "Green"-this and "Garden"-that, pass easily for the promise of new developments.) Instead, you see warehouses, whole blocks of them, windowless white boxes. Some people bring all their worldly possessions—according to my mother—all that dark ugly old furniture, all their dark heavy winter clothes. And then: "Who needs it?" They put it all in these warehouses, and store it—as she says—"forever."

So I feel the way I would if I didn't know the people who live here. Not sure where to sit, what to touch. I walk around looking for things familiar to me. The pots and pans, heavy hammered aluminum (they never looked new, so they don't look old): the Portable TV (a suitable "momento," it does nothing but snow). Pictures of weddings and graduations. The decanter has a gold star pattern, it must be from Israel, where my sister lives now. (She'll be back; she moves around as much as I do.) Maybe those demitasse cups were housewarming gifts, like—I'm sure—the two bottles of Sabra they take out when company comes, and put back when company leaves.

I keep looking at the things in the china cabinet. I look so much, I make them nervous.

—Psst. Watch out. Knock it off. Here she comes again.

—What? Her? Oh no, not again. What's she up to, anyhow?

—She wants to see if we're worth anything, dope.

—Of all the nerve! I like that!

So that's the way it is? That's a fine how-do-you-do. My parents are getting on in years, they're living in a Retirement Village. My father is lying at this moment in a hospital bed—they just took out half his gut; here is my mother, hands nailed together atop her breast, napping on the couch, with a mouth like a punctured tire. The Last Act.—And I'm inspecting their possessions? Looking it all over, to see how I like it?

So that's the kind of person I am.

That's nice to know.

All of a sudden I caught on: my parents have never had *things* before.

Not like other people have; not like everybody else; possessions, acquisitions, matters of taste—

choice—pleasure—pride. Considerations of a sort which rarely entered our lives. No wonder all this is new to me; no wonder it's such a strange sensation. I'm not used to looking upon their belongings as anything of value, sentimental or otherwise. But especially sentimental. As anything to be kept; worth keeping; to be passed on; potentially mine.

Some day, in the ordinary course of events, it will fall to my lot to get rid of all this. And what am I supposed to do with it? Will someone please tell me? Where can I put it? How can I keep it? I have no place of my own. I've been storing belongings in this one's basement, that one's attic, for years. And I don't want to get rid of it; dispose—disperse—give away—I don't want to separate it—any of it. I want it all just as it is, every last bit. Intact.

This is the scene of their happiness.

Maybe I can rent a warehouse?

What funny people. My parents. Still don't understand my sister and me. How come we live the way we do. Why we don't "have anything"; never seem to settle down. (Why we can't be like other people's children, acquiring things, habits, for a lifetime.) The same way they can't understand why and how come we never learned to speak Yiddish.

Our grandparents spoke a crude and broken English, and we thought that that other language they spoke—harsh, guttural, to us—was crude and broken too. Our parents spoke Yiddish for privacy's sake. How else could they conduct this grim business of their grownup lives? They talked about us in Yiddish, all the time; but never to us. Sitting at the table in morning darkness, my father dragging the spoon through his cup, stirring the sand in his coffee. Oh, we knew what they were saying all right. Someone had gotten sick, or died. Someone had lost money, or a job. Someone had done something wrong—though she didn't know what; and was going to get a licking—though she wouldn't know why.

Like oars thick in weeds, the sound of their voices slapped in our ears, tangled in sleep.

They had learned Yiddish at home; their first language, the primary language, the expression of feeling and family life. For them it meant a separation between that life and the rest. (What they called "this cockeyed world.") But for us it meant a division within the family itself; barriers between parents and children; bitterness fated; something banished and denied.

And yet I knew all along that Yiddish was the primary language, an original tongue. All other speech would never be more than a polite translation. This was the Source. Things were named by their rightful names, names that could hurt: given their true weight and force. Nothing could be taken back. It was all Last Words.

My mother, for all she looks like a stabbing victim, is making a purring noise, humming to herself—her motor left running. If this is old age, she sounds contented. And I forgot to say: we took off our shoes when we came in the door.

Family. What a discovery.

There is nothing here I would ever choose—and nothing I can ever part with.

7.

So. Here we go again. The distant, the steadfast, the enduring. My father's stern and rockbound features. Elevated. Snoring. His head is huge—precipitous. Steep banked brow. Broken nose. Quarried cheeks. The skin not so much pocked and pitted as granular, eroded; the mica flash of whiskers beneath.

A pile of sandstone on a high white pillow.

His lips are smooth in his rough face.

My father's snoring is an old scenario. Action-packed adventure. Good guys vs. bad guys. Hair-raising rescues, narrow escapes. Also: storms at sea, sword duels, catapult and cannon. All this and more courtesy of *Liberty Comics*—*Wonder Woman*, *Batman & Robin*, and *The League of Justice;* James Fenimore Cooper and Victor Hugo in *Classic Comics* editions; fairy tales dramatized over Saturday morning radio to the whistle and swoon of sound effects; and all those mealy-papered, close-printed books that began with dashes—and took my breath away: "One day in the year 177—, in the village of M—."

My father was David *and* Goliath. Samson *and* The Philistines. Jack *and* the Giant. Daniel *and* the whole damn den.

And to think he had been such a puny kid.

At the time of his Bar Mitzvah, almost fourteen, he was still the shortest in his class. He posed for his photo in cap, knickers, prayer shawl, some tome open on the lectern table beside him; and you can see how he has to hoist his elbow and hitch it up in order to lean against the table. The face is already his face: a mug, a muzzle, a kisser. It's as if he had stuck his head through a hole in a cardboard poster, like those trick shots you take at carnivals and amusement parks.

He sprouted, in the proverbial manner, overnight. It took the rest of him a while to catch up. At the time of his marriage, ten years later, he weighed one-hundred-eighty-five pounds and looked gaunt. Starved. The heavy-boned, hollowed cheeks, the lumpy throat and cliffy brow of the young Abe Lincoln. There are props in this one too; his white bowtie, the white carnation in his buttonhole, the stiff paper cone of his bride's bouquet and the swirling train of her veil (a curtain someone swiped off a window)—all belong to the photographer. Like the studio backdrop they are standing in front of: a waterfall, a stream, frothy bushes, frills of trees. After this is over, after the click, after he yanks his head out of the box, he's going to take it all back.

It was the stock story; told in all those comic books. *Superman, Captain Marvel* (there was a whole *Marvel* family, and I'm not sure but what there may have been a *Marvel* dog), and all the rest, had ordinary everyday identities; but when they tore off their shirts, or their specs, or shouted out the magic word *(Shazam!)* they became their true selves—hero selves—and invincible. A story retold in the smudgy back pages as well. Those ads featuring the famous "97 lb. weakling," in his roomy bathing shorts, with legs like white worms, and two little—oh pitiful little!—dots on his chest. On the beach he is mocked by bullies; they laugh at him and kick sand on his blanket. He sends for the Charles Atlas Course; and the next time those wise guys show up, are they in for a shocker! They get the surprise of their life.

There would be a photo (actual) of Charles Atlas himself; legs solid in skimpy trunks, chest massy, head bowed; looking all in all surprisingly like my father—something grim-lipped, stoical in this self-made strength. What had worked for him could work for you.

Mind Over Matter.

There was a moral to these stories (Is there any one in the world who doesn't know it by heart?) All those pip-squeaking, four-eyed, timorous alter egos; all those heroes who could fly through the air, who laughed at bullets. Escape! Escape from the weak and helpless condition of childhood. Growing up was growing invulnerable. That's what we thought.

My father used to emerge from these struggles victorious. Now it seems from the rattles and sighs and phlegm catching in his throat—those two noisy excavations, his nostrils—that he might be getting the worst of it; taking his lumps, I hear blows.

The room overlooked the entrance to the hospital—three or four stories of pink stucco, sticking out for miles around. The usual landscaping outside the glass doors; grass laid down in patches—squares—rough green toupees; spindly, scantily-clad palms bending and bowing in colored spotlights. (These were buttressed with poles as thin as they were.) And the usual digging seemed to be going on: a new wing being added, the parking lot expanded, white mounds and pits all over the place. Today the holes were water and clay. The roads were still slimy with mud, the grass and fields blubbering with it. Everywhere, stranded tractors, bulldozers, trailers, and the rusty beat-up trucks of the migrant workers. The green peppers stood row on row, polished to ripeness. But the bosses weren't taking any chances on sending their equipment into all that muck; they were afraid of ruining their machinery. They walked up and down in squelching boots, talking here and there to angry pickers. Most of the pickers weren't talking to anybody; not even to each other. They sprawled on the trucks they had come in. Some of them seemed to be wet—soaked to the skin—as if they had spent the night out in the rain. It was their stocking-hats and processed hair, stuck to their heads like large wet leaves.

All along the roads lay frayed flattened shoelaces that turned out to be dead snakes. Hundreds of dead snakes, and pale pink blood-prints.

My father quarreled with his mother. Never mind the whole story—because what's the whole story?—but anyone would have said he was in the right. For all the good. And shouldn't he—of all people—have known better? Who was it who was forever telling me? Might Made Right. Two Wrongs Didn't. Sleeping Dogs Lied.

He had been the dutiful son; he had *shown respect*. (One of the truly mystical phrases of my childhood. I had never *seen* any *respect*.) How was he supposed to know she would make so much of it? Backs turned; doors slammed; telephones banged onto receivers; letters torn up and sent back in shreds.—How was he to know she would die suddenly, the result of a bus accident?

The passengers were taken to the hospital. The

old woman complained of pain, but they said she was only bruised and shaken up, and they sent her home. Some time during the night she tried to get out of bed and a broken rib pierced her lung.

The phone call. The rush to the house. The trucks standing outside. A long red fire truck, a hook-and-ladder, motor running—shuddering—pumping noise by the gallon. The street seemed flooded and dammed.

It was a stone-fronted two-flat with a brief front lawn and on the steps a couple of plaster urns for geraniums. All the doors and windows were open. My father ran up the steps. A fireman in shovel helmet and hip boots was coming out backward, an ax at his belt, carrying one end of something. Black rubber or oil cloth, same as his slicker. Two men were holding up the other end and they shouted directions at him as he came backing and bumping down the stairs.

Keep Going—Watch Out—Easy Does it—Keep Going.

He glanced over his shoulder.

His boots sank in soft mud and sprinkled grass seed.

The next morning I heard my father getting up. He always rose mute, with a mouthful of phlegm, and headed straight for the bathroom—holding up his pants, holding out his lip—looking neither left nor right until he'd had a chance to spit. I heard the floors resounding under his heavy bare feet, then the hoarse rash hawking. First thing he always did.

That had been the hardest blow of my father's life. He told me so himself. (Sometimes he forgets when he's talking to me and when he's not. And who wouldn't get confused, off-and-on, on-and-off, after all these years?) It had been a dark period, he said; it had seemed like a lifetime. Why he would want to pass on such pain; why he should be so bound and determined to inflict this bitterness—I can't say. But we have to pass on something, don't we? Otherwise, what's the good? What are children for?

A plastic bag was slowly slowly seeping light-sap, one clear liquid bead leaked at a time, into a plastic tube. Another, larger bag, clipped to the side of the bed, was sudsing and slushing. His arms over the covers hairy and sunburned; a circle of sunburned skin round his neck. A sprinkle of grizzled hairs—singed, frizzed—they'd crumble if you touched them. The width, the depth of his chest—the rough sheet-blanket stretched across it, arm to arm—seems pretty much what it has always been; the forearms still viny with tendon and vein. But the upper arms and shoulders don't bear the load as they used to, don't pull their own weight. They seem to slope and slump from the humped muscles of the neck.

His hair is cocoon white, and of that texture. It looks frivolous above porous yellow earthworks.

An eyebrow tugs.

A lid lifts.

I see blue.

"Oh, Bet. Well well well. Look who's here. 'Lo, Bet."

His voice is unexpectedly hoarse, almost a whisper.

"So you made it, I see? So you got here all right? Everything all right, then?" An iron door scraping on its hinges. "Where's your mother at?"

A little trouble with the car. I'm not supposed to mention, among other things, cars and floods.

"She's coming. Don't worry. How do you feel?"

"Aw, this? This is nothing. A Rough Customer, that's all."

"But who's the Rough Customer, Daddy? It or you?"

"Oh oh. My daugher's here. She's ribbing me. She's giving me the business."

Still looking at me out of one eye. Lip stiff, as if he has to spit.

There is a deep dent over the bridge of his nose, right between the eyes. From the accident, still? Or is this from his specs? We're used to the spectacles by now; so used to them we forget. We think it's the lenses that make his eyes so blue—blinking—on the brink. The truth of the matter is, the new nose is an improvement. Not so rough-hewn. High-crested, flattened at the top. Abrupt. Abutting. If you'll pardon the expression, a real butte.

I put my hand on the middle of his forehead. (The middle of his forehead is the size of my hand; a slope, a saddle.) Damp but cool, smelling of headsweat. In his mortared face the niche of blue eye is like a glimpse of the sky in whiskered stone walls; monuments or ruins.

I see what it is. I see what it is. With my mother age is a disguise. She puts it on with a wink. (Some joke.) But with my father it is another matter altogether. Age is revealing him; the essential in him; completing the job. It scares me. Hacked, chipped, chiseled—gouged. The mark of the craftsman's hand, the craftsman's tools.

The heavy ridge over each brow smoothed as with the stroke of a thumb.

He doesn't mean it.
This hurts him more than it hurts you.
You know he really loves you.
He's *still* your father!

Who would have thought? That all those things my mother said would turn out to be true.

This is the way my father shows his love.

What's more. What's more. This is the way he feels it.

I saw her coming, her white head moving along briskly with the rhythm of her steps. Florida white. White as gulls' wings. Her arms abrupt and swinging, alternating at her sides. She was wearing slacks and flats and turning out her feet smartly, the way she does. Such conviction in her step I could see the soles of her shoes.

Whaddayaknow. Taps on her toes.

And she shall have music wherever she goes.

I opened the vent. "Here she comes now."

Very distinctly the taps could be heard, singing out on the sidewalk—announcing and identifying. Arms, legs, elbows, shoulders, smooth brown cheekbones, Indianhead-nickel nose—all of her seemed to be pointing one way, heading in the right direction.

My father must have heard the sound, familiar enough to him; and it must have brought to mind what I was seeing. And a whole lot more. Because he shut his eyes and laughed to himself, his chin and his voice in his chest. His thick forehead bunched in a frown, as if it hurt him some, all the same:

"Know her anywhere."

The glass doors glided open; she glided through. Puddles were beginning to gleam in the parking lot. In the colored spotlights the palm trees bent their bundled sheaves. Over the chilled dried racketing of the air conditioner the night air was coming in: mammal warm. You could all but catch it and keep it.

I put my hand out. I shut my eyes too.

Yes. Please. Give them ten years.

Sacred Texts

Alte Bobbe

Charles Angoff

How old she was when she died in 1915 I don't know, and neither does anybody else. Whenever one of her thirteen children, ten grandchildren, and about twenty great-grandchildren asked her for the date of her birth, she would smile and say, "Who knows such things? Only in America they remember birthdays. I was born when the good Czar Alexander II was a little boy, God have mercy on his soul. Don't ask me any more foolish questions."

Her oldest daughter, my grandmother, however, who also didn't know her birthday, once gave her brothers and sisters more detailed information; and on the basis of that, Great-grandmother Jeannette must have been ninety-five at the very least when she died. Very likely she was more than a hundred.

In Yiddish her name was Yente, or Alte Bobbe Yente, Great-grandmother Yente. Her family called her that in Russia and in Boston, until the census man came around in 1910. He asked one of her grandchildren what Yente's name was in English.

She knew hardly any English, but this question she did understand. It made her laugh. "Tell him I'm too old to have an English name," she said.

The census man persisted. He claimed he couldn't put it down just Yente Schneider. Finally an idea struck him. "Why not call her Jeannette?" he asked.

"Jeannette," my great-grandmother repeated and laughed. The census man also laughed, because in those days at least in Boston, Jeannette was a name assumed by girls who thought they were better than they were. For a while the mention of Jeannette would cause guffaws of laughter in the house. Then, for some strange reason, the name lost its potency as a laugh inciter, and great-grandmother became Yente again to her friends, and Alte Bobbe to all her offspring, near and far. It sounded more respectful, yet more familiar. Anyway, I, her oldest and favorite great-grandchild, always called her Alte Bobbe. The name Jeannette never appealed to me. It was at best a joke for grownups, while it lasted, not for us younger fry.

She was short, about five feet two, and she had remarkable bearing to the very end. She weighed only about 100 pounds, walked erect, never wore glasses, and her face was round and kindly and had fewer lines than many women half her age. In accordance with orthodox Jewish rite, her hair was closely shorn and she wore a kerchief instead of a hat. She used a wide variety of kerchiefs, some of them quite colorful, though on Saturdays, Yom Kippur, Rosh Hashanah, and other holidays, she

Alte Bobbe

always wore a pure white woolen kerchief. It gave her a truly angelic appearance. She was meticulously tidy, manicuring her fingernails every Friday afternoon in order to greet the Eve of the Sabbath in a worthy manner.

She lived with her oldest daughter, my grandmother, but she really managed the house as if it were her own. She was not dictatorial, but she took an interest in everything that went on, helping out with the housework wherever possible. As long as she lived, her house was the center of the whole family, including all the relatives. Every one of her children and grandchildren visited her at least once a week, and she visited them at least three times each year: on Rosh Hashanah, Passover, and Chanukah, three important Jewish holidays and feast days. On the first two holidays she would bring sponge cake and a little wine to each family, take a sip of wine, and continue with her visits. On Chanukah she used to carry a bag of pennies and give each of the youngsters two or three cents as a present.

Of course she would visit a family more often if there was need for her services or advice. She settled domestic difficulties, made sure that the children got proper religious training, and occasionally administered to the physical ailments of young and old. As far as I know, she was never ill herself. She was a great believer in sleep as a healer, and after that she put most stress on chicken soup, boiled beef, black bread, and tea. The only three vegetables that made sense to her were potatoes, carrots, and horse-radish. I often heard her say, "If chicken soup and sleep can't cure you, nothing will. They are God's gift to the poor man." She had little respect for doctors, and there was a slight touch of superstition in her. She cured mild colds and toothaches with a knife and magic words. She would make three circles with the knife around the head or throat if the patient suffered with a cold, and around the jaw if the patient had a toothache, touching the skin in each case lightly, and whispering holy Hebrew words as she did so. However, she never relied completely on this magic. She insisted on chicken soup and sleep in addition, saying that the incantation wouldn't work otherwise.

While she made sure that all the children got religious training, she didn't push her piety upon the oldsters. She would never light a match on Saturday or even carry a dish across the street. Both were work, which was forbidden on the Sabbath. But she didn't object to her children and grandchildren going to their jobs on the Sabbath. "God does not want the poor to starve," she would say. "He understands and will forgive." The children and grandchildren returned this consideration by not smoking cigarettes or sewing or doing any other forbidden thing on Saturday in front of her. This pleased her so much that she at times violated her own convictions. Some of her sons and grandsons, she knew, were heavy smokers, and she was sorry that on Friday night they had to abstain on account of her. So around nine o'clock she would say, "Harry, Fishel, don't you want to take a little walk?" They always did. They knew it meant that if they went into the street and had a cigarette or two, it would be all right with her.

My own only religious disagreement with her took place when I was seven years old; she was

Alte Bobbe

then in her late eighties or early nineties. One of my sisters and I had arrived in America with her, in steerage, of course. (My mother and two other children had to remain in Libau, Latvia, for a few months.) As was customary in those days, steerage passengers had to spend a day or more in Ellis Island for medical examination, and some organization sent over baskets of fruit and cookies for the poorer immigrants. Each unit received one or more baskets. I ripped open the basket allotted to us, and was immediately fascinated by a long yellowish object. I examined it from every angle, and the girl who brought the basket peeled it for me. It was a banana, of course, the first I had ever seen. I began to eat it, and offered it to my sister to taste. Whereupon Alte Bobbe seized it from my sister, and turning to me said, "You don't have to be in such a hurry to forget your Judaism." She thought it was pork done up in a special way.

Her advice in the realm of marriage and love helped to smooth out many difficulties. She herself was married at fifteen, and while she thought that was perhaps too early an age, she believed that every girl should have a husband by the time she was eighteen, "A woman must have a man to make up her mind for her," she used to say, "and to give her children." She looked upon childless marriages as a curse. Any family with less than six or seven children was not a real family. She said that in all her life she never knew a woman who was really happy without a flock of her own children.

She had clear and definite ideas about the relationship between husband and wife. I once heard her say to an aunt of mine who complained about her husband, "I don't care what he did or what he said. If there is a quarrel between a wife and her husband, it's always the wife's fault. Look into your heart and change your ways." To the men she spoke with equal plainness, and sometimes with sharpness. To one of them who was a bit of a miser she said, "Yes, they'll erect a golden gravestone in your memory." To another who was mean-tempered and selfish she said, "Consider how small you are. When a fine Jew says, 'Good day,' to another, the other replies, 'A good year to you.' A whole year for one day! You don't even reply, 'Good day.'"

While she lived in this country only six years and knew only a few words of English, she loved America almost from the day she arrived. "A country that has sidewalks," she said, "is God's country. I'm sure there are sidewalks in Heaven," she would add with a smile. The village she came from had no sidewalks. The roads were muddy nearly all year around. She admired President Wilson: "He has so much grace and learning. It's a wonderful country where a professor, a man like that, can become the head. When he makes mistakes, it's only like bad weather. It goes away." Her pet, however, was Louis D. Brandeis, upon whom she looked as a neighbor because he lived in Boston. She said that his face was "like evening on a mountain." For a while she regretted that he didn't have a beard. "A Jew should have a beard, as a mountain should have foliage." But she soon overlooked that. I often think what a pity it was that she didn't live long enough to be told of Brandeis' elevation to the Supreme Court. She would have been thrilled as only a woman in her nineties can be thrilled.

Alte Bobbe

A year or two before she died, she began to weaken perceptibly. I used to walk with her almost every Saturday morning to the synagogue—a journey that meant going down a steep hill and crossing a congested streetcar junction—and I began to notice that she held on to my arm more firmly than before. In the synagogue she used to sit in the balcony, where all women sit in an orthodox synagogue, and I noted that she would doze off occasionally, a thing she had not done previously, to the best of my knowledge. When she returned from the synagogue, she took longer rests before dinner. In the evening she would amble over to the hot water boiler by the coal stove in the kitchen, lean against it for hours, and apparently go to sleep, though she maintained that she heard everything that was said.

Her children pleaded with her to permit Dr. Golden, the family physician, to examine her thoroughly. She would say, "I'll see him. He's a fine man, but I won't let him examine me. There's nothing wrong with me. I'm only a little tired. When my time comes, he won't be able to help. And besides, I've lived long enough. All my children are married happily, and that's all a woman really wants in life. So don't disturb Dr. Golden."

Dr. Golden knew Alte Bobbe very well. He used to talk with her at length when he visited others in the family. Once in a while she'd allow him to put the stethoscope to her heart, but no more. He told the men folk in the family that Alte Bobbe's heart was none too good, that age was beginning to take its toll. A few times he told her to rest more often. She replied, "I'll take a good long rest when I'm dead. You'll die before me with all your medicines. Now tell me how your wife is, and the children. You don't look too good yourself. You should sleep more and have more chicken soup."

The inevitable last day came. She was unable to get up from her bed to wash and go to the front room, where she used to pray by herself before breakfast. She asked her oldest daughter to give her a little tea. She finished the tea and then said, "Call the children. This is the end. I'm not afraid. Don't you be afraid. It's God's will. I thank God I am dying in my own house, with all my children around, and in a good country, where Jews are treated like human beings. I'm sorry I'm not leaving anything of value. I make only two requests: remember me every year by burning a lamp on this my last day, and put a picture of the whole family in my coffin." The entire family had had a group picture taken two years before, at her suggestion.

Her oldest daughter protested such talk.

Alte Bobbe said, "Do as I tell you."

We all came over as soon as possible, some thirty of us, young and old. Dr. Golden was also called. He examined her. She did not object. After the examination he walked out of Alte Bobbe's bedroom, his eyes red. Three, four hours later Alte Bobbe died, fully conscious to the end and as peacefully as anybody could have wished. Her two oldest sons picked her up from the bed and put her down on the floor, in accordance with orthodox Jewish custom, and placed two candles at her head. All of us then walked by her and asked her to plead for us in the other world. My turn came, and I said the Hebrew words my mother told me. I wasn't afraid. Alte Bobbe looked the same as I had always known her, calm, kindly, and as beautiful as snow on a hill not far away. I saw the family picture by her feet. I was inexpressibly glad I was in it, and I always will be.

The Retired Gentlemen

Molly Berg

Grandpa Mordecai had been drinking schnapps since he was ten years old. By the time he was eleven it was a habit. He needed his few drinks a day just as some people need their coffee. It wasn't that he was addicted. I suppose he could have done without it if he wanted to—but he didn't want to. He took four drinks a day; that was his ration. As he got older the doctors told him to stop; his wife begged him to stop; and after she died the government took over. They declared prohibition.

Grandpa was a great believer in the law. If the government said you couldn't buy schnapps, so all right, you couldn't buy it. But! Where was it written that you couldn't make it? If you showed him in black and white that there was a law against making liquor, he wouldn't believe you anyway. The government had better things to do than to torment him.

Grandpa's retirement and the Eighteenth Amendment came at about the same time. The retirement left him with lots of time on his hands. And prohibition gave him a hobby, a cause, a project, to amuse him in his old age. At that time his children had all grown up and got married. He was seventy and a grandfather many times. So he moved from the empty house in Jersey City and took a small apartment on the Lower East Side, near Norfolk Street. The apartment was on the first floor. He didn't like to admit that he was getting old. He had a tacit understanding with age: he paid no attention to it and hoped maybe it would go away. But four flights of stairs was a little too much even for him. Also the apartment he took had a nice large closet.

Grandpa took some bits of copper pipe, his tools, his imagination, and his thirst and built a still. He made his own schnapps from everything and anything that sounded good: potatoes, raisins, grapes, prunes. If it could ferment, it went into the still. The still worked, and he liked what came out of it.

There was always a fragrance about Grandpa's apartment when he was in the process of making a new supply for himself. Sometimes I would visit him in the middle of one of these operations. I loved to tease him about what was going on in his closet.

"What are you cooking, Grandpa?" I would say to him when I came in.

"Cooking? A little prunes for stewing."

"They smell very good."

"For prunes they're all right. Roses they're not."

"Prunes they're not, either."

"A couple there are."

The Retired Gentlemen

"For schnapps?"

"What do you think? Soda water?"

And then, very carefully so as not to disturb what he called "the works," he would open the closet door and let me look. There, on the upper closet shelf, was a hot plate. On top of the plate was a copper kettle he built. Attached to the kettle was a shiny coil of copper tubing that looked very scientific. The tubes coiled downward to the lower shelf and the end of the tube was fitted into a glass jug where a colorless liquid dripped slowly. The only sound was a constant faint "plop, plop" as the schnapps filled the jug.

"A little drink maybe?" he asked, knowing that I wasn't that brave. I always said, "No," and he always said, "A young girl like you shouldn't drink anyhow." No matter how old I got I was always a young girl to Mordche and that saved me from hurting his feelings and gave me the excuse I needed to refuse his very special four-star product.

Grandpa was a sociable man and he didn't like to drink alone. Everybody who knew him knew that and it saved Grandpa the trouble of inviting people to his apartment. People just dropped in. Because of all the comings and goings it didn't take long for everybody on the block to know that Mordche was making his own schnapps. Even the landlord found out that Mr. Edelstein was using the premises not as per the words in the lease and he came storming in to put a stop to it. The landlord, a Mr. Stone, was a little man with a big sense of responsibility for other people's business. If he was a little late with the heat in the morning, that was all right. If someone was a little late with the rent, that was not so all right. He knocked on Grandpa's door and as soon as the door opened Mr. Stone became a moralist.

"Mr. Edelstein," he said, "I'm surprised at you!"

"Mr. Stone," Grandpa said, "come in. You'll catch a draft in the cold hall. What's the surprise?"

"There's a still in this apartment!"

"That's the surprise? For that you're huffing and puffing?"

"It's against the law, Mr. Edelstein!"

"Have a little drink, Mr. Stone?"

"How could you do such a thing?"

"Mr. Stone, I'll ask you a question? You have a little drink sometimes?"

Mr. Stone said he took a little drink once in a while, but just to be sociable.

"So where does the drink come from, Mr. Stone?" Grandpa asked him and answered for him. "From bootleggers, from gangsters, from public enemies, no?" Mr. Stone couldn't disagree so Grandpa became the moralist. "Shame yourself, Mr. Stone," Grandpa told him. "I'm surprised," and he shook a finger at the poor little accused man, and the more Mr. Stone tried to point out that a still wasn't legal, the more Grandpa accused him of dealing with gangsters. It wasn't more than five minutes before Mr. Stone was practically an uncle to a rum runner. Grandpa, according to Grandpa, was doing his patriotic duty by having a still in his closet and once he got Mr. Stone to agree that having a little drink every once in a while was part of human nature he also got him to agree that making whisky was better than buying from crooks. Grandpa's version was that Mr. Stone had a drink and then apologized.

The Retired Gentlemen

Being a retired gentleman, Grandpa spent his winters in Daytona Beach with his sister and her family. During prohibition this winter trip was something of a problem for him. His sister, Channa Beana, Channa for Anna and Beana for Beatrice, was a very strict lady. To her, when the government made a law, it was a law. There was no drinking in her house.

Within the same family you couldn't have found two more different people than Grandpa and his sister. He was tall, broad, and by now in his sixties he was beginning to look like Mark Twain with a full, white mustache, flowing white hair, bushy eyebrows, and, in the summer, a Panama hat. Channa Beana was tiny, delicate, like a good-natured but very busy bird. She drank tea. Before prohibition she didn't mind when the men of the family had a little drink. But now the government had said, "No." To her there was no place even for a little "Yes."

Channa Beana knew her brother. She was positive that Mordche was getting his daily drink from someplace. When letters came from up North telling her about the still, she was impressed by his ingenuity but shocked by his nerve. She called it *chutzpa*, which is more than nerve; it's closer to having a hole in the character than just being brave. Channa Beana wrote her brother a letter before he was due for his visit.

Dear Mordche,
You are very welcome to come for the winter and to stay with me and mine. Stay as long as you like. Don't bring the still. I am very good friends with all

the people in Daytona Beach. You know what I am talking about.

> Your loving sister,
> *Channa Beana.*

Grandpa wrote back:

Dear Sister,

Thank you for the invitation. I'll be very happy to come. I will not bring the still.

> Your loving brother,
> *Mordche.*

Grandpa loved his sister. He would never tell her an untruth. He said he wouldn't bring the still, so he wouldn't. But love or no love, he couldn't change the habits of a lifetime just one, two, three. Of course, there was no harm in promising not to bring the still—it was too big anyway. But there must be another way, and if there was, Grandpa would find it. He thought about the problem, and then he found the solution. He took an old leather valise and lined it with copper. It wasn't an easy job, but it was a labor of love. When the valise was filled with his latest vintage, he was ready for his vacation. Grandpa and his schnapps went south.

Channa Beana never found out about the contents of the suitcase. Grandpa wouldn't have hurt her for the world. So he kept his secret and the suitcase to himself. For a sociable man that must have been very hard. It meant that he had to have his four drinks a day alone. Luckily his room had a mirror. The way Grandpa told the story, when he took a drink he could look at himself in the mirror, raise his glass, say "Lachaim," and have a little

The Retired Gentlemen

company. The drink made him feel like a new man. So he had to toast the new man with another *lachaim*. And that's the way the winter passed, with plenty of company.

When prohibition was finally repealed, Grandpa put the suitcase back in the closet. His still was taken apart and stored, just in case. What had happened once could always happen again. Mordecai prided himself on always learning by experience.

If Grandpa was ever alone, it was when he was walking from one man's house to another's. Even when he lived by himself in later years there was always somebody to talk to or to have a little drink with. If it wasn't a friend, it was a parrot, a cat, a dog, or a fish. The names he gave his animal friends were the result of a simple logic. The parrot he called "Polly," the dog he called "Dog," the cat was called "Cat," and the fish, two of them, were called "Ike" and "Mike." He always used both names, Ike Fish and Mike Fish.

The parrot never learned to talk, but it got to be very good at listening. Grandpa would tell Polly stories about what had happened to him during the day. The bird's main use, however, was as a third person, a judge who was supposed to arbitrate Grandpa's arguments with his friends.

One of Grandpa's favorite people to argue with was Joe Shuster. Grandpa had known Mr. Shuster since they were both children and the two of them had been arguing since the cradle. There were two things Grandpa found to argue about with Mr. Shuster. The first was that Shuster had changed his name. In Lublin the family was known as Shuister and when they came to America Joe dropped the "i" and picked up a fight with Mordche. The second thing that Grandpa didn't like was that Joe Shuster kept saying he was younger than he really was. Instead of saying he was seventy he said he was sixty-eight and Mordche resented it. Mordche's whole object was to make Joe Shuster say he was seventy. It was a matter of honor and Grandpa finally did it with the parrot and a little subtlety. Mordche's idea of being subtle was to invite Mr. Shuster to his apartment, give him a drink, make him comfortable, and then ignore him. He talked only to the parrot and the way Grandpa told it the parrot was the Supreme Court and he was Emile Zola.

"Polly," he said he said, "how many years do I know this man?"

Mr. Shuster saw what was going to be. "Don't start Mordche," he said.

"To you I'll talk later, Shuster," Grandpa said and kept on talking to the bird. "I know him already seventy years, Polly," and he held up seven fingers so that the parrot would be able to understand.

"Mordche, please! The bird has to know everything? She's a stranger!"

"You're ashamed yourself, Shuster?"

"What's to be ashamed?"

"Listen, Polly, when does a boy become a man?"

"Mordche! How should a bird in a cage know such things!"

"Don't worry. A boy becomes a man when he has a *bar mitzvah*. You had a *bar mitzvah*, Shuster?"

"Of course."

"You know where, Polly?"

"The bird knows geography?"

"In Lublin, Polly. . . ."

"Some smart bird, Mordche. So far I haven't heard one word."

"Polly, you know when I had my *bar mitzvah*? No? When I was thirteen."

"What do you want from life, Mordche?"

"You know who was with me when I was *bar mitzvahed*? Shuster! So how old were you, Shuster?"

"Ask the bird."

"Thirteen, no?"

"So?"

"So! Polly if I was thirteen and he was thirteen and today I'm seventy, so how old is Shuster?"

"The bird is Einstein, he can add?"

"Better than you. . . ."

"Mordche, please. . . ."

"Joe Shuster, me you can tell, and believe me, the bird wouldn't say one word."

Mr. Shuster finally said he was seventy and the only other people in the whole world besides Mordche and Polly who knew were my mother, my father, and myself. Mordche had to have somebody to talk to about his victory. After all, how much can you say to a parrot?

Grandpa had his differences with everyone he knew. Sooner or later somebody was bound to do or say something he didn't like. And then Polly, and sometimes myself, would hear about it.

Many times members of the family borrowed money from Mordecai. He was always willing to lend, the only condition he ever placed on a loan being that it should be repaid, and in a family this can lead to some terrible resentments. One particular relative took his time about repaying a loan, and Mordecai got mad. Since I had a husband by that time and should know a little about life, he would talk it over with me and ask my advice, which he didn't need because he had already decided what to do: He was going to court and let the law decide who was in the right. He would describe to me exactly what he was going to wear to court—his working clothes, his overalls. In this role of a poor working man he was going to walk right up to the bench and say: "Judge, Your Honor, sir, look at me. I'm a poor old man. Out of the goodness of my heart I loaned this man money. You tell me, you are a judge of people, is this right or is this wrong? Should he or should he not pay me back? Last week he bought his wife a fur coat while I haven't even an overcoat to wear in the winter months. Tell me, Judge, Your Honor, do I need a lawyer to plead my case?"

He was positive that there was no judge or court in the land that could resist his dramatic plea for justice. Probably he could have won his case, but he never went to court with it. Once a year, at least, he would rehearse his courtroom drama for me, and then decide to forget it for another year. The relative never paid him back. I think it would have spoiled Grandpa's fun if he had.

One case did get to court. Grandpa retinned a whole roof on the house of a lady-in-law. He repaired the ventilators too and fixed the cornices. When he finished he handed in his bill. She refused to pay. She said it wasn't a good job. That was the last thing in the world to say to Mordche, the Tinsmith. Maybe you didn't like him, maybe you just postponed paying him, but you never said he did a bad job. He sued. First the case was taken up before each member of the family, but Grandpa absolutely refused to have it settled out of court. He prepared his case without a lawyer by making two models, each about three feet high and exact replicas of the house he had fixed. One model was before, and the other after. When the case was tried, Grandpa showed the two models to the judge and made him a speech. He told the judge among other things that if he didn't believe him it was a good job, he should go up to 97th Street and Lexington Avenue and take a look at the building himself.

Grandpa won his case, without the judge going up to Lexington Avenue and 97th Street to take a look at his craftsmanship. He was vindicated. He told Polly all about his triumph. Then he solemnly swore to her that he would never fix that woman's house again—not that it would ever need fixing, because, he assured Polly, when Mordche Blecher fixed something, it stayed fixed.

The Gift Horse

Judith K. Liebmann

What can I tell you? My grandmother never locked her door.

"But Bubba," I'd say, "they come and pick the place clean on a regular basis."

"So, David-the-boy-genius," she would answer, impatient. "You think a few locks make a difference? They get in just the same, with their special keys and their tricks. Look at Salowitz. So many locks it takes her an hour just to get into her house or get out. Always the newest model she gets, and what good does it do? No good it does. Ha! Some day they'll catch her with a bag of garbage, on her way to the incinerator, in her bathrobe like she always is, and they'll sneak in behind her and lock her out. That way they can take their time. So that's better?"

This was her reasoning and there was no sense arguing with her. Even Salowitz gave up after a while, though never completely. She'd still take a stab, if she caught her waiting at the elevator or at the washing machine in the basement.

"You'll be sorry, Miss Know-it-all," she'd say. "You'll tempt fate once too often, mark my words. God watches over those who watch over themselves. He's not gonna bother with a stubborn old lady who don't care enough to take precautions."

To my grandmother, Salowitz was a coward, a busybody and a yente. "Like an onion she is, that grows with its head in the ground. She thinks if you put ten locks on your door and carry a baseball bat in your shopping cart, though you can't even lift it with your skinny arms like sticks, then they'll leave you alone. Look at her. A pile of sticks she is inside those schmattes. Who's she gonna scare off? Nobody, that's who. She got it backwards. The truth is, if you let people have what they want, they take, and then they leave you alone. That's the way it is. A way of making things come out even, so nobody gets too much and nobody gets too little."

This sounded to me just like something my grandfather would have said. When he was alive Bubba would shake her head over his wild ideas. Now she sounded just like him. He was a socialist. A communist really. He kept telling everybody who'd listen his Marxist theories and the advantages of sharing as the basis for society. This was a terrible thing in the eyes of his family and everybody else, too. He had a bunch of cronies, old men in black suits and beards who would come to the apartment and sit at the wooden table in the dining room, drinking tea and eating my grandmother's herring salad and strudel, talking and arguing, endlessly, in Yiddish. To them he was a traitor to the Jewish religion and to America. That didn't keep them from coming, though. They came and drank tea and ate, and called my grandfather names. They are all dead now, like him, and their families moved away, like ours.

Now Bubba was left, the only one, living up to his theories. There was even some truth to what she was saying. Salowitz was broken into just as much as Bubba. She called in the police every time and made terrible scenes. But Bubba just shrugged and let it pass over her. They kept coming, picking over whatever was left from the last time, taking even the toaster and the electric wall clock with two yellow roosters on it from the kitchen and finally, out of frustration not meanness my grandmother said, even the souvenirs—kewpie dolls and enamel ashtrays with pictures of the parachute jump and the roller coaster on them—that my grandfather had won half a century ago shooting ducks in the Coney Island arcades.

She never replaced what they took. Just adapted her ways and got along with whatever they left.

"What I need, I got," she would say, and I guess it was true, though the apartment got emptier and to me it seemed like she was shrinking her life down to fit the emptiness. Or maybe she was just getting old and her needs were shrinking and shriveling up like her body.

There was one thing, though, she kept getting new. The television. It was always on, never too loud, in the corner of the living room, all day and all night, sometimes in color and sometimes black and white. I asked her once how she could just keep buying all those TV sets, some of them big, fancy things.

"I got a connection," she said.

"What connection?" I wanted to know.

"A connection. It's like recycling. You're all excited about recycling, saving your bottles and tin cans and newspapers like a junk man. So we recycle TVs. They take mine out, I get one they took from someone else. I got a connection. It doesn't cost too much. It works out fine."

It went on like that for years. The neighborhood got worse and worse and everyone but Salowitz and my grandmother moved out. The apartment got emptier and emptier. After a while, they just stopped coming to take things. Even the television sets got recycled less often. Maybe the word got out that there wasn't anything left in 4B to bother about except a hot TV. The door was still open, but there just wasn't anything inside worth going in for.

So they left her alone then, pretty much. She would sit all day long on the worn-out green sofa they'd left her, between two floor lamps from Kresge's, with her feet dangling down not quite to the floor and her hands clasped in her lap, the TV blinking but the sound turned low. She really began to look old to me then, with her thin, white hair and her tiny face wrinkled up, and her skin like a piece of paper you roll up in a ball and spread out again. Her eyes seemed to fade and film over, and she just didn't seem to pay attention to things any more.

The biggest event in her life was the Friday night visit to our house. I'd drive down to get her after school. I liked the ride to her house, on the Bronx River Parkway. You drive along next to the river, and even in winter there are ducks and geese on

The Gift Horse

the grass, and the woods that you go through make everything quiet. Then even before you get into the Bronx, it all starts to change. The city spreads out and the ugliness grows like a fungus, eating up everything, leaving the burned-out buildings and broken glass and the dirty billboards and boarded-up stores. I was the only one who went there. My mother stopped going a long time ago, not because she was scared, she said, just depressed to see what had happened to the place where she grew up. She always imagined the worst, even worse than it was, and was always trying to make Bubba leave and move in with us.

"You'll get killed one of these days," she would say, "or you'll die of starvation. I won't set foot in that jungle. You're crazy to stay there."

"If I'm crazy, so let me be crazy. What should I run from?" Bubba would answer. "I had my life, what difference which way it ends. As long as it's in my own house where I'm my own boss, I don't care when or how it should be over. Now leave me alone and light the candles."

The argument was part of the ritual, and they both knew nothing would come of it. Bubba was stubborn, and in a way even my mother knew she was right. What would she do living with us? None of us was home during the day, and you needed a car to get around. At home, Bubba could walk everywhere. She knew her way around, and everybody knew Bubba. I have to admit, I don't think any of us really thought something awful would happen to her. We thought she would just kind of waste away, she ate so little and got so skinny.

I'm sure that's the way it would have been, too, if

it hadn't been common knowledge how she never locked her door. I mean, that's how it happened that Siserene and the baby came into her life in the first place. One afternoon Bubba came home from shopping and found them, Siserene and Roy Little, asleep on the green velvet couch.

"There they were," Bubba told me, "like a pile of Tootsie Roll candy."

Siserene was lying on her back on the bottom, in shorts and a halter, and the baby on top, on his stomach, his fat little arms and his fat little legs hanging down.

So what could she do? She went and got a chair from the kitchen and put it next to the couch and sat down and watched Siserene and the baby and waited. She just sat there and watched them, she told me, the way you can watch people when they are asleep. She looked at them carefully, at the baby's fat little cheek pushed to the side by the swell of his mother's stomach, and the little mouth, like a rosebud, and the shiny blister inside it from sucking his bottle. She touched Siserene's hair, a short curly mat, and was surprised at how soft it was, not scratchy the way she'd imagined, and let herself stroke the fudge-brown skin of Siserene's face.

Finally Bubba got up and went into the kitchen to put away the groceries she had bought. Siserene had put a carton of milk and a baby-bottle half full of juice in the ice-box, its cap screwed on a bit crooked so it took on a jaunty appearance. An assortment of boxes of instant pablum and jars of baby food stood on the counter and on the floor was a box of disposable diapers, torn open, one of them pulled half-way out. All the boxes and jars had the same picture of a blue-eyed, smiling baby on them.

Bubba straightened the cap on the juice bottle and went back to sit again in the chair by the couch.

Much later Siserene opened her eyes.

"What you lookin' at, Mrs. G.?"

"So? Looking hurts?"

"What you gonna do?"

"What's to do? I notice you put in supplies."

"I gotta stay here a while." Siserene hitched herself up against the arm of the couch. The baby still clung to her, sleeping. "Gotta stay outta sight, Mrs. G. Got myself in a real fix this time." She shook her head and started rocking back and forth. "Ooooh Je-sus. Ooooh, shit."

My grandmother just sat there without saying a word. Siserene stopped her rocking. "Don' you wanna know what happen?"

"You want to stay, you can stay. The first time something comes in the door instead of going out, I'm not gonna look a gift horse in the mouth."

"Jus' like that?"

Bubba nodded.

"Listen. This here is a *serious* problem. You got no idea what you gettin' yo'self into." Siserene swung her legs around, hoisted Roy Little up with one arm, and leaned over, putting her face a few inches in front of Bubba's. "Sea Cat, he after me," she hissed. "Oh Lord! He say he gon' kill me!" She sank back again into the couch. "He find out I been cuttin' out on him with Tally, you know, the numbers guy in the Take-Out. Charlene, from upstairs with the four kids, she call me up an' tell me how Sea Cat he come in all fired up, fumin' and carryin' on like crazy, callin' me names an' tellin' everybody how he gon' teach me a lesson. As if that nappy-headed, thin-brained son-of-a-bitch knew anything worth passin' on. Hah!

"Anyways, after he finished screamin' an' rantin' he took out this big long knife an' he sit down an' lay the knife across his knees, an' he wait. When Tally come in, Sea Cat let out a whoop an' go after him. Cut him up pretty awful, Charlene say. The others, they finally pull him away, an' then he start screamin' 'bout how he gonna come an' find me an' kill me, too, shoutin' how he gonna go after me now, an' Roy Little here, 'cause he sure Roy Little ain't his, but he is I swear it.

"Charlene, she run an' call me up when she hear that. She say I better not let him find me. So I get a few things and I grab the baby and I start goin' down the stairs. I ain't got very far, when I hear him comin' up, screamin', 'Where's that bitch, where's that fuckin' bitch.' I jus' stood there, sure it was all over for me now. But then, then it come into my head how Mrs. G. never lock up—so I quick run in here, jus' in time."

Roy Little, who had slept through his mother's entire story, woke up as soon as she finished, roused perhaps by the sudden silence, and began to cry.

"He'll hear him, he'll hear him," Siserene yelled and clapped her hand over his mouth.

"No he won't," Bubba said, and took up Roy Little from the couch. She carried him into the kitchen, got the juice bottle from the ice-box and settled him onto her lap. "A baby is a baby," she explained later, and while he wrapped his baby fingers around her thumb, she sang one of those songs I remember her singing to me years ago, *Oif'n pripetshok brent a fayerl.* . . .

Siserene came in after a while and sat down at the kitchen table. She listened, nodding her head.

"I like the tune alright," she laughed, "but I can't make head or tail of what it say."

So my grandmother told her about the little rabbi sitting on the oven tiles to keep warm, telling stories and teaching the alphabet, and Siserene liked it well enough to learn the words, and though her inflection wasn't quite right and she had a bit of trouble getting the ch's gutteral enough, she was a good mimic and soon she was singing the whole thing, in a big, dusky contralto that filled the kitchen. Siserene was a real singer, it turned out, doing church solos on Sunday mornings and an occasional late-night show at small-time local clubs, and Bubba couldn't get enough of hearing her sing. They sat there for hours that first afternoon. Bubba taught Siserene "Rozhenkes mit mandlen" and Siserene had my grandmother singing "Gon' up Yonder" and "Big Feelin' Blues," which she rendered, much to Siserene's delight and despite a slight Yiddish lilt, with real gusto.

That's how it happened that they set up housekeeping together. At first they made do with the little my grandmother had, because Siserene was so scared that she wouldn't go near her own apartment. They made a bed for the baby in a cardboard carton and Siserene slept on the couch, in a nightgown my grandmother lent her, that she filled like a sausage.

These makeshift arrangements were fine for a while, but after the first few days, when things started taking on the appearance of being long-term, my grandmother decided, in spite of Siserene's pleading, to go up to the apartment and bring down a few necessities. She brought some clothes for Siserene, some of the baby's things, and some extra dishes and pots.

She especially needed those, because as Siserene and Roy Little moved in, Bubba started cooking again. She started making all the dishes I remembered from years ago, like potato pudding, tsimmes, and stuffed breast of veal. I could smell the good things in the hall when I went like always to pick her up for Friday night dinner. She still came, because she didn't want my mother to find out about Siserene. The whole time Siserene lived with her, Bubba never said a word to my parents. We never even discussed it, and I joined the conspiracy as a matter of course. She'd stay overnight, like always, and then I'd take her back on Saturday after breakfast.

With all the shopping she was doing now, it made sense for her to wait and do it with me on Saturday. We went to the Co-op on Siskin Street, three blocks away. I couldn't believe how much she would buy. Sometimes we would fill the shopping cart and I'd have to maneuver a second. At first I would try to make her buy less, but she just went on aisle after aisle, loading up the bags and boxes and cans, stopping at the meat counter for long discussions about the relative quality of this piece or that, making them cut things special for her, scolding them if something didn't meet her standards. She'd squeeze and sniff at the fruit and vegetables, and check every bottle of milk to make sure it wasn't after the fresh date. By the time she headed for the check-out counter, like a queen at the end of a state visit, the whole store knew she had been there. The funny thing was, they didn't seem to mind. She enjoyed it so much, the abundance of all that carefully, lovingly chosen food, and the clerks and butcher enjoyed it with her. "I got something special for you today," they would say. Or, "Wait, I just got some in fresh, let me get it from the back."

My grandmother took pleasure in every detail of that weekly shopping trip, but the best part of all was when we got home. We'd line up the bags on the floor, and all of us, Siserene and Roy Little and Bubba and me, we'd unpack it all and lay it out on the table, and Bubba would praise each piece as if it were a work of art. "Just look at that pepper," she'd say. "Did you ever see such a green?" Or she'd roll a grapefruit on the floor to where Roy Little was sitting and tell him how round and yellow and juicy it was. He would laugh, and Siserene would laugh with him, and then we'd all laugh, even Bubba.

As time went by, and they got used to each other, and they eased into or around each other's rhythms, and Roy Little started calling my grandmother "Bubba," their life took on a comfortable feeling of habit. When they weren't busy in the kitchen, Bubba cooking up something, chopping onions or liver or stuffing a chicken, and the two of them singing some song in Yiddish or belting out a Bessie Smith blues, and Roy Little chewing on whatever tidbits Bubba found for him, then they would play cards, poker mostly, but also gin rummy and pinochle. They were both very serious about their card playing, and they'd sit for hours, each with a heap of pennies on the table, smaller or larger depending on whose luck was running that day, not saying a word except for a bid here and there or a grunt when somebody showed a winning hand or completed a trick. Otherwise they watched TV or played with the baby.

Of course, things weren't perfect. It was really hard to Siserene to be cooped up all day and not be able to go out, so it wasn't surprising she had some low times, too. She'd sit sometimes in front of the living-room window, looking out at the garbage-littered courtyard and up at the patch of sky that showed between the buildings, singing in a melancholy voice.

> Picked up my bags, baby, and I tried it again,
> Picked up my bags, baby, and I tried it again;
> I got to make it, I've got to find the end,
> It's a long old road, but I know
>   I'm gonna find the end.

But she still wouldn't dare to go out, though sometimes she'd go up to the roof at night for a breath of fresh air. Whenever Bubba went out on an errand, to stop for a couple of items she may have forgotten on a Saturday shopping trip or to cash Siserene's welfare check at Walgreen's, she'd report back every detail—the weather, the people she'd met, any gossip she'd heard, Mrs. Salowitz's latest doomsday warning. Charlene came by a lot, too, to pick up Roy Little and take him out for a walk, or to leave off a couple of her own just to keep him company. But I think it was still pretty hard on Siserene, especially at first.

The Gift Horse

Once the cold weather came, and it got dark early, she didn't sit at the window so much. It was also around that time she started cooking, out of homesickness she said, adding her own specialties to Bubba's cuisine, cooking up a mess of collards to go with the braised flanken, or corn cakes and black-eyed peas for the roast chicken, and, after Bubba had locked herself in the bathroom to discuss the matter with the Almighty and had gotten his OK, ham hocks to go with the kasha varnishkas, and chittelings to nibble while they watched TV. After that she didn't seem to have much time left for feeling blue.

The result of all the shopping and cooking and eating was that Siserene and the baby got fatter and fatter and Bubba filled out so much even my mother stopped telling her she was starving. Not that Bubba's new robustness and apparent satisfaction made my parents any less anxious about her. In fact, it seemed to me, the better Bubba looked the more my parents put on the pressure for her to leave the old neighborhood. They cited every newspaper report of a mugging, and were particularly thorough about retelling stories of rape and torture of the elderly. The worst part was that instead of wanting Bubba to move in with us, they started talking about nursing homes.

"It's like paradise, Ma," my mother would say. "You don't have to do a thing. Everything's taken care of—your meals, cleaning, everything. And there are plenty of people there to make friends—play cards, sit in the garden. Much better than where you are."

But Bubba wouldn't hear of it. She'd sit there,

looking rosy and sleek, nodding her head a bit to show she was listening but refusing to be drawn into any discussion.

"I'm fine where I am, enough already," she'd finally say, putting an end to my mother's entreaties, at least for the moment.

My mother didn't give up, though. She started asking her friends about all the places they had put their parents, even visited the ones that sounded good, and wrote away for information to scores of others. Brochures on "Sunnyview Meadows" and "Vista View" piled up on the kitchen counter. It wasn't until Passover, though, that things seemed to turn serious. And it was partly Bubba's fault.

I don't know what put it into her head, but she was convinced that Roy Little would be a terrific guest for the Seder. I tried to tell her that the tradition of inviting strangers to the Seder celebration didn't usually include fifteen-month-old black babies, but she was as stubborn as ever. She told my mother she was going to bring "a poor baby from the neighborhood," and that was that.

It might even have turned out okay, if Bubba hadn't gone too far. I could see it coming, watching her sip away at the wine until her face was bright pink, and the way she winked at me when everyone else was too busy reading the Haggadah to notice. It was hard to keep a straight face, I can tell you, with everybody looking so pious with their noses in the books and my pink-faced grandmother winking at me over Roy Little's black, curly head.

They didn't keep their noses in the books for long though, not once Roy Little started fussing a bit and Bubba started to sing to him. "It's hard to love another woman's man," she began in a whisper. "It's hard to love another woman's man." The whisper got louder. "You can't git him when you want him, you got to catch him when you can." Bubba's voice rose up, sweet with a hard edge, and my family sat there listening open-mouthed. "Have you ever seen peaches grow on sweet potato vine. Have you ever seen peaches grow on sweet potato vine—yes, step in my backyard, and take a peep at mine." She finished with a shake of her shoulders and a chuckle.

For my mother this was the final straw. She was convinced Bubba was going crazy and started screaming about putting her away. Bubba lost her temper, too, and yelled at my mother that she was the crazy one, thinking she could run everybody's life for them. I've never seen Bubba so angry. She muttered and trembled and cursed all the way back in the car, and threatened not to come any more on Friday nights, just to be insulted.

They both stayed angry this time, my mother watching for any more signs of Bubba's "senility" and Bubba tight-lipped and unforgiving. Things were going to come to a head, I knew, so I can't help feeling that what happened, awful as it was, came just in time. And out of the blue. I mean, nobody had seen Sea Cat since the day he killed Tally. The police never showed much interest, but everyone knew the guys Tally worked for wouldn't let Sea Cat get away with it. It would have been suicide for him to hang around the neighborhood. Somebody told Charlene he went back to Georgia, and somebody told her he went to stay with his brother in Detroit.

So nobody was expecting him.

I didn't know what to think when I came for

Bubba on Friday and saw the police cars outside and Salowitz standing there with a wild look in her eyes.

"Don't go up! Don't go up!" she wailed when she saw me, wrapping her skinny arms around me like a vine. "It's terrible, terrible. You can't go up there."

I unwound her arms and she folded up onto the front stoop and sat there weaving back and forth. "I kept telling her, lock your door, keep to yourself, don't tempt fate. Would she listen? No. Stubborn like a mule always. Oy, oy. Now look what she's done."

I went in and took the elevator up. The policeman in front of 4B wouldn't let me in at first. He told me I should get my mother or father to come down. But Charlene spoke up and we convinced him.

They had left Sea Cat's body where they found it. He was lying face-down on the living room floor, his arms and legs spread-eagled, one hand still holding a long thin-bladed knife. The muscles of his shoulders stuck out like eggplants from the sleeves of his tee shirt, and the right side of his head had a dent in it, as if someone had stepped on it. Next to him, outlined in white chalk, Bubba's iron meat grinder lay on the floor, still coated with scraps of the onions she must have been chopping when she threw it at him. There was hardly any blood, except around the dent in Sea Cat's head and a little smeared on the edge of the funnel of the grinder.

What more can I tell you? Bubba was sitting in the kitchen with the other two policemen, each of whom had a glass of milk and a piece of apple strudel on a plate in front of him. Bubba waved me into the kitchen, and introduced me as her grandson-who's-going-to-college-in-the-Fall-and-shouldn't-be-upset-because-she-had-no problem-taking-care-of-the-burglar-*all-by-herself*-and-everything-was-fine. I got the message and kept my mouth shut about Siserene and Roy Little, who'd gone back to the old apartment upstairs. They figured it would be better all around if Siserene didn't get involved in the whole furor, and I guess they were right.

As it turned out, Bubba became quite a celebrity. Even my mother had every neighbor she could find watching the evening news that night. Nobody talked about "Soundview Acres" any more, and for years the front page of the *New York Post* hung like a souvenir on the wall above the kitchen table:

GRANNY
BEANS
BURGLAR

and under the headline a picture of Bubba smiling.

The Prayer Shawl

Gloria Goldreich

Their father grew old suddenly and sadly and they were oddly unprepared for it. They spoke to each other worriedly on the phone, and their voices trembled as though they had been mysteriously betrayed. Richard, the older brother, was a psychiatrist and his voice was measured and reasonable when he counselled families who came to him swollen with anger and grief because a father had Alzheimer's, a child was suicidal, a sister betrayed a dangerous depression. He sat erect in his brown leather chair and offered them suggestions and alternatives. But when his brother, Alan, and his sister, Miriam, phoned to discuss their father, he felt his tongue grow thick and he slid down in his seat and played fretfully with his silver pen.

"I should have expected it," Miriam said. "Why should I have thought that he was different from the others?"

"The others" were their aunts and uncles, their in-laws and their parents' friends who had succumbed slowly to the melancholy infirmities of age. Their hearing faded, their eyes grew weak, they moved with difficulty. Their father's brother, Uncle Avram, who had swung them high above his head when he visited and wept openly at their graduations, could no longer remember their names when he died. The sister and brothers went to too many funerals with their faces masked in sadness but their hearts light with relief.

But their father was different, as he had always been different. He had, it seemed to them, grown stronger with each passing year, and Richard, who spoke with authority on such matters, confirmed that some men achieve a new vibrancy when they are freed from the routine of work, the responsibility of family. His hearing was keen and his blue eyes, the color of a burnished beryl, were often dangerously bright. Miriam thought it sad that of all her father's children and grandchildren, only Richard's autistic son had inherited the glinting sharpness of their father's eyes.

He read two newspapers each day and sent them clippings about tax shelters and nutrition. He circled articles on the real estate page for Alan whose law firm handled condominium and co-op conversions. Once every two weeks he walked to the Sheepshead Bay branch of the Brooklyn Public Library where the librarians greeted him by name and suggested new biographies.

They worried because he was alone so often but he scoffed at their concern.

"These last years are the best years of my life," he told Miriam and she had not challenged him because she knew the terror of his other years, although his assertion seemed disloyal to her mother who had died before the best had come to be.

Their father's hair had never thinned and Miriam and Alan could not remember a time when it had retained a trace of the rich chestnut color, although Richard had often spoken of it.

"Brown hair, like ours, but with tints of red in it. And then overnight it was the color of ashes." His voice would become vague, puzzled, the voice of an analysand recalling childhood mysteries. "In Portugal," Miriam always added, in the special familial shorthand of memory and association.

It was in Portugal, in the refugee transit camp, that their father received the letter that told him of the deaths of his parents. They were not cruel deaths, for those times. Typhus had swept through the narrow streets of Prague with swift democracy, killing the rich and the poor, the young and the old. Richard, a small boy who trailed after adults, heard their father read the letter aloud. The writer, a cousin, confided that he envied the dead.

Miriam was only a year old then yet she has retained a memory of her father as he prayed beside an open window. He was wrapped in his *tallit*, his prayer shawl, and he swayed with slow grace, causing the sun to move in liquid rhomboids of light across the white wool and the broad black stripes. Sunbeams were trapped in the fringes. He pulled the prayer shawl over his head and when he lowered it his hair was dusted with grief, the color of ashes. Miriam has acknowledged that the memory must be woven of dream and fantasy. She was, after all, a baby, just beginning to take slow uncertain steps.

A barber in Sheepshead Bay clipped their father's hair but he trimmed his neat square beard himself, using the stainless steel scissors he had brought with him from Prague. There, he had sharpened the blades nightly and Alan had watched sparks fly as the blade met the whetstone. The scissors had been his insurance policy and he had told his children that he would have used it to kill them and their mother and then himself if their visas for Cuba had not arrived. He would have preferred poison but there was none to be had in the pharmacies of Lisbon.

"Would you really have done it?" Alan asked once, keeping his voice light and mocking although his eyes were hooded and searching.

Their father did not answer but Miriam knew. He would have donned his prayer shawl and stabbed each of them neatly through the heart as they lay sleeping and then he would have killed himself. The certainty had been frozen in her mind since childhood when she overheard her mother telling a neighbor the story of the Finkelsteins of Riga, their neighbors in that Lisbon compound.

The Finkelsteins had not received visas and in the darkness of a summer night, the father of the family, a ritual slaughterer, drew the sharpened blade of his profession across the throats of his four-year-old twin daughters and his pregnant wife and then killed himself. He was a skilled man and they did not cry out. He wore his prayer shawl for these last sacred acts of his life and the blood that spurted from the severed arteries formed crimson streaks on the soft white wool. There had been much discussion as to whether the bloodied prayer shawl should be buried with its owner according to tradition. There were those who felt that it should be burned but in the end the stained *tallit* was placed in the coffin. The man's blood was on the fabric and Jewish law holds that a man be buried with every discernable corporeal remnant so that he might rise up intact to greet the messiah. Their father's friends argued the question for years afterward and Richard and Alan imitated them but Miriam put her fingers in her ears so that she would not hear.

Years later, at a New England university, Miriam took a course in the sociology of religion and the instructor, who was not Jewish, dwelt briefly on the Jewish messianic tradition. *They* hold, he said (and Miriam winced at the pronoun, at the slyness of his tone), that the dead will rise from their graves and dance after their messiah until they reach Jerusalem.

Miriam dreamed of the slaughterer that night. He was naked, his skin as white as the prayer shawl that draped his shoulders. He danced down the streets of Lisbon and his two small daughters followed him. They wore blue organdy dresses, like the one Miriam had worn for her first day of kindergarten. Their dark hair was plaited and tied with blue ribbons and they wept as they danced. She awakened, trembling, and wondered how she could dream of people she could not remember. *I was only a year old,* she told herself but she did not sleep again that night.

She met her brothers for dinner in a Cambridge restaurant.

"Do you really think he would have killed us?" she asked.

"Yes." Richard's voice was bitter and Alan did not

raise his eyes from the castle of bread crumbs he had built on the pale blue cloth.

Miriam had briefly belonged to a consciousness-raising group where the deepest intimacies were discussed by women who were strangers to each other. One evening the women passionately explored their relationships with their fathers.

"Did your father really love you?"

The question was tossed, like a rubber ball, from woman to woman. There were tears and laughter, bitter replies and silences but Miriam simply said "yes" with a certainty that no one else could offer. Her father, after all, had loved her enough to kill her.

Because their father had at last acknowledged that he could no longer shop for himself, Miriam drove to Brooklyn from Connecticut each week, her station wagon loaded with sacks of groceries and biographies printed in oversized type from her local library. His eyes were too weak to read the regular print yet he lifted each can and carton and searched for the label that guaranteed it to be kosher and struggled to read the list of ingredients.

"He's becoming a fanatic," Miriam complained to Alan.

"He was always a fanatic," Alan said bitterly. Alan's wife, Nancy, converted to Judaism and although they were married by a rabbi and Nancy kept a kosher home, their father had never visited them.

Richard offered another suggestion.

"He thinks he was saved because he believed."

He had told them often enough that even during the weeks of flight he never broke the Sabbath. In Portugal he had eaten no meat. He had stood guard

The Prayer Shawl

beside the bodies of the dead, draped in his prayer shawl and murmuring the Psalms. Richard remembered that throughout the long journey to Cuba, their father had prayed three times a day. He had climbed onto the deck and faced eastward to Jerusalem, indifferent to waves that buffeted the small ship and cast their spray across the pale planked deck. The saline scent of the sea clung to his prayer shawl and a veil of rime settled on the leather-cased phylacteries.

Miriam remembered how her father donned that prayer shawl each morning, first kissing its ritual fringes and then draping it over his head so that it formed a tent of darkness, enclosing him and his God in its folds. She watched her father place the black leather phylactery box in the center of his forehead and tie its mate to his upper left arm, parallel to the heart. He wrapped the frontlet seven times around his arm, three times around his middle finger, crossing the remaining strip about his outstretched palm. She thought that the strip of black leather formed a cruel harness of submission, rendering him powerless because her father, like herself, was left-handed. She saw that when he removed it, there were red markings on his left arm. He did not chant his prayers but murmured them so softly and rapidly that she could not discern them and she imagined that he offered a furtive secret to his God.

He never glanced at the prayerbook he held open in his hand and she wondered still if he thought about the words. Her brothers doubted it.

"He thought about his *tallit*," Richard said. "He spent more time folding it than he spent praying. Typical obsessive-compulsive behavior." Richard's profession gave him the instant wisdom of the throw-away phrase. It was not so simple for Miriam who remembered still how carefully he had examined it each morning before placing it again in the faded burgundy velvet bag that his mother had embroidered with his name.

The prayer shawl had been his bar mitzvah gift but he had selected it himself after carefully holding lengths of fabric up to the sunlight to be examined for defect of weave and blend of thread. The shopkeeper had not wanted to sell him the prayer shawl he finally selected, arguing that it would be too large. But her father had insisted.

"A boy becomes a man, I said, and a man carries his *tallit* from his bar mitzvah to his grave."

Miriam thought of the bloodied *tallit* buried with the slaughterer in Lisbon and she wondered if the fabric had disintegrated into the earth, if the blood stains had faded and turned the ochre color of the Portuguese soil. She wondered too if a Jew died at sea, whether his body would be draped in his prayer shawl and cast out on the waves. And when the messiah came would the dead rise from the waters as they rose from the secret places of the earth? She had been a morbid child, intrigued by death, dreaming of spectres and wraiths.

Their father carried his prayer shawl from Prague to Lisbon, from Lisbon to America. When he was establishing his business he often slept in his loft and he packed the burgundy velvet bag with the change of clothing and food he carried with him. Miriam imagined him at his morning prayers in that stark space where their fortunes were made. He rose in the pre-dawn hour and the white prayer shawl glowed in the half-darkness. Perhaps he shouted his prayers then, into the silence, the emptiness.

His business prospered. He bought a house and he bought their mother a fur coat. She was a small, quiet woman and she felt lost in the folds of dark shining pelts but she wore it to please him. And then she wore it because it was very warm and somehow she always felt cold. She wore it when she went to the hospital for "tests."

Miriam took two buses from Brooklyn College to Maimonides Hospital. Her father met her in the corridor.

"It is serious," he said, "but there is a cure."

"There is no cure." Richard's voice was harsh. He was a second-year medical student and his knowledge overwhelmed and angered him.

But their father had heard there was an alloy of gold which, when blended with penicillin, could shrink carcinomas like the one that had taken possession of their mother's pancreas. The capsules were illegal in the United States but he would get them from Antwerp. He had already made calls, sent telegrams. The burgundy velvet bag was under his arm. He was going to synagogue. He strode away from them and did not look back. He believed in the efficacy of prayer coupled with the power of money. He was encouraged because the capsules were expensive. Their visas too had been expensive. He had cheated death once and he would do it again.

He came to the hospital every day. He shouted at the nurses because she would not eat. He shouted at her because she could not sleep. He shouted at the Hungarian Jew in Antwerp who had undertaken the task of finding the magic capsules. In the interim he prayed. He sat beside her bed, sometimes wearing his prayer shawl and sometimes not, and read the Psalms. "Weeping may endure for a night but joy cometh in the morning . . . Thou hast turned my mourning into dancing . . . Thou hast put off my sackcloth and girdled me with gladness." Miriam saw her mother's waxen white fingers touch his *tallit*.

"You must take care of yourself," she said. Her fingers worried the fabric and she slept the shallow sleep of the very ill.

The capsules arrived from Antwerp and their mother swallowed one and vomited it up. Their father poured the second one into a cup of hot tea. She retained it and even Richard agreed that a new brightness stole into her face. She said their names aloud in a strong voice and that evening she rose from her bed and went to the bathroom herself to the shocked amazement of the nurse. The next morning she took another capsule and smiled and brushed her hair as she sat up in bed.

"You see," their father said triumphantly. He had prayed the morning service in her room and he drew his prayer shawl close as though he were indeed girdling himself in gladness. But their mother frowned.

"Give me your *tallis*," she said. "It is dirty."

She rose from her hospital bed, her shoulder blades protruding like fragile wings beneath the white batiste nightgown that Miriam had bought in the children's department but which was still too large for her shrunken form. She carried the prayer shawl into the small hospital bathroom and washed it in the sink.

"You must use cold water and liquid soap," she

The Prayer Shawl

told Miriam, who stood beside her. "Let it soak. Don't rub." Miriam nodded dutifully. But the weakened woman could not lift the soaking fabric from the sink and Miriam took over the task and wrapped it in a large towel.

"Take it home, her mother said. "Stretch it on a clean towel on the porch. Let it dry in the sun. There should be lemon juice in the water when it is washed but who has lemon juice in a hospital?" She laughed and Miriam laughed with her.

She died the next morning as their father prayed the morning service, draped in the newly washed prayer shawl that smelled of soap and sea and sunlight.

Miriam was married a year later and the fragrance of her mother's death chamber suffused her marriage rites. The prayer shawl formed her wedding canopy and the stretch of white wool was held high above her head by her brothers and her husband's brothers. She and Stan stood beneath the symbolic tabernacle of shelter which slipped dangerously low as the plain gold band was placed on her finger. She inhaled deeply and thought that she smelled the scent of lemon juice but she remembered that her mother had not used lemon juice. *Who has lemon juice in a hospital?* She wept then and Stan brushed his lips against what he considered to be her tears of joy. She did not tell him that she cried because her mother had washed her wedding canopy on the day before she died.

It became her habit to go to her father's seaside home each year at the approach of the high holy days, to wash his prayer shawl. She always sprinkled a few drops of lemon juice into the soapy water and then spread it out on a thick towel to dry in the sunlight. She took pride in its whiteness and she was troubled when, at her son's circumcision, a tiny fleck of blood stained the fabric as her father bent forward to bless the child, at the moment the foreskin was severed. *Why was he wearing his tallit?* she thought angrily. The other men, even the rabbi, wore only their skullcaps. *He has to show that he is holier than everyone else.* The small stain faded from scarlet to rust as the years passed but she did not forget her brief and bitter anger.

Her father grew older, and now, at last, they worried about him, and called him often, awakening him from sleep at odd hours. They visited with their children. Alan's son carried a tape recorder and a notebook, interviewed him about his flight from Czechoslovakia, the long year in Lisbon, the dangerous voyage to freedom. The others had their own questions. They were taking courses in anthropology and sociology, in religion and the holocaust.

Miriam's son, whose droplet of blood had stained the prayer shawl, was doing a research paper on the reactions of individuals to catastrophe. His grandfather told him about the slaughterer and the boy whistled softly. He looked at the old man as though he had discovered a new hero but Miriam, who was hemming a skirt, took up the famous scissor to cut a seam. She examined the blade and decided that it could not ever have been sharp enough to kill.

Richard visited the Brooklyn house one afternoon. Their father was still in his pajamas. He had not taken in the milk because the bottle had been too heavy for him to grasp.

"He is not disoriented," Richard said, resorting

The Prayer Shawl

to the language of his profession because he was more comfortable when he spoke as a doctor than when he spoke as a son or a brother. "He just seemed debilitated and fatigued."

"He is 82 years old," Miriam replied irritably.

She and Stan drove from Connecticut to Brooklyn the next day. It was very hot and her father sat on the porch wearing gray cotton slacks that slipped from his waist when he rose to greet them. His white shirt was misbuttoned and his blue eyes were faded, reminding Miriam of the gaze of her autistic nephew under the influence of a tranquilizer. Her lips brushed his cheek and his skin was as dry as newsprint which has been exposed to rain and left to bake in the sun.

"How are you, Papa?"

"How should I be?" His voice was not querulous. *How should he be?* He was an old man and it was a very hot day.

"Pop, we want you to come home with us," Stan said.

He held his hands out in mute acquiescence and followed Miriam inside where she washed the few dishes in the sink and made the bed.

"I was too tired to do it," he said apologetically and his newly faded blue eyes grew moist. It occurred to her that she had never seen her father cry. He had prayed when other men wept. She comforted him, as she had comforted her children when they were small. She stroked the hair that had lost its color that grief-stricken night in Lisbon and envied Richard because he could remember their father when his hair and beard had been chestnut brown.

She packed for him—shirts and pajamas, underwear and slacks. A neat stack of socks and handkerchiefs carefully placed in the drawer before he was so overtaken by weariness.

"My *tallit*," he said. "My *tefillin*." The matching burgundy bags, their holy burdens gently bulging, topped the hillock of white handkerchiefs.

He slept all the way to Connecticut and went to bed and slept again when they arrived. But the next morning he awakened early and dressed carefully. He prayed on the screened porch, pacing back and forth across a ribbon of sunlight. The prayer shawl enveloped him and his shoulders sagged beneath its weight. When he had finished the morning service he sat down but did not remove it.

"It's heavy," he said. "It needs to be washed."

Miriam lifted it from his shoulders.

"Go rest, Papa," she said. "I'll take care of it."

She watched as he made his way to the patio and closed the sliding doors behind him. The glass panels were heavy yet he pulled them shut with the force of a single gesture as though he had received a new infusion of energy. She had forgotten how strong her father was and the small demonstration of a resurgence of that strength comforted her.

The phone rang but she did not enter the house to answer it. Instead she draped the *tallit* about her own shoulders and arranged it in graceful folds. Her fingers played with the fringes, fondled the intricate knots; she kissed the corner fringes and tasted her father's breath. She too felt its weight. It was laden with the prayer-filled days of his life, with the memories interwoven with its threads, with the supplications for the newborn and the dead, the newly married and traveler. She pulled it

The Prayer Shawl

close about her and thought of her brothers' secret angers and the fearful dreams of her girlhood. Briefly, she pulled it over her head and closed her eyes. She remembered how the prayer shawl had enclosed her father in a tent of darkness; she had watched, frightened and alone, a child hovering in a doorway.

She bowed her head and swayed from side to side but no prayer came to her lips. The sun beat down on her as she stood there and the light wool was harsh against her bare skin. She took the prayer shawl off and carried it inside.

She washed it gently in soapy water and added a few drops of lemon juice. Gently, she kneaded the fabric, and studied each newly cleansed area, holding it up to the sunlight. She rubbed at the tiny speck of rust until at last it disappeared. She spread the prayer shawl to dry on a towel in a corner of the lawn where the sun burned the brightest. It was gleaming white against the newly mown grass.

She went to the patio and saw that her father had fallen asleep on a chaise lounge covered with a light blue mat that was almost the same color as his newly faded eyes. Sunlight splayed across his hands and slashed his outstretched arms with brightness. The phone rang again and this time she went inside to answer it, pulling the glass doors open with both her hands. Patiently, she reassured her brothers. He was fine. He had eaten a good breakfast. He had prayed. She thought to tell them that he had closed the glass doors with ease but it seemed, now, a foolish observation.

Two hours later she returned to the garden. The prayer shawl was dry and it seemed to Miriam that it rested more lightly in her arms. She folded it carefully and carried it out to the patio. It was time for her father's lunch.

"Look, Papa. Your *tallit* is clean," she said. Her voice was childlike, eager to please.

She went to the chaise and draped it over his shoulders—the teasing, flirtatious gesture of a small girl. He did not stir.

"Papa?"

She reached for his hand. The vein-striated flesh was golden with sunlight but cold to her touch. She wept then and pulled the prayer shawl closer about his frail body so that it would warm him; her tears darkened the white wool.

Her brothers helped to wrap the prayer shawl about his lifeless form. Richard's hands trembled and Alan's eyes were moist with unshed tears. Miriam looked at her father as he lay in the unfinished pine coffin and bent forward. She loosened the *tallit* and spread it loosely about him. She did not want her father to be restrained. She wanted him to soar on the wings of fragrant whitened wool and look down with vigilant compassion, with protecting anger, on all the joys and sadnesses of their lives.

Afterword

Many societies associated age with wisdom: the "elders" were also the governors and the judges. Others had complex hierarchies that linked different ages with different accomplishments and intellectual attainments. The statement by Rabbi Judah ben Tema in the Jewish "Ethics of the Fathers" (5:24) is particularly illuminating:

> At five years the age is reached for the study of scripture, at ten for the study of the Mishnah, at thirteen for the fulfillment of the Commandments, at fifteen for the study of the Talmud, at eighteen for marriage, at twenty for seeking a livelihood, at thirty for entering into one's full strength, at forty for understanding, at fifty for counsel, at sixty a man attains old age, at seventy the hoary head, at eighty the gift of special strength, at ninety he bends beneath the weight of years, at one hundred he is as if he were already dead and had passed away and vanished from the world.

Note that aging, from the rabbi's point-of-view, was only a mixed blessing. Some people, to his mind, were "too old." Today, of course, classifications of this sort have mostly been rejected. Age-based expectations and rituals, which typified Judaism in past generations, have lost much of their meaning. Instead, puberty is prolonged; marriage and child-bearing are delayed; and old age is filled with roleless expectations.

Jewish tradition generally encourages respectful treatment of the elderly. The Bible, for example, in telling us that Abraham was 175 at his death, and Sarah 127, apparently intended to indicate that both had become wise as well as old; the Hebrew word *zaken* embraces both meanings. Sarah and Abraham, according to the biblical account, were thus wise beyond their years. Moreover, their "old age" did not curtail their activities. They loved in old age. They bore children in old age. And in old age, they even guided their children. They refused to allow stereotypes of old age to beset them.

The *locus classicus* of the biblical view of aging is found in Leviticus: "You shall rise before the aged and show deference to the old. You shall fear your God; I am the Lord" (Lev. 19:32). One was compelled actually to rise when an old person approached, and was not permitted to speak before the elder had spoken. Indeed, the text implies that there is a direct relationship between respect for the elderly and reverence for God. Ecclesiasticus, the apocryphal Wisdom of Ben Sirah (25:4–6), makes this link appear even stronger:

> How beautiful a thing is judgment for gray hair, And for elders to know counsel! How beautiful is the wisdom of old men and thoughtful advice to men who are honored! Much experience is the crown of old men, their enhancement is reverence for the Lord.

It is further strengthened in the Midrash Genesis Rabbah: "Concerning he who welcomes an old

Afterword

man, it is as if he has welcomed the Shechinah" (Gen. R. Toledot 43.6). In general, then, Judaism demanded considerable deference before the aged. It thus helped to establish the basis for what would eventually become a social system of caring for the elderly.

For all of the glowing statements in Jewish literature suggesting an almost absolute deference to the elderly, sources are, at the same time, realistic about the maladies of old age and the lack of communication between the generations. For example, a Levite could not work in the Temple past age fifty (Lev. 8:25–26). According to the Talmud, the very old could also not serve on the *Sanhedrin*, presumably their judgment at that time in life was considered inadequate (B.T. Sanhedrin 36b). The Psalmist likewise speaks of the infirmities of old age (Ps. 71:9–18). And in Ecclesiastes, chapter twelve depicts in a striking if depressing metaphor, the physical changes which accompany old age:

> The sun grows dark, the light goes from moon and stars, and the clouds gather after the rain. The guards tremble in the house, when its upholders bow, the maids that grind are few, and they that look out lose their luster. The doors to the street are shut, and the sound of the mill runs low, the twitter of the birds is faint, and the daughters of song are dull. There is fear of that which is high, and terrors are in the way. The hair is almost white, and he drags his limbs along and the spirit fails. So a man goes to his long home and mourners pass along the street. The silver cord is snapped, and the golden lamp is shattered, the pitcher breaks at the foun-

tain, and the wheel breaks at the cistern. The dust returns to the earth as it was, and the spirit to God who gave it.

This moving description, perhaps the most powerful depiction of old age in all literature, paved the way for all early researchers (sixteenth to eighteenth century) eager to understand how change comes about.

Like Ecclesiastes, the talmudic rabbis often speak of old age in metaphors and euphemisms. In Tractate Shabbat of the Babylonian Talmud (152a), for example, old age is referred to as a crown of willow rods (which are heavy by nature). Ecclesiastes Rabbah, commenting on the above passage in Ecclesiastes 12, generated new metaphors even as it sought to explain old ones:

> "Before the evil days come" refers to old age. "And the years draw nigh" refers to the time of suffering. "Before the sun is darkened" refers to the nose. "And the moon" refers to the forehead. "And the stars" refers to the cheekbones. What does "And clouds return after the rain" refer to? According to Rabbi Levi, who explains it in two different ways: one refers to scholars, the other to fools. According to the first interpretation, when the scholar comes to weep, his eyes flow with tears. According to the second interpretation, when the fool comes to ease himself, his movement anticipates him.

Old age, according to this view was dark and dull, without music or the sounds of the world. In a like vein, the rabbis also proclaim (B.T. Shabbat 152a) that "The intelligence of the aged is dissipated. The speech of the old is faltering. The ears of the elderly are unreliable. . . . To an older person even a little hill seems like the greatest of mountains." Perhaps for this reason, the midrashic collection of *Tanhuma* (Mi-ketz 10), urged a young man to pray that "in his older years his eyes may see, his mouth eat, and his legs work, because in old age, all powers fail."

If old age in the Bible and Talmud was considered no more than a mixed blessing, death at a young age was understood to be a punishment meted out personally by God. According to the rabbis, the number of one's years on earth depends on one's goodness and meritorious deeds. Each individual, according to tradition, is allotted *about* one-hundred twenty years: "The righteous ones may be granted a few extra years and the wicked may be restricted in their years on earth." Another Jewish tradition suggests that one's stay on earth is limited to seventy years or three-score and ten. Should an individual be given an extra ten years for a total of four score years, it is, according to this passage (Ps. 90), by reason of unusual strength.

These approaches, however fraught with theological problems, do offer insight into the rabbinic perspective on aging. There is, however, no monolithic view of the subject in rabbinic literature. Instead, the rabbis present individual insights and opinions, generally derived from personal experiences. What unites these texts is an overwhelming *reverence* for old age that is expressive of Judaism, regardless of time and place. This view is epitomized in *Yalkut Shimoni* to Isaiah (156), where we find written ". . . the Holy One, Blessed be He, forgives all Israel for the sake of one elder." Lack of respect and courtesy to the aged, by contrast, was in the eyes of the rabbis a sign of troubled times, such as those preceding the coming of the Messiah (B.T. Sotah 49b).

Beyond inspiring reverence, Jewish tradition viewed the aged as a group imbued with a special purpose: to pass on to the young traditional wisdom and sound advice. The rabbis viewed the past as a guide to the present: "Remember the days of old," the Bible teaches, "consider the years of ages past. Ask your father, he will inform you. Your elders, they will tell you" (Deut. 32:7). Given the choice between listening to the old or heeding the impetuous voices of the young, the rabbis almost invariably went with experience and listened to the elders. A famous Talmudic text (Avodah Zarah 1:19) referring to the rebuilding of the Temple in Jerusalem in Hadrian's time explains why: "If young people advise you to build a Temple, and old men say destroy it, listen to the latter. The building of the young is destruction and the tearing down of the old is construction." While this sounds like a prescription for generational conflict, the traditional Jewish ideal was actually far more harmonious. The goal was a world where young and old worked together for common ends, as envisioned by the prophet Joel (2:28): "And it shall come to pass afterward, that I will pour on my spirit on all flesh; your sons and daughters shall prophesy; your elders shall dream dreams and your young shall see visions."

The rabbis understood that adult learning was slow and much might be forgotten. "Respect even the old man who has lost his learning," the Talmud teaches, "since not only were the two perfect tablets of the Law placed in the Ark of the Covenant, but also the fragments of the tablets which Moses shattered when he saw the people dancing before the Golden Calf" (B.T. Berachot 8b). Lifelong learning, nevertheless remained the ideal. The "Ethics of the Fathers" likened one who studied at an advanced age "To one who eats ripe grapes and drinks aged wine" (Avot 4:20). Tractate Shabbat teaches that wisdom actually improves with age. "The older a scholar grows, the greater his wisdom becomes" (B.T. Shabbat 152a). It was clearly recognized, however, that no amount of learning could make a wise man out of a fool. "There is old age without the glory of long life; and there is long life without the ornament of age. Perfect is that old age which has both" (Gen. R. 49).

Early on, caring for the elderly who were without means and bereft of family was considered an important act of tzedakah. The poor suffered most in old age because of their vulnerable position: many ended up in a community supported *Hekdesh*, an asylum for the poor. Medieval persecutions and massacres brought added suffering upon them. Yet, it was not really until the late seventeenth century that Jewish communities sought to create *organized* care for the aged. The Council of Lithuania thus passed a resolution in 1650 to support the elderly who survived the Chmielnicki massacres. Around the same time, the Jewish community of Rome introduced care for the aged as one of its four major divisions of community charity. A century later, in 1749, a Jewish Home for the Aged was built, apparently for the first time, by the Sefardic community of Amsterdam. By then, European Jewish communities had begun to realize that care for the aged had to be separated from the various other problems associated with poverty and physical disability. The ensuing decades witnessed the development of foundations specifically created to finance and support a home for the aged (the *moshav zekenim*) in many communities. The majority of major European cities with substantial Jewish populations had established homes for the aged by the end of the nineteenth century.

Institutional care for the adult Jewish elderly began to emerge on American shores at about the same time. In 1855, for example, one of the earliest Jewish Homes for the Aged was founded in St. Louis. Built to fill the multi-faceted needs of lonely elderly German-Jewish immigrants, it provided an old-world style haven for these old Jews. Like its counterparts that slowly began to develop around the country, the home reflected the unique group culture from which its residents originated. This trend did not continue in the United States. It seems that there was a resistance, in general, to professionally employed social workers. As a result, care for the aged was impaired. Social service agencies displayed reluctance to deal with the aged—one which took, many years to change. The pattern changed in the twentieth century, and now the work of providing services to the elderly rests for the most part with communal service professionals.

There has been a trend in the United States to avoid even the mention of "old age," a result of the American emphasis on youth. The aged are referred to as "senior citizens." Specialized housing communities are called "retirement communities" and "senior citizen resorts." The familiar Home for the Aged has become a refuge of last resort. Professionals now emphasize the need to provide services to the elderly in their homes and communities, so as to keep them "supportively independent" at home, among family and friends.

The modern discipline of social gerontology has taught us that the aged, like other age cohorts, are not cast in one mold. The elderly reflect a diversity of life experiences; they are far from uniform in character or disposition. Their responses to the situations forced upon them by the exigencies of life are no less diverse. This is what makes the study of the elderly so fascinating.

In this collection, I have sought to gather sources which *authentically* explore the life of the Jewish elderly, avoiding sentimentality and nostalgia. These stories speak of what it means to grow old in the American Jewish community, the laughter and the tears. In a sense, these stories represent the mosaic of Jewish life: a carefully constructed menagerie of Jewish pain and jubilation.

I have tried in this volume to avoid stereotyping the elderly. We find such stereotypes wherever we turn: in literature, in the media, in popular culture. Old people are assumed to be poor learners, poor employees, stubborn and nasty. Actually, we know that most people maintain their same dispositions and outlook on life, good or bad, from young adulthood well into old age. This diversity is well-illustrated by juxtaposing Gertrude Berg's fun-loving "Grandpa Mordecai" in "The Retired Gentlemen" and Seymour Epstein's taciturn "Mr. Isaacs." In dealing with his landlord about a still that he [Grandpa Mordecai] had built in his apartment,

Grandpa takes control of events suggesting that the landlord is the criminal, since his occasional drink (during Prohibition) comes by way of bootleggers, gangsters, and public enemies. "Grandpa, according to Grandpa, was doing his patriotic duty by having a still in his closet and once he got [the landlord] Mr. Stone to agree that having a little drink every once in a while was part of human nature he also got him to agree that making whisky was better than buying from crooks." Epstein's Mr. Isaacs, on the other hand, sits placidly, a family cast-off. Like a household dog, he was consigned to an outside chair from morning 'till night, coming in only for a meal at the end of a solitary day. He sits, rehearsing in his mind the experiences of his past, waiting for the final visit from the angel of death. "Deliberately, Mr. Isaacs invokes memory, and he is like a man stumbling around in the darkened rooms of his own house."

We also now know—and this too is illustrated here—that length of years provides individuals with a lens, yellowed or rosy, through which to view the entire world. Where young people may make judgments based on a single experience, the aged learn from their whole lives. This leads to a certain resilience in character on the part of the elderly, a self-assurance that may be difficult to challenge. Moreover, older people are sustained by a strong will to survive. Many have the uncanny ability to take the hand dealt them in life and beat the dealer, in spite of overwhelming obstacles. Character after character in the stories here makes the best of a bad situation, struggles on, and lives to fight another day.

Older people are not so much afraid of death as

Afterword

of dependence. After a lifetime of independence, they are unwilling to turn to others for assistance or help. Some overcompensate and become fiercely independent, refusing to yield to circumstances that might strike fear even in younger individuals. Thus, "Bubba" in Judith K. Liebmann's "The Gift Horse" continues to leave her door unlocked even as the neighborhood deteriorates, and thieves march off with her belongings. "I had my life," she explains, "what difference which way it ends. As long as it's in my own house where I'm my own boss, I don't care when or how it should be over."

In this volume, I hope to recapture the spirit of elderly Jews, many of them first generation immigrants, through true-to-life fiction. I want readers, especially students of aging to identify with the characters they meet here, to think of them as friends or next door neighbors. I echo what Gertrude Berg wrote in her own introduction:

> The best thing I can do is start at the beginning and hope. But starting at the beginning isn't always easy. People don't just appear, they come from someplace. Everybody has ancestors and everybody is descended. I must have come from a long line but the furthest back I can remember is my father's father, Mordecai Edelstein. So I start with Grandpa for two reasons: because he would have liked it and because he was the first one of us all to come to America. He started us here in the New World. It was his discovery and he was our link to the past on the other side.

It is my hope that these stories offer readers new insight into old age as well as into "beginnings" and "hopes." Instead of seeing old age as a "problem," I hope that they can now see it as experience, filled with challenges to be overcome, friendships to nurture, and family to love.

Social science research supports the selection of these stories as fairly representing the life experiences of the elderly. Social research, however, can never quite capture the emotional qualities of aging—the passion, the rage, the intense resolve to survive. For these we must turn to literature—to characters who, even if fictional, make old age seem real. Research tells us a great deal about old age, but the statistics and dry prose sometimes rob the subject of life. Here we seek to restore the balance, by allowing authors and characters to speak for themselves.

Kerry M. Olitzky
New York, New York
June 1989

About the Contributors

Charles Angoff (1902–1979) Born in Minsk, he received his education in Boston and became associated with the *American Mercury* there, eventually to serve as its editor, as well as an editor with *The Nation*, the *American Spectator*, and the *North American Review*. Only late in his life did he begin to write short stories, turning to subjects he encountered early in his Boston childhood.

Gertrude Berg (1900–1966) Actress and scriptwriter, she was best known for her "The Goldbergs," which played on radio for seventeen years and on television for five years. She played herself in an autobiographical Broadway play, which she also wrote, entitled *Me and Molly*.

Seymour Epstein (1917–   ) Born in New York, he has taught creative writing at various institutions, including Princeton University and the New School for Social Research (where he also studied). Author of a group of very insightful and sensitive novels about the American Jewish experience, he won the Lewis Wallant Memorial Book Award in 1964. This is from his first collection of stories.

Edna Ferber (1887–1968) Born in Michigan, she began as a newspaper reporter at seventeen, and became the well-known writer of plays and films, including "Showboat," "Cimarron," "Gigolo," and "Dinner at Eight." She won a Pulitzer Prize in 1924 for *So Big*, the story of a woman's struggle for independence.

Gloria Goldreich is a well-known popular novelist and author of *Leah's Journey*, which won the National Jewish Book Award in 1979. Her fiction appears in many publications, including *Redbook*, *McCall's*, and *Midstream*. *West to Eden* is Goldreich's most recent novel.

Bette Howland (1937–) Born in Chicago, she has received fellowships from the Guggenheim and Rockefeller foundations, among others. Her semi-autobiographical novel, *W-3*, was based on her attempt at suicide. She also contributes to *Commentary*. This story is from *Things Come and Go*, which includes three novellas.

Dan Jacobson (1929–) Born in South Africa, and a critic of its politics, as this story clearly indicates, Jacobson spent time in Israel before returning to South Africa to spend most of his career as a journalist. He now lives in England. He has written novels, short stories, and essays, in addition to a travel book about California. In 1964, he shared the Somerset Maugham Award. What is perhaps his best-known story appears here.

Bruno Lessing [Rudolph Edgar Block] (1870–1940) Born in New York, Lessing earned his living as a reporter for *The Sun* and *The Recorder*. In the mid-1890s, he worked for the Hearst newspapers as an editor of the Sunday comics. He is the author of *Children of Men*, a collection of short stories, from which this selection is taken.

About the Contributors

Judith K. Liebmann (1943–   ) Born in Brooklyn, a poet and fiction writer, Liebmann received her Ph.D. from Yale University in 1969 and taught there until 1975. Her work has appeared in *Orim* and other journals.

Ruth Miller (1921–   ) Born in Chicago and now living in Israel, Miller taught at SUNY-Stony Brook from 1969 until recently. She is a former Fulbright Scholar and has taught at Hebrew University. Primarily a poet, this story is one of her early and few published pieces of short fiction.

Hugh Nissenson (1933–   ) Born in New York, Nissenson later became a Stegner Literary Fellow at Stanford University. His first collection of short stories won the Edward Lewis Wallant Memorial Award for fiction in 1965. Now living in Israel, many of his more recent stories grow out of that experience.

Grace Paley (1922–   ) Born in New York, she has been on the faculty of several institutions of higher learning including Columbia University, Syracuse University, and Sarah Lawrence College, where she currently teaches. She has received numerous awards for her writing and a Guggenheim fellowship.

Sylvia Rothchild (1923–   ) Born in New York, she is a lecturer and writer. Her biography of I.L. Peretz, *Key to a Magic Door*, won the Jewish Book Award in 1960.

Frank Scheiner's first story was published in *The Menorah Journal* in 1928.

Isaac Bashevis Singer (1904–   ) Born in Poland, Nobel Prize laureate, well-known for his Yiddish short stories and novels.

Jerome Weidman (1913–   ) A novelist and playwright, he received the Pulitzer Prize for Drama in 1960, the same year he won a Tony. He has written over twenty novels, eleven volumes of short stories and essays, and several plays.

Anzia Yezierska (1885–1970) Born in Russia, she immigrated to America at the age of sixteen and published her first short story fifteen years later. *Hungry Hearts* (1920), a portrait of Jewish immigrant life, was her first and most famous book and later became the basis of a motion picture of the same name. Later in life, she wrote a number of short stories dealing with the challenges of the Jewish elderly.

Eugene Ziller (1935–   ) Born in Harlem and raised in Brooklyn, Ziller is the author of *In this World*. His prize-winning stories have appeared in numerous publications.

About the Editor

Kerry M. Olitzky, an ordained rabbi, is Director of the School of Education at Hebrew Union College-Jewish Institute of Religion, New York. Trained as a social gerontologist and well-recognized as an authority in Jewish education, he is the author of numerous books, monographs, and articles. Dr. Olitzky is also the editor of the *Journal of Aging and Judaism*, an executive editor for *COMPASS: New Directions in Jewish Education*, and an executive curriculum consultant for *Shofar Magazine*.

Claude D. Pepper (1900–1989) Congressman from Florida at the time of his death, who also served in the Senate from 1936–1951. Trained as an attorney, he practised and taught law until he sought political office. He is best known for his work as an advocate for the elderly and has received awards from various organizations in tribute for his work.